the
BECKONING
SHADOW

the
BECKONING
SHADOW

KATHARYN
BLAIR

KATHERINE TEGEN BOOKS

An Imprint of HarperCollins Publishers

Library of Congress Control Number: 2019934617
ISBN 978-0-06-265761-9
Typography by David Curtis
19 20 21 22 23 PC/LSCH   10 9 8 7 6 5 4 3 2 1

First Edition

For my husband.
Thank you for being the guard dog of my fever dreams.

the BECKONING SHADOW

ONE

If I think about it, it's always been there. Something wrong, something I kept locked behind my ribs. I could feel it brushing up against my lungs when I took a deep breath to laugh with my older sister, Carmen, or when I was getting ready to shout at a game to *be aggressive, be be aggressive.*

I could feel it wrapping around my heart when I saw my weekly crush in the hallways and it would beat faster. It was a vine made of temptation, a vice made of terrible promises.

I knew, somehow, that there was something wrong with me.

That's a nice way to start a story, right? It situates me exactly where I want to be—the person this *happened to.* The person who suffers. The person who fears.

But that's not the whole truth.

I have fear inside me, but not the way you'd think.

My life used to be filled with the normal kind of fear. When dusk seeped out of the air and left night in its wake, my mom would reach down and grip my hand in the parking lot. There was something about the evening, the hum of the streetlights that raised something in my mother. The kind of fear that is learned—the kind that is taught.

But I abandoned that fear along with everything else the night I destroyed my family and ran away. I hid in the dingy bathroom at the bus station, cutting off my hair with the pocketknife my dad had given me when daylight savings ended and cheer practice started ending when it was dark. Shivering and covered in ash, I tried to shed who I was because I knew I could never go back. Everything my parents ever told me to fear was no longer useful. So I unlearned it.

After all the warnings, all the lessons, all the looks over their shoulders—the thing they should have feared the most was next to them, the whole time.

Me.

I was the scariest thing.

TWO

I've been on the run for nearly two years. I've slept under freeway overpasses and in abandoned churches. I have learned how to pee in empty alleyways and how to steal a ripe avocado without getting caught.

But I don't know if I'll ever get used to interstate bus rides. I've been in this seat for twelve hours, and I've been sitting in front of a seven-year-old who has *also* been on a bus for twelve hours. And he's acting like a seven-year-old who has been on a bus for that long. I babysat a lot back in Los Altos. Kids like me, and I'm generally a good person.

But if he kicks the back of my seat one more time I'm going to unleash the full fury of hell on him, tear his sanity down to the studs, and make him rethink all the decisions he's made in his tiny little life. I could move, but I get carsick if I don't have a window seat.

I take a deep breath, lean against the window, and shut my eyes. I'm heading south. If I stay in my seat, I'd wind up back in Los Altos. Home.

I slip my tongue between my front teeth and bite the tip until I wince, hitting the rubber heel of my Chuck Taylors on the plastic bottom of the seat. I know it's stupid, but I read an article about operant conditioning in the waiting room at the dentist office. I figure if I bite the crap out of my tongue every time I start missing the home I can never go back to, I'll start associating homesickness with pain. The woman in the article stopped craving cigarettes by snapping a rubber band on her wrist, so, I mean, it's the same principle.

No, it hasn't worked yet. I just have welts on my tongue.

We stop, picking up another batch of people before we roll into our final destination.

I look out the window to keep my mind off everything else. It's a pretty drive, at least. And we're almost there. I just have to get through San Francisco to get to Paynes Creek—a little farming community. They have an opening at the almond-packing plant . . . the perfect place to throw my hair up under a baseball cap and blend in. I'm not stupid enough to think that the recent stories about weird things happening with Oddities—the rumors traveling on quickly deleted social media posts—haven't reached small farming towns. I'm hoping they'll be too busy to ask questions.

The fog has started to slip over the hills like curious

tendrils of the ocean looking for a taste of the city. I pull a piece of Big Red gum out of the pocket of my hoodie and pop it into my mouth. If I close my eyes, I can almost pretend I'm in the back of the bus with Lindsay and Jenna, getting ready for Regionals, or something. Hannah would be stretching against the front seat. Coach Amira would be joking with Phoenix, our driver. But that life is gone. Every day away from it makes it easier to let it slide back into the part of me I keep locked behind a steel door.

Someone plops down in the seat next to me, and I jump. He's not bad looking, the guy. But he smiles at me in that way that always preludes speech, and I'm not here for talking. I look back out the window, hoping he'll get the hint.

I don't turn back to look at him. I shouldn't have used my last stick of gum. The breath I've got all worked up from twelve hours of gas station Butterfinger coffee and buffalo bleu chips would surely be all I needed to shut down conversation.

I snatch a magazine from the pocket of the seat in front of me. It's some Bay Area business periodical . . . not something I'd ever choose to read on my own. But it's a distraction, and suddenly those glossy pages feel like my most valuable possession. There's a guy on the cover standing in front of a massive structure covered with scaffolding. He's older and beautiful, like he just stepped out of one of those ridiculous perfume ads. The ones where a salt-and-pepper male model lounging on a speedboat is seduced by a mermaid. You're like, *What's the point of this commercial?* Then they show you a bottle and you're confused about what it has to do with mermaid boat sex, but you still kind of want to know what it smells like? That kind. My eyes rove down the page. The headline reads *Ananias Ventra: Real-Estate Mogul, Breaking and Making His Own Rules.*

I keep my eyes on the words, thinking that maybe if I don't look up, he won't—

"Where you headed?" the guy next to me asks.

"More south." Two syllables. I think of them as stand-ins for the other two-syllable phrase I want to utter, but it's like I just tossed toast at a hungry pigeon. Here he comes, looking for more.

"Got family down there?" he asks, scooting closer as two more people squeeze past him on the narrow walkway. One guy stops at the row behind us. A woman with a "Resist" sweatshirt heads toward the back of the bus. I run my eyes over them, almost like I'll be able to tell. It's a habit now. I read once that there's a certain type of Oddity that has weird irises you can see in certain lights. Two years, and I've never seen it. Maybe it's just an urban legend.

Though, in all fairness, up until two years ago, I thought a lot of stuff was urban legend.

I look out the window, hoping my seatmate will get the hint that I'm not really interested in talking. I stare hard at a sign near the road that reads *San Francisco—18 miles*. Fog roils over it, and I see a familiar graffiti tag in the lower left-hand corner.

It still makes me freeze up no matter how many times I've seen it. It's a purple flower engulfed in flames—a queen of poisons.

To people who aren't like me, it's nothing to stop and stare at. There's nothing particularly interesting about it.

But it's a calling card that's been showing up more and more lately. On street signs. Bumpers. Bus stops. Public bathrooms. Baselines—regular humans—won't know what it is.

They never lived in fear of waking to find a queen of poisons bud nailed to their door. That's a fear reserved for Oddities. That fear is one of the many reasons I had to run from home. The graffiti is supposed to send a message: *Things are changing*. But I'm not willing to bet my life on believing it. I'd heard rumors that the dissidents are in San Francisco—which is exactly why I'm *not* stopping in San Francisco.

I shove the magazine in the pocket and sit back.

I don't know much about the scary underbelly of the Oddity world. But I do know that the Wardens don't just disappear. My chest tightens as I let the word bounce around in my thoughts: *Wardens*. Just the sound of it echoing in my mind brings bile to the back of my throat.

The bus lurches forward, and the sign with the graffiti rolls out of my view as I realize my seatmate is *still talking*;

ohmygosh he is *still talking*. But there has been one positive development. Mr. Seat Soccer has shifted seats behind us and is now this guy's problem.

". . . So I figured I'd come down to San Fran to help out, since, you know, he helped me out so much in my chem lab. Some people would say it's not my problem, but I say it was the right thing to do. I'm Kolby, by the way."

My seatmate stops and looks at me, smiling. The ball is in my court. The hungry pigeon is expecting more bread crumbs. I lower the hood of my sweatshirt—the one the whole squad got at State Championships right before I ran—and pray that he can't read the name I blacked out with permanent marker on the pocket. "Vesper," it says, in the most cheerful font imaginable. Greasy strands of my blond hair fall out of the topknot I'd finger-combed together, and I can feel at least three new zits blooming on my unwashed forehead.

Maybe there's a silver lining to the fact that I ruined my life and took off running, never to look back. Because two years ago, polite me, the me who wore ribbons in her hair on game day, the one whose biggest concern was keeping her knees straight in her back walkover, would've felt like she had to talk to Kolby.

Nice. Polite. But that girl is gone. Long live greasy-hair-don't-care Vesper.

"Look. I get that you're excited. But I'm not into talking."

I expect him to be a little taken aback. Maybe irritated.

But the guy *smiles*. Smiles. Like what I said is cute.

And just like that, I feel it pulsing around in my fingers like flickering electricity wound around my bones. Like my hands are asleep, but that's not it. This is a familiar feeling. This is a dangerous, hungry feeling—a feeling I have tethered back with as much yarn as I can muster. I ball my fists and look out the window.

"You don't have to talk. I get it. But I'm here if you need to talk. I majored in women's studies in college, so I get—"

Kolby lurches forward as the kid kicks the back of his seat. His forehead thuds against the seat in front of him. The smile comes off his face like it's been wiped clean. I look over my shoulder at the kid who had, just an hour before, been the bane of my existence. In this moment, he's the dearest thing I have in this world. He'd jostled my seat, but he'd never kicked like *that*. The kid smiles at me like he gets it. I can't help it. I smile back.

Even though the buzzing in my palm still flits around under my skin like a trapped bee. Even though I'm reminded that if there ever is a war between Oddities and Baselines—humans with magic and humans without it—

I'm on the wrong side.

THREE

It's dark when we pull into the bus station, and the fog is a curtain of breath so thick I can barely see a few feet past the glass of the window. Kolby tried to talk a couple more times during the ride, but he eventually got the hint. And by hint I mean I sneezed in his coffee. I'm excited for him to get off the bus, though. I'm going to stretch out and try to get some sleep.

"Last stop of the night!" the burly bus driver shouts as he stands.

No. That can't be right.

"We were supposed to get to Stockton tonight!" I call out. The bus driver gives me a weary look.

"Supposed to. Can't. Major flooding on the roads. We'll get going first thing tomorrow."

I can't stop here. I can't be in San Francisco.

"You need a place to stay?" Kolby asks as I step out into the freezing night. I don't answer him as I walk quickly to the station. Maybe I can get a ticket to a different town tonight.

CLOSED, the window reads in all caps, like it's shout-laughing at my misfortune.

My heart sinks in my chest as my thoughts spin in my head. *Calm down. Just think.*

I lean against the building, watching as all the passengers gather their bags and head off to the street to wait for their rides. I step as far back into shadow as I can. I press the light on the cheap Marvel watch Jack gave me as a gag gift on my birthday. It tells me it's almost ten. I sigh. Spending the night on the street is not what I wanted to do today, but it doesn't look like I have a choice. I tighten the straps on my backpack and take off down the street. I'm looking for a church or train station—some place I can sit until sunrise.

I walk, my high-tops silent on the pavement as I pass a giant mural of the Virgin Mary painted in bright fuchsia and hot pink. I stop, captivated by the image and how the color seems to cut through the darkness of the night. I've always heard things about the vibrancy of San Francisco, but I never expected this. I want to keep my head down and my feet moving, but the energy of this place begs for me to look, and I can't help it. There are rows and rows of Victorian-style houses, all different shades of blue. I pass by a bodega with golden window boxes bursting with peonies and fresh cilantro. I walk under a lime-green fire exit and stop as an orange cat missing a chunk of its ear meows, putting its little paw through the grate toward me. I smile, stopping for just a moment to reach up and give it a high five. The wires of the streetcars hiss as electricity crackles down the lines. For just a few minutes, it's like the reality of who I am and what I've done slide to the back of my mind, pushed there by the smell of sourdough and sea air so thick I can almost taste the bay on my tongue.

I hear a skitter that snaps me back to reality. I whip around. The streetlights are hazy halos through the earth-bound clouds.

It's a city. There are lots of sounds in a city.

I turn around and quicken my pace even more, hoping that no one saw me jump at what was probably just a cat. Then, I hear it again. Not so much a skitter as a set of foot-steps lightly skimming the concrete. Right behind me, and getting closer.

I turn around one more time, the fear filling my veins so fast that I hear my choked heartbeat in my ears.

"Someone there?" I call out. My voice wobbles, but I make my breathing steady.

It's not them. It's not them. It's not them.

The Wardens are gone. Everything is different. You don't have to be scared.

Just breathe.

I need to calm down, but I can't shake the fact that right now I'm the quintessential first victim in a horror movie. The camera is coming up fast behind me just so that I can spin around and see a small animal coming out of the shadow. I'll breathe a sigh of relief only to turn back around and see some murderer in a mask and a battery-powered drill, and someone will find my half-eaten corpse washed up under the Golden Gate Bridge. And that's the best-case scenario. Because if it's the Wardens, no one will ever find my body.

No one has seen the Wardens in almost two years, I remind myself.

A sound makes me jump and spin. A gray cat scuttles out from behind a dumpster. I jump, biting back a scream. Okay, so it was a cat. Now, I just need to turn—

I turn back around. No mask. No power drill.

There's a very distinct chance that I might have been overreacting.

I'm in a new place. Everything is strange. It's natural to feel weird in a new place, right?

But then I hear it again. I look up, and that's when I see it—a silhouette barely visible, caught on the edge of the streetlight's glow. I could swear I see something. Someone. I can't tell if it's my imagination or not, and I don't give myself time to figure it out. I book it as fast as I can, scrambling blindly down the sidewalk.

I can hardly see anything through this thick fog, but I

make out the lights of a small lavender building across the street. *Aloa's Café*. It looks like the only place still open.

I rip open the door, the little tinkle of the bell feeling horribly out of place against the background of my terror.

I stand here, breathing hard as the warm, deep-fried air envelops me. Two hipsters sit at a table near the back, with what looks like seven different electronics plugged into a wall painted the color of eggplant, and a guy in a sweatshirt is reading a book near the opposite window. I step inside, my Converse squeaking on the scuffed wood floor. The bell tinkles once more as I let the door shut and shuffle over to a table near the front window. It's tucked close to the corner, under a theatrical poster of *The Fellowship of the Ring*. From here, I can keep a look out into the street without being out in the open. I peer through the glass, but there's nothing out there but swirls of fog on the black street. The guy across the café looks up from his book. He wears a dark beanie and a gray hoodie. He's got a butterfly bandage over his eyebrow. Even from this far away, I can see the purple bruise seeping out from under it. He's got a barely healed scab on his lower lip. He brings up his paper cup and takes a sip. It looks ridiculously small in his huge hands, which are also covered in bandages.

Oh, good. This is fine. He doesn't look like a serial killer at all.

I look back out the window, half expecting to see the

silhouette standing in the mist. There's nothing, but the sight of the empty street feels more like a threat than reassurance. I know someone was watching me. Someone who can scale buildings.

I startle again as a man's voice cuts through my thoughts.

"Coffee?" he asks, holding up his free hand as he reads the panicked look on my face. He's older—bald with fading tattoos on the sides of his head. Each ear has at least three piercings, and a thick red beard covers the lower half of his face. His name tag reads "Gabe."

I swallow hard as I shake my head. I have some money saved up, but I need to be smart with it. "I'm sorry. I'll be out of here in a minute, if that's okay?"

He regards me for a moment before filling the chipped mug at the edge of my table. He sets it in front of me.

"Oh, I—" I start, but he shakes his head.

"We close in two hours, and this coffee is going to get thrown out. You're doing me a favor."

I look up at him, meeting his eyes for a moment. Kindness is rarely free, especially when you're a woman. I've learned not to take favors, not like that's ever spared me from unwanted attention. But he isn't winking with subtlety he obviously learned from a porno. In fact, he's looking out the window, almost like he can tell I'm scared of something that lurks behind the swaths of shadow.

"Thank you," I whisper.

He nods once and heads over to the hipsters. I wrap my freezing fingers around the cup, gasping slightly as the heat bites my skin through the ceramic. For a moment, I remember slipping into Ashtyn's hot tub at the end-of-the-year slumber party.

I bite my tongue. Not now.

I haven't cried about this for months. I don't think I could even if I tried. The pain is buried so deep in my chest that I'd have to dive to reach it—and I don't think I could find it with one held breath. It's lost to me until I really go looking for it. I'm fine with that.

I pull my backpack off my shoulder and open it gingerly, like there's something dangerous inside that's going to lunge once it has the room.

I eye the envelope I paid almost three months' wages for when I was living up in Seattle. The one I haven't had the guts to open. I take one breath—just long enough to remind me that I'm a coward and I can't do what I'd been planning when I bought it. It's been fifteen months since I was home. I thought I'd get braver as time wore on, but the opposite is true.

It's been twelve months since I saw the last "Missing" poster with my face on it. It's been nine since I saw my face on the news. "Local Girl Disappears After Massive Fire," the caption said, accompanied by the picture my mom took at Manhattan Beach, the one where I'm wearing a tube top, so it looks like I'm naked. I rolled my eyes when I first saw it, because my mom probably didn't even realize it when she grabbed it and handed it to the police officers. For a moment, I imagine teasing her about it with Carmen. And then reality sinks over me, heavy enough to dent the floor under my feet.

I can't laugh with them ever again. Not after what I did.

The memory of the screams brings with it the stench of burning wood that makes my fear of the Wardens feel almost laughable by comparison.

I knew what I'd done warranted a death sentence from the Wardens. Honestly, I'd been expecting it. I found myself waiting for the telltale queen of poisons flower nailed to our front door. For months before I ran away I'd been waking up early and checking, just so my mom wouldn't find it first on her way to work.

It was only a matter of time before I screwed everything up and lost control. I just never imagined—not in a thousand nightmares—how devastating losing control could be.

I bite my tongue so hard I taste blood.

I don't know how long I sit, sipping the coffee and staring at the writhing mist brushing up against the glass. It must be a while, though, because the hipsters pack up and leave. Gabe comes over and pours more coffee into my mug. I mutter a soft thank you, and he nods before heading back to the counter.

I watch Bloody Knuckles as he reads. He runs his thumb over his bottom lip, and I find myself staring. Despite his bruises, he's actually kind of . . .

Something long-forgotten churns in my gut. I was *not* going to say that he's cute, because the last thing someone on the run needs is a useless crush.

I had a boyfriend back home for a couple of months. Nathan Perez. Football player, totally gorgeous, *terrible* kisser. We broke up sophomore year. He cried. I didn't. I've kissed a few boys since then, but not since I left home. My eyes lock on Bloody Knuckles's lips, again.

Okay, now I'm staring.

Don't look up. Don't look up, don't—

Oops. He looked up.

We lock eyes again. I bristle, going from *I literally ran away from fog about an hour ago* to *I can and will shank you if you get too close to me* in ten seconds flat. Another little trick I've learned over the year I've spent traveling alone.

He cocks a scarred eyebrow at me and then smirks. Like he thinks my carefully cultivated look of menace is intriguing, or something.

"What?" I ask, because the best defense is a good offense, right?

He looks up again, surprise on his features. He makes a show of looking behind him and then back to me, amusement creeping up his features.

"Nothing," he says.

My hands go back to my coffee cup, and I spill some over the edge as I lift it to my lips. Crap.

I look back up, hoping he didn't see that. But of course he did. I swear I see him smile as he looks down at a Mole-skine notebook on the table in front of him. I wonder what he's writing. *Dear diary. Update—women still spill things in my presence.*

"Ouch," I whisper, because the coffee was still hot. This is just not my night. Or my year. Or my life. I'm about to get up and chance the creepy-ass fog outside when someone sets a napkin on the table. I look up at Bloody Knuckles.

"You okay?" he asks.

"Fine," I say, scooting back out of instinct as he sits in the chair across from me.

"I told Gabe not to serve it so hot," he says, reaching his hand out. I don't move. He doesn't expect me to ask for his help, right?

"I'm fine," I repeat, and the intonation says, *Eff off, please.* Another trick I've picked up on the run.

Bloody Knuckles rolls his eyes. "I'm not trying to be creepy. I was an EMT for a year. I just want to make sure you're okay."

"And I've been the owner of this hand for seventeen, so I know it's fine."

Bloody Knuckles stands. "Okay then. I can take a hint. If

you change your mind, there are ice packs in the freezer in the back."

"I don't need your help. I didn't need the free coffee, either. I'm not a helpless stray, okay? I can take care of myself."

Bloody Knuckles holds his hands up in surrender. "No one said you couldn't." His eyes search mine, and I see a question rising in them as he looks me over. It makes me want to squirm in my seat, like he can see things I've tried to keep hidden. Up close, he looks less like a murderer. He looks wholesome, like Captain America or something. But I make myself sit still. I'm about to open my mouth when we hear it. It's a *thud*, followed by the clatter of metal rattling from the kitchen, like utensils spilling across the tile floor.

Bloody Knuckles freezes, listening hard. I do, too. There was something wrong about that sound. Then—

Click.

I know it's not as loud as I hear it in my head. It can't possibly be loud enough to echo in my skull from that far away, but maybe that's just how the cocking of a gun always sounds—like the snapping of teeth, hungry to decide things no human should be deciding. A noise like that can't possibly be quiet, no matter how hard it tries.

"Don't move," someone snaps from the kitchen. I see through the cook's window—a man with gray-and-black gloves. He has a small pistol in his right hand. He hasn't seen us . . . yet.

Just like that, Bloody Knuckles is across the room. He didn't make a sound. I move, too, but he puts a finger to his lips.

Get down, he mouths. I stop for a moment, then drop down to a crouch near the table.

He moves closer to the kitchen, and I inch toward him. He spins, looking over his shoulder.

"Stay there," he says. His voice is a deep, ragged whisper. He crouch-runs to the counter, then scoots as close as he can get to the kitchen.

I know I should chance the sound of the bell that hangs over the entrance and run as fast as I can away from here. At best, this is going to bring cops—I can't afford to be seen by cops. I don't think news of my disappearance went this far north, not with so many kids my age disappearing—but I don't want to risk it.

But the sound of the *thud* plays over again in my head. Someone hit Gabe, and he's hurt. And if Bloody Knuckles is going to attempt some heroics, he's going to get himself killed. I've seen too many people get hurt. I can't just walk away, even though I know I should.

I inch forward.

Bloody Knuckles whips around, the concern melting off his face, replaced by naked irritation.

He waves wildly at me. *Run*, he mouths.

Okay, now I'm annoyed. Sure, he's the size of a small

redwood, but this close I can see that he can't be more than nineteen, at most. I don't take orders from anyone anymore.

I don't know when I moved closer to Bloody Knuckles, but I'm right behind him, flush with the counter. The man with the gun in the kitchen is muttering, but I can't see a second figure. He's either talking to Gabe or cussing into a cell phone.

Bloody Knuckles realizes I'm behind him and jumps.

"You," he says, his tone incredulous. "I said get out."

"Do you have a phone?" I whisper back. He shakes his head and narrows his eyes at me. I stare back, not even trying to bristle, now—it's just coming naturally. Bloody Knuckles opens his mouth to say something, but I put a finger to my lips as the guy in the kitchen stops talking.

I ball my hands into fists at my sides. A low hum in my head rolls along the bottom of my skull, and my palms pulse.

"Last warning. Get out. I don't want to be responsible for you," Bloody Knuckles says, but I barely hear him as I stare down at my hands, feeling the power build under the skin.

Bloody Knuckles moves to the kitchen door. I look up just as he sneaks inside. I'm frozen to the spot.

Get up. Do something, I tell myself.

Do something. Do something.

Another voice answers back, like blood ringing through my ears. *You can't control it. You could make it worse.*

Who says I need it? I can help without my curse. People

help all the time without freaky powers.

I make myself stand. I make myself move, despite the fear in my muscles fighting to make me stand still.

I lurch toward the door, not really even registering that my feet are moving until I'm standing at the kitchen door. Gabe is on the ground, dazed, holding a hand to his bleeding head. Bloody Knuckles has the intruder against the wall, an arm pinned behind his back.

I slide across the floor, grabbing a dishcloth to put on Gabe's bleeding forehead.

"You're going to be okay," I whisper, though he's as white as a ghost. I pull the towel back. The gash is deep, but he'll be fine if he gets to a hospital. His shaking hand takes mine and squeezes once. His eyes are distracted and wide, but they focus on something just over my shoulder, like a warning.

"Sam," Gabe breathes, and then blacks out, going limp against the freezer door. I turn to look at Bloody Knuckles. Sam. His name is Sam.

The intruder throws his head back, hitting Sam in the face and knocking him off-balance. The intruder spins, snatching his gun and pointing it square at Sam's chest.

As my mouth opens to scream I feel something spring from my palms. Before I can stop it, it snakes across the room and locks on to the intruder's chest. My mind is filled with a deep thrumming—a low rumble of thoughts running together. I hear voices, see glimpses of faces. I see underwater—a tumble of ocean—the roar of the waves. Then, the thing I released pulls back, like a muscle twitch. My eyes spring open as the tug from my magic causes the intruder to lurch forward, like he's been shoved from behind.

My stomach plummets as I realize what I've done. I'm still tethered to the intruder's chest, my magic still linking us as the sound of waves grows louder in the back of my head.

"What the fuck was that?" the intruder shrieks, lowering the gun to look behind him, as though he's going to find someone there. There's a look of pure terror on his face. I shove myself to my unsteady feet. His red-rimmed eyes lock on mine, like he's noticing I'm here for the first time. His bleached hair falls in his face, a faint line of stubble lining his quivering upper lip. If I was fully present, I might feel bad for him.

"What are you afraid of?" I ask the intruder. His eyes settle on me for a moment before darting around the room again. He isn't listening to me.

"Run," I whisper, looking at Sam.

"What? Why?" he presses, and I know he sees the look of terror in my eyes, because he takes a step toward me.

"Take Gabe and go," I beg. I try to break the connection between me and the intruder, but it's useless.

The guy raises his gun at my chest. "No one is going anywhere," he spits.

Okay, maybe I wouldn't feel bad for him.

That underwater feeling is getting stronger, pulling me deeper as my hands shake and I feel the connection between us tighten. Sweat drips down the back of my neck as I see the intruder's angry expression slipping—I know he's feeling the same thing I am. He's hearing the waves . . . the screams.

I hear the roar of the ocean in my ears. He cocks the gun and points it at Sam's head.

"Back off, or I blow your boyfriend away," he says, but something else has his attention. He looks down at the sound of trickling water. It's gathering around his feet, swirling in a torrent around his ankles like a whirlpool conjured out of thin air.

"What is this?" he asks breathlessly.

I stare at the water, a strange thrill coming over me. I feel the current in my hands—every move it makes, I feel under my skin. He tries to move, but I bring my hands up and the whirlpool around him rises to his waist. I raise my hands higher, focusing on the water. The water rises, covering his shoulders, pinning his hands to his sides as he shouts.

I stretch my fingers, and the water spins around him faster. A slight hope sparks deep in my chest—I've never before been able to control what I bring out. This is completely new.

Energy spins in my palms as I bring my hands higher.

The thick, unforgiving water churns around him. This is what I found inside of him—the fear born of a memory deep inside this guy from ten summers ago, when a riptide yanked his legs out from under him and sent him spinning into darkness. The moments when he thought he was going to die—the roar of the ocean heave in his ears, filling him until he didn't know what was the ocean and what was his own scream. The salt burning his throat, stinging his eyes. Somewhere in the darkness of his fear, I hear a woman screaming his name. *Mitch! Mitch! My son! He's caught! Mitch*—

Mitch. That's his name.

I come back to the kitchen as I open my eyes. I chance a look at Sam—who is looking back at me, a curious expression on his face. I don't have time to try to place it. I turn back to Mitch.

Drowning. He's afraid of drowning.

"It's not fun having someone play with your life, is it, Mitch?" I ask, and his eyes widen.

The power thrums through me, my muscles stretching and pulling with the weight I haven't used since I ran away, but my body remembers this.

"How do you know my name?" he sputters as I let the water rise to his neck. I take a step, and the water moves with me, inching backward. My shoes squeak on the wet tile. I'm going to push him and the water outside, let the fear snap back to its place in his chest, and then I'm going to take his gun and let Sam hold him until the police arrive.

I never thought the day would come when I'd be able to do something good with it. That I'd be anything but a danger. I'm almost giddy at the thought, almost triumphant. I close my eyes, focusing on the water.

The sandy water, icy and angry. The water, filling my nose and leaking into my lungs and wrapping them tight—

I feel it, the moment when something goes wrong. It's like I feel the hold I have creaking, and then it snaps, and I tumble, the deafening roar of the ocean ripping through my mind. In a moment, I am back in his memory. Back under the water, tumbling. My fingers dig into the sand, trying to gain purchase, to set myself right. But I can't set myself right. I can't fix this. I might never be able to set myself right again.

I fall to my knees, and the pain yanks me back to the present just in time for me to see the water cyclone collapse in front of me, sending Mitch sprawling onto the floor. There's a beat, a moment, when I think that's the end of it. But then a roar rushes in my ears, and I turn.

A wave of water bursts through the door leading to the dining room, knocking Sam off his feet and tipping the metal table, throwing it against the back wall, blocking the back door. Water pours in, flooding the kitchen in seconds. It's like we're in a sinking ship, the ocean ripping our pathetic vessel to shreds as it claims us.

I hear myself scream, but it sounds far away. I squeeze my eyes shut, trying to get control back, but it's pointless. The terror ripping through my chest isn't letting me get a hold of anything. I'm choking on Mitch's borrowed fear.

The water rises—shit, it's freezing. Sam's in front of me, then, Gabe limp over his shoulder. He's shouting something that I can't hear. He moves closer.

"We have to get the table away from the door!"

I nod dumbly, and we wade over to the flipped table. It's huge.

"Hey! You have to help us!" Sam yells at Mitch, but he's not listening. He's frozen, shivering as he looks at the water barreling through the door like it's a monster from his nightmare. It is.

I shove my own terror as far back as I can, focusing on how to get the hell out of here alive.

"Pull on three!" he shouts. "One, two, *three*!"

Sam and I yank on the table, but it's wedged between two shelves that sit on either side of the door.

The water is to my collarbone now, and it pulls me off my feet and knocks the air out of my lungs.

Sam adjusts Gabe over his shoulder to make sure he stays above the waterline.

"Let me try from below," I rasp, taking a deep breath and plunging beneath the surface. I open my eyes, but sand swirls through the current and I can barely see anything. Salt water invades my mouth and nose. Of course—he was afraid of the ocean, so that's what I conjured up. I pull on the table's leg, but it's no use. Stuck.

I break the surface again. We've only got inches left. The fluorescent lights sputter and die above us, and everything is thrown into darkness.

"We'll have to try through the other door—maybe the

water will let us through once it's full in here," Sam sputters. But I know it won't work. I know it because I still feel the fear raging in the base of my chest, a mirror current of the water ripping through the door. It won't stop until I do, and I can't get it to stop.

We're going to die because I'm scared. Because I was dumb enough to think for one second that this was anything other than a curse.

The water rises over my mouth. I take one more deep breath, my lips brushing against the foam lining of the ceiling, and I go under.

I sink, letting myself drift to the bottom. It's so cold that I'm not even shivering anymore. The floor is against my back, the water whipping my hair around my head.

I pull once more against the table, but it's not budging.

The sound of the water pummeling, rushing against itself fills my head, and it's almost soothing. Terror is rippling through me, and I hear the faint screams of Mitch's mom echoing through my head—the remnants of his fear that still link us.

It wasn't supposed to end like this. I'm not ready for it to end like this. My lungs burn, and I scream out, bubbles slipping through my lips. I yank on the edge of the table as hard as I can. Nothing.

I stop. The water doesn't even feel cold anymore. That's a bad sign, right?

I wonder if my family will ever know what happened. If

they'll have to come identify my body. I'm such a shit daughter for making them do a trip on top of breaking their hearts. Of course, I'm a shit daughter for other reasons, too. I picture my mom and her smile from the stands at games. I see my dad across the fire pit at the beach. I hear Carmen's laughing shriek as Jack puts his arms through the legs of his boxers and chases her around the kitchen.

My heart slows. Everything slows.

And then, the fire in my gut fades. I'm still scared, but the panic loosens its grip on my spine. It's just for a moment, but it's enough of a gap in my panic to get a hold of the fear.

Just for a second, I have a grip on it, and not the other way around.

I reach over and pull on the table leg, and it yanks free. If the fear has lost its grip on me, then it's lost its foothold in this world, too. I pull the table free and shove myself to the door. I throw the bolt and pull as hard as I can. I get it open a couple of inches, but it's not enough. Terror flares up again. Then, Sam is next to me. The feel of someone fighting alongside me silences the fear still swirling deep in my chest, just for a moment. And a moment is all we need.

He wedges his fingers in the gap and pulls.

We're sucked out into the night as the water spills into the parking lot.

I hit the asphalt, and everything goes black.

FOUR

Up until I was fifteen, the worst thing I'd ever done was buy a couple of G-strings without telling my mother. The worst thing I'd ever seen was when my best friend Lindsay found her cat's lower half in the gutter outside her house.

My life was caramel Frappuccinos, cheer practice, and Friday-night sleepovers.

I played with my younger sister, Iris, and my younger brother, Jack. Carmen was the oldest, and we made it our mission to annoy her as much as possible.

Up until I was fifteen, everything I thought about my life was a lie.

I was raised on stories about Oddities. Everyone was. I think that's the weirdest part of the whole thing. I grew up hearing tales about the freaks, the anomalies—Oddities—the magicians. We talked about them like they were weird, but we all wanted to know what it was like to have power. I remember joking about the silly-sounding ones. A kid who realized he could pop a bag of popcorn by putting his hand on the bag, or a girl who could break glass with her voice. Then there were horror stories told in the dark during camp, like the one with a girl who woke up early one morning with yellow eyes and a thirst for blood so intense she tore the family dog apart. Those stories kept me up at night long after I'd laughed about them over campfires.

But the stories always had a hero . . . the reason Oddities could never hurt us. The Wardens—Oddities who protected humanity. Shadows in black who made sure nonmagical people would never be hurt by the magicians.

For most of my life these stories were just fun things we whispered in the dark over the edge of our sleeping bags at a sleepover. Until I woke up one morning and started feeling a pulse in the center of my palms that felt like it was *latching on* to other people . . . like it was somehow *inside* them.

I stayed in denial for as long as I could. But I wondered, as I lay in my bed late at night, if the stories might be true. Parents tell their kids about Santa Claus knowing that, at some point, they'll realize it was just a game—something sweet to make childhood more wondrous and magical. As the sharp, humming *something* pulsed under my skin, I wondered if parents were betting on the fact that we'd realize the reverse about Oddities: that they *were* real. If they told us it was just a story because they wanted to keep our childhoods safe and carefree for as long as they could.

I begged my parents to take me to the doctor, and I prayed it would be nerve pain, maybe something from cheer. But they didn't find anything. Next, they took me to a psychologist, who was convinced I was nervous about college applications and this was my way of acting out.

Nothing is wrong, Vesper, my mom whispered to me. But I felt a thirst in me I was worried about controlling.

One night, my dad sat me down and told me to do it to him—whatever I was afraid of being able to do.

"You can't be serious, Dad," I remember saying.

He set his hands on his knees on the couch across from me. "Very. I'm going to show you that there's nothing to be afraid of."

I raised my palm. It tingled, a singsong threat threading through my blood. And I focused . . .

But nothing happened. The power fizzled out, and I looked down at my hand.

"See? There's nothing to worry about," he told me.

It wasn't that I was controlling my power. It was that there was something much bigger than me stopping me from showing it to anyone.

But on July Fourth, everything changed.

It was ravenous that night. I could feel it—hunger pangs in the tips of my fingers that stretched to that place deep in my chest. The last thing I wanted to do was go to the Independence Day party by the lake, but my whole family was going, and I knew that getting out of it would be harder than just saying yes.

But right before the fireworks, Lindsay grabbed my hand. She had found the best spot down by the water. At the feel of her skin, the hungry thing leaped out. It coiled around her, and she had no clue. I remember watching her talk about how hot the new lifeguard was, completely unaware of what I'd done. Completely unaware that if I wanted to, I could let whatever it was loose on her. I stopped walking; stopped breathing. If I was still, I could keep it where it was—slack in the way it surrounded her whole body, as if waiting for orders. I choked out that I had to pee and I would meet her in a few minutes.

Someone called her name, and she ran off, breaking my hold on her. The power shot back into me like a lightning bolt, and I fell to the sand, clutching my chest as I let the sobs build in my chest like a storm.

That's how my dad found me a few minutes later.

"It's real. I know you and Mom don't believe me, but it's real," I gasped.

He tried to calm me down. He brushed the hair off my forehead like he did when I was little and running a fever. He tried to tell me, for the thousandth time, that it wasn't possible. I shoved myself upright, broken shells digging into my palms.

I held my hand out, letting the power snake from me. Looking back, I see how dangerous that was. I wasn't really thinking about that—I just needed my dad to believe me. He couldn't stop this from happening if he didn't even think it was real.

As it grabbed him, his eyes widened as a strangled sound slipped past his teeth. In my mind, I saw hints of something inky and dark. My senses were full of the smell of wet stone and something coppery. Metallic.

Blood.

I saw a man in a black suit walking down an alleyway, his back to me. He stopped at a door under a fluorescent sign that read *Sue's Pawn Shop* in neon green.

"Vesper. Pull it back." I heard my dad's voice, but it sounded far away.

The man in the suit started to turn. He started to say something.

"Vesper!" my dad screamed. His hands shook my shoulders, and I was back at the lake, my dad's face inches from mine.

I knew then that I was right. I saw my own heartbreak reflected in his blue eyes—the ones that were the same shade and shape as mine.

"What's happening to me?" I hiccupped out. He pulled me tight to his chest. Above us, the fireworks went off. Shouts and cheers echoed up from the lake, and the sound of the free, careless joy felt wrong against the refrain playing in the back of my mind.

I was anything but free.

FIVE

I must not have been out long. I open my eyes, my cheek pressed against the soaking pavement. Water rushes over me—the last remnants of the current I pulled from Mitch. A slight breeze rustles the trees above my head, and it feels like razors grazing my exposed skin. I shove myself to my feet as I remember what has just happened, my thoughts clinking together like falling dominoes.

Sam. Gabe. Mitch.

I whip around, my chest tight.

I see Sam then, not ten feet away, his back against a tree that's on the edge of the parking lot. Gabe is lying beside him.

"Are you okay?" I call, stepping toward him. I ignore the look in his eyes. I ignore the way my shoes squeak as I step closer, and the way I sink in the mud with every step. If there's anything worse than this feeling—this complete exposure, I don't know it. I don't want to look up. I don't want to have to answer the questions. *What was that? How did you do that?* Or, even worse, I don't want to deal with the terror. The way he might avoid my eyes and look for the quickest escape route.

He nods, looking down at Gabe.

"He's breathing."

That's it.

No questions. No panic. It's a look I understand well now. Most people who were told terrible stories about Oddities outgrow them and cast them aside with all the other things kids outgrow. But there are a few people who can't leave the stories behind, and I can see in Sam's eyes that he's one of them. I wonder who it is. A family member? A friend? I take a closer look. Him? Could he be an Oddity, too?

"We need to get him to a hospital." I say. Maybe he can take Gabe. That will give me enough time to disappear before the cops show up. And maybe parks and recreation services. The Coast Guard? Who do you call when a giant tidal wave rips through a parking lot? I doubt there is protocol for this kind of thing.

Sam pulls his sweatshirt over his head and tucks it around Gabe. He wears a black tank top with the word "Duncan's" emblazoned on the front. His wide shoulders are peppered with bruises and scars. He stands, slowly, turning to face me. I take an involuntary step back when I see the look on his face. It's something between anger and disbelief.

"What was that?" he asks.

"A burst pipe." The lie is easy and feels right, even though I know he won't buy it.

"Bullshit," he counters, stepping closer.

"I don't owe your unshot face an explanation for anything. You're welcome, by the way," I say, refusing to take a step back on what is probably a misguided principle. I hold my ground, hoping I look more certain than I feel. "Because your half-cocked plan almost got you killed."

"I'm missing how that was better than your fully thought-out plan that almost had *all of us* killed."

"Spare me the hero act," I shoot back, so very painfully aware that I have no moral high ground to stand on. My power was been a monster inside me, prowling restlessly since the night I ran away. Using it was a panic move, and I should've known better than to think I could control it now.

Something catches Sam's attention, and he turns around at the sound of coughing. Mitch. I don't really want to look over my shoulder. If I look over my shoulder, I'm going to see the extent of my damage.

I wince and turn.

Yep. It's as bad as I thought it would be. Metal grinds against metal as the cars in the parking lot settle into the mud. The back door of the café hangs loose from its hinges. At the edge of the flooded lot, I see Mitch, pushing himself up into a sitting position. He's coughing, sputtering, cussing, and having a total mental breakdown, but he's not dead.

I don't have much time here. He doesn't move—doesn't try to run. He looks around. He flinches when he spots me and drops his eyes to the concrete. Sirens ride the wind, pricking my ears. Slowly, I walk closer.

His eyes are wide as I kneel next to him. In his daze, he looks like a declawed kitten. I almost feel bad for him.

But not enough.

"What happened?" His voice squeaks and breaks as he looks at me. I know he's looking at me for comfort—for answers. I could make him feel better, right now. I could ease the inky panic that will follow him, clinging to his heels for the next few months—maybe years.

Nah. If I feel bad about this, he's going to, too.

I lean forward.

"You're going to leave this town without telling anyone what you've seen. Do you understand?"

He stares at me with a mixture of fear, awe, and barely veiled contempt. "You shouldn't be out here, mixing with regular people. You should be locked up in some government facility somewhere."

A smile slides up my mouth, and I know I look a little unhinged. I roll with it, letting the confusion on his face edge closer to fear. A small laugh escapes my lips. "That's true. How about this? We'll go turn ourselves in together. That sound good? They'll book us and keep us in processing for at least a night before we part ways. That's plenty of time for you to mysteriously drown in your cell's toilet water. Or you could shut your mouth and disappear."

Fear wins out on his pasty face as he nods reluctantly. I clap him on the shoulder, and he winces. I stand, pausing for a moment as I look down at the man who would've easily taken a life tonight without a second thought.

"If I see you around here again, Mitch, you won't see me coming."

He looks up at me, taking in a deep breath before he spits out, "What are you?"

So he has no clue what I am—even better. I force a demure smile on my face and take a couple steps backward, really hoping that I don't trip over my untied shoelaces.

He doesn't need to know that I'm an Oddity. And I'm certainly not going to tell him that I'm a Harbinger—an Oddity who can make someone's worst fears come true.

I turn when I'm back in shadow. Sam looks at me, peering at me in a strange way that makes me want to cross my arms over my chest. He's not afraid, and I realize that I kind of prefer fear. Whatever this is—this *figuring out* look—I don't like it.

"You should go," he says lowly. "I'll make sure Gabe's safe." Behind me, I hear the sounds of Mitch trying and failing to stand in the thick sludge. He's not going anywhere.

I want to ask why he's willing to cover me, but I swallow the question down.

Despite the massive property damage, I'm almost feeling

like I might actually get away with this. Mitch won't say anything. Sam is covering for me. I might be able to get a ticket out of this town, get to Paynes Creek, and disappear.

For a moment, my mind flits back to the moment before I lost control, when the water bent to my will and my power was just that . . . power. I was in control.

I shove the thought out of my mind, because it's a stupid hope to have. I can't risk having regular hope at this point, let alone the stupid kind. Nothing good comes from a Harbinger. We only bring fear. That's why my best shot at a life that doesn't hurt anyone means slipping into the shadows until I'm dead. If I can do that, things might be okay.

This is what I'm thinking when the sirens pull me out of my thoughts and I hear the shouts. Paramedics, cops, and firefighters surround the parking lot, and I know there is nowhere to run. I feel the bright glare of headlights, accompanied by the two worst words I could imagine, cut through the freezing night:

"Police. Freeze."

Previous optimism redacted.

Dad told my mom I was feeling sick and that he would take me home. I curled up in the back seat and watched the smoke from the fireworks smear across the moonlit sky as he drove home in total silence.

It wasn't until we were safe in his study that he finally

looked at me. Then he started riffling through his drawers. He opened his laptop and clicked the keys at a furious pace.

"Something's happened then," he said.

"What's happened?" I asked, frustration rising in me like a scream. Finally, my dad kneeled in front of me. He took a deep breath and then unbuttoned the top two buttons of his Tommy Bahama shirt.

"You know the story of this scar," he said, more a statement than a question. I knew the story. Everyone did.

Knotted pink tissue weaved and curled in a mass the size of a dinner plate just below his right collarbone, a permanent reminder of the motorcycle accident that almost killed him when he was in his twenties, right after he met my mom. He'd been in a coma for over a month.

I nodded, and he shook his head.

"You don't. It's a lie."

It was the first of many.

SIX

My forehead is pressed against the brick of Aloa's Café, my palms resting on either side of my face, as an officer older than my mom pats me down. I can't tell if I'm shivering because I'm freezing or scared. Getting on that bus was the worst mistake I've made since I decided to try gas station sushi two months ago. If I get out of this mess, I'm hauling my ass down to the middle of nowhere. I'll work on an almond farm and never speak to another human as long as I live.

"This is just a precaution. We have no clue what the hell happened here, so you need to stay put until we figure it out," the officer says, clicking handcuffs around my wrists and securing them to a drainpipe. She narrows her eyes at me and flips her no-nonsense braid over her shoulder.

"What do you mean 'what happened here'? It was a burst pipe," Sam replies. He's in the same position next to me.

Another cop kicks a soggy loaf of bread next to his foot as he pats Sam's legs. "One hell of a burst pipe," he says, eyeing the officer who cuffed me. They don't believe us. She meets my eyes as the cop finishes patting Sam down and pulls him toward the patrol car behind her.

A sound rips through the night. One of the headlights on the patrol car shatters. *Crack.*

Then the other. *Crack.*

It's so fast I can't see what's doing it. Then the streetlights around the parking lot are gone, and we're left in a dull darkness, the glow of the city lights nothing but a vague promise through the thick fog. There are shouts and the sound of cocking guns. I look up—a girl with cropped black hair appears on the edge of the café above me and lifts her hands. A strange hum rolls over us. The pressure in my head changes, like my ears need to pop.

"Where did they go?" the officer behind me screams. She is looking straight at me but not seeing me. Something is blocking her vision. Her words become muffled, like there's thick glass between us. I can barely hear her. The girl above has shaded us—blocked us from view. I pull against my cuffs to look over my shoulder. I don't know why I look, why I care—but I turn to Sam. He's muffled as well, his eyes darting over me, unseeing.

"Madam, are these people bothering you?" a voice asks from the darkness. A guy steps out of the shadow. He's tall and broad, with dark skin that looks luminous in the orange light. His black hair is pulled back into a ponytail at the base of his neck, and tattoos stretch up both arms.

"I said no attempted wit, Aldrick. In and out," the Shader calls from the rooftop. Her hands shake.

"I'm being polite. *God*, Alanna," the guy named Aldrick calls back in a fake Valley girl accent.

"Let me rephrase—hurry the hell up."

"Who are you?" I ask, trying to step as far back as I can with these cuffs on. He steps closer, and I can see that he's only a little older than me. He throws his arms out into fists at his sides. His skin crackles and stretches, turning an ashen gray. His tattoos fade, becoming shadows. He's a Stoneskin.

"The good guys." He reaches over to yank my hands free of the pipe, and then the cuffs. He snaps the metal with his fingers like he's breaking a pretzel.

"*Good guys*? Do I look twelve to you?" I reply sharply.

"Now is not the time to debate the very complicated nature of good versus evil, so how about I just start with the basics? You're an Oddity. We're Oddities. You were arrested. Now you're not. Shall we?" As he gestures to the alleyway, I decide I've had my fill of *hilarious* male repartee tonight. And for the rest of my life.

"Theo!" Alanna shouts. The officer with the blond braid lifts her gun as she steps closer to us, breaking through the shade for just a moment. Alanna shrieks as the shade shatters, and the police officers see us again. A red-hot stream of what looks like reddish liquid glass streaks through from the dark alley behind the café and knocks the gun out of her hand, though from the look of horror on her face, I can tell the cop has no clue what just yanked it from her fist. The snake of glass whips out once more, knocking the other gun from the other officer's grip with a clatter. There are more shouts—more chaos—but Aldrick's running, and I'm following him. I stop suddenly, my arms pinwheeling as I whip back around. Sam is still by the cop car, his eyes wide with confusion.

"I can't leave him," I call out to Aldrick. He skids to a stop at the sound of my voice. He grabs my arm and pulls me behind him. "He's not the one about to eat a bullet, hon." I swallow down the gross feeling that I'm abandoning someone who tried to help me, and we run, following the whip of glass as it slinks back to its owner. A boy with dark skin steps out of the shadow, calling the glass back into his palm. I've heard of Vitrifases but have never seen one. He can convert the air around him into glass—that's what knocked the lights out.

The Vitrifas—Theo—looks at the roof as Alanna jumps down, throwing her palms up once more. The hum is back—we're shaded again. The boy called Theo lifts his hands, and a disc of blue glass sprouts and multiplies under Alanna's feet, creating glass stairs down from the rooftop. She lands softly on the ground, hands still out, though they're shaking.

"I don't have much left," she says.

We run until we're at the end of the alley, Alanna keeping one palm extended backward, covering us from sight. Before us is a wide street, the wires of streetcars crisscrossing over our heads. Town houses are pressed together in a smattering of different colors, and a bright blue bodega with a flickering fluorescent sign sits on the corner. This street is more open, and it looks like the theater on the other end of the street has just let out. There are dozens of people here. There's no way Alanna can hide us from everyone.

I'm about to tell them to leave me, to run—when the sound of squealing tires cuts through the night. We turn as a white van rips around the corner, shrieking to a halt right in front of us. A girl opens the driver's side door and hangs out the side, one arm on the wheel while the other grips the bike rack on the roof. Her long blue-black hair whips around her head in the windy night.

"Time to go!" she shouts, jumping out of the van.

"I'm losing—" Alanna's words are lost as she faints. Theo catches her in his arms, and the shouts of the police officers behind us escalate as they see us.

The cop who cuffed me holds up her Taser and fires it at the driver.

Aldrick shouts as I jump forward, knocking the girl aside. The cop swears as we roll out of the way. I help her scramble up, and we both run to the van.

Theo rips open the van door while Aldrick runs back into the alleyway, throwing his arms out as he goes, his skin thundering back into stone.

He tips a dumpster on its side and lifts the other, stacking it until the alley is blocked. He turns, triumphant, smiling as he runs back to the van, his skin returning to normal. The police are trapped behind the barricade. It won't take them long to get around it, but it's bought us a couple of minutes.

Aldrick hops into the passenger seat. "Get in, Waterworks," he says to me.

I don't have a choice, and I know it.

I get in the van.

SEVEN

I sit in the back seat, wondering where the hell this whole night went so terribly wrong as the girl Aldrick calls Sapphira drives us through the streets, taking all the street signs more as suggestions than rules.

Theo and Alanna sit in the middle seat in front of me, her head cradled in his lap.

"Is she going to be okay?" I ask quietly, and he looks over his shoulder at me.

"She depleted herself trying to shade so many people at once," he explains, looking at her. His glasses slide down his nose. He scrunches his nose to move the lenses up and eyes me with as much contempt as someone who just scrunched their nose can muster. *A* for effort, dude.

"She'd be better if we'd grabbed you at the bus station like I said," Theo retorts, raising his voice, so I know he's talking more to Aldrick and Sapphira than to me.

"The bus station?" I ask, my mind rewinding to earlier this evening. I can't believe I was just on a bus this evening. It feels like years ago. I remember the feeling that someone was following me.

"That was *you?*" I ask, and anger seeps into my voice. "You scared the shit out of me." I knew there was someone there.

"There are a lot of Oddities arriving in San Francisco. Dozens a week since the Stirring. You're lucky we found you before someone else did," Theo responds, brushing the hair gently out of Alanna's face.

"The Stirring?" I ask. I already don't like the sound of that. It's like the title of a M. Night Shyamalan movie.

"Independence Day. Two years ago," Aldrick says, shifting in his seat again.

Pinpricks slip up my spine.

"You know what I'm talking about then?" he asks, a smile inching onto his lips before I can think to adjust my expression.

It wasn't just me. I knew it, but it's weird to hear it from someone else out loud. It was the night I used my powers on my dad. I was never able to really get answers about it.

Does it even matter now? A small voice in the back of my mind asks.

I lean my head against the split vinyl seat. Someone's drawn a burning queen of poisons flower on the inside roof of the van. It feels like a bridge too far. "Okay. Can you just let me out at the next light, please?"

They all turn to look at me, except Sapphira, who is eyeing me through the rearview mirror, her ice-blue eyes unreadable as we veer left . . . closer to the coast.

"That's a hell of a 'you're welcome,'" Aldrick says, raising an eyebrow.

"I am *not* heading back to some secret headquarters for a revolution against the Wardens. I will take my chances with the police."

Aldrick cocks his head to the side, his eyebrows knitting together as he looks at Theo.

"You're planning a revolution, Theo?" he asks.

"Not that I was aware of, Aldrick. You, Sapphira?"

Sapphira pulls her eyes up from the road to look at Aldrick. A little smile plays on her lips as we pull up to a red light. "Always. But against the Wardens? No."

She puts her clicker on to merge with another lane as we come up against a construction zone.

I point to the drawing above me. "No?"

Aldrick cranes his neck. "Ah. That. Well that is just a celebration of our freedom. The Wardens are gone."

"Or they are biding their time. They've done it before."

"Wow. They sure got you scared," Aldrick replies.

"If you're not scared of the Wardens, you're an idiot," I snap. "They've gone silent before. And when they came back, they didn't take kindly to the people who defied them."

I sound like my father as the words tumble out of my mouth.

"It's different this time, darlin'," Aldrick says turning to face front. "It's a new day."

Maybe he's right. The fact that we can show our powers to humans now when we couldn't before, does say something. Maybe the Wardens just decided to stop nailing queen of poisons flowers to doors. Maybe they stopped taking out those of us who pose a threat to our secrecy.

But even as I think those words, another refrain pulses at the base of my throat.

Unlikely.

"Damn," Sapphira says as the traffic slows. I look out the window. Construction crews line the road. A huge wall of opaque sheeting dangles from a crane, blocking the work from view.

"I should've reminded you not to take this way. It's impossible for the next six blocks," Theo says.

"Yeah, that's super helpful right now, Theo," Sapphira shoots over her shoulder as she merges again, checking her blind spot as she accelerates.

"Where are you taking me?" I ask, because burning fear is rising up my throat at the thought of the Wardens, and I need a distraction.

"The Grotto," Theo answers, turning around. "Headquarters for the resistance." He makes a ridiculous sweeping gesture with his hands that end in a salute. He's making fun of me.

I roll my eyes. "A safe house?" I ask.

"Something like that," Theo agrees as he faces forward.

I've been on the run for a long time, and I've seen the different ways Oddities have learned to survive. Safe houses are one of them. All the Oddities use their powers to protect each other and keep the house hidden. Freaks of a feather, I guess. I saw one in Portland operating out of an abandoned shoe factory, and the Oddities there passed themselves off as a construction crew for a solid six months. Once or twice, I've come across a kind, naive stranger who thinks I would be a good addition to the community, or whatever. I always turned them down, citing my lone-wolf tendencies, which is complete bull. I hate being alone. I hate the moments when my voice cracks and false starts because it's been days since I talked to another human. I wish I could sink into a community like that. To have friends again. To be known right down to the shadows that are bone-adjacent. But my power is too dangerous.

"It's where the cool kids live, darlin'," Aldrick calls over his shoulder. "And with that mini-flood stunt, *you* just made the cut. Settle in, we'll be there before you know it."

They don't know what they're saying. They don't know what I am.

"My name is Vesper," I shoot back. "Spare me the *darlin'* crap." That's the second time he's called me that tonight. I'm so very done with it.

"Vesper?" Alanna sits up groggily, rubbing her forehead. "I hate Aldrick's nicknames, but even I'd take darlin' over *Vesper*."

I bite my lip and lean back against the seat as Sapphira pulls past a rusted gate. A sign with scrawled pink spray paint is drilled over the entrance:

Abandon all hope,
ye dumbasses who venture past this point.

I'll stay for the night, regroup, and get out of here tomorrow. As much as I'd hate to admit it, I'm exhausted. And judging by all my calls tonight? Consider me a dumbass.

I don't remember the exact wording my father used to completely unravel my life that night. I was in such a state of shock that the words just hovered around me, refusing to sink in and take root until much later. But I remember the moment he told me I was a Harbinger.

I remember the moment when I screamed at him and asked him how he knew, how he could possibly be so calm about it.

I remember the moment he told me he used to be one, too.

I remember the way the floor tilted and how my breath burned with every inhale.

Tears rolled down my cheeks, filling the crease of my lips

as I shut my mouth tight. He'd lied to me. He'd known for months what was happening and didn't say anything.

"Used to?" I finally asked, hope flaring in my chest. "Can I get rid of it?"

The sorrow in his eyes doused it immediately. "No, Ves. You can't."

I sat there, letting the weight of the disappointment settle over me like concrete. Heavy. Sticky. Lethal.

My father reached for a notepad and a pen from his desk. His lawyer voice kicked in then, almost like he saw me fading and knew I needed an anchor.

"But you can learn how to control it."

I looked up, an ember of something like hope on the tip of my tongue.

We said we were working on a project for AP English, but instead my father taught me about the shadowy world that existed in and underneath our own.

From him I learned there are different types of us. Dozens, at least. Maybe hundreds. They're called clans. Each can do different things, and all started in different places on the map. Stoneskins in the Pacific Islands. Miasmas in Central America. Vertiasmas in Ethiopia. *Oddities have always been there*, he explained. *You just had to know where to look.*

I learned that Oddities have their own wars, their own myths—their own heroes and villains. Secret histories tucked between stones and buried in unmarked graves. They ran parallel to the world I thought I knew, slithering alongside the well-worn narratives we had all been taught in history class. I drank it all in, learning everything I could. Oddities helped Edison invent the light bulb. Shifters aided in a famous search-and-rescue mission in World War II.

And we had our own nightmares—our own monsters to fear in the shadow.

And then, one night as a storm rolled in, he told me about the Wardens.

No one knows when they arrived. It's not like there was some secret ceremony where a dude pulled a cloak over his head and decided to give Oddities rules *or else.*

All we know is that some Oddities banded together and decided that in order to be able to live the lives we wish, we should stay quiet. Shadow-ridden.

It wasn't a request.

It starts as a warning—a purple bud of aconite, or queen of poisons, on your door. Nailed right through the petals. *We've seen you,* it means.

You're not given a second chance.

My father paced in front of his desk, covered with open books, as he explained it to me.

"The Wardens have a multitude of Oddities working for them, enforcing our silence, but the Rippers are the scariest—and most valuable, because what they do is dangerous. They can pull your power from you. Separate it from your bones, your DNA, and make you Baseline. Ripping certain powers can kill. A Ripper puts that part of you in a jar and takes it to the Rippers' Athenaeum; they keep the power under lock and key."

I thought I was scared by the lake, but this was worse.

Even now, I like to picture the stolen magic in mason jars, glowing like centerpieces at a rustic barn wedding. But that's just because it's less terrifying that way. In reality I think it's much worse. That's why my dad didn't linger on the *how* or *why* of the Ripper's Athenaeum. I got the gist. A library of all our bloody, most dangerous parts. Endless rows of raw power.

My dad pulled out the encyclopedias Carmen, Iris, and I used for the school projects that annoyingly didn't allow for electronic resources. He opened them to different pages and turned them toward me on his desk.

"Pisa, 1347, when victims of the bubonic plague suddenly came to life.

Ning'an, China, 1840, where it was reported that a camp of Russian defectors disappeared in the space of two minutes. Three hundred tents, gone." He turned the books so I could see the pages better.

"All these were Oddities?" I asked, running my hands over the pages. He nodded, his salt-and-pepper hair falling into his face. "I wanted to keep you shielded from this, Vesper.

You and your sisters and brother. But since that's no longer an option, then you need to know about this world. The best way to survive is to understand."

"Carmen, Iris, Jack . . . ," I started, but my dad looked down.

"No, Vesper. None of them are Oddities." For some reason, that made me relieved. At least they wouldn't have to go through this, too.

For months, I was in denial. But now that all hope of denial was gone, I was desperate for answers. If this thing inside me was real, then I wanted to know everything about it.

He gave me his handwritten notes. He drew me maps. He showed me old books hidden in false bottoms of his desk drawers. Our history was kept on scraps, written in margins. There was an old story about an Oddity—the Chronicler—who kept our stories in one place, but no one alive could confirm an Oddity like that ever existed. So we learned what we could.

My dad opened doors to this world, but he wouldn't tell me what I'd almost pulled out of him. I tried to ask him about what I saw—the alleyway. The man. My dad's gaze hardened then, in the way it did when I knew I pushed him too far.

I'd been nursing a hope for months, and I finally got a chance to ask about Rippers; my father saw the look on my face and quickly shook his head, dousing any spark of an idea that he worried might be blooming in my mind.

"That's what happened to you?" I asked, pointing to the scar on his chest.

I knew I had him. He'd walked right into the questions that had danced between us for months. Finally, my father nodded.

"Mom said it was a motorcycle accident."

"Mom thinks it was a motorcycle accident." He looked down, fingering the pages of the notebook in front of him.

"Did you want to lose your powers?" I whispered. The moment was fragile, made of the kind of glass I worried I'd break if I spoke too loudly. He looked up, his eyes blazing.

"It wasn't my choice, at the time. But now? I would risk death a thousand more times to stop being a Harbinger, Vesper. It was the only way I could've married your mother. The only way, I thought, I could have kids." His eyes filled with tears. "I thought when they pulled it from me, there was no possibility of me passing it on." He took a deep, shaky breath. "I'm so sorry."

I reached out, my cold fingers finding his over the paper. After a moment, I found my voice.

"I want to do it, Dad. I want to try."

He looked up, eyes bright. I sensed an argument coming, so I pulled my fingers from his and stood.

"If you could survive it, then so can I. I'll find a Ripper and—"

He stood up then, all traces of the tears gone. "The only Rippers still alive work for the Wardens, and you had better pray you never cross one. He didn't mean to leave me alive."

We locked eyes—a stare-down I could feel myself losing with every second. I wondered if the man I saw in my father's fear had something to do with it. There was a thick, inky layer of terror that came up the back of my throat at the thought.

"How do you know so much about the Wardens?" I pressed.

I didn't expect an answer from him. After all, I'd asked the question dozens of times before and simply fumed in silence as he changed the subject. I don't know why it was different that night. I don't know why he closed his eyes, the crepe-paper skin around them looking thinner than it ever had before. But when he opened them, there was heartbreak in his gaze.

And he told me that he'd once killed for them.

EIGHT

I wake up with a jolt; I'm in the back seat of the van, which is now still. I blink, my heart beating in my throat as my eyes adjust to the dark. Something moves near the door, and I raise my hand, searching for something to latch on to. It's instinct.

"You really don't want to do that." Sapphira's voice is low, almost bored. As my eyes adjust, I see her sitting on the track of the open sliding door, her mess of blue-black hair thrown over one shoulder. Beyond her is darkness tinged with flickering light.

"Did someone drug me?" I ask, not lowering my hand as I shift. I was curled up in a ball, and both my legs are asleep.

She turns to face me slowly. "No." Something about the simplicity of the answer makes me believe her. I was exhausted. I've been exhausted for months. Maybe longer than that. I don't know if I can remember when I wasn't tired down to my bones. I'm just usually more careful about where I let my guard down.

"You okay? I was going to let you sleep, but you kept thrashing around," Sapphira says. She hands me an unopened bottle of water. I take it and wrench the cap off. She's quiet while I drain the bottle.

"What do you mean, I 'don't want to do that'?" I ask when I finally come up for air. I can see farther through the van windows. We're in a gutted parking garage that seems to go on forever in each direction, lit by a handful of trash can fires. There's no one else around.

Sapphira stands, pushing the sliding door all the way open. It's an invitation to step out with her. "I mean, you wouldn't like the fear you'd bring out of me."

I eye her for a moment. I don't really want to get out into the open with no clue where I am, but it all seems an equal amount of unsafe at this point.

She waits for me, and I jump out after her, my legs buckling slightly as I hit the gravel. Sapphira reaches out to steady me, and I let her. Her grip is stronger than her frame would suggest it could be.

"How do you know what I am?" I ask.

Sapphira levels a look at me. It's unreadable. Normally, that would feel like a threat. Harbingers aren't exactly welcome company in most circles. *Hi, thanks for inviting me. By the way if I get too worked up I might accidentally pull out your*

worst nightmares and make them material— Is this the door?
Cool, I'll just show myself out.

"And I don't *like* anything I pull out," I correct her, because I can't seem to deny it.

"I didn't say you did. You might want to calm down—Vesper, right?"

We lock eyes. Hers glitter in the dim light.

"Hell of a name," she says.

"Sapphira, right?" I shoot back.

She laughs. It's a nice sound, and I find myself letting out a snort despite myself.

She turns and walks, her Magdalena boots crunching the gravel beneath her. "Usually, Aldrick does the introductions. But he's helping Theo get Alanna to the medic."

I look down. "Is she going to be okay?" I didn't want anyone to get hurt because of me tonight. Or ever. But tonight especially. Sapphira stops and looks over her shoulder. "She signed up for this. You don't have to feel bad. She'll be better after some rest."

When I don't move, she holds her hands out. "We're all monsters here. You're going to have to learn to stop worrying about what we're going to think of you." She turns and keeps walking, without another backward glance. Without another plan, I've got nothing left to do but follow her. Besides, as much as I hate to admit it to myself—I'm intrigued.

"I'm not staying," I call after her as I jog to keep up.

"That's what everyone says when they first get here."

"And what is *here*?" I ask as soon as I've reached her side. "I've seen dozens of safe houses . . . but none like this."

A faint smile curves up the side of her lips.

"Some entrepreneur started this huge business development over fifteen years ago, only to have the whole thing crash two years in after they discovered an uncharted, defunct gold mine deep in the ground right next to the property. San Fran is full of them. Watch your step," she says, pointing to the ground where rebar is sticking out of the pavement like a forest of naked trees. We veer left—me following, her leading.

"So they just . . . left this here?" I ask.

"They didn't have the money to fill the mine, didn't have the money to take this place apart." She stops and turns to me when we reach the elevator shaft at the farthest wall.

"Do the cops know you're all here?" I ask.

"They did," she says, a lilt in her voice that tells me there is so much more to the story, but I stop as she flicks the toe of her boot under a crowbar and catches it before spinning it deftly and sticking it between the elevator doors. With a yank, they both open, revealing a shaft.

"Um . . . ," I start, inching toward the opening to look up, then down. "Where's the elevator?"

I back up as Sapphira reaches into the shaft and grabs a knotted rope.

No. No way. No way in hell.

She steps back and holds the rope out to me.

"You can't be serious," I say.

"For a Harbinger, you sure are scared of a lot of things."

"Yep," I say, moving back.

"It's two stories down to the Grotto. No big deal. You've probably been on diving boards higher than this at your country club, or something."

"Why would you think I belonged to a country club?" I shoot back.

"Did you?" she asks.

"That's beside the point," I grumble. She holds the rope out again, and I take it. I swing out into the shaft, and darkness whips around me, carrying with it shouts and music from below. I chance a glance downward—there's light spilling in from a cracked door on the ground floor.

"Hold on tight," Sapphira says.

I open my mouth to ask what the hell she thought I was going to do, when she hits one of the gears above me with the crowbar and I plummet down.

My stomach clenches as it rushes up against my lungs as I slip down the shaft, and I close my eyes—then, as quickly as it happens, it's over. My feet touch the ground, crunching the leaves and other debris trapped at the bottom. I didn't even realize I had closed my eyes until I open them and look up.

"You could've killed me!" I gasp. The doors next to me roll open, and music, shouts, and laughter ring out into the metal tower.

Aldrick leans against the doorframe, his arms crossed

over his chest. "Yet look at you, alive and lovely." I'm full of adrenaline and pissed off, so I do the only thing I can think to do. I flip him off and push past him. I have no clue where I'm going, but I can't just keep standing there. It's a good flip-off, with the proper amount of wrist flick and everything. I grind to a halt two feet later because . . . I was not expecting this.

I hear Sapphira land behind me. "Welcome to the Grotto," she says as she steps up next to me. This was once the massive foyer to a fancy hotel. The marble is all cracked and uneven, and the chandelier hangs sideways from the ceiling, clinging to life by one rusty chain that looks like it will inevitably give way one day and kill the person below. The walls are covered in string lights, glow sticks, candles, and a smattering of glow-in-the-dark stickers. It smells like mildew, like the ocean slipped in here to see what was going on, got stuck somewhere, and died. Surprisingly, it's not entirely a bad aroma.

It's teeming with people—all around my age. It looks like someone stole the mattresses from the unfinished rooms above and lined a section of the sunken-in floor to my left, making a pillow-filled pit where a red-haired white girl and a lanky black kid with glittering red tattoos practice throwing fire and water at each other from their palms. Like one does.

Across the lobby, through cracked glass windows, I can see several skateboarders using the empty pool as a half-pipe. Couches line the walls—Oddities sit on the edges, on laps, kissing and talking and laughing and acting like this is completely normal.

"Silas?" Aldrick calls.

A tan boy with wild hair and a twice-broken nose gets off one of the dilapidated couches that form a circle to the left of the mattress pit, atop a pile of overlapping Persian rugs that retain none of their original color or structure. Aldrick motions for me to follow as we walk up to the circle of couches. Silas plops back down next to a girl who is engrossed with a book in her lap. "This is Lucy."

Aldrick points to a boy who looks about fourteen, with long blond hair tucked behind his ears. "And this is Joey." Aldrick turns to look at me and I see, for the first time, a genuine smile on his face as he snakes his arm around Sapphira's waist. It's like he's introducing me to his family. "Guys, this is Vesper."

"Nice name. I knew a Whisp named Prudence. You a Whisp?" the boy named Joey asks. Whisp. I remember my dad's notes. It's an Oddity who can talk to other dead members of their clan.

All their eyes are on me. Their faces open. *We're all monsters here.* Sapphira's voice echoes in my mind. No matter what Oddity clan we belong to, we all know what it's like to be reborn as something not of our choosing. They look up, expectant, waiting to hear me spill out the story, to show them my gaping wounds.

I wish I were a Whisp. Talking to ghosts seems much less dark.

"Um . . . ," I start, and I feel a flush in my neck. Lying usually comes so easily, but the words are stuck in my throat.

I feel a hand in mine. It's slight and soft. Tentative. I don't pull away.

"I think she's exhausted. I'm going to show her to her room," Sapphira says, smiling up at Aldrick as she pulls me away. She leads me across the foyer to a flight of stairs.

"Thank you," I say once we're clear of the group.

She doesn't say anything as we near the exposed stairwell on the opposite side of the room. A group sits near the steps, passing an amber bottle between their hands.

"*Feer-a*," a girl with golden hair calls out. I turn. Her voice is low and throaty, and despite her lilting tone, she doesn't sound at all glad to see Sapphira. She's easily one of the most beautiful girls I have ever seen up close. I didn't think runaways had access to that kind of brow sculpting, but I guess I was wrong.

"Just keep walking," Sapphira says lowly.

"What kind of skulking sob story did the Greyhound bring us today?" the girl asks, and with a gloved hand she takes the bottle from the guy next to her. She takes a swig, her eyes not leaving mine. The edges of her irises light up red—a vague threat.

"This is Vesper," Sapphira answers. She puts a foot on the

first step, but the girl doesn't seem satisfied with that answer. With a movement so fluid I almost don't catch it, she pulls her glove off one hand with her teeth and sets a fingertip to the step. It crumbles to ash, and Sapphira stumbles, catching herself on the wall.

"Mavis, what the hell?" Aldrick calls from over my shoulder, his voice tight with rage. The room stills. Mavis glances at him and smirks, her matte-black lips curling up in the corners as she slips her glove back on. She's a Demo—like a reverse Midas. Everything her fingertips touch turns to dust.

"It's fine, Aldrick," Sapphira says, turning to motion for him to leave it alone.

"I just wanted to meet our new friend," Mavis says, standing up. Her tone suggests the opposite, but she holds her gloved hand out. A challenge. I look around—everything has stopped. The Oddities in the corners are now focused on us. On what will happen next.

I know that nothing can hurt me while she's wearing gloves. Still. I can feel everyone around me sucking in a breath. I also know it doesn't matter—this is a power play, and I won't be here long enough to be worth it.

"Mavis. Don't . . . ," Sapphira starts.

But something about Mavis's expression plucks at my chest—something about how she kind of looks like she thinks she's the scariest thing around. She thinks I can't possibly understand what it's like to be feared. I smile as I reach out and grip her hand. Her fingers wrap around mine as she meets my eyes. It's a vise grip, but I don't back down. I look downward. On the inside of her forearm, I see it—a burning queen of poisons flower tattoo.

"So you're here for the show?" she asks.

I have no idea what she's talking about, but I don't want her to know that. Mavis seems like the kind of person you don't admit ignorance to. I opt for a blank stare as she releases my hand.

"I know Aldrick has a soft spot for strays. But if you think you can just come in here and secure a spot when the rest of us have been training for *months*—"

"You don't make the rules," Sapphira says quietly.

I have no idea what the hell is going on, but I'm not about to let that show. Mavis smiles, tonguing her incisor like she's double-checking that it's still sharp.

"That's enough, Mavis," Aldrick says in a voice I haven't yet heard. It's thick with warning—all his playfulness is gone. Mavis looks slowly to Aldrick, her smile widening.

"What are you going to do, Aldrick? Get hard with me? Been there, done that."

The room erupts with snickers, and I feel rage kindle in my chest.

Sapphira steps closer to Mavis.

"Sapphira, leave it," Aldrick says, coming up behind her and setting a hand on her shoulder.

Sapphira doesn't listen. "Do not talk about him like that," she says.

Mavis leans down, meeting her eyes. "And what are *you* going to do, little one? You're too good to show what you can do in the Beneath, but you'll do it here?"

The Beneath. What the hell is the Beneath?

Mavis raises her voice, bringing the room into her question. "You'll *finally* prove that you even belong here?"

"I'm the one who doesn't belong here," I say, stepping forward. "And I'm not planning on staying. They risked themselves to save me tonight, and they've been through enough without having to deal with any of your shit."

Mavis turns her head slowly, her eyes locking on mine like a lion locking on a dangling piece of meat. She was looking to lay into someone, and I have just volunteered to be that someone. With a grin, she slowly pulls off her gloves again.

I hear Aldrick crackle into Stoneskin form behind me. On the couch, Joey stands up, his fingers slowly turning to blades. Two Oddities who were sitting next to Mavis stand. The girl's eyes go flat black as electricity crackles over her fingers, and the guy smiles, revealing fangs.

The pulse in my palms beats as rapid as a rabbit's heartbeat. *Let me out let me out let me out.*

The magic senses others like it. It would be easy to let it slip here. And I can't let it slip. Not after what I just did two hours ago. I look around the room. The world's freakiest freaks all in one place, filled with hormones and anger issues and misplaced senses of justice.

Abandon all hope, ye dumbasses who venture past this point now makes *so* much more sense.

"What is going on here?" a voice sounds from above us. All necks crane upward as the foyer falls silent. A woman leans over a half-finished wooden banister that circles the open second-floor atrium. She wears a blazer and a pencil skirt, and her bleached hair falls in perfect ringlets down her shoulders as she gazes at us, her lips curling up in something between a sneer and smile. The outfit ages her, but I can see from her expression that she's got to be only in her twenties.

"I know there is no possibility that you latchkey losers are starting shit in this Grotto. Because then I'd need to pull out my ridiculously expensive phone and call him, and I don't think he'd like that. And I don't think you'd like him not liking that."

"It's nothing, Tessa," Aldrick answers, snapping his arms out as his skin returns to normal, and the whole Grotto follows suit. Joey sits back on the couch, the blades retreating back into his fingers. Mavis puts her gloves back on, her irises glittering red and focused on me as she does it.

Back home, we had a squirt bottle we kept for when our cat, Inigo Montoya, jumped up on the counter. It only took a couple of good shots to the whiskers to get him to never jump up again. We'd only have to reach for the bottle and he'd freeze before slinking away. That is kind of what just happened. This Tessa chick pulled out the squirt bottle, and no one is thinking about jumping up on the counter anymore. Something about it feels really wrong. Since none of these people are cats.

I bite my tongue at the memory of Inigo as I look at Sapphira, letting my eyes plead the question I know she can read on my face: *Who is* he? She looks down.

"That's what I thought, but I had to check," Tessa says, pushing herself up and straightening her blazer. "By the way—you? What's your name?" she asks, pointing to me. I look behind me, just to check.

"Yes, you, the pretty one with the desperate need for dry shampoo," she replies. I look up at her, all sorts of confused. I mean, she's not wrong about my needing a shower. But, okay, rude.

"Your pathetic little kitchen is out of those hun-cal brownie things. Fix that, okay? If I have to trek down here to make sure you're behaving, I should at least have that to look forward to."

"I—" I start, but she looks down at her phone and holds up a finger, motioning for me to *wait*.

Okay. No.

"She's not staying, Tessa," Sapphira cuts in.

Tessa looks up. "You're gonna miss the Beneath tomorrow night?"

I open my mouth, but Sapphira steps up next to me and grabs my arm. "She is."

"Fine. I don't care who gets the bars. Just make sure

they're there. And not the caramel-crunch type, those are effing disgusting."

With that, she turns and leaves.

The Beneath.

There's that word again.

I don't care. I don't want to know. I want to pack almonds and be the weird girl who doesn't talk to anyone, doesn't hurt anyone, and is basically invisible.

Slowly, the room around me comes to life. Joey turns the music back on, someone drops into the half-pipe, and the sound of wheels scraping against the concrete rattles my bones.

"I'll show you where you can crash," Sapphira says.

I follow her to the steps, and then up the winding stairs. Sapphira opens a small door just off the third-floor landing. It's a modest room. A twin bed and a desk rest on the far wall, and the floor is concrete. Through the window, a lighthouse sends twisting beams of light into the otherwise dark space.

"It's not much," Sapphira says, her eyes roving over the walls.

"It's perfect," I say. I mean it.

When she leaves, I curl up under the covers and stare at the ceiling as the light bounces off the unfinished beams overhead. I briefly wonder what the Beneath is before my eyes slip shut.

NINE

I'm at the park behind my house—the one where I kissed Trevor Martineau in seventh grade. The one where Carmen and I tied ribbon into the branches of a pine tree we named Jasper.

But I'm not home, because it's snowing. It doesn't snow in Los Altos.

I'm dreaming, I think to myself in the way you only really can when you're dreaming. *I want to wake up.*

But I can't. I can't stop walking, one foot after another, each step a painful bite of ice on bare feet as I pass the toddler park with harness swings. That's when I hear the rhyme whispered on the wind.

She smiled at blades.
She kissed the rope.

She danced with arrows.
She sang though smoke.

I know this rhyme. "The Legend of the Queen of Poisons."

It's my younger sister's voice—I hear it in the way her voice hitches when she says *kissed.* I feel the same horror I felt in the moment when I heard it from the living room and realized that I left my dad's notebook out on the coffee table, open to the worst of our stories.

The tune stops, and the memory of my father's anger at my slip fills my head.

What were you thinking, leaving it out like that?

I walk deeper into the forest, the flaming flowers my only guiding light. The song continues, bouncing off the frozen trees around me, rattling like a femur on prison bars.

In flames she lit her chains and then
They slipped the petals deep within.

The air smells like smoke.

She feared no wrath.
She feared no rage.
They locked her deep
In shadow's cage.

Up ahead, there's a clearing. This is where Jack, Iris, and I used to pitch tents and pretend to camp. We never made it past dusk before we packed up and went home.

Home.

Dream thunder clapped overhead, and I knew I couldn't escape the memory lapping at my feet.

It rained the night I ruined my entire life: the night I set everything on fire and ran. You'd think it would make it better, right? That maybe the rain would help? It didn't.

For a few months, my powers didn't cause any problems. Sure, sometimes my younger sister, Iris, would piss me off and I'd feel the latch. I'd feel myself link to the innermost part of her chest, where the things that terrified her dwelled. And I'd have this urge to pull back, just like I did with Mitch. To pull it out, whatever it was, and let it roam free.

But I could shut that down. I could swallow it back. My monster stayed coiled at the bottom of my gut like that one octopus Carmen loved at the aquarium—the one that seemed to know exactly where it was and was like, *Eff you guys, I'm not swimming around for your entertainment.* It stayed put.

I went to homecoming with Hunter Cadilli. I made varsity cheer. I barely managed to pass Algebra I, and they let me in to Algebra II. I was starting to think about what colleges I was going to apply to. Dad and I talked less and less about our world, though there was one question we still were never able to figure out: why I was able to manifest my powers in front of him—a Baseline—*now*. Why that had changed, all in one night.

I would see his office light on, late into the evening as he searched for answers. Before, I would softly knock and then go in. I would close the door and ask questions until he insisted I go to sleep. But now I knew there was no hope of ever ridding myself of this power. I think the knowledge of that made me want to pretend I was normal even more.

I should've known the pretending wouldn't last long.

It was November. I was wearing pajamas I should have put away in August, but I had a huge duvet and didn't quite notice how frigid it was, even for Southern California. I texted Jenna and asked her a question about where the cheer squad was meeting the next day before the pep rally, and my mom poked her head into my room to check if I'd unplugged my straightener. Satisfied, she blew me a kiss and reminded me to take the trash out in the morning. I blew a kiss back and then I fell asleep.

And I had a dream about fire. I dreamed of it in sheets, licking the air with raging tongues and twisting closer to me. Even in sleep, I could feel my power snaking out from my chest. I couldn't move. Maybe I didn't want to. I felt it on my skin, a warm kiss that thrummed in my palm as I twisted it around. The fire knew my name, and I knew its secrets. I wasn't afraid of it. I spoke to it, coaxing it closer. Then I woke up smelling smoke. I woke up hearing screams.

When I opened my eyes, I was more afraid of the fact that I knew where the fire came from than the fire itself.

Ever since I was little, my mom never let us use the fireplace. She never let us play with sparklers. She barely even let us light candles. There'd been a fire in her family cabin when she was twelve. Someone knocked over a little butane lantern, and it caught her blanket, setting the whole place up like a tinderbox.

And somehow, I'd found her fear.

In my sleep, I'd reached it. I don't know how—maybe the fact that she'd checked on the straightener before I fell asleep. I don't know. I just know it was my fault. My powers, my *curse* . . . it yanked it out and lit my whole house on fire while we slept.

I don't remember running downstairs, where I'd found Iris. Where my dad tried to get us to go outside while my mom ran to get Carmen.

I fought. I pulled against him, ripping his skin with my nails as I shrieked, begged to let me help get Carmen.

This is my fault. My fault. This is my fault.

Those are the words I kept screaming, sucking in ash between heaving breaths. My dad lifted me over his shoulder and carried me outside, setting me down on the soaked, freezing grass. I grabbed his arms, slick with ash and sweat.

It was me, I cried. He met my gaze, and I knew he

understood. There was no anger on his face. Not even surprise. He didn't flinch, and it was so much worse—the moment when I watched his eyes dance between mine, trying to find something to say. It was just a second, but it felt like longer. My dad put a hand to my cheek and then pointed to a firefighter, motioning for him to help me before my dad got up and took off into the house, shoving a firefighter aside.

My feet slipped in the wet grass as I tried to shove the firefighter off, and I landed on my knees. I looked up just in time to see Inigo Montoya in the front bushes. He was covered in soot. Alive, but limping. His eyes were wild with fear as he looked at me, almost like he knew I was the reason this was happening. I was the spark that set this whole thing ablaze. It was like he was an animal sensing another animal. Sensing danger.

"Inigo," I called, sobbing. A paramedic pulled me up to my feet, and Inigo skittered away. "Inigo, I'm sorry," I cried as the firefighter scooped me up into his arms.

The rest of the night was a smoky smear in my memory. My mom, screaming at the top of her lungs as she walked out behind a firefighter carrying a limp Carmen in his arms. Dad, sitting with Jack and Iris—both covered in ash and wrapped in blankets.

The paramedics examined me in the back of an ambulance. Blood pressure cuff, heart monitor clipped on my finger, oxygen mask strapped on my face. Cold gurney sheets biting at the back of my legs as the world spiraled outside.

Are they okay? Is my family okay? Are they going to be okay?

My questions sounded foreign because my voice was ripped to shreds from the smoke.

No one answered. No one would tell me. They unwrapped IV needles and adjusted the mask on my face and talked about my vitals. I knew what my father was thinking as he touched my cheek. I could read it in his eyes—he was wondering if the Wardens would come looking for me. Accidentally or not, I'd broken the number one rule and used my magic in front of Baselines. And I'd wreaked havoc on my family. That was a thousand times worse than the Wardens.

I almost didn't care if they came.

I sat up as the other paramedics led a gurney to the back of a waiting ambulance, the wheels scratching on the pavement.

Then I saw Carmen's face. It was blacked and raw and incurably burned by the flames I'd conjured. The flames *I* created. My mom hopped in the ambulance and grabbed my sister's unmoving hand.

Unmoving. Still.

I did this, and I couldn't control it.

The monitor above me let out a small *beep beep beep*, but I knew then that something in my heart had died. Something had changed, and I would never be able to bring it back.

As soon as I was left alone, my fingers moved of their own

volition, shaking as I pulled the IV out of my veins. I yanked the mask off my face, slipped out of the ambulance, and ran.

I ran as fast as I could. Through backyards. Over fences. Barefoot and half naked.

I couldn't ever put my family at risk like that again.

I went to the school and changed into clothes from my locker. I hadn't taken my competition duffel home, and I had enough spare cash at the bottom to get a bus ticket to Seattle.

The thunder claps again, and I'm back in the dream, on my hands and knees in . . . a circle of burning aconite buds. I hold my hand out, and snowflakes flit to my palm. No. Not snow-flakes. Ash. Ash is falling from the sky.

I am the scariest thing. I am the nightmare.

Me.

I sit up in the dark, breathing heavy and drenched in sweat.

Since that night, I've been a light sleeper. Anything can wake me, and I don't let myself sleep for more than about two hours at a time.

I thought the upside to that would be that the nightmares would lighten up, but that isn't how it worked out.

Everything feels too closed in. Everything is too still. I have to move. I slip my feet into my shoes and throw my jacket over my shirt, wincing at the feel of the heavy fabric on my soaked shirt.

I'm up and out the door in seconds, walking down the hallway.

I have no clue where I'm going, and I don't really care. The air out here is cool and damp, and it feels good on the back of my neck. I walk through an unfinished stairwell made of plywood steps as laughter bubbles up from below. I hear wheels on concrete—people are still awake in the lobby.

My knees wobble, and I rest back against the wall, sliding down to a crouch as I wrap my fingers through my hair.

The wall opposite me is covered in tacked-up fliers— everything from missing-people posters to passive-aggressive *To the person who stole my sub sandwich out of the fridge: do it again at your own peril.*

There are several blank sheets of paper fluttering against the perpetual breeze wafting through the corridor. Curious, I push myself back up and walk over to the wall. Leaning close, I breathe out over the paper—a trick my dad showed me. Swirly black letters appear—*Twenty bucks for fake IDs. Call 909-555-9831.* It's in umbra ink. Invisible writing that's meant to reveal itself under an Oddity's breath—those with magic to write it are called Scribes.

My eyes move over the board, stopping at a piece of thick paper with an embossed queen of poisons flower on it, flames licking up near the edges. I take a deep, shaky breath before I exhale on the paper. Thick gold letters appear in seconds.

THE FESTIVAL OF THE QUEEN OF POISONS.

Come out of the shadow and into the light.

Fangs, teeth, and all manner of misbehaving welcome.

There are directions, and they involve counting trees. It's off the Ewoldsen Trail in Big Sur.

My gaze fixes on that damned flower—that symbol I've been seeing everywhere.

I want to blame it for my nightmare, but I know it's more than that. I pulled out another fear tonight. I haven't done that in over a year. But it makes me feel better to hate that flower, so I pull the flier from the bulletin board and look down at the drawing.

The queen of poisons. The flame that lit the fuse of a civil war that nearly destroyed us all.

"'In flames she lit her chains and then they slipped the petals deep within,'" a voice behind me says. I jump at the sound. Sapphira stands on the landing, her hand still on the railing. "I hate that poem." She steps up closer.

"Me too," I agree. "It feels like whoever first said it said it with a sneer."

Sapphira is quiet next to me as we take in the expanse of the wall.

"Do you think they're gone?" I ask quietly, looking over at her as she gazes up at the wall. Her eyes flit over to mine.

"You don't?"

I press my lips together. Maybe it's my constant guilt about what I did to my family, but I always feel like the Wardens are watching. "I would rather play it safe. Better than having my head on a spike." I gesture to the flier.

"The Stirring has people thinking something new is going to happen," Sapphira says softly. She steps closer, her black leather boots making almost no noise. Leggings with a mesh-cutout run up the sides of her legs, and an oversize sweater hangs on her frame, the sleeves overtaking her hands. She shakes her arm, and a bracelet jingles down past the hem. It's a gold bracelet with brightly colored dinosaur charms dangling from the links.

"I would give cold, hard cash to never have to hear another cryptic name like 'the Stirring' ever again. 'Oddity' is bad enough."

Sapphira snorts. "It's kind of obnoxious, right?"

"It's *so* obnoxious," I agree, and she smiles. "Aldrick seems excited about it, though." I say after a moment, wondering only after I've said the words if I've overstepped.

Sapphira is quiet for a moment, biting her bottom lip before running her teeth over it as she juts her lower jaw forward.

"He deserves some hope," she says quietly. "We all do."

"But . . . ?" I ask, because I hear one in her voice.

"The devil you know is better than the one you don't, right? If the Wardens are gone . . . then we just have the devils we've never seen before."

I open my mouth, the start of a thousand questions revving up in the back of my mind, but she shuts them down as she sighs and looks at me.

"Come on. I need some air."

After grabbing a bag from her room, she leads me through the Grotto and up a ladder that cuts through a maintenance shaft. It opens next to the bluffs near the ocean. I stop short, taking in the sight. The fog was so thick before that I didn't see it. I had no clue we were this close to the water. The moon is out tonight, throwing a gorgeous smear of white on the water and lighting up the night. I look at the sky as I step into the cold night—we're at the base of an abandoned lighthouse. Shouts and cheers sound on the icy air, and I take Sapphira's hand as I climb off the ladder and let the metal door drop back down with a *thud*.

"The hotel was never finished on this side," she says, pointing across the rolling hills covered in long grass. I can see lantern lights dotting the skeletal face of the hotel's edge. "They built another half-pipe out of the supplies lying around," she explains as the cheers start again. A girl on a bike jumps down on the three-story drop. She loses her grip halfway down, and a boy on the edge of an unfinished balcony throws his arms out. Her momentum slows until she gently rests on the ground. Must be nice—all the risk, none of the broken bones.

"Come on," Sapphira says. I follow her toward the lighthouse. The door at the base is unlocked, but the hinges shriek as she pushes it open. She cracks two glow sticks and hands me one as we head up the pitch-black stairs. When we reach the top, my breath catches in my throat. The view from up here is unlike anything I've ever seen. A sheet of fog rolls over the water, splitting just enough in places to let splinters of moonlight hit the water. Lone headlights pass over the Golden Gate Bridge, and the wind whips the water into tiny whitecaps. Sapphira sits on the edge, letting her feet dangle over the side as she rests her chest on the railing.

She reaches into her bag and pulls out a thermos.

I settle next to her, my back stiff as I cast a sideways glance at her. I realize now that I've been waiting for the hammer to drop—waiting for the catch, with all this. No one is nice for free. Not in this world.

"Why were you following me?" I ask, my voice feeling like a blade cutting through the serene night.

Sapphira smirks. "We check all the bus stops around here. Too many runaways wind up on their own, and it's dangerous to be alone."

"Sometimes it's dangerous to be around people," I add without really stopping to think.

Sapphira looks at me, a dark eyebrow raised, like she knows there's a story buried under those words. Something on my face must tell her that I'm not going to talk about it, because she turns back to the ocean.

"So you have nightmares too, huh?" she asks.

I don't answer, and she takes that as a yes. She unscrews the lid of the thermos and pours some liquid into the lid.

"Do you want to talk about it?" she asks finally.

I shake my head.

"Want some?" she asks, holding the lid over to me.

I shake my head again, and she raises her eyebrows. "Think I poisoned it or something? Because I promise you, if I wanted you dead, I'd just tell Mavis where you were sleeping."

"No, I just—"

"You don't trust anyone," she says, swirling the liquid in the lid.

I let out a small laugh. "The opposite. I don't think people should trust me. Especially when you mix in alcohol."

She snorts. "Wow. You assume it's alcohol."

"Is it not?"

She smirks as she brings the cup to her lips. "Nah. Totally is. It's just cheap wine."

I smile then, and it feels at home on my lips. I've missed this.

She looks out at the water, and I follow her gaze. We both watch as fog slowly slithers over the waves. The silence isn't hollow—it's not begging to be filled.

She takes a drink of the wine, wincing as she looks down into the cup.

"Bad?" I ask.

She shrugs. "My mom used to make it in a pan with fresh spices, so . . . microwaved with dried stuff isn't the same."

Home. My gut twists painfully at her words, and I lean on the railing as I look out into the night and bite the tip of my tongue.

"So how long have you and Aldrick been a thing?" I ask, desperate to change the subject.

A smile creeps up her lips. "We're not a . . . thing. We're . . ." She shrugs, and I laugh. Oddity or not, some things are never simple. "We're friends. I met him in a McDonald's after I got off a train."

"Was he collecting strays even back then?"

She snorts into her wine. "No. He just loves their breakfast sandwiches."

The image of Aldrick, his frying-pan-size hands gripping a tiny little egg sandwich, makes me laugh, too.

"He took me in. Unlike Mavis, who demanded I announce my clan and show my abilities . . . he's never pushed me to use my magic. Never demanded to know my clan." She stops, taking a deep pull from the cup before she refills it. She doesn't like using her magic, either. "With everything that's happened . . ." Her eyes are far away as she thinks. "He's made me feel like I'm home. Like this life could still be mine, even though it's so different from the one before."

"Do you like him?" I ask, only because I can't resist the normalcy of the question.

She smirks. "I do."

"Then what's the problem?" He's hot—there's no question.

"Aldrick is a protector. It's just his nature. He'll protect those he loves fiercely. Stupidly. And he loves easily. He doesn't need any more danger in his life." She reads the question on my face. "Aldrick has been leading a team to intercept runaways at the bus stations. Some have been disappearing."

"Disappearing?"

She picks at the paint on the rusted-out railing. "They get on the bus, and then they're not at the station when it pulls in. We've been expecting a couple of people—friends or relatives of kids already here . . . they never made it."

My mind instantly reacts. "You think the Wardens got them?"

Sapphira barks out a laugh. "You and the Wardens. You know there are worse things, right?"

"In theory."

"In actuality," she counters.

"What could be worse than a group of death-wielding control freaks?"

Sapphira levels her gaze at me like I just issued a challenge. She squints for a moment, considering. "There are rumors around that some of these kids might've made bad deals in order to get here. Maybe with a Ledger."

"Ledger?" I ask, my mind flashing back to my dad's notebooks. I've never heard of a Ledger before.

"Ledger—an Oddity with binding magic. You make a deal

with a Ledger, and you can't go back on it," Sapphira explains.

"Wow," I say, gripping the railing in front of me. Sapphira takes another long drink.

"They have a dark history of travelers and gamblers making deals with the unsuspecting or desperate. They carry a briefcase with them, filled with their contracts. All Ledgers have a mark on their inner wrist—an emblem of a bleeding pen—they're marked by their clan when they come of age and can start . . . ruining lives, I guess," she says. "And they weren't allowed to make deal with minors . . . before."

"Before the Stirring?" I finish.

Sapphira nods. "They couldn't. Before the Wardens disappeared," she says simply. "Now what's stopping them? What's stopping any of us? It's a selling point, unless you're at the bottom of the food chain."

"Is there any way to find the kids?" I ask. Suddenly, almond packing doesn't seem that important.

Sapphira shakes her head. "No." She takes a sip. "But the devil you know." She eyes me over the edge of the cup.

I think about it—the rules and the consequences. The power and lack of.

Who wins and who loses when the restraints come off.

I shake my head, not wanting to think of the Wardens anymore.

"How do you guys"—I gesture to the hotel below—"survive?"

Sapphira's eyes harden at my question. I'm not naive. I've visited several safe houses all over different states. Oddities do what we have to do to survive. Move less-than-legal merchandise, or remove merchandise from places by less-than-legal means.

"You're leaving tomorrow, Vesper. It's better if you don't know."

There's nothing sharp about her words. Nothing sharp about her gaze as she looks up to meet my eyes. Her blue irises are earnest. Pleading, almost. Like she's begging me to believe her. Like she's begging me to let it go.

She holds the cup out to me, and I look at it for a moment before taking it. Her dinosaur bracelet catches the moonlight.

"That's cute," I say, pointing to the bracelet.

A smile spreads across her rosy lips as she looks down at it. "It belongs to my brother," she says, fingering the T. rex softly. "Nolan. He gave it to me."

"You miss him," I say, the words leaving me like an exhale before I can think of a thousand reasons why I shouldn't say them. She fixes her ice-blue eyes on mine, and for a moment I wonder if I overstepped again. Geez, for someone looking to keep everyone at an arm's length, I sure am having trouble keeping my effing mouth shut.

She nods, looking back down. "I'm going to get back to him. Eventually." She takes a slow breath as she holds her hand out, letting the bracelet dangle in the breeze. "Do you miss home?"

I start to bite my tongue but opt for a swig of wine instead. "Yes," I say. "Yes, I do." I hand the cup back, and she takes it.

"You know what's dumb? I miss stupid things, too. Like my cafeteria had these burritos on Fridays that were absolutely *terrible*, but it was a tradition."

I smile. "Were they the ones that came in the cellophane wrapping?"

She turns, her eyes alight. "*Yes*," she says, pointing. "And they were hot as balls—"

"—And your fingers would get all caught in the steam?" I finish, laughing at the memory of Lindsay and Jenna trying to open theirs with their protractors.

Sapphira wraps her hands over the railing as she throws her head back. "I miss not ever having to talk about the things I miss," she says quietly as she sits up. "Sometimes I come out here and pretend I'm just . . . ditching class."

I haven't thought of it like that, but it's exactly right. I miss living without constantly trying to crawl back to when things felt simpler.

Tears sting my throat. I miss not missing anything.

We're quiet for another stretch as the fog gets closer, passing the wine to each other after each swig.

"So," she starts, lifting her legs out straight. "That math test, huh?" She looks over at me, and I don't know if it's the wine or the simple absurdity of it all, but I smile.

"It was a bitch," I answer, nodding.

"Think she'll curve it?" Sapphira asks.

"Nah. And Hilary would screw that up anyway," I throw out, thinking of one of my best friends from home. The words feel good on my tongue. "But at least Isaac is still having that party on Saturday, right?"

Sapphira doesn't skip a beat. "It'll be nice to blow off some steam. Though . . . whatever shall we wear?" she asks, gesturing to her tattered black yoga pants and old Hotshot sweatshirt.

"I'm sure Lindsay will have something," I croak out. Old phrases from a life I never thought I'd resurrect.

Sapphira points her toes and leans back on her arms. "But if not, I have some money from babysitting Nolan. We could go to the mall."

"I'll borrow my mom's car and come get you at six?" I rest my head on the railing and look at her. She closes her eyes against the wind, lifting her chin. Pieces of hair slide across her face, but she doesn't push them away. She opens her eyes and looks out across the ocean.

"Six is perfect."

TEN

I let myself fall back asleep a couple of hours later, after Sapphira and I walked back to the Grotto. I don't have more nightmares.

I slept longer than I meant to, and no one woke me. I guess the weeks of getting four hours of sleep per night finally caught up to me.

There's a note on the end of my bed along with a Chewy granola bar: *Shower is at the end of the hall.* She's left me half a bottle of Dove shampoo and a disposable razor.

For a moment, I wish I could stay. This place is ridiculous, but I almost didn't feel completely alone for a few hours. I forgot what it felt like to be part of something. And this is something—I can say that, at least.

Aldrick knocks on my door.

"Hey," he says as I crack the door. I open it and walk back

over to the bed. He leans on the doorframe.

"So I wanted you to know that, no matter what Mavis said to you—you're more than welcome to stay. There are some pretty awesome things happening here—"

"Aldrick." Sapphira's voice cuts through the room as she comes up behind him. She doesn't look pleased as he turns to give her enough room in the doorway beside him.

"I told you that she has to go," she hisses. "It's bad enough that you signed up for it. Leave her out of this."

It stings a little—the thought that maybe Sapphira *wants* me to leave. Not that I can blame her. I wouldn't want a Harbinger under the same roof as people I love, either.

I shrug one shoulder. "It's nice of you, Aldrick, but I have to get going."

Sapphira gives Aldrick a death glare as he holds his hands up in surrender and backs out of my room.

She tosses me a set of keys, and I catch them against my chest. Then she tosses me a little cell phone.

"Take the van to the bus station and just leave it there. We'll come get it tomorrow. It's a burner. Prepaid. All our numbers are already loaded on. If you need help, ever . . . just call," she says. I nod, fingering the keys and phone. I almost got her and all her friends killed yesterday, and she still wants to make sure I'm okay. When I look up to thank her, she's gone.

A little later, I use Joey's refurbished tablet and the

absolutely abysmal Wi-Fi to check the bus schedule—there's a bus headed south leaving at eight tonight. Perfect timing. I shower in the communal bathroom, making sure to use the towel on the shelf labeled *THIS BELONGS TO MAVIS, DO NOT FUCKING TOUCH.*

I leave the towel in a wet heap on the floor, and that small act of defiance, paired with freshly shaved legs, makes me feel like I could overcome the world.

I put my hair up in its usual bun and throw my bag over my shoulder. Time to go.

The lobby is empty, but a deep bass pounds from somewhere in the unfinished hotel. I stop for a moment and listen.

It's a metal version of "We Will Rock You."

What? Where is everyone? I check my cheap watch again—I have time. And while I should probably have learned not to let curiosity get to me by now . . . I want to know.

I follow the pounding bass ripping up from the floor. It gets stronger with every step, as does my growing sense of dread. But I keep going, following winding hallways that lead farther into the hotel. At the end of the hallway, a stairwell leads downward. I open the door and step inside.

The music gets louder, and the lights get dimmer. The walls shake with the bass. I reach the bottom of the stairwell, and then I push the door open and my breath catches in my throat. I don't know what I was expecting, but it was not this.

It's a room that looks like it was once part of the sub-
terranean parking garage—everything is cement and stone,
but it's been repurposed for this. Whatever *this* is. Dozens of
people mill about, blocking the center of the room from view.
I step farther in, letting the door close silently behind me as
I slip between people, unnoticed. I'm good at that.

Music pours through speakers attached to the walls with
vines hanging from the ceiling. I reach up and touch one
that hangs right in front of me, turning it with two fingers.
A purple queen of poisons flower rests between two leaves,
and I let go as if I'd been burned. Who has queen of poisons flowers as a decoration? A pit forms in my stomach as I
notice a small line of stadium seating that reaches up to the
lofted ceiling. The crowd in front of me thins, and I see what
rests in the center of the room. It's a slightly lofted cage,
edged with eight fenced-in sides. I've seen this before—it's
something like the MMA fights Iris and my dad used to love
but . . . different. There's a purple light emanating through
the links. Every couple of seconds, the links shimmer in a
wave, sending ripples along the edge of the cage. It's not a
regular octagon. I back up to the far wall, my eyes still fixed
on the cage, like if I look at it long enough, I'll piece everything together.

Everyone is waiting for something—I can feel the anticipation crackling in the air as I edge alongside the wall. The
outline of a queen of poisons flower hits the back wall in an

electric blue as two spotlights dance around the room, finally landing on the base of the cage, where two figures stand.

The lights flash, and applause rips from the crowd. Two girls in green satin gowns enter the cage and hold their hands up, and a screen projects from their palms. It's the size of a movie screen, shimmering silver with the outline of a queen of poisons flower above the cage.

There's a hush over the crowd, and I feel something in my gut that tells me I should leave, but I can't move. I don't know if it's curiosity or panic—maybe a mix of both, but I'm watching as darkness overtakes the room and the screen shows a little town. A woman's voice comes out of the speakers above us. "In eighteenth-century Brasov, there lived a woman with hair the color of old blood. No one knows her actual name."

The screen flickers, showing a red-haired woman walking stone streets.

"Some called her a witch; others thought she was a prophet."

The woman smiles as she leans down to pet a dog and turns to eye women who are gathered in the doorway across the street, watching her skeptically.

Isn't that how it always is with powerful women? We're feared or worshipped. Pitchforks or roses.

There doesn't seem to be much in between.

The screen swirled then, and the voice continued. "Her transgressions were small, at first—showing her power to a Baseline. She woke up to a purple bud nailed to her door. Aconite. Wolfsbane. The queen of poisons. The flower of the Wardens. She knew what it meant. Who it was from."

I remembered the legend my dad told me, but I was mesmerized watching it on-screen, watching the woman reach out and pull the bud from the nail. Liquid from the flower's blood ran down her dirt-smeared hand. And then, she smiled.

The smile bloomed into a laugh.

"If she didn't kill herself, the Wardens would do it for her. But she did not fear them. She pulled the nail from the flower and put the flower in a vase in her window. She started growing it in her garden, as well. It grew, too, despite the cold. Despite the fact that ice kissed the window in the middle of the night."

The woman kneeled in her garden, inspecting the buds.

My mind spins as I try to understand what I'm watching. Why they're showing this.

I know the rest of the story—it's one I read from Dad's notebook until the edges of the pages were curled from the way my nervous fingers ran along the curve of the paper.

"Her next transgression is unknown, but it was enough to send one of the Rippers through her window on a frosty night."

I could finish this story in my sleep.

Sometimes, I do.

The next morning, the villagers walked out to the square

to find his body sitting next to the frozen fountain—

An aconite flower in his mouth and a wide, smiling slit across his throat. Her own kind of message, it would seem.

They sent another.

Another body in the square.

That went on for seven days. Seven Rippers, seven bodies.

The Baseline villagers were confused and scared, though the Oddities knew what it meant. The Wardens soon realized that the more they tried to get her to be quiet, the louder she was.

Other Oddities moved to Brasov. There was something about the Queen of Poisons that made them feel free—the woman the Wardens couldn't kill. The handful of them—the Wolfsbane Court, they called themselves—started showing their powers to Baselines.

A strange thought—the missing part of the puzzle— started forming in my mind as the two girls came together, their palms getting closer and closer as the story continued to crescendo.

"It was slow, at first. A Miasma and a Renderer had a public duel in the town square. The next day—people were gathered around in the square. They wanted to see more."

The shot showed two men—one blond, one bald with ink covering his skull—fighting on the cobblestone. The Miasma held his hands up, and green light streamed toward the Renderer, who drew a doorway next to him with a sweep of his palm and stepped through, stepping out behind the Miasma. The Renderer moved his fingers, drawing a blade into existence so quickly the Miasma didn't have time to turn around before he put it to his throat.

"They wanted to see these creatures that were like them, but *more*."

The projection shows a quick succession of Oddities fighting. I catch a Stoneskin and a Vaper, but can't place the others. I know my father's scrawled list was incomplete, but I had no clue that my knowledge was so limited.

I turn to move, but the voice stops me. I don't know why. I know how the story ends. I don't need to see it.

But I'm frozen.

"And so they started fighting. Soon they moved from the town square to a field, where they built stands. It became bigger than just the Queen of Poisons, though they say she was at every tournament.

"It was there, under her gaze, that the world saw us openly for the first time. It was then that we stepped out of myth and set our feet on the cobblestone. And, as it always is, it was fine for a short while. A few months passed, and nothing. No bodies, no flowers.

"Just stillness, like a deep intake of breath, with the tournaments continuing. Oddities walked around without fear, and the Queen of Poisons was our emblem—our liberator. She didn't seem to see it that way, though, as she continued to frequent the pub and take lovers and walk the street barefoot, her blood-colored hair catching snowflakes like nothing had changed.

"No one knows how it happened because, despite the town being full of Oddities, the Wardens showed themselves to no one else."

The projection fills with black smoke, coiling around itself to darken the screen.

Then, it clears, and I stop breathing.

"The next morning they found her lying in the middle of the square, her eyes open and milky, ice already clinging to her irises. And around her, in a perfect circle—aconite buds. In her mouth, seven flowers."

I want to look away, but the sight of the vibrant redhead lying still in the snow keeps my eyes locked on the screen.

A man's voice comes over the speaker.

"I'm sure the Wardens thought it was over. I'm sure they thought no one would be stupid enough to challenge them after that. But they were wrong, because something happened—Oddities had a taste of sunlight, and they were tired of shadow. Tournaments started happening everywhere. But the Wardens didn't like that we'd acquired a taste of freedom."

The projection filled with a scene that stilled the stadium. Hooded figures, faces hidden, with queen of poisons flowers in their grasp.

The Wardens.

"In the span of one night, they used every Oddity at their disposal to wipe out everyone who had ever fought in one of the tournaments. The light of dawn washed over heads on spikes, aconite buds in their mouths, a warning from the head of the Wardens himself—Ivan Illeria. From then on, we've lived in fear."

The girls in the cage lower their hands, and the projection fades. The silhouette of a man steps inside the cage. He's speaking now. His voice is smooth and sure.

"They used all their magic, combined, to create a rule that said we cannot use our powers in front of Baselines. And since that day, we've lived under that rule. Because while our hands were bound, we still lived in fear of the Wardens. Any misstep that could alert Baselines to our existence would warrant a queen of poisons bud on your door. But those days are over."

The spotlight finds him then, and recognition sparks in my mind as I realize I've seen him before. My mind searches as he smiles.

Applause fills the room, and I recognize him.

Ananias. Ananias Ventra. The mermaid seducer from the front of the magazine on the bus. The real-estate guy. He's an Oddity? *Him.* He must have been the one Tessa had been talking about. I get it.

"We come here to mark the beginning of a new era. Baselines, we're excited to see you among us. I know many of you have heard about this tournament. You're probably wondering if the whispers are true. I assure you, they are."

Ananias reaches up and plucks a queen of poisons bud from the vine above him. He crushes it in his palm and rolls it between his hands. He holds it up to show the audience.

It's ruined.

"We don't live in fear anymore."

Then he lifts the flower higher, and the whole stadium falls completely silent. I thought it was quiet before, but it's nothing compared to this. I can hear my own heart beat in my chest as the crushed flower unfurls, its petals springing back to life.

The crowd gasps, and several people jump to their feet.

Botivasts can't do that. They can create new plant life, but they can't bring the dead back to life. My mind spins, searching for an answer, my memory flitting over pages of scratched-out histories and coffee-stained maps. I come up empty, except for one, and it makes no sense. There's only one group of Oddities in the world who could do that, but they were on the list of the extinct clans on the last page of my dad's notebook.

"I've known about the fights in the Beneath for years now. The gladiators"—cheers erupt at the word, and Ananias smiles—"that's what they are—warriors. Daring to use their powers as they pleased without fear. That is why I came here and asked to start this tournament in *this* cage." He gestures

to the cage around him.

I think back to my talk with Sapphira. How she didn't want me to know what they did here. That's why. This safe house is an underground fighting ring.

"Welcome to the Tournament of the Unraveling," Ananias's voice rings out, and the applause is deafening.

My instinct for self-preservation tells me, *Get out.* I can still make my bus if I leave now. But the other thought is louder and more powerful—the one around the word *unraveling.* If that means what I think it means, then Ananias is an Unraveler.

He's not supposed to exist. And if he exists, then everything in my dad's notebook wasn't completely correct. That means my dad was wrong about something, and in that thought there is both terror and hope. After a moment, terror wins out, and I start to slink toward the door.

Tournament.

Suddenly, I piece it together. *Night one.* The queen of poisons flower. He's turned a fighting ring into a re-creation of the Tournament of the Queen of Poisons.

It's a giant "eff you" to the Wardens, and I'm standing in the middle of it.

Aldrick joked that this place isn't a revolution, but that's exactly what it is.

"Before we get to our first fight, I want to lay out some ground rules, because this tournament will be different from regular matches held in the Beneath."

The room is more crowded than it was when I came in, and moving is difficult. I duck behind a man in a gray suit.

"All participants have signed an agreement with my Ledger, Mara. This is for their own protection."

Ledger? My conversation with Sapphira comes rushing back.

"If a gladiator signs a waiver, they are entered into the tournament for as long as they are an active participant, and they are protected until they forfeit or lose. That means that no harm can come to them outside the ring for as long as the tournament progresses."

Ananias stops and smiles, and the crowd cheers for him.

"And there will be no referee. My assistant, Tessa, will give her incredible commentary, but she will not call the fights. This is a real tournament of the will as much as it is a tournament of magic. How much can one withstand? How much can one inflict? We'll find out." He stops, smiling as the applause ripples over the crowd once more. His smile is wide. Genuine. If it wasn't for the pit in my gut, I would almost want to believe in the hope he's selling.

"Let's start with a bang, shall we?"

The lights go out again, and a roar of applause rips through the small space. The spotlight locks on the cage as a familiar face steps in, and a rock song splinters out of the speakers.

Aldrick.

"What?" I breathe, stopping as I look up at the cage. Another guy steps in from an opposite opening in the cage, pacing next to the fence as an announcer's voice fills the room. It's Tessa—the girl who stopped the mayhem last night. She circles the floor around the cage.

"First up, we have Aldrick versus Gregory."

Everyone has stopped moving, so it's harder for me to get around them. I'm so desperate to get out of here that I might start pushing.

"Reminder: there are no referees here tonight. All gladiators will fight until the other yields."

Aldrick steps into the ring, a smirk on his face.

Gregory runs his tongue over his teeth and makes a foul gesture with his hips, and the intro music stops. Aldrick and Gregory go still.

Tessa raises her arms and drops them, signaling for the fight to begin. The fighters start circling each other.

Aldrick's a Stoneskin, so he has the advantage. At least, I think. Gregory is taller than Aldrick, and broader, as though that's even possible. I bite the edge of my sweatshirt's sleeve. A thick, dirty beat rips from the speakers, and Aldrick steps forward, clenching his fists. His skin turns an ashy gray, and he rushes Gregory, throwing a punch that Gregory ducks just in time.

Stoneskins can turn their skin as hard as stone—hence

the name—but they can't keep it that way for long, and they can't cover their whole body. I'm hoping that Gregory can't tell which part of Aldrick is vulnerable. Gregory pulls his hand back and throws a dark sphere at Aldrick.

"What a way to start the night, people! We've got a Stoneskin versus a Charger! Those little bombs are called chrysalises. Like grenades of varying intensity. But don't worry!" Tessa yells into the microphone.

One of the chrysalises hits the chain-link, and the metal ripples as the chrysalis falls to the mat inside, harmless.

"The cage is protected. Nothing will get out that's not supposed to get out."

End it, I think, watching Aldrick dance around Gregory with a smirk on his face. But from the gasps and roar of the crowd, I can see that's not what people came for. The usual patrons of the Beneath don't want fast; they want bloody.

And that's what they'll get if Gregory hits Aldrick.

This place is sick. What the hell is wrong with people? I always wondered who went to the Colosseum back in Rome. What awful person willingly goes to watch someone else suffer?

These people. These people do.

Gregory throws a chrysalis and it skims Aldrick's earlobe. The crowd gasps, but Aldrick doesn't seem fazed. He connects with Gregory's jaw, sending him sprawling against concrete, but Gregory rolls and takes out Aldrick's feet before Aldrick can finish the job. A Chrysalis goes flying but stops when it hits the metal links of the cage. The chrysalis sizzles, disarms.

I look down, shutting my eyes tight.

I think it's worse with my eyes closed, honestly. The cheers. The gasps. The hoots and boos and shrieks. The sound of bloodlust; the sound of thirst. The sound of humanity at its worst, looking for spilled blood, dented honor, and crushed bodies.

I turn. I'm getting out of here. I run right into the guy standing next to me.

"Oh my gosh. I'm so sorry," I say. The crowd erupts, and I purposefully keep my eyes low so I don't look back at the ring and see what made them so excited. At this decibel it has to be at least a broken tooth.

"No worries," the guy says, and I know the voice.

He turns and sees me, his eyes widening with recognition. Sam.

Of course. The guy who witnessed my only slip in over a year—a guy I thought I'd never see again—is here.

And now I'm scrambling past strangers as I try to get to the door. He turns around all the way, like we're going to have a conversation here, or something. No way.

"I have to go," I mumble, and it gets lost in another round of screams and applause.

"Wait! Hold on a minute!" I can hear him muttering

apologies as he squeezes past people to follow me, and judging by our sizes, it's a lot easier for me than it is for him.

Keep moving, Vesper. Keep moving. Don't answer him. Don't. More gasps from the crowd. This thing isn't over yet. I chance a glance over my shoulder. Gregory is holding on by a thread, and Aldrick is just dragging this thing out. It'll be over in minutes.

I turn back to Sam.

He didn't tell the cops about me. He didn't even seem that surprised when I used my magic. He's seen Oddities before, then. Maybe he's a regular here when the Beneath is just a regular fighting ring.

I look over at the cage. I can't see from this far on the floor, though I hear the viewers from the ringside seats start to chant *Aldrick, Aldrick, Aldrick,* so at least I know he's okay.

"Wrists?" a gruff voice asks from behind me. I whirl around. A tall bouncer with dark braids holds up a small flashlight. The bouncer looks at me. "Wristbands, please?" he asks again, slowly, like I'm an idiot.

"I was just leaving," I say, moving to push past him. But he blocks my path.

"Nah-uh, sweet cheeks. You watch the fight, you pay for the fight."

My stomach sinks. I am running low on cash anyway. I already have to buy a new bus ticket. I can't imagine the price tag for an underground fighting ring.

Sam steps in front of me and grabs my hand. "Actually, she's with me. And she really doesn't like being called *sweet cheeks*, right . . ." He turns to me, a question on his lips.

"Vesper," I answer through gritted teeth.

The bouncer looks me up and down for a moment, then seems to decide I'm not a threat. I stand there for a moment, unsure. This happens often, and I'm never sure how to feel about it. I'm shifty and skittish, but I still get the benefit of the doubt. I'm still a small blond girl. I don't fit the mold of what seems "dangerous." The fact that my appearance gives me safety when I know how deadly I really am makes my stomach churn.

The bouncer walks away, and I cross my arms over my chest, reeling from the idea that this guy has helped me *again*.

"You're a regular, huh?" I sneer, turning to face him.

"Nope."

"Are you here to fight?" I press.

"Nope. I'm Baseline."

I eye him. He's got no reason to lie about that.

"I didn't need your help." I need to get a new catchphrase. This one sucks.

"Didn't say you did," he replies, crossing his arms over his chest. "You know? You could just say thanks."

I force a smile on my face. The thought of him coming here to watch Aldrick and others like us beat each other up for survival's sake makes me sick. "Hey, Sam, thank you for supporting local Oddities. Thanks to patrons like you, we can beat the crap out of each other for basic necessities like food and medicine. You're a true hero."

I turn, and he's following me as I make a beeline for the door I came through.

"That's kind of a sweeping generalization, don't you think?" he counters.

His voice is close to my ear. Sweet mother, he's following me.

"No," I say over my shoulder. I'm not answering any more questions. I am getting the hell out of here, though it's taking forever, since the floor is packed.

"Really? You've asked the other Oddities here how they feel about the fights?"

I open my mouth but don't get to say anything else because the lights around us dim and the crowd lets out another deafening roar. Ananias enters the now-empty cage, twirling his resurrected flower between his fingers.

Aldrick stands off to the side below the cage door, smiling through bloody teeth as the people around him slap him on the back. He won.

I need to get out of here. This is all too much.

I turn away from Sam and make my way to the door. It's slow going, since the crowds are thick.

"This is a new world, guys. This is *our* world. No more fear. It's an age with tremendous potential. But I know that some of you are tentative. You're scared, and understandably so, that the freedom you've felt lately is just temporary. It seems like a great risk to fight in this tournament—and that's why I'm offering a great reward for those brave enough to fight. To the winner of the final round, Tournament of the Unraveling, I am offering one unraveling, along with one million dollars of prize money."

I stop and whip toward the cage.

The applause is deafening, but all I can hear is my heartbeat in my ears. My mind spins as I try to process what I've just heard. The money means nothing, but . . .

An unraveling.

A do-over.

A rewrite.

I close my eyes and taste ash. I smell smoke, I hear roaring flames, and I see Carmen's face. I see my family together, uninjured, and whole.

I could undo it.

The thought is ravenous inside of me, the hope catching and spreading through me before I can let logic tell me that this might be a bad idea.

I don't know when I started moving again, but I'm pushing through the crowd and making my way to the edge of the cage, leaving Sam somewhere behind.

When I open my eyes, I see Aldrick standing at the base of the bleachers, high-fiving people who are congratulating him. I put my hand on his arm. His eyes widen at the sight of me, surprised that I'm here.

I bring my mouth to his ear as he leans down.

"I want in," I breathe.

He pulls back and smirks down at me.

I don't hear a thing as I follow Aldrick and a guard named Demitri to what Aldrick calls the bullpen—the place where the competitors wait for their name to be called. On a normal night of fighting in the Beneath, you can pick who you want to challenge to fight. But this is not a normal underground fight anymore, so the pairings are random. I'm lucky, Aldrick tells me, since there was a no-show in the fifteenth slot. My one shot.

He explains that only winners from tonight go on to the second fight, but that from there it goes down to four, and then two. His voice sounds far away as I imagine myself in the cage. I got so nervous before cheer competitions I almost always threw up, and the worst that could happen there was that I face-planted a back handspring or something.

Now I am sitting on a worn-out couch staring at my hands. I told myself I wasn't going to use my magic again—the dangerous, uncontrollable, life-ruining magic that almost kills me every time I use it. But here I am.

I was going to leave to go work on an almond farm today. How the hell did I wind up here? I put my head in my hands and replay the last fifteen minutes.

Aldrick walked me to the sign-in table; I looked around as I waited. Medics in off-duty clothes talked and laughed as they stood along the hallway, drinking free beer and watching the fights on a live-feed TV screen mounted on the wall. The Ledger, a girl with pink hair, stood behind a leather-bound book and explained the rules.

No outside weapons, no time-outs, and—no referees.

I blanched at the last one, and she smirked at me. "You don't have to sign if you don't want to."

But I want to. I need to. This is redemption, and I know it might not come by again.

With a shaky hand, I took the pen as she rattled off the rest of the rules—winners from tonight advance to night two. There are wild-card entries possible in the second round, but the entry fee is ten thousand dollars. I snort. I'd better win tonight then. I skim the rest of the paper, wincing as I read the standard part where it's like *Yeah, we know we could die, and, no, we won't hold you accountable if we are killed or otherwise maimed.*

I should've left when I saw the words *death or other severe forms of bodily harm* on the paper, but every time I think about bailing, I hear Carmen's screams in the back of my mind, flitting and crashing against my thoughts like a trapped bird. I thought I had limits, but I never had the chance to fix this before. Now, faced with this chance, I will do just about anything to undo this. And if it means using the magic to fix what the magic destroyed . . . so be it. I pull on a hangnail until blood pools near my cuticle. I lift my finger to my lips and suck the drop as I look around. There are a couple of couches to sit on and contemplate your fate, a screen with the live feed of the fights to scare the shit out of you, and a buttload of energy drinks to pump you so full of caffeine you're either ready to go kill someone or run a half marathon. Maybe both? Simultaneously? One right after the other?

A warm body sinks into the couch next to me. "Okay, we probably only have a few minutes, so listen up." I jump at the contact but turn to see Aldrick. He points to a group of Oddities standing in the doorway. "There's Brittany, the Duster. She breathes a glittery dust that induces hallucinations. Not so bad. Also, she's nice. She helped me get my M&M's out of the vending machine when they were stuck once. Kate, the Shader. Scot, the Shifter. Diana, the Levitas—she can literally float." He mentions a few other Oddities—ones I have heard of, and ones that are completely new. I watch, trying to take it all in. He points to a girl with wild curls and a pink fur jacket, wearing purple sunglasses even though we're inside. And it's night. "That's Jill. Don't worry about her— she doesn't fight other women, on principle. So she would forfeit before she'd fight you. I've seen her shred a couple of men, though."

I smile, liking the sound of that. A dark-skinned guy in

jeans and a sweater hands her a Diet Coke and sits next to her.

"And that's Rob, an Animus and the only male Oddity she'll talk to."

I take note, just in case I'm in the cage with him. I run over all their names in my head, trying to keep them straight. Kathy. Luke. Jo. Aldrick is, for some reason, giving me a heads-up, and I should take it. I'm struck yet again by how everyone's power seems to suck exponentially less than mine.

"Wait," I say, holding my hand up. "Why are you helping me?"

Aldrick shrugs. "You helped Sapphira when the cops came after her." He says it like it's the most natural thing in the world. "Also she'll rip my balls clean off if anything happens to you in there, seeing as I didn't send you packing the moment you stepped foot in here."

"Where is she?"

"Around here somewhere. She's a Botivast. She's the one who made the queen of poisons vines," Aldrick says, motioning to the ceiling. I realize I never asked Sapphira what her power was. I stare up at the vines covering the ceiling. If they weren't completely deadly and the symbol of the people who probably want me dead, I'd think they were pretty. "She makes herself scarce, though. She, um"—he looks up at the vines with me—"she doesn't exactly like watching the fights."

"I wouldn't like watching someone I care about getting pummeled, either."

"I did *not* get pummeled," Aldrick replies, reaching up and batting softly at one of the vines.

"Right. You still got some dried blood on your chin," I retort. Aldrick rolls his eyes, but I see him wipe his scruff with the back of one massive hand.

"It's the beginning of something good. Soon, she'll see that. This is all worth it."

"You're pretty certain."

"This is the future, Vesper. We're free now."

"Again. You're pretty certain," I counter.

Aldrick shifts toward me, and I turn to look at him. He leans forward, earnestness on his bruised face.

"I *know*, Vesper. Haven't you put it together yet? I pegged you for a thinking type."

I press my lips together and give him my best *I have no idea what you're taking about* face.

"Ananias used his power to unravel the Rule of Shadow. Two years ago. This man is single-handedly responsible for changing the tide of history . . . and the Wardens haven't killed him. In two years. You know why?"

The Rule of Shadow. My memory races back through the books and countless internet searches. It was the rule that bound us to keep our powers secret. It was the reason I couldn't show my parents what I could do before that Independence Day when everything changed.

I look away, trying to process the thought. An Unraveler isn't supposed to exist, but I just saw one with my own eyes.

And the Wardens have been gone before, but never for two years.

"Because the Wardens are gone."

His dark eyes light up with excitement, the kind that only stems from a deep faith. I had faith like that once. I believed that there was a point and purpose to things, and that good would always win. I don't think I'll ever feel that kind of faith ever again.

My father's warnings were too deeply laced to be pulled free by one wild hope. He was wrong about Unravelers. But he was right about so much more. I shake my head.

"I'm going into this knowing what I'm risking, Aldrick. You should, too. The Wardens aren't gone."

Aldrick smiles at me. "Agree to disagree then. And in a couple of months, when the world is different and we're livin' large . . . I'll accept your apology."

His grin is so easy, and it contrasts strangely against the cuts on his lips, that I can't help but smile back. I wish I could have this kind of faith in something.

We both stop to watch the screen as Mavis is called up against Theo. I grab Aldrick's arm. The music starts, and Mavis circles Theo. She's dressed in black leather. He, however, looks just like he did when they picked me up last night—jeans and a white T-shirt.

My feet move on their own as I get closer, trying to get a better look.

Theo lifts his hand, spinning his palms. Two razor-thin disks of glass spin toward Mavis's neck. She ducks, the disks hit the metal links of the fence, and the glass splinters over the ground of the cage. Shards fly past Mavis, slicing her cheek open. She shrieks, losing ground for a moment as she wipes the blood with her forearm.

Even from this far, I can see Mavis smiling. She pulls off one glove with her teeth. Theo shoots glass out from his palms, ducking as he shoots the stream at Mavis's feet. She jumps, flipping over the cooling stream and reaching for Theo. He dodges, but she lunges, tripping him.

He falls, raising his hands and making a block of red glass and holding it up like a shield. Mavis puts a hand on it and lets out a horrendous shriek. The glass disintegrates into dust. Theo tries to roll, but Mavis is on him too quickly. Her finger is inches from his throat when he reaches out and taps his fingers to the mat.

Tessa blows a whistle from outside the cage, and Mavis stops.

"Mavis with the win!" Tessa calls through a microphone. Mavis smiles and flicks her finger against Theo's shirt. It crumbles to dust, revealing his bare chest peppered with dark hair.

She slips her glove on and reaches down to pull Theo to his feet. Whistles and catcalls peel down from the bleachers, and Theo blushes, crossing his arms over his chest as Mavis gestures to him with a sweeping arm. A reluctant smile slides up the corner of Theo's mouth, and he flips Mavis off as they both leave the cage.

Mavis walks by me with a smirk on her perfectly lined, matte-black lips. They didn't smudge even a little bit in her fight, because life is completely unfair.

"This is too good." And then she doubles over in laughter, her blond hair falling over her shoulder. "You're going . . . to get . . . eaten alive . . . ," she wheezes through her fits of laughter.

"Enough, Mavis," Aldrick says, pushing himself to his feet.

I'm about to open my mouth, but someone calls my name over a speaker.

Vesper.

I stand in a chain-link-surrounded cage, blinded by a spot-light. Voices chatter in the darkness around me, and my heartbeat is now just one continuous thrum in my chest. I'm like a deadly hummingbird hopped up on Monster Energy and the couple Sour Patch Kids Aldrick handed me to cover the taste of bile after I vomited into a trash can on my way up.

Another body steps inside. I move to the side to be able to see him clearly. He's taller than me, but not by much. His dirty-blond hair is tucked behind his ears, and he wears a black motorcycle jacket over ripped jeans. He shrugs it off and hands it to a girl waiting on the stairs. He's shirtless under it. Of course. Her orange hair falls over her eyes as she grabs it from him and pulls him in for a deep, completely inappropriate kiss.

Tessa says something I don't comprehend, and the cage door closes.

Clink clink clink. It's locked.

Why the hell would they lock it? What purpose can that serve?

Focus, Vesper.

"Carl versus Vesper," Tessa calls. The lights dim, glowing purple as they shoot up toward the ceiling.

Carl grins at me, though it's not so much a grin as that look Inigo Montoya got when he spotted a lizard on the deck.

"Ready?" Tessa calls as she raises her hands to the ceiling. Before I even have time to think, Carl flexes his wrist. A stinger lowers from his skin, black and gleaming.

He's a Chigger. If he stings me with that thing, I'm out of the fight. And also maybe dead. Tessa drops her hand.

Carl swings his hand, and the stinger gets longer. He lunges at me, but I sidestep him. He hits the fence with a growl.

I launch myself toward the other end of the cage, my fight-or-flight instincts kicking in, though it seems like they're all screaming, *Flight! Flight! Are you kidding?* There's little to no fight. Almost none.

I hear Sam's voice behind me then, his lips close to my ears through the fence. He's in the corner where I've seen coaches stand in the movies, his fingers laced in the metal links.

"He wants you to keep running. He wants to tire you out." I chance a look at him over my shoulder. His eyes are dark and intense—the eyes of someone who has done this before.

I nod, because I can't think of anything else to do.

Carl rushes me, and I step up to meet him, faking left before launching myself right and sticking my hand out. The pulse in the center of my palm latches on to something. A voice sounds in my mind. It's faint but menacing. *You useless piece of shit*, it says.

I turn, and Carl's knuckles catch me right in the mouth, sending me flying to the ground. Blood swirls against my tongue, hot and salty, as Carl stands over me. He launches himself on top of me, pinning me to the ground. I try to push him off, but he has my hands pinned to the sides of my head. I scream, partially in anger, partially because I feel my one chance at redemption slipping out of my grasp.

It's a terrible, hopeless feeling—being trapped beneath someone. Knowing no screams in the world will bring them down. Carl's enjoying this. I turn my head to look away from his hateful grin as he leans down. I shut my eyes tight.

"You scream like a bitch. Is that standard for all activities on your back?" he whispers, his breath tickling the shell of my ear.

I open my eyes and see Sam, his fingers laced in the chain

links, his expression tight. The roar of the crowd shakes the ground, but I hear his voice as I watch his lips move.

Buck your hips, he calls.

I have no clue what that will do, but I scoop all my remaining strength into my core and, with one huge push, buck upward.

Carl wasn't expecting that. He loses his balance, and I scramble out from under him. I throw my hands up once more, latching on to his chest. He staggers, eyes widening as my grip on him gets stronger.

I see it now. A woman stands in a kitchen, her apron covered in flour. Hair falls in her face as she spins around, hatred gleaming in her green eyes—eyes that look just like Carl's. This is his mother.

She pulls a metal spatula from the counter and raises it over her head. "Get out of here, you useless piece of shit!"

The tingling in my hand gets stronger, and I feel the urge to pull. To yank this terror out of him.

But something stops me, just for a moment.

There has to be something else. Something less . . . awful. I close my eyes and sift through his dark corners for other fears. I see clowns, a stuffed bear with red eyes, and the view from a twenty-story window. Those are all better than this woman—this woman who broke him apart when he was too young to fight back. I try to grab on to the clown—God help us all—but I can't get a grip on it.

It keeps slipping, and I find myself grabbing on to the woman.

Carl rushes me, picking me up and body-slamming me down to the mat. My whole body contracts in agony as the air rushes out of my lungs. I writhe for a moment, breathless, before a crashing inhale inflates my chest just in time.

Carl throws his stinger down, and it lands where my head was, sinking into the spring-loaded mat like it's butter.

He was going to sting me in the *face*? Okay. I don't have time to worry about being his childhood shit. I don't even really have time to worry about what I can do, and what might happen if I let my magic out. This place is a pit full of monsters, so I need to be a little more of a monster. I roll to my feet and latch on to him. He stumbles as my magic grabs hold of the sickness in his chest—an abusive mother. I wonder if he knows what I've found, because he looks up at me, and all the cockiness is gone from his emerald eyes. All that's left is wide-eyed terror. A child, afraid. My resolve buckles as I try for one more moment to search for something, *anything* else. But there's nothing. Carl's sneer curls up his lips again as he lunges. I dodge, but he sticks out a foot and trips me. I go sprawling, my teeth sinking into my lip. I cry out as I roll over, and Carl snaps his hands out. The stinger comes straight for my chest, and I freeze.

I reach out and tap the mat, and Carl stops the stinger inches from my chest.

We have a winner! Carl advances!

Just like that . . . I'm done. It was over before it even really started.

I push myself to my feet as his orange-haired girlfriend jumps into the ring, throwing her legs around his waist as he raises his hands in victory.

I hobble over to the exit of the cage. I step on the first step but lose my balance. An arm wraps around my waist. I look up as Sam helps me down the last three steps.

"Easy," he says lowly, tightening his grip.

Ahead of us, Carl turns. "Hey, blondie, maybe no one told you, but this is the kind of activity you *don't* win by being on your knees."

Sam steps forward, but Aldrick is there then, putting his hands up between them.

"Enough. Carl, you won, asshole. Go crawl into your hovel and tell all three of your fans how you beat up a rookie on her first go. I'm sure that'll get you laid."

"Piss off, Aldrick," Carl replies, his smile fading as he turns.

The next fight is called, and amid the roar, I slip through the crowds, my body screaming with every step—though it's nothing compared to the shuddering disappointment racking my heart.

I hear Sam calling my name, but his voice gets lost as the place erupts in applause when the next fight starts. I grab my backpack from where I'd stashed it below the bleachers and walk down the hallway. I don't know where I'm going, but I know I'm moving, and that's enough.

I don't think I actually thought I would win. I didn't actually think that I would be able to fight my way through all those Oddities. And maybe part of me is relieved, and that's what's worse. If I won the tournament, I'd have to go home, and I didn't stop to really think about what that would mean. I'd have to face what I'd done, even if I could fix it. I'd have to answer to disappearing in the middle of the night. I'd have to own the things *I* did to my family. Not my magic. Me. My magic hurt them, but I let it. I walk through the back door, into the dark, wet night. Of course it's raining now. I throw my hood over my head. I'm twenty feet from a street, with the ocean behind me. There's a gas station at the corner, right next to a Purrfect Auto Service and Koala-T-Water, so my plan to walk to a bus station isn't looking too great. Not that it would matter. My bus left an hour ago.

The door opens behind me. "Vesper?"

"I don't want to talk about it," I say, looking over my shoulder. It hurts to twist in any direction.

Sam holds the door open with a foot as he slips an arm back into his green military jacket. "Come back inside; it's freezing out here."

I realize now that I'm soaked. I step under the awning near the door, but I'm not going back inside. There's just no point in standing here getting drenched until I have a game plan. I cross my arms over my chest.

"Look, I know how that feels. I've had my ass handed to me more than once," Sam says.

Really? You know what it's like to lose your only chance to put together your shredded life? Doubt it.

"I don't want to talk about it, okay? It was a dumb idea, and now I'm leaving."

Sam steps out and lets the door close. I make an incoherent noise as I reach for it, but it's weighted and slams shut. And locks.

"We're locked out," I say, looking at him with as much accusation as I can muster.

"You didn't look like you were planning on coming back in, so I don't see how I screwed anyone over other than myself."

"I didn't ask for your help," I say quietly, knowing I'm not just talking about right now. I don't know why he decided to try to get me through that fight, but every time I close my eyes, I see his taut face looking at me through the chainlink.

His eyes shift as I hit the core of what we've both been circling. He looks like he's going to say something, but I cut him off.

"How do you know about this place?" I ask. My voice drops, even though there is no one else around. "How do you know about Oddities?"

"I have a friend who has . . . abilities," he says, looking down.

"Baselines aren't supposed to know any of this," I say lamely.

"I don't know if you've noticed, but things have been changing lately."

The rumble of the crowd is so strong that it shakes the doors. "What do you want, Sam?" I ask, my voice finally finding the words that have been dancing around my chest since I met him.

"To make sure you're okay."

"I'm fine." I say it too quickly. No one believes you when you're too quick about it. And he knows. He narrows his eyes at me like he's waiting for me to revise and tell him the truth. I shrug, and the moment goes on for a second too long. The crowd roars inside, and I lock eyes with Sam. What is he doing here?

"So your friend introduced you to the wide and compelling world of desperate, freakish youths trying to kill each other, and you, what, got a taste for it?"

"No. It's not like that."

"That's my favorite phrase. Because it almost always is." I walk back out into the rain.

Sam follows.

"I know you don't want to hear this, but you have potential, Vesper."

I can't help it. I burst out laughing. "Oh yeah? What part gave you that idea? When I was literally running from my opponent, or when he had me pinned to the ground?"

"I'm serious. That was your first fight, right? I'll bet you hadn't even seen a cage before tonight. Will you stop for a second?"

I reach the street and hit the button at the crosswalk, and he comes up next to me.

"God, what's it going to take for you to leave me alone?" I say, whipping around. "We aren't friends. We're not even acquaintances. I thought I might try something, and it failed. Not the first time I've made an ass of myself, and it won't be the last. On to the next town," I call, raising one hand over my head to signal *onward* as I hit the crosswalk button with the other.

"And why did you do it?" he asks.

I freeze, because the real answer is on the top of my tongue. I swallow it back. "For one million dollars?" I ask, forcing levity into my tone. It sounds wrong, but I'm hoping he won't notice. "I'd do a hell of a lot worse for that kind of money, Sam. As would most homeless runaways—huge shocker. It's been real, but I'm gonna go lick my wounds in private now."

The crossing light turns green, and I start across the street.

"And where are you planning on licking those wounds?" he calls.

I turn around and look at him, my soaking hair whipping around my face. A lone truck rolls up to the stoplight and freezes. Its headlights light up the space between Sam and me.

I don't answer, and it's an answer in and of itself.

"Thought so," he says lowly. "Come stay with me."

The light turns green, and the trunk honks. I step out of its way but don't walk all the way to Sam. "I'm sorry? I said lick my own wounds, perv."

Sam shakes his head. "Not like that. I mean, I have a place you could stay. We have a loft above the gym. You could crash there."

I want to be incensed at his offer, spit that I couldn't possibly because I don't know him at all, and storm off.

But I'm cold, and my head is pounding, my muscles burning from the beating I just took. And I'd had all these great "in theory" ideas about where I was going to go, but now that he's put it into words, I realize I have no real plan, and that underpass sounds like misery right now. And I can't go back to the Grotto. I just can't. Not after that.

I step forward, onto the median.

"Why would you want someone like me staying with you?"

"Because . . ." He stops. "You held back."

I glare at him, and he steps closer, raising his voice a little more. "You had something, and you decided not to use it. You could've won, but you held back."

Tears burn my eyes at his words. Not because I'm amazed that he's right, but because I realize how close I'd been to winning. I didn't just stop for Carl. I did it because I wasn't sure I could control what I brought out.

I look back at the gas station just as the light on the *g* goes out. It's not like I'm signing a lease. I just need to get dry and make a plan. One more thought drags me down.

"I'm not a safe person to have around," I say, the words coming out haltingly. It's one thing to take a risk around a bunch of Oddities. But he's Baseline, and he could get hurt if I'm around.

Sam sees my hesitance, because he steps closer, palms up. "Whatever you are, I've seen worse."

"You can't know that."

"I'm willing to risk it." He eyes me.

I lick a drop of rain off my top lip. The promise of warmth is too much to pass up. The thought of not being alone is too much to ignore.

"Just for one night," I say, more to myself than to him. He motions to the parking lot and points to his truck. I walk behind him, my hands in my pockets.

One night, then back to the road. Back to what I know—and I'll make sure to leave hope here when I go.

ELEVEN

We pull up in his beat-up white Chevy and park in front of a small brick-covered building across from Aloa's. I stare at the café through the rearview mirror.

"He's okay, you know. Gabe. Couple of stitches, but it's better than what would've happened had you not been there," he says, like he can read my mind. I bite the inside of my cheek and turn to look at the gym. There's no name on it, no huge *HAWT PEOPLE WORK OUT HERE* logo, or something. Light streams through the front windows.

"Welcome to Duncan's," he says as he kills the engine and opens his door. "Let me do the talking."

I grab my backpack and step out into the frigid night. The rain has leveled off to a drizzle, but I'm still so thankful when he opens the door to the gym and the warmth slips around my shoulders.

It's bigger than it looks from the outside, with mats covering the floors. Punching bags hang from a scaffold on the ceiling. A thudding sound, mixed with staccato breathing and "one, two, three, four, one, two, three, four," fills the air, and I look over. A tan blonde in a black crop top and bright purple boxing gloves is beating the shit out of a water bag while a shirtless, muscular guy with dark skin and a knee brace stands behind it.

I follow and keep my eyes on the floor, because otherwise I know I'll wind up staring at the guy's freakishly cut abs or something. I don't want to be that *eyes up here* kind of girl. Eyes on the floor seems best.

Oh my God. Is that blood?

That's blood.

There's blood on the floor here. It's dried, too. Like . . . they didn't even properly mop it up. What kind of sport allows blood to be so commonplace that you might actually *forget* to mop it up?

"Duncan," Sam says. "Can I talk to you for a minute?"

"Take three, Abagail," Duncan says. The thudding stops and I look up. I can't look at the blood anymore. The girl lifts her shirt to mop the sweat from her forehead. She's got a bruise under one eye. She looks at me with mild interest before squirting water into her mouth. I didn't know people did that in real life. I've only ever seen it on commercials for sports drinks and stuff.

I hang back. I don't need to listen to Sam's *can we keep her?* speech, just in case Duncan decides he doesn't want a shady girl crashing here. I turn around and stare at a dusty trophy case. There are several awards lined up on shelves—regional championship plaques in everything from judo to Jiu-Jitsu to Muay Thai. I'm not surprised, really, but . . . okay, I guess I'm surprised. From the outside, it looks like nothing. But this gym is super legitimate. My eyes scan the shelves and land on a picture of a much younger Duncan holding a silver metal. The wording on the frame tells me that he was a medalist in wrestling at the Olympics. *What?* Geez, you'd think I'd be less of a snob now that I fully have to buy all my underwear from the Dollarstore.

Below, there's a picture of Sam in a cage. He's wearing MMA gloves and a mouth guard.

I turn around. Duncan is listening intently as Sam spins my tale of woe. I didn't even think to ask if he was going to tell Duncan about the Beneath. About me. Does everyone in this gym know about Oddities?

As if on cue, Duncan looks over Sam's shoulder. Sam turns and motions for me to come talk to them.

Duncan crosses his fully tattooed arms as I walk up. "Vesper. You got a last name? And maybe a real first name?"

"Vesper is my real first name," I shoot back, chancing a quick look at Sam, who does nothing but step back and smile. Okay. So this is some sort of test then. Like how I can take Duncan busting my balls. Fine. I cross my arms, too.

"Sam says you're in some sort of trouble but didn't want to tell me too much without your permission. Now, I get that he's nice like that. But I have a bit of a conundrum, because I am not usually the type to let people I don't know stay in my gym. So I'm going to give you a chance to tell me what you think will give me the best picture of you, so I can get a sense of whether this is a good idea."

The girl he was fighting with, Abagail, comes up next to him as she tightens the hot pink wraps around her wrists. Does this girl only own Barbie-colored fighting gear?

I look back at Duncan.

"I ran away from home. No criminal record. No mob ties. No Liam Neeson trying to get me back at all costs. And I don't even plan on staying long. I just need a place to crash for the night."

Duncan narrows his eyes at me. "That's it? That's your best pitch?"

"I promise I'm housebroken?" I shrug.

Duncan nods, surveying me with this weird look that I can't quite place. Then he closes his eyes—

And disappears.

"What the hell?" I scream, stepping back.

Sam covers his mouth in an effort not to laugh, and Abagail concentrates on her wraps, a smirk on her face.

Duncan reappears, arms out as he takes a slight bow. Ta-da.

He's an Oddity.

"You're a Fader?" I ask. I don't care how many times I run into freaks like me, it will still weird me out when I see powers in action. I look out the front window, as though someone in a black suit and Taser is waiting to drag him to some government lab. Or Wardens, ready to come in and kill us all. But there's no one out there.

"So. You want to revise your statement?" he asks.

He might be okay with being open about his freakishness, but I'm not. And I never pretended to be. He looks too smart to think that trust is something everyone gives, but then again, this gym looked like a hole-in-the-wall and inside is an Olympian Oddity. So looks aren't everything.

I just stare back at him. "Either you're okay with me crashing here, or you're not."

Duncan smiles. "Fair enough."

The two most unhelpful words in the English language. I'm about ready to turn and walk out when he looks up and motions to the loft that rests above the punching-bag scaffold.

"That's the loft. There's a cot under the sofa. Door locks from the inside. You can crash there as long as you need." He leans down to adjust his knee brace. "Abagail, that was way more than three. Let's keep going."

She rolls her shoulders, and I step back just before she does a one-two punch on the water bag that shakes the floor. Sam reaches out, his fingers light on my forearm.

What? He's just going to let me stay here? No more third degree?

"Um . . . thank you. And I'd be happy to pay my way. I don't expect you just to let me stay here for nothing—"

Sam pulls me back as Duncan waves me off and starts counting for Abagail.

"If you give me a mop, I'll be more than happy to wipe up that blood over there—"

"Okay, Vesper. Come on," Sam says, dragging me behind him.

"She's not an Oddity, is she?" I ask, eyes glued to Abagail as he leads me to the staircase up to the loft.

Sam motions for me to walk up ahead of him. "Nope. Just a regular badass."

I remember when sleeping at someone else's house used to be a thing. My friends and I would try so hard to coordinate a sleepover—getting all our parents to agree and let four or five preteens crash in the living room and watch movies and giggle until dawn wasn't always an easy feat.

But we'd eventually wear one parent down. Then we'd plan the whole night. What movies we were going to watch and what games we were going to play and what ghost stories we were going to tell.

But something would happen once the lights were all turned out. It had nothing to do with being an Oddity, or even being afraid of them before I knew I was one. No matter how much fun it was or how much I loved my friends . . . something about the lights turning off made me want to be home. The bed wasn't mine and the blankets were scratchy and the house smelled different and just knowing that my parents were asleep somewhere else weirded me out.

Most of the time, I could suck it up until morning. But sometimes . . . sometimes I would stare at the ceiling, or look at the illuminated time on the cable box and wait for the morning. I just couldn't sleep somewhere else.

That feels strange now, considering how many places I've had to sleep in for almost two years. Gas station bathrooms. Bus stops. Trains. A line of shrubbery in a nice neighborhood.

And every time I start to fall asleep, I wonder what will happen if I pull something dangerous out of a stranger while I sleep. Often, all I can do is remind myself that my mom came in to check the straightener before she went to bed. I tell myself that that little reminder is what kept the temptation of her fear in my subconscious. It might be bull, but it's the only way I can get to sleep sometimes, so I take it.

I wake suddenly, the familiar panic overtaking me as I sit up.

Is everyone okay? I look around the dark room, waiting for smoke. Waiting for screams. When none come, I twist, putting my feet on the cold floor.

Thud. Thud. Thud thud thud.

I slip off the cot, pulling the blanket around my shoulders

as I creep to the window in the loft and look down.

The gym is empty, except for Sam. He's wailing on one of the punching bags. Fists, elbows, knees, spinny-kicky-things. He's shirtless, with tape wrapped around his wrists, and he's dripping sweat. It looks like he's been doing this for a while.

I look at the clock. It's five in the morning.

I could go back to bed. I don't need to get further into this than I already am.

But something about the tightness of his shoulders and the way his jaw is set as he punches is something I recognize, down in my bones.

There's a desperation in the way he hits, like he's trying to jar himself so hard he'll forget what's keeping him awake.

And that's why I stand there, entranced. I *see* him.

That's the thing about being haunted. Once you're marked as deeply by scars of your own making as I am, recognizing those same wounds in others becomes a lot easier.

I should go to bed *now*, because standing here staring at him is creepy and if he looks up—

Crap. Crap, he looked up.

He stops, chest heaving, and waves up at me.

I have to go down now. Or this just gets weirder.

"I promise I wasn't just standing there watching you work out." Those are the first words out of my mouth. Much to my own horror.

He takes a deep pull from his water bottle. "I didn't think

you were. Did I wake you up?"

I shrug, trying to play it off. I need to go back to bed. Nothing good can come from talking to him more.

"Sorry," he says.

"You fight?" I ask finally.

"Used to," he says simply.

I hug myself, pulling my arms as deep into the sweatshirt as they will go. I changed my clothes, but my hair is still damp from the rain. I shiver.

Sam sets his water bottle down, and a silence fills the space between us. I didn't think this far ahead. I didn't think at all, really. I should get back upstairs. Nothing good can come from getting to know him better, since I'm leaving in the morning. But my mouth keeps moving.

"Do you live here?"

He picks his water bottle back up, like he's unsure about what to do with his hands. He wears a long chain around his neck, with an oval pendant at the end.

He smirks at the question through a mouthful of water. He swallows. "It feels like it, sometimes, but no. I have a flat near here I share with my friend Wex."

"And do you have a job?" I ask. I know it's coming out like an inquisition, and I am really not meaning for it to. I just can't place this guy, and I want to. I want to know what the hell his deal is.

Sam eyes me up and down. We're on the brink of joking,

and we both know it. Any further, and we've waded into murky waters. "I do. Down at one of loading docks on the western bank. Want to see a W-2?" he asks.

"Not yet. But you should have one on hand, just in case I change my mind."

He turns to set his water bottle down again, and I catch a glimpse of a tattoo on his tricep. It's in thin script, so thin that I wouldn't be able to read it if I weren't so close.

Elisa, it reads.

He turns back, and I drop my eyes before he can see what I've been staring at.

I'm done asking questions. But there's one more thing. One more thing that's been eating at me since we arrived here.

"Why did you go to the Beneath?" I ask.

"For someone not keen on answering questions, you sure ask a lot of them."

"You said you weren't there to see the fights. What else is there to see?"

He pulls at the Velcro straps of his wraps and unravels them. "I was looking for someone." He still has the black band around his wrist.

"Someone? Oh good; I was worried I was going to get an infuriatingly vague answer from you."

He lets out a staccato breath. "You're the one who said we aren't friends. You saved my ass when that guy put a gun to my chest, and I saved yours when you were looking at hypothermia. We're even." He runs his thumb knuckle over his lower lip.

Take it and run, my good sense says. *He's giving you an out. Take it.*

I step back. Sam looks up, slight annoyance in his gaze. He motions to the bag. "If you're not going back to bed, I'll start another set." The irritation he brought into my gut that first night at Aloa's is back, and I bristle at his tone.

"Hey. You woke me up, okay? I just wanted to make sure you were all right. And maybe . . ." I stop. The next words are ones I can't take back. I push onward. "You just looked . . ." I stop again, trying to find the words. What can I say? "I just wanted to make sure you were okay."

He stops and then lets out a small, hollow laugh.

"I'm fine." His words seem defeated. There's no anger in them now. His tone is something different. It's brittle and raw, and I should back off. I should nod and take my leave and go upstairs. I should pack my things up and get to the nearest bus station. That should be that.

I should go back to being alone. I lived in a decrepit studio apartment above a pizza place in Seattle, where the only friend I had in the whole city was a spider that made a web on my ceiling. I named him Winston and talked to him when I got lonely, and look—no one got hurt while I was there. No floods, no fires.

I think I forgot, even in that short amount of time, what it feels like to be with people. Sapphira reminded me, and now Sam feels like he's snagged on me or something. I'm caught, a little. Stuck here, drawn by the way he looks as broken as I feel.

I don't feel alone. I like being around Sam.

I like how he went to protect Gabe. I like how he didn't rat me out to the police, and how he's friends with Duncan and the fact that Oddities don't scare him. I like that he tried to help me. I like that he's still talking to me.

He hits the bag one more time, shaking the scaffolding above.

"Tell me."

He stops and looks at me, and the words are splinters in the air between us as he considers.

"I was looking for a gladiator," he says, lifting his arm and showing me the black wristband I'd seen earlier. Suddenly, the way the bouncer acted makes sense.

I step back. "You want to enter the tournament?"

"*I* can't enter. I'm a Baseline. But I was looking to sponsor an Oddity, yes."

"You trying to win the million?"

He lets out a sigh. "Not looking for money."

There's something he wants to fix. Something he needs to change.

"Is that why you followed me out?" My chest drops. If this

whole thing was a ruse to get me to fight for him—

But the way he looks at me silences that fear. "No, Vesper. I followed you out because I wanted to make sure you were okay."

"Well, didn't you blow your chance to find someone?" I ask.

"No. There's still the wild-card entry on the second night."

I remember the rules on the waiver I signed.

"You're going to drop ten thousand dollars on a chance to win this thing?" I ask, my voice rising an octave.

His expression is dead serious, and it's all the answer I need.

"Do you know who you want?" I ask.

"Jeez, you're relentless," he says, rolling his wrists. They strain against the athletic tape. "I did, and then she told me if I tried to convince her, she'd kick my ass," he says, his eyes meeting mine.

I should be pissed that he brought it up again, but something in his eyes stops me. I freeze, the hint of an idea pulling at the corners of my mind.

"He beat me, Sam. I lost."

"Because you pulled back," Sam says. "I saw what you did at Aloa's. You could flatten any of them."

"You don't know anything about me."

Sam stops, running his knuckle over his bottom lip as he turns to me. "You asked the guy at Aloa's what he was afraid of. Right before everything started."

I don't move. I don't even breathe as I stare him down, almost daring him to call it.

"You're a Harbinger," he says.

"How do you know what a Harbinger is?" I ask, my voice small.

"I know a bit more about Oddities than your average Baseline," he counters.

I feel a buzzing in my head as adrenaline shouts into my ears. I look around, trying to pin my thoughts down as they spin around my mind. Should I deny it? Tell him he's wrong? I could say he was hearing things.

But when I look at Sam again, deflections ready on the tip on my tongue, I stop at the sight of him—at the way he stares back expectantly and without a hint of fear.

Before I can think of the thousand lies I probably should use, I nod.

He steps forward, excitement plain on his face. "I didn't think I'd ever meet someone with that kind of power."

"Yeah. It's not as great as it sounds, Sam. Exhibit A being the fact that I could have killed you less than two days ago."

He shakes his head. "But you didn't."

I laugh humorlessly and look up at the ceiling, bringing my index fingers up to wipe any remnants of the mascara I stole from Mavis from under my eyes.

"I pulled back because I couldn't control it. I can latch on when they're close, but the second they back away, it's like I can't get a grip on anything—I have to find the fear that's the strongest. It's usually the worst, and then . . ." I don't finish, because I don't know how to. *And then my fear feeds it and it won't disappear. It becomes bigger than me. I unleash a monster.*

Though that's not the only thing that makes me a monster. The idea that blossomed a few minutes ago grows larger in the back of my mind as Sam steps closer to me, his eyes alight. "So I'll teach you to get close. Jiu-Jitsu is all about the smaller person using their opponent's body against them. Throw some Muay Thai and Krav Maga in there? You'll be in complete control. Hell, you might not even need to use your powers, Vesper. I've watched those fights for months. They only rely on their powers, and most aren't even that great at that. They'd have no clue what to do with a real fighter. Chigger or not, get Carl in an arm bar and he'll tap out."

There's a beat of silence between us as I look down at my hands. I can't believe I'm considering this.

Sam steps closer. "I'll buy your wild card. You let me train you. You kick some ass. You walk away with one million dollars and I walk away with . . ."

He stops as I look up and meet his eyes. He swallows, and I know that look. He was sucking words back down his throat. There's more to this story than I know.

"With what?" I ask, because I have to know if I can even

go through with this. "What do you want to use an unraveling on?"

Sam eyes me for a moment and then looks down, weighing his words. "My girlfriend left," he says carefully.

I eye him. "That's it?"

A girlfriend. Suddenly, the tattoo on his bicep has a different meaning.

"*It?*" he asks, tilting his chin down as he eyes me. "You ever had your heart broken, Vesper?"

"I'm not minimizing, okay? I just didn't take you for the type—" I stop, struggling to find words. "The settle-down type," I finish primly.

Sam smiles then, and the tension diffuses. "Well. I didn't take you for the nosy type, so I guess we're both wrong."

"How does it work?" I press, desperately trying to change the subject. "The tournament?"

Sam eyes me. "You write your tragedy down in the Ledger before the fight. You win, the unraveling happens, and then I give you the cash prize."

"*I* have to write it down? Why me?" I ask.

"Only an Oddity can inscribe in the Ledger."

My mind weaves the idea further before I can stop it. There's a beat, and I fill it with words that seal my fate.

"Let's do it," I say softly.

"You're serious?" he asks. I recognize that look in Sam's eyes, now—the same rabid, reckless hope I felt when my dad told me he was ripped. It's a snarling, starving hope that will take any scrap of a whisper of a chance you toss at it.

This girl must have had a grip on him.

I look around the gym, at everything from the sweat on the bag to my own bare feet. "I mean, don't get too excited. None of this matters if someone's afraid of an atomic bomb and I cover this half of the country in a nuclear winter." It's a bad joke. This isn't the time for a joke at all, let alone a bad one. But I say it because I want to warn him of the reality of what I carry in my bones, but, I mean, I need it to be light-hearted. As lighthearted as a nuclear winter can be.

"That won't happen," Sam assures me.

"When is the next fight?" I ask.

"Two weeks."

I could back away. I could tell him he was right in thinking that I didn't want to hear more. That he's crazy. But there's a power buzzing in my chest, like the thrill of a high. And, if Sam's right, I could maybe—maybe—do it without loosing a swarm of horse-size killer bees or spider-clown hybrids, or whatever other pit-of-hell horrors that linger in the deepest parts of the other gladiators.

Sam walks over to me. He's sweaty and breathing hard as he looks down at me. And it's not like he's looked at me before. In the coffee shop, I was just a girl who wound up in the wrong place at the wrong time. Then I was the girl who almost drowned him in an industrial-grade kitchen. Last night, I was a girl who needed a place to stay.

But right now?

His eyes are on mine, and I know I am the only one in the world who can stitch him back together. I can give him the antidote to whatever poison he's been breathing in since she left.

"It's a big decision. Don't make it now," he says. "We'll talk later?"

I nod, even though I've already made my decision. I should make it look like this is more difficult than it is.

As Sam's walks away to take a shower, the thought that was a shadow in the back of my mind blooms, spilling down my throat and into my mouth with such force that I actually gasp.

Am I really considering this?

I'm not just going to fight in this tournament. I'm going to win.

And then?

I'm going to take the unraveling for myself.

TWELVE

"Mary Lou Wiles Memorial Recovery Center, this is Marcie."

The voice on the other end of the phone is way too chipper to belong to the receptionist in the burn ward at Baldwin Hospital, and it catches me off guard. I pull the phone away from my head and look down, making sure I got the number right.

It takes me a minute to find my voice. I've called my mom's work once before but hung up right after she answered. This is the first time I've had the guts to actually say something. "Um. Is the recovery group meeting in the West Room today?"

"Yes."

I look up from the file. Before me, the Golden Gate Bridge splits through the fog like one of those titans from the old stories. I'm sitting on the grass on the eastern side of the bay. I fell asleep for a few hours after talking to Sam, but I feel completely rested. I woke up, grabbed a granola bar, and came here. It was the safest place I could think to open the envelope. No one looking over my shoulder.

"Can you transfer me over?" I ask, my voice shaky.

"Absolutely," the nurse says.

It took me three weeks after I left to summon the courage to read newspaper articles about the fire, and even then I could only do it two sentences at a time, with a ten-minute walking break between. When I read that my whole family was alive, I sobbed. But once the sensational story of the burned house and missing daughter wore itself out, I had no other way of checking on them. I did a little social media stalking—enough to know that they haven't stopped looking for me—but not enough so that it might become traceable. This envelope is the only real look I've had at my family in almost two years. I'm scared.

I look back down to the photos in my lap that the hacker I hired was able to get of Carmen. I used all the money I'd saved working as a restocker in a small convenience store, and it was barely enough. Most of the pictures are in the hospital, her blond hair twisted in a braid behind her head. I know from the log the hacker provided that Carmen leads a recovery support group with a guy named Tim on Sundays.

She's smiling, in these photos, which is so like her. The left side of her face is pink and raw, the scars still healing. It does nothing to dampen how radiant she looks here. A little boy with bandages around his hands sits on her lap, a grin on his face. Another is Carmen with my dad, walking out to the car after the group. He looks . . . normal. Happy. He has a cup of Starbucks in his hand, and her arm is looped through his. The back of her hand is marked with deep, purple scars. Before my cheer competitions, I'd see Carmen in the bleachers, and she'd put both hands over her heart— one right after the other. She'd leave them on her chest for a beat, then pull them off at the same time. *I love you*, it said. And it always made me feel strong. Now the sight of her hands reminds me of how weak I was.

They were probably on their way to the new home they bought a couple of months after I left. They probably picked up some takeout and ate on the porch with my mom, Iris, and Jack.

I bite my tongue hard as the receiver is picked up on the other end.

"Hello?" A voice comes over, half breathless with laughter. "Ty, sit down!" Carmen says to someone in the room.

Tears well up in my eyes as I fight not to breathe. To not make a sound.

"Hello?" she presses again. "Is someone there? I can't hear you."

Her voice is the same. It's the same voice that pulled me out of sleep in the mornings as she sang and jumped on me. *Riiiise and shine and give God the glory-glory*, she'd sing into my ear, mimicking the infuriating way our father used to wake us up as kids. The same voice that screamed and screamed that night, filled with pain and terror.

"Well, whoever this is—we are meeting today until about four thirty, so stop on by!" She laughs. "Ty! I'm serious—"

Click.

The line goes dead, but I keep the phone to my ear for another minute, tears streaming down my cheeks.

She sounds alive, though I can't imagine what kind of pain she carries daily, both physical and otherwise. But at least she's alive.

I look down at the grass, letting the full realization of what I'm about to do sink into my bones.

I thought I had reached the level of monster I'd never be able to pass, but now I know there's more of my soul I could lose. There's more monster to become. Not because of what I *am*, but because of what I'm going to *do*.

It's probably best that I don't find out.

I finger the folder in my lap and look down at the paper, at the photos of the charred remains of my house. I'm not going to just reverse the fire. I'm going to reverse *me*. I'm going to make it so I was born a Baseline.

Then I'm going to watch as every monstrous thing I've

THIRTEEN

I take the streetcar back to Duncan's, where I find Sam on the mat, sparring with another guy, whose hair is pulled back into a twisted braid, with an undercut on the sides. He has a tattoo on his back right shoulder—some saint I've never seen before peeks out from his black tank top. Another fighter, one with a thick beard, stands on the edge of the mat, a knife tucked in his workout shorts. Why the hell a guy needs a *knife* in his workout shorts is anyone's guess, but I have stopped asking questions ever since I saw the dried blood on the floor. Some of this stuff I'm just never going to understand.

They're not just boxing. Sam throws a kick, but this guy blocks it and lunges, his elbow rotating right at Sam's face. Sam ducks, shoving forward and ducking, catching the guy around the waist. He picks him up and throws him to the mat with a sick, heavy *thud*.

Suddenly the bloodstains are no longer a mystery.

"Move your feet," the bearded guy calls.

Sam's opponent lets out a grunt, and for a moment I wonder if they're going to keep fighting. But the guy laughs.

"I cry foul, sir," Undercut says, going limp against the mat. Sam reaches down, holding a hand out.

"You can't cry foul just because you lost, Wex." Wex. Sam's roommate. He reaches up and takes Sam's hand.

"Um, Sam?" the bearded guy warns. But it's too late.

"I didn't," Wex answers, yanking Sam down. His legs shoot up and wrap around Sam's shoulders, pulling him into a sort of really painful-looking bear hug.

Sam struggles, but Wex has his feet locked behind Sam's shoulders, and Sam can't move.

"That's some shady crap, Wex," Sam says. It's muffled, though, since his mouth is shoved against Wes's shoulder.

"Krav Maga is all about being shady, Sam," Wex says through clenched teeth.

Sam shoves but can't get his footing. His grunts turn into laughs, though, and he slaps the mat three times.

"See? *Now* we're done," Wex says, releasing Sam. "And I win."

Sam stands and helps Wex to his feet. They're both laughing. I clear my throat, trying to get Sam's attention. He looks at me, noticing me for the first time.

He motions to his opponent. "Vesper. This is Michael

Wexler. Wex. My friend and resident sketchy-ass cheater. And this is Roy, who is just plain sketchy-ass."

He does a double take at my face, and I realize too late that it's probably very evident that I've been crying. I blink and force a nod, like that will magically clear up the puffiness and red splotches. Roy nods as he rolls his shoulders and warms up on the now-vacant mat.

Wex laughs and holds out a hand. "I guess that's easier for you to say than 'guy who routinely beats me,' so I guess I'll take it. And you're the weird destructress we have living in our attic?"

I look to Sam. "That's my name from now on, okay?"

He nods, playing along, though I can see his concern.

"Can I talk to you for a moment? Or do you have an appointment to have your ass handed to you again?" It feels good to joke, like I'm able to conceal the darker parts of me, even if just for a little bit.

Wex brings a fist up to his mouth. Sam playfully shoves the side of his head. As Wex backs away, he points to me. "I like you, Vesper."

"He does know my name," I say as Sam leads me to the corner of the gym, where I tell him I'm in. He takes a deep breath, like he's trying to balance his excitement with apprehension.

"You sure you want to do this?" he says as soon as we're out of earshot.

"If you ask me that again, I'm going to punch you in the face."

"You don't know how to punch someone in the face."

"Well. You've got two weeks to teach me."

A smile slinks up the side of his mouth. It's a good look.

"Is this this movie montage where I become a kung fu master?" I ask, walking toward the stairs.

Sam rolls his eyes. "Go get dressed. And don't let Wex hear you call it kung fu."

It is safe to say that while I've never been much of a physically intimidating person, I haven't been afraid of other people, either. When it comes to fear, I am the scariest thing out there. When it comes to MMA, the scariest thing around is Abagail Gaines, the Barbie-colored badass.

"You have to move your feet," Sam calls from outside the cage.

"Focus, Vesper," Abagail says, throwing a left jab that would have shattered my cheekbone had I not ducked. I step to the side, trying to remember everything Sam has taught me these past three days.

Gloves up, protecting the face at all times.

Do not keep your thumb in your fist when you punch. (Rookie mistake. Still hurts.)

Move your feet, and stay light on your toes.

If you can reach your opponent, you can punch. If you can punch, you can kick.

Abagail throws another punch, and this time it grazes my ear.

Sam told Abagail and the others he needed them to help train me, and they all signed up to help without any further questions. I don't know how much he told them. I don't know if they know the stakes. But Sam asked for their help, and they are here. I get why. There's something nice about seeing these guys throw each other across the room with reckless abandon while knowing they have this familial allegiance that surpasses needing to know all the answers. I wasn't there for very long, but this place already feels different from the Grotto. This fighting is about getting smarter and stronger, not trying to outmagic your opponent.

"You've got to move! Get on the offensive!" Another voice calls. Wex stands next to Sam as they watch me barely surviving a pity round with Abagail—my first actual practice fight. Wex is the resident Muay Thai expert.

"Don't let her get you in a corner!" Roy calls out, sticking his fingers through the links of the cage and leaning back. I still don't know what his expertise is. Maybe he doesn't have one. He's just shady as hell and showed me how to counter a knife attack.

It's now or never. I can't keep bopping around and avoiding Abagail forever. I close my eyes and throw a punch as hard as I can, missing wildly.

"You're going to throw out your elbow if you punch like that!" Sam calls.

"Will everyone just . . . ," I breathe out, ducking another blow from Abagail, "shut up!"

She kicks, catching me behind the knees and throwing me to the ground.

I look up, covered in sweat, as Wex and Roy come to stand over me.

"That was better than the last time, right?" I ask feebly.

"You didn't run out of the cage," Abagail says, coming up and kneeling next to me.

I sit up and look at Sam. "I'm going to give you very specific instructions on how I'd like to be cremated, and I want you to follow them, do you understand?"

He helps me up. "You're not going to die."

That's what he's been saying. I don't quite believe him. I see Duncan standing at the bottom of the cage stairs, his arms crossed over his chest as he looks at me. As the days go by, he's been getting colder. He seemed fine with me staying here in the beginning, but that doesn't seem like the case now. I don't know what I did to make him change his mind, but I can't really worry about it right now.

I look up at the large calendar Wex stapled to the bulletin board by the lockers. Three days down. Eleven to go.

"Jiu-Jitsu is the art of the using another person's strength against them. It's more like chess than boxing," Sam says as he paces the cage, rolling his shoulders. He's wearing a gray tank top that is fraying at the collar and sweatpants slung low on his hips.

"Okay, so chess," I say as he carefully steps closer. My fingers tingle, but I ignore them.

"Come at me like you're trying to knock me down," he says, motioning for me to come closer.

I lunge forward, and Sam grabs my wrists, pulling me close as he falls back to the mat, rolling over his shoulder and taking me with him. We somersault together, and when we stop moving, he's above me, pinning me to the ground. This close, I can smell him—he's like mint and firewood. It's a good smell.

Remember what you're doing here, I let the refrain play over and over in my mind.

I see a future without a ruined past. A life without fearing my own two hands.

I focus.

"Now, ideally, there'd be no space between us," Sam explains, and I lock eyes with him. "Because the more room your opponent has, the more chance for escape."

The tingle in my palm heats up. I can feel it reaching.

No, I tell it. It's listening. For now, at least.

"Not a chance of me escaping," I say. And there's not. His huge hands are gently locked on my wrists, and his thighs spread over mine.

He shifts, and the tingling in my palms intensifies as my

heartbeat rolls to a boil in my ears. I feel the magic snake outward, slithering toward his chest.

"I need a minute," I shout, hating how my voice sounds panicky. Sam is off me in half a second, pushing up to a crouch as I scramble back toward the edge of the cage.

"Are you okay?" he asks, his brows drawn together as he regards me.

My heart slows, and I feel the magic retracting.

"I'm fine. I just need to . . . I just need to see it, maybe?" I say, trying to keep my voice as light as I can. *I'm trying not to kill you while I'm in the process of stabbing you in the back*, I think.

"Yeah, sure. Aba, can you help?"

Abagail finishes putting her hair in a ponytail and jumps into the cage.

"Hip escape into arm bar. Ready?" Sam says. Abagail nods and lies on her back. Sam climbs over her, locking his knees around hers and placing his elbows on either side of her head.

"On three. One, two, *three*," Sam says.

It happens so fast. Abagail bucks her hips upward, then pushes back on her side. She pulls Sam's left arm with her, flipping him as she rolls, until his arm is between her legs, her calves tight across his chest.

"An arm bar," Sam explains. "She pushes her hips upward, and my elbow breaks."

Abagail gestures slowly, and Sam taps the mat. She releases him, and I wince, shaking my arm as I imagine my elbow snapping backward. Could I really do that to someone?

You've done worse, I think.

"I don't care what kind of magic you have. A broken elbow will floor anyone," Sam says with a smile. Abagail nods next to him. "Want to try?" Sam asks.

The tingling in my fingers flares up, and I shake my head.

"Mind if I watch a couple more times?" I ask, my voice tight. His eyes skim over my face. He knows I'm not telling him everything, but he rolls his shoulders and gives Abagail a questioning look.

I watch them spar, and then we practice shoulder rolls and hip escapes. Somehow, I manage to stay away from him, and I know he notices.

I eat a pack of peanuts that I bought at the bodega down the street and wait until everyone is in bed before I go back to the gym and practice a few shoulder rolls on my own. I'm not an overachiever—I just can't sleep.

I fall backward, turn my head, and feel the satisfying *swish* as I push myself over the mat. I haven't moved my body like this since I left home. My muscles are stretched and tired.

"Those look good." Sam's voice comes out of the darkness near the lockers. It's been hours since we sparred. I thought he went home.

I whip around as he climbs the steps and gets in the cage.

His hair is wet, and he's changed. "Your punches look great, too."

"Thanks," I say, backing up against the chain-link.

"Want to run some release moves?" he asks.

"No," I say quickly, my eyes darting up to meet his.

He takes a tentative step closer to me. "Why, Vesper?" he asks, his tone softening. "Did I hurt you last time?" His eyes search mine, regret slipping into his gaze.

"No. No," I say, shaking my head. And when he doesn't say anything, the silence hangs between us. "That's not it," I add, because I guess I'm not a fan of quitting while I'm ahead.

"What is it, then?" Sam asks, stepping closer to me and sticking his hands in his pockets.

"I don't trust myself not to hurt you, okay?" I say, shutting my eyes as I blurt the words. He doesn't answer, and I open my eyes. "When we were close, earlier, it felt too easy to grip on to . . ." I don't know if I want to say it. I hate how the words sound when they click past my teeth. "Your fear," I finish at last.

Sam cocks his head. He doesn't look afraid. More . . . curious? Could he be curious instead of terrified?

"And what do you feel?" he asks.

"I can't . . . I haven't been able to feel it. My magic *wants* to grab on to it, but I stopped it."

"You can stop it?" he asks.

"I mean, sometimes. But . . ."

"How many times have you practiced getting a rein on it?" he asks, turning around and pulling his sweatshirt over his head. His T-shirt reads "Danbury Softball League." He must see the confusion on my face, because he looks down at his shirt and then back up to me. "I coached my sister's softball team back home."

Sister. Home. Two words I can relate to. Two words that make it harder to do what I need to, so I shake them off and try to focus on the question he just asked.

"I don't exactly *practice* with it, Sam. You wouldn't want to play hacky sac with a grenade."

"I wouldn't want to play hacky sac with anything, because I hate hacky sac," he counters. "But have you ever thought that that's why you have so little control over it?"

His words are like little sparks in a dark room. Dangerous. Illuminating. I hope they catch something, and I hope not.

"That's not how magic works," I reply finally.

"You won't know until you try," he says, stepping to the center of the cage and gesturing to me. "Come on. Let's try some escapes."

"Do you know what you're asking?" I press, anger slipping into my voice. It's the equivalent of him asking, *Hey, Vesper, you know that fanged creature you keep in your chest that devoured your whole life? Can I pet it?*

I cross my arms over my chest as he lies flat on his back.

"I know I'm looking at a girl who could wipe the floor with any opponent stupid enough to get in the ring with her, but she won't because she's afraid."

"I'm smart," I shoot back, my hackles rising higher. He doesn't know. He doesn't know what kind of destruction he's poking at. "And if you wanted someone to wipe the floor with the gladiators in that ring, you shouldn't have picked me. There was absolutely no shortage of burly dudes in that cage to pick from."

"They aren't what I was looking for," Sam replies, tilting his head. He shoves himself to his feet.

"You said you could show me how to fight. So show me and stop trying to get me to unleash this . . . thing." I hate that tears spring up in my eyes, but the words conjure them, and I have no choice. This *thing*. This *curse*. *This life-ruining force I can't get rid of.*

Sam takes a step toward me, and I jerk back. He stops, putting his hands up.

I wipe my eyes, furious that he's seeing me like this.

Sam steps back, and puts his hands in his pockets. "I picked you because, believe it or not, I know a fighter's spirit when I see it."

"Bullshit," I spit, blinking back the rest of the tears.

"No. Cheesy. Very, very cheesy, but not bullshit," Sam corrects. He chances another step toward me, and I don't step back. He leans down to meet my eyes, but I look down at my hands.

"I think you could win this without your magic, because you're smart. I've seen enough fights where David beat Goliath to know it can be done. But you can't be at war with other people and yourself at the same time. You can't get in the cage with two opponents. So if you want me to shut up about your magic and just teach you release moves, we'll do that."

I finally look up and meet his eyes.

"But I think the more afraid you are, the harder this is. And I'm not scared of you."

I clench and unclench my fists. He's right. I won't be able to think about my next move in the cage if I'm too worried about my powers slipping out. I need to learn to control them. I can do that, at the very least.

"You're sure?" I ask finally.

"Only one way to find out. And, hey, if I'm wrong, I'm wrong." He motions for me to come closer.

"How do you know this is even a thing?" I ask.

He shrugs. "I know more than your average Baseline, remember?"

"That's vague," I say, stepping closer as I roll out my ankles against the mat—something Abagail showed me.

"I like being mysterious. Makes up for my lack of personality." Sam lies on the mat and motions for me to get into position.

I laugh, though my heart is pounding at the thought of approaching the monster in my chest. I've never thought of it as something I should practice. I thought that you were either born with something you could control, or you weren't. I figured I was just horribly unlucky. Or cursed.

While the night at Aloa's was a disaster, I was able to release it. True, I could have killed myself in the process, but I have to admit that I was able to latch on to Mitch before I decided to pull it out. I was able to sift through Carl as I tried to find something to pull out. Maybe I can get better at this. I step closer to Sam and put my feet on either side of his hips.

I lower myself to my knees, straddling him. Abagail and Sam took this position dozens of times today, and neither looked uncomfortable. They've both done this so long that straddling an arguably not unattractive guy probably didn't faze her at all.

But I've distanced myself from all human contact for more than a year. Going from not talking to anyone to pressing my skin against his like this is giving me whiplash. I think Sam sees that.

"Are you okay?" he asks.

I nod.

Slowly, he reaches up and puts his hands on my waist, his calloused fingers accidentally skimming the skin above my yoga pants. My breath hitches, and I clamp my mouth shut.

Please, in the name of everything good, please let him not *have heard that.* I chance a look down at him, and he's looking at me with a strange intensity, his jaw clenched tight.

Something deep in my gut spins at the sight, but I shake the thought away. He's offering himself up as bait to hell-raising magic. He's just nervous, and he should be.

"What will I pull out of you if you're wrong? I want a fair heads-up in case we're dealing with land sharks or Freddy Krueger."

"Land sharks. With wings," he says, pulling me down. I settle over him, his hip bones digging into my inner thighs. I take a staggered breath and lean forward, putting my elbows on the ground next to his head.

"Those would be air sharks then," I correct, my voice shaky as my cheek brushes the side of his head. This is a bad idea. For so many reasons, I'm realizing as I take a deep breath and taste him in the back of my throat.

"They're flightless winged land sharks," he says, a laugh riding his voice. His breath tickles my ear.

"Like a chicken-shark?" I snort, despite myself.

He bursts into laughter then, and I sit up, putting my hands on his chest to keep from falling off him.

"Yes. My deepest fear is the elusive chicken-shark. One-foot-wide bite radius, *juicy* thighs."

I can't help it. I don't know if it's because it's been forever since I laughed, but I lose it, and so does Sam. I fall over onto the mat, gasping for breath. Sam rolls over on his side.

"Wait, would it have thighs?" I ask, raising my head off the mat through gasping laughs.

Sam snorts then, falling to his back. "*No*," he admits. "That makes no fucking sense."

We lie there for a few minutes, cracking up. When we catch our breath, Sam pulls himself up onto his elbows and reaches for me.

"You can do this, Vesper. I know it."

I wipe tears of laughter from my eyes as I look at him. It's worth a shot. I lie on my back and motion for him to climb over me. He does. The tingling in my palms heats up. I can already feel it lifting off my skin.

"One. Two, three," he says, tightening his grip as I buck my hips and slip sideways. I whip my leg around, and the magic lashes out. I get Sam in a perfect arm bar before he knows what's happened.

"Excellent!" he calls, his voice full of excitement, and I let go. I'm about to get up, but I freeze, because I feel a latch. I have him. His eyes widen, and I know he feels it, too.

"Don't move, Sam," I whisper. I stand up, and he stays on his back. I hold my palm out, and it finds him like a magnet. I hear voices in my head. Lilting, like a laugh, but it's not distinct. I shut my eyes.

Pull. Pull.

The desire is so strong I almost want to fall to my knees,

but I grit my teeth and look down. Sam's eyes are open, boring into mine as he lies in front of me, completely exposed.

"Don't just shut it down. Don't try to stop it. Just let it . . . run its course. You said yourself your fear feeds it. Then . . . try to not be afraid."

"Easy for you to say," I spit through gritted teeth.

"You can do this. Breathe, Ves," he replies.

Ves. No one has called me that since I left home.

I take a deep breath and let the magic flow through my veins.

Not now, I tell it. *This far and no farther.*

I'm still for a few minutes, and nothing happens. Sam lies there quietly. I'm about to give up and tell him to run—not like that will do any good—when the magic relaxes. It's just a hint, at first, but then the latch on Sam's chest evaporates from my hands.

I look down at my hands. "It worked," I whisper, looking up and smiling. Sam pushes himself to his feet.

"I knew you could do it," he says. Then he does something I'm not expecting. He reaches out and pulls me into his chest. He wraps his massive arms around me and lifts me off the ground. And before I can tell myself not to, I raise my arms and throw them around his neck, because *I did it.*

Maybe there's a chance I can do this.

He sets me down and grabs his sweatshirt off the edge of the cage.

I stand there with a sliver of confidence and a newly hatched, raw hope. For a moment, I'm selfish enough to forget my plan. For a moment, I pretend we're friends and that I'm not planning something awful. And when Sam mixes the *Jaws* theme with the tune of the chicken dance, I lose myself in a fit of laughter.

The rest of the days blur together as I form some strange kind of routine. I wake up at five o'clock in the morning and slip downstairs to warm up. Abagail is there before work. If it's not her, then Roy. Wex and Sam come after their shifts at the docks. But despite their ins and outs, I'm starting to figure out that this isn't just a gym. This is home for them. A refuge from the rest of the world that spit them out.

I don't have much time to talk, considering how much of the time I spend getting pummeled, but somehow I've learned a lot about these people. Abagail was once a gymnast for UCLA, but stopped after a knee injury and never went back. Her family wanted her to come back home to Tennessee, but she had other plans—she has her debut UFC fight later this year. She's in nursing school now. So, basically, she spends half her days sewing up cuts and the rest of them causing them.

Duncan wasn't just an Olympian. He also served as a captain in the navy, where he met Jeffry Wexler—Wex's father. They were best friends, so Wex kind of grew up in this gym, except for when he was doing two tours in Iraq.

Roy was in foster care and has a gnarly scar up his torso. I don't ask him where it came from. I don't know if I even want to know.

I practice boxing with Sam and get the crap beat out of me.

I practice Jiu-Jitsu with Abagail and get the crap beat out of me.

I practice Muay Thai with Wex, and I'm actually getting pretty good.

Just kidding. I still get the crap beat out of me.

All the while, I practice keeping the magic at bay. I feel it reach forward, but instead of freaking out and shutting it down, I let it run through my veins. I don't pull, but I can latch and retreat. That feels good enough for now.

Roy and Wex show me Krav Maga. Wex was right before. It's sketchy as hell. You use whatever you have; it's street fighting at its barest. That's what Roy's knife is for. It's rubber—I found that out only when he mock-stabbed me in the kidney and for a split second I thought, *I can't believe this is how I'm going to die.* They all had a good laugh at that one. Krav Maga is the dirtiest but also my favorite. The only rule is that if someone comes at you, finish him before he finishes you.

I'm surprised to find my muscle memory waking up, eager for the movements that in cheer used to feel as natural as breathing. The rolling of Jiu-Jitsu feels a lot like tumbling, sometimes, and the different grips of krav maga remind me of stunting. It's not easy, by any stretch of the imagination. But I saw the way Wex's eyebrows shot up when I pulled a hip escape from under Roy.

"All right, Pom-poms. Not bad."

"Pom-poms? What happened to Destructress?" I called out.

All day. Early wake-ups. Breakfast. Fight. Lunch. Fight. Dinner. Fight.

Fight fight fight sleep.

Then, on the Monday before the second fight, I stop Roy when he tries to stab me with that rubber knife.

I slip away from Abagail when she has me in what's called "full guard," that painful bear hug that is, in fact, painful. I even manage to get her into an arm bar.

I land a kick on Wex.

And the only thing I keep seeing is Sam's face through the cage, his eyes intent. He believes in me, and somehow that makes me get up every time I get knocked flat on my back.

The Xs fill the calendar.

It's the night before.

I told Sam I was going to bed, but I came back down. There was no way I could just drift off when I know what's coming tomorrow. I'm sitting in the middle of the grappling mat, drinking from a plastic water bottle that I'm sure I should've thrown away days ago. The paper wrapping is gone, leaving behind just the grimy adhesive. I look at the painted brick wall. For the first time, I notice the words in thin permanent marker that line the wall next to the lockers:

Out of the night that covers me,
  Black as the pit from pole to pole,
I thank whatever gods may be
  For my unconquerable soul.

In the fell clutch of circumstance
  I have not winced nor cried aloud.
Under the bludgeonings of chance
  My head is bloody, but unbowed.

Beyond this place of wrath and tears
  Looms but the Horror of the shade,
And yet the menace of the years
  Finds and shall find me unafraid.

It matters not how strait the gate,
  How charged with punishments the scroll,
I am the master of my fate,
  I am the captain of my soul.

It's "Invictus" by William Ernest Henley. I remember hearing it once in English back home, but it didn't hit me then like it does now.

I'm exhausted, but it's better this way.

I've been working so much, I haven't had time to stop and think. Think about what I'm doing and what the hell it could all mean.

I feel someone come up behind me, and jump. It's only been two weeks, but I roll to the side and push myself to my feet in the space of two seconds.

Duncan stands at the edge of the mat, his hands in his sweats pockets.

"Not bad," he says.

I nod. I should've said thank you or something. Too late. The moment is passed. Now I'm just standing here, my arms crossed over my chest.

Duncan looks up at the ceiling. "Two weeks is not enough to know everything you'll need to know to survive in a fight," he says simply.

I just stare at him.

What am I supposed to say to that?

I wonder if he can tell what I'm planning on doing if I win this thing. I wonder if I could explain it to him—that Sam winning his girl back is not as important as the world being rid of one less monster. Of my family coming back together.

I just nod.

"But that doesn't mean you're helpless out there. Against a trained fighter, you'd have nothing. They'd flatten you." He looks up, surveying the ceiling before letting his eyes drop down to me again. "But tomorrow night, they won't be trained fighters. They're powder kegs, thinking they are the masters of the universe. They won't be expecting you. Remember that."

And with that, he turns and leaves. He's gone. I can't tell if he meant to help me or psych me out.

Perhaps that is his entire plan.

FOURTEEN

After a fitful night of sleep, I wake up and walk down to the bag, but Sam stops me as I'm putting on my wraps. He's coming in from a shift at the docks. His hands are covered in dirt.

"No. Not today. Today, you take it easy."

"But today, of all days, is the day I need to hit something. Besides, aren't you tired?"

He shakes his head. "Nope. And you need to save your energy for tonight."

I look around the gym. It rained last night. Through the front windows I can see that the streets are still soaking and the sky is a dark gray. "I'll go crazy if I just sit here waiting for tonight."

"Then we'd better not sit around."

Pier 39 is kind of a tourist trap, but that means there are plenty of faces to blend in with. This is the one place in San

Francisco I remember liking on our road trips when I was a kid. No one is looking for locals, and it's usually crowded. I'm worried it'll be a thinner crowd, since it's so cloudy, but it's San Francisco. It's always cloudy.

The smell of bread wafts through the air. Music from a carousal in the center of the square rings out, along with a hostess calling out the name for a reservation at a seafood restaurant. Sam and I walk through the wonderful chaos, taking it all in. It's weird, walking like we're friends or something. We're just hanging out. Like regular people. Kids run between us, trailing balloons behind them, and Sam steps aside. Great. There's this weird gap between us now.

Sam crosses over to me as we pass a table selling souvenir Pier 39 baseball hats.

"The day of a fight, you just need to get out of your head," Sam says finally.

"What would you do?" I ask.

He eyes me, and I bring my shoulders up around my ears.

"I saw that picture of you at Duncan's," I say. "You used to fight, right?"

"Nothing professional. Rookie stuff. Wex and I did underground fights—just to make a quick buck."

There's a tightness in his voice, a wavering that tells me there's more to this story. He looks over at me, and it's like he's trying to decide if he should tell me.

"When Wex and I were doing the amateur circuit, we went go-karting on fight day."

I snort at the idea of Sam and Wex, two of the biggest, most built guys I've ever seen, smashed into a little go-kart.

"Together?" I ask, the mental picture quickly sending me from snorts into full-fledged giggles.

"Separate cars," Sam corrects, enunciating each syllable.

"Wait. Did you go to an arcade? Like a place where they have little kids' birthday parties and stuff?" I'm laughing now.

Sam fights a smile as he shakes his head profusely. "No. No—it has drag racing, which is specifically for adults. If an establishment has drag racing, it's not *just* for kids."

"*Just*?" I smirk. "Oh my *gosh*, you *did* go to an arcade! Did you win tickets? Did you buy slap bracelets?"

"Okay, never mind. Let's go back to the gym and sit and stare at the wall." He moves like he's going to turn around, but I laugh and grab his arm, pulling him along. It's the first time I've touched him casually outside the ring.

I don't know if he realizes it—but I do.

And I look over at him as I drop his arm, almost like I should apologize or something.

"No, I'm sorry. I'm sorry. No more teasing. Thank you for bringing me out here."

I stop to look over the railing. Sea lions lounge below, oblivious to the seagulls that swoop down and perch themselves on their massive torsos.

I rest my elbows on the railing. "This was my mom's

favorite part of the pier. She always made us stop here on our way back from the cabin we rented in Oregon."

As the words roll off my tongue, it's almost like I'm back here with them. Iris on my left, shivering despite the fact that it's eighty degrees. Carmen smiling at some boy across the way, Jack scaling the railing, my dad getting us cotton candy while my mom struggles to find the sunscreen she *knows* she put in her bag before we came.

I bite my tongue. It doesn't work. I want to stay in this memory a little longer. Especially today. I need to remember what I'm fighting for. What I'm being a villain for.

"For her fortieth birthday my dad asked one of the wild-life rangers to let her get a little closer. My sister Carmen, she cried. She was so mad at my dad for putting my mom in danger—she was convinced that sea lions ate people," I say before I can stop myself.

The words hang between us, awkward as they refuse to dissolve in the sea air. They just sit there, bulky as they wait for further explanation.

I bite my tongue harder as I look over at Sam. His eyes search my face.

"You miss them," he says. It's a question and a fact all in one. He's figuring me out, despite all my efforts to stop him.

I want to deny it, but I'm tired. I'm tired of pretending and hiding and remembering pseudonyms and fake addresses and cover stories. But I don't want him to get too close to my reasons. He might see the truth. Also, if he gets closer to my reasons, it means *we* are getting closer. And that just makes everything harder. But the words slip past my lips before I can swallow them back.

I nod. "I do."

Sam nods and looks out, and I pretend I'm looking at a family of sea lions while I'm really looking at him. The cut on his eyebrow, the one from the fight with Mitch, is healing nicely. There's a scar on his lower lip, a little to the right of center. I want to ask how he got it.

I look down at my hands. It's so cold I can barely feel them, but I know if I say something, he'll insist we get warmer. And I don't want to lose this moment.

"So. Sob story for sob story. How did you meet Elisa?"

So much for not getting closer, I think. But maybe I want to hear about Elisa. If she let Sam slip through her fingers, she can't have been that smart. Maybe I won't feel so bad for sparing him a terrible unraveling. *The lengths I won't go to to justify my own bullshit*, I think.

Sam looks over at me, his eyebrow cocked as he considers my question.

"Yours wasn't a sob story. Yours was a sweet childhood memory."

"There was crying in it. Technically it was a sob story," I argue.

Sam smiles, his eyes far away as he considers my words. "I

met Elisa at a party my parents were throwing—for themselves, of course. I grew up in the part of Connecticut where
all the kids wear collared shirts, and every dog is hypoaller-
genic and so purebred that they're actually inbred but no one
wants to say anything." He reaches down and touches the
pendant on the chain around his neck.

I try to picture Sam in a prim-and-proper house, but it
doesn't quite compute. I smile when he looks at me, encour-
aging him to go on.

"Anyway. We weren't really good for each other."

Aha! I knew it.

"My parents wanted me to date the daughter of my dad's
investment partner. Actually, they would've been okay with
me dating just about anyone except Elisa. Probably because
she was genuine and called nonsense when she saw it. Anyway."

Never mind.

"We got more serious as the question of college came
looming up. My parents weren't thrilled, you can imagine,
especially since my dad had to pull a thousand strings and
even got me into Brown, if you can believe it."

A thousand questions. I have a thousand. Connecticut?
Brown? I swallow all of them down. If I talk, he'll stop. If I
move, he might stop. I freeze.

"I decided to take a year off. I graduated early—I was only
seventeen. Elisa had some work to do out here for her family's

business, so I followed. My parents flipped. Disowned me. Duncan hired me to clean his gym, and I started working out there, too. Met Wex and Roy and Abagail. I was out here for a year and then . . . things just started getting hard. We fought."

I look down at the railing. Sam grips the wood, his knuckles white. This is the part I desperately wanted to hear . . . and seeing how much it hurts him makes me feel sick.

"We had a fight one night. She left, and I didn't . . ." He stops. "I didn't stop her. I should've. I'd give anything to go back and stop her." He looks to me. "Obviously," he says with a smile, gesturing to the air between us. He runs his knuckle over his unshaved cheek and looks out at the water. He blinks and swallows and rezips his jacket and coughs and does everything he can to not hear the words he just said.

And just like that, the Sam I saw punching the bag—the one who carried a wound I couldn't fully understand—makes sense. "That was a lot heavier than a story about sea lions, so . . . I'm sorry." His voice is soft, like he's unsure of himself. Like maybe he's worried he's said too much.

I open my eyes. The air around us is still full of his deepest wound, pulsing with expectant silence. My mouth moves before my brain, and I say the words I've been keeping clamped down in the bottom of my lungs for months.

"I burned my house down," I say, looking over at him. "My mom was afraid of fire, and I accidentally pulled that fear out of her while we were sleeping."

He looks at me, his expression softening. "Shit, Vesper. I'm so sorry. Was anyone hurt?"

Abort. Abort. He's getting too close.

"No," I choke out. The lie is acrid on my tongue. "Just our house."

"Well, then. A million dollars would be kind of nice then, right?"

I force a smile onto my face. "That's the plan."

The wind blows, carrying the sound of thunder as it claps above us. It startles the seagulls into the sky, causing a flurry of wings around us as I look at Sam.

"We're a sorry team, huh?" he asks, looking out over the bay.

"The sorriest," I agree, hooking my fingers around the wooden edge and leaning back.

And I hate myself, because the words stick. I hear them as they vibrate through my lungs and in my mind. *We.*

I am the worst person alive because I want to hear them again.

FIFTEEN

Sam and I drive in silence. He seems to know I don't want to talk.

I don't ask where we're going. Sam got a call earlier to tell us where to go, but I didn't want to know. There's nothing he can say that will make me feel less scared.

It's a foggy night, the kind where even his headlights do little to cut through it. I lean against the window and close my eyes.

I can do this.

I can do this.

Sam slows down, and then kills the engine.

I lift my head. The fog thins slightly, and I see what's ahead. We're at the northern harbor, at a shipping yard. It's huge. Ships are lined up at several different docks, separated by black water, their bodies dark and still.

Sam leans forward on the wheel and peers forward. "It's an industrial shipping yard."

I zip up my jacket. "I take it the owner of this place has no idea we're here?"

"I think that would be a safe assumption," Sam says darkly.

We get out of the car. Sam pulls a duffel bag from the trunk and closes it with a *thud*. The night is cold and thick, but I welcome the chill into my lungs. It's better than the burning adrenaline that's been coursing through them all day.

We walk together in silence, slipping through a hole in a chain-link fence that seems to be cut just for this occasion, and then through a path of shipping containers. It's creepy, like we're being guided despite being the only people around. I wonder if it's magic, or just fog.

I mean, maybe this is better. What did I expect? That I'd walk up to this with the other gladiatorial candidates? That we'd share small talk like nervous little kids on the first day of school?

What's your power? Cool! Do you know what heat you're in? Do you think the officiators are going to be nice? Well, it was nice to meet you. I hope I don't have to brain you in the cage to win this thing. See you later.

So yeah, maybe it's better we're alone.

Sam turns past a line of forklifts, and I follow.

We both stop when we see it. The cage is set up on the concrete outlet on the water between two huge ships. Spectators line the decks of both vessels. Waiters wander the area, providing the spectators with bubbly champagne. String lights are suspended over the cage, fastened to the railings of each ship.

"What the hell?" I ask breathlessly, looking to Sam.

"He said it was going to be a tournament unlike any other," Sam replies.

"How are we not getting arrested for this?" I ask.

Sam points to the bow of each ship. Three people stand on each end, arms raised high.

"Shaders," I say. No one will see this who is not supposed to see this.

We turn a corner. Ahead of us is a metal barricade sandwiched between two shipping containers. The entrance.

"Halt," a voice calls. Sam and I stop. The built guy from the qualifiers—Demitri, I think his name was—walks forward. His beanie is fraying on the edges, and his eyes are a vibrant green. Matrix green. He's a Screener. Like a human TSA machine. He points to two figures in black manning AKs secured to the top of the containers, pointed at us. Nice.

A light *tsk-tsk-tsk* comes from behind the metal barricade. It's Tessa. She leans forward, draping her forearms on the railing like she did at the Grotto.

"I'm afraid I must advise against *that* jawline entering a

battle as dangerous as this," she purrs. And I don't say that lightly; it sounds like a purr. Like the words ride a hum out of her throat. I shift uncomfortably.

Sam coughs and looks down. "No, I'm the sponsor. Sam Hardy. She's the gladiator." He points over to me.

I wave. It's curt, like, *Over here, a-hole.*

"Gladiator name?" Tessa asks. Her lips are a bright purple that contrast well with her emerald heels.

"Vesper," I answer. Her eyes flick up, and she stretches the gum out with her tongue.

"Real names, pumpkin."

"That is my real name, buttercup," I shoot back without missing a beat.

Her eyebrows arch up as she blows another bubble and runs her eyes down the screen. "Sorry. You're not listed."

"She's a wild-card entry," Sam counters. Tessa looks up from the tablet.

"It's ten thousand to enter a wild card," Demitri grunts. This isn't news to me, but I still flinch at the sound of that kind of money.

"I know," Sam says.

"Cash," Tessa reiterates.

Sam doesn't break eye contact with Demitri as he tosses the duffel bag at his feet.

Demitri looks over his shoulder at Tessa. They share a skeptical look at Sam before Demitri kneels down and unzips the bag. I see the surprise on his face as he looks at the contents. He gives Tessa a thumbs-up.

"Okay, then. You and one other are the wild-card entries. Your name will be pulled at random. The gladiator from night one with the worst time will be replaced by the wild-card entry with the best time. You understand?"

I look to Sam. I wasn't expecting to have to do this on a timer, but I nod.

Tessa hits a button on the tablet, and the barricade slides open.

"You're certainly going to need *your prayers* tonight," she says, smirking as I walk past her. It's not unkind. In fact, I'm pretty impressed that she even knows what *Vesper* really means.

I cock my jaw by way of agreeing with her, and she motions us inside.

We're just past the entrance when —

"Yo, Waterworks!" a booming voice calls from a tent on my right. Over the door, there's a sign with the words *Gladiators Only.*

Aldrick saunters toward me, arms outstretched. "You're here. We thought you bounced."

"I guess I bounced back," I reply.

The floodlights over the cage flicker twice. "You'd better get to the stands," he says.

"I'm fighting," I reply. He stops for a moment, looking to Sam and then back to me. I see the hesitancy in his eyes, but he covers it well with a shrug and a smile. "Then you're with me," he says.

I look back at Sam. This is the last time I'll see him before the fight. I don't want him to leave. I want him to stay here with me and distract me with stories about Connecticut. He leans forward. "You can do this," he whispers, and I nod. He sounds so assured that I almost believe it.

Then, he's gone and Aldrick is walking me to the tent.

I spend the next hour stretching with Aldrick and avoiding Mavis, Carl—the asshole to end all assholes—and the orange-haired she-demon who's permanently glued to Carl's side on the opposite side of the tent.

Mavis lounges on the couch, sipping an energy drink and throwing a small knife at one of the wooden tent posts with a gloved hand. She rolls her eyes when she sees me and throws a bull's-eye.

Then the lights flash. We walk out to the holding area near the cage, where Ananias stands on the cage's steps.

I stop, eyeing the structure. It's the same one as in the Beneath, rebuilt here. The metal links shimmer under the floodlights.

Ananias takes a microphone from Tessa.

"Night two," he says, smiling down at us. His gaze stops

when he sees me, and I feel unsettled as his eyes lock on mine. "Remember to keep it as civil as you possibly can while beating each other up, and smile for the camera!" He points to three different mounted cameras that cover every angle of the cage.

"Let us begin," he says, smiling widely as he tosses the mic back to Tessa as he walks toward the scaffolding that leads up to the deck of the ship.

"Who is up there?" I whisper to Aldrick. We both look up at the deck. Most of the faces are obscured, but I can see suits and flutes full of champagne.

"Investors," Aldrick answers back. I look over at him. "I heard Tessa talking about it earlier."

"Investors for what?" I whisper back.

Aldrick smiles. "I don't know. But I told you that this was only the start, didn't I?"

I look up at Aldrick, who waggles his eyebrows excitedly. What would happen if I got paired with him in the ring? Could I take him down when he's been nothing but kind to me?

You've done worse. You'll do worse, I think.

Tessa calls out the first match. Brittany, the Duster, and Scot, the Shifter.

I scan the deck above for any sign of Sam, but I can't see anything against the floodlights beating down on us.

❁ ❁ ❁

After that, everything happens fast.

The fight between the Duster and the Shifter doesn't last long. He can separate himself into seven different pieces, but it's nothing against her hallucinogenic effect. He swings a wide arc toward her, but she ducks and blows dust from her palm, knocking the Shifter to the ground in a convulsing mess.

Then Aldrick is against a Miasma, and Aldrick knocks the Miasma against the chain fence so hard I wonder if it's going to snap, but the shimmering links absorb the blow. Aldrick raises a stony hand but stops at the last second, returning his fist to normal before knocking the Miasma out cold. He won, but he didn't do as much damage as he could have. There's polite applause from the deck above as Demitri pulls the Miasma off the floor of the cage. And then it's my turn.

I'm up against someone named Briony.

As I step into the cage, the orange-haired girl who was trying to plaster herself to Carl the first time I saw her enters on the other side. She tips her chin to the side with her knuckles.

"You got this, Vesper!" I hear Aldrick call out. I look over my shoulder. He nods at me. Next to him, Mavis runs her index finger over her throat while she mouths, *You don't got this.*

I turn around. If I lose now, I can't get back in.

Briony runs her tongue over her top teeth and laughs at something Carl calls out to her. I close my eyes and picture home. In this moment, I unlock the door I've kept barricaded in the name of self-preservation and let little things slip out. I make myself remember Carmen's laugh and the smell of my mom's favorite coconut coffee creamer. I remember the feel of Inigo's fur and the squeak my front door let out when someone opened it. My family.

I'm going to win this, and I'm going home.

I don't hear Tessa's commentary as she announces, but I nod when she looks at me. Then Briony and I walk to our corners and wait for the start.

Go.

I'm up against the clock right now. I need to end this quickly.

She leans back against the fence and shoves herself forward. I step forward to meet her. She won't be expecting me. Sam and I worked on takedowns all last week. I'll get her in an arm bar or full guard, or—

Briony lifts her hands and smirks. Flames lick down her arms, trickling up her fingers like water in reverse. My heart jumps up into my throat and I stop.

A Fire Fury.

The heat coming off her blasts my cheek as I turn my head, struggling to breathe.

She steps closer, and I step back. "Come on!" she screams,

and I can see a light at the back of her throat as she laughs. It makes the air shimmer.

I hear Carmen's scream, then. I hear the ragged gulp of her frantic breathing, the terror that shattered through the night like a piece of glass in a hurricane.

Is this how she felt when she had nowhere to go? I shut my eyes.

"Wow. This is embarrassing," she says as she gets closer. I open my eyes and look down. Her legs are still clad in dark jeans. I feel a flicker of hope. She's just like Aldrick. She can't maintain Fire Fury form across her whole body for very long.

It's a chance.

I can work with a chance.

I duck, rushing forward as I grab her behind the knees. She shrieks as she falls to her back. I land on top of her, pinning her arms at her sides with my legs as I wrap my hand around her jaw, keeping it shut. With her hands and mouth out of commission, she can't reach up and burn me, and she can't spit.

My fingers tingle, and the sensation reaches out, diving into her chest.

We're not in the cage at Duncan's. It's not just Sam and me. This is high-stress, and I have less control of my magic. But I have enough for now.

The crowd roars with approval.

Rage registers on Briony's face. She shuts her eyes and

when she opens them, her eyes are bright yellow. Heat kicks up under me as she lets the fire run to her torso. I cry out as I roll off. She tries to get to her feet, but I sweep her feet out from under her and twist, grabbing her elbow. It will be a matter of seconds before she refocuses the fire to where I'm touching, but I've worked this with Sam enough to know that I only need a couple of seconds. I maneuver her arm between my legs and put my calves across her upper body.

Arm bar.

The crowd goes wild.

I push my hips up, and Briony screams. With an inhale through gritted teeth, she closes her eyes. When she opens them, I can tell something is happening. She's stronger than I gave her credit for, and she's holding on longer than I thought. And I have to end this. Fast.

With a wild shriek, she arches her whole back. The skin under my fingers heats up in seconds. She's using the rest of her energy to light her whole body. I hear the sickening sizzle under my fingers, but I scream to cover the sound. Smoke plumes from my grip. She's hoping to burn me into letting go.

But that's not going to happen.

Her skin flies past fever-hot in seconds, and I let out another yell as I push my hips up farther and shove my thighs together.

She's not giving up, and neither is her effing elbow.

I feel the heat of her chest pushing past my jeans, burning my calves and the back of my thighs.

I push harder, though the heat searing through my grip is almost unbearable.

The magic in my fingers is screaming, begging to be let out. The cords of my power slip away from me, digging into Briony before I can stop it. I feel myself plunging through the darkest parts of her, sorting through memory and terror. Her fears sound off as my magic passes them, calling out to me.

I know Briony feels me sifting through her, because she stiffens and lets out a small cry. Her brief movement is enough for me to get a better grip on her arm, and I pull harder.

"What was that?" she screams. But I don't answer. It takes everything I have not to let my magic wreak havoc on her.

I could end this in seconds if I released it. She'd never see it coming. But I know I can't control it right now, either. I won't be able to stop it. I pull my magic back, and it listens.

I look up, and I find Sam's face. He's at the edge of the deck, his eyes intent, full of something between horror and disbelief. I'm in agony, but I manage to lock eyes.

I got this.

He nods once. I want to believe it's because he's worried about me. I want to believe it's because we're friends. But I know better. He's using me to fix his relationship with Elisa. I'm using him to then stab him in the back.

Something about that thought sends rage down my spine,

and it's a domino effect. I'm angry that I have magic. I'm angry that I'm afraid of myself. I'm angry that I ruined my life and that I love the way Sam sounds when he laughs and that it's going to hurt when I know he hates me, and I'm *angry* . . .

I let out a final scream and push my hips up as far as they'll go.

And with one final cry, Briony collapses to the mat in a smoky heap, the fire inside her going out. She's spent all her magic—she's passed out.

I go limp, letting out a soft cry of relief. I didn't have to break her arm. Thank God, I didn't have to break her arm.

I let go of Briony's elbow, my hands raw with burns. I roll onto my knees as the crowd erupts in cheers.

I don't know how I got to the medics' tent. Did Sam carry me in here? Did I walk? It's all a blur. All I know is there's a thick bandage around each of my hands and a salve around my calves. The skin between my shoulder blades starts to itch, and I sit up.

"Whoa," Aldrick says from beside me. I look over. He's on a gurney next to mine. "Don't push it, Vesper," he says, reaching out. I can see a freshly stitched cut up his forearm. There's a matching one on his cheek.

I sit long enough for the room to stop spinning. Outside, the crowd cheers as the sound of flesh hitting metal rips through the night. I wince.

"Deep breaths," Aldrick says, and his voice is low. There's no smirk in it . . . not a hint of a joke. I look at him, and he smiles. "That was one hell of a match. Talk about a comeback."

"Yeah." I roll my eyes and lift my bandaged hands. "I'm a pro."

I don't know if it's the magic, or if maybe the adrenaline made the fire feel hotter than it was, but the burns aren't terrible. They're less *I did battle with a Fire Fury* and more *Crap, that cup of noodles was in the microwave too long.*

They aren't that bad. It could've been worse.

"The Menders fixed you up as best they could, but the rest of it's going to have to heal on its own," Aldrick says. I look up, and he reads the question in my eyes. "Menders. Magical medics? Healing powers?"

"I've never heard of them," I say. Add them to the list of things I have no clue about.

"You didn't use your magic," Aldrick says.

"Is that a question?"

He shrugs. "You didn't use it in the Beneath, either."

"No," I reply.

"Why not?" he presses, putting his hands on the bed on either side of his legs and leaning forward.

I swallow hard. I don't know how much I want to tell him. Wait . . . should I be telling him anything? He's my competitor. "Umm . . ."

He's smiling now, like he's reading my thoughts. "Vesper, I'm two hundred and sixty pounds and I can turn my body into granite. Psychological warfare has never been my forte."

I narrow my eyes at him, and he holds his arms out, showcasing his bare chest. "I'm not trying to screw you over. It just seems like . . ."

"Like what?" I shoot back.

He tilts his head. "It seems like you're afraid of your magic."

"I've got it under control," I reply. The skin on the back of my neck prickles.

"No, you've got it caged. It's different. You're at odds with it."

"No shit, and you would be, too, if you were me," I blurt. The words are out before I can stop them.

Aldrick is still. I should apologize for biting his head off. He didn't realize he was tap-dancing on the part of me that still bleeds.

"I don't know *how* to let it out without hurting someone," I say, looking up and meeting his eyes.

He nods, pursing his lips as he considers my reply. "Well. You want to learn?"

I regard him. Is he for real? *He could be trying to screw you over.*

"How?"

Sam wanted to help me, too, but it feels easier with Aldrick.

For one, he's an Oddity. And getting closer to him doesn't scare me as much as the thought of getting closer with Sam. I know how to lock my power down, but Sam was right. I can't keep going in with two things to fear.

"Come by the Grotto. I'll spar with you."

It's quiet for a moment as the words bounce around in my skull. "Why would you help me?"

He shrugs. "I already told you. You saved Sapphira when we were running from the cops. Plus, I know what it's like to be afraid of your powers, and I know what it's like to be alone. Both suck."

"And if my time is good enough to make it to the next round and we get matched to fight?" I ask.

Aldrick's smile widens. "Honey, if we get paired to fight, I'd want someone worth fighting."

"No one is that noble in real life, you know," I reply.

We hear a roar as the next match starts, and Aldrick and I both get up to watch the final fight from the door of the tent.

It's Mavis versus a Slitter they call Riles. He rolls his shoulders and razor-sharp edges poke through his skin. He's like a porcupine, but with razors instead of quills. He smiles, sticking out his tongue. There's a razor at its edge, too. Mavis cocks a perfect eyebrow as she peels off her black gloves and tosses them aside.

The Slitter swings his arm in a wide arc toward Mavis's face, but she ducks, her sheet of golden hair following behind her in a perfect arc. She reaches for his leg, but he lifts his leg and pivots, bringing his elbow down over her. Mavis rolls, her eyes flashing red as she braces herself on the ground. The cage pulses purple as it absorbs her power. Otherwise, the whole thing would crumble under the Demo's touch.

"Shit," Aldrick says, his voice low. He steps out into the night, and I follow him as we move closer to watch the fight.

The Slitter smiles as he whips around.

"Mavis just has to touch him, right?" I ask.

Aldrick shakes his head. "Her fingertips have to touch him. And that's going to be difficult if she no longer has fingers."

His voice is dark, his expression taut. Aldrick seems like the kind of person who handles violence well. But now I see that he's just a good fighter. He doesn't like watching this any more than I do.

Mavis does a dive roll, swiping her hand over the flat edge of one of Riles's blades. It crumbles to dust, and he cries out in rage as she spins, bringing her hand back and touching the other blade on his shoulder, reducing it to the same fate.

She gets to her feet, smirking as Riles lifts his hands and more blades grow out in their place. Mavis's smirk fades. His blades will grow back as fast as she can destroy them.

The Slitter cocks his head for a moment before launching himself at Mavis once more. This time, though, she doesn't roll. Instead, she reaches up, stopping his hand with her own.

I gasp, grabbing Aldrick's arm as Mavis lets out a scream.

Riles pushes his blades out farther, cutting into her palms, but she doesn't let go. She touches the blades with her fingertips, and they turn to dust, only to be replaced by another within seconds.

Riles brings his arm around, aiming for her face. Mavis grabs that arm, too, slicing her skin with another scream as Riles's razors bite into her hand. Blood runs down her arm, dripping onto the mat at her feet and mixing with the dust of Riles's demolished blades.

"Give up, Mavis! Stop this!" I hiss, digging my fingers into Aldrick's arm.

He shakes his head. "You don't know Mavis. She won't quit for anything."

And she doesn't. She pushes against Riles, shoving him to the middle of the mat and then to the opposite side. They crash against the metal, Mavis tightening her grip as they go. She's gaining, now—her powers are destroying his razors just a millisecond faster than he can re-create them, but that's all the time she needs.

If she gets to his skin, she will destroy him.

I look up at the deck, wondering if Ananias realizes how close they are to destruction. He watches the fight, his expression unreadable as he fingers the flute of his champagne glass.

Riles tries once more to push back against Mavis, but she holds fast, tightening her grip. We all know the moment her fingertips touch his skin. The scream he lets out is the terrible, keening kind. I clap my hands over my ears, but I can't tear my eyes away.

Mavis steps back, and I can see what's left of Riles's arm.

Almost nothing. Blood pours from his shoulder, and his breath comes in gasps as he looks down, his eyes blank with shock.

He staggers and then falls to his knees. Mavis watches for a moment, swaying slightly as she looks at her work.

Tessa winds her finger in the air, signaling for the Menders and the end of the fight. Announcing that Mavis won seems unnecessary. Mavis steps back as the Menders step in and pull a now unconscious Riles onto a gurney. One slips in blood but manages to keep herself upright.

Mavis watches as they carry Riles away and then makes a beeline toward the cage door. Her face is smeared with blood, and her dark lips are void of a smirk.

"Mavis," Aldrick says as he reaches for her, but she shakes him off and walks away. I lower my hands, eyes fixed on the blood spattered over the mat.

The tinge of my burned hands and the sight of the bright blood invade my senses, and I feel sick. I knew this was dangerous when I signed up, but *knowing* and *seeing* are two different things. Ananias said on the first night that this would be a tournament that tested our own limits. Now I know what he means. And the truth is, I can't even be disgusted at what Mavis just did. Because I would do the same. We all would.

The thought makes me sick, and I turn, walking into the night as I pull the bandages off my hands and let them flit to the ground. Floodlights crash on around me, and I'm blinded. And in that second, it's so familiar I could swear I'm back on the football field at Northview, huddled with my girls before a game, sharing glitter glue for our temples. I'm in my cheer uniform, the gold sparkles catching the floodlights. I hear Lindsay laughing as she fixes one of my curls that's stuck in my zipper. It's freezing, and the icy air bites into my burns in a way that feels both good and terrible. I throw my hood over my head and take several deep breaths.

"Very impressive," a soft voice says, and I almost jump out of my skin. Ananias is walking toward me. He stops near the medics' tent and crosses his arms over his chest. "For a moment, I thought you were really going to snap her arm."

I look at him, trying to find my voice. "I would have," I say finally, trying to figure out why he's talking to me.

Ananias stops in front of me, champagne glass still in hand. He tosses the rest of the liquid into the shadow. The medic sticks his head out of the tent.

"We'll transport him, Mr. Ventra. He's beyond our help, here."

"My car is out back. Don't wait for an ambulance. He doesn't have that kind of time," he says. The medic nods and disappears back inside. I am still as I watch Ananias look at the tent. His expression is still unreadable as he turns back to me. His eyes are a dark brown with yellow rings around the pupils that expand as he talks. His jaw twitches as he smiles slightly.

He looks at my burned hands. "To an untrained eye, it would almost seem like you're a Baseline. But I felt that shift toward the end. Whatever is inside of you wanted out."

I meet his eyes, and I don't answer.

"You had the best time, so you advance to the next round. And I hope you decide to let it out. I want to know what a girl like you keeps as a secret." With that, he walks past me. I follow him with my eyes.

I turn back, getting ready to slip into the tent, but I stop when I see someone standing in front of me. Sapphira.

She is in a black hoodie, her face obscured by shadow. She'd even moved like a shadow; I didn't hear her footsteps. When she turns to look at me, her bright blue eyes stand out even against the darkness. "Aldrick said that I should let you make up your own mind about the fights. He thought I should've told you and not tried to get you to leave."

"But you didn't," I reply.

She steps closer to me and touches my shirt. I look down to where her hand points to a red fleck of blood from Mavis's fight that had landed on me in the crowd.

"Everyone I care about has been entranced by this fight.

I didn't want that for you. You have no idea how consuming this whole thing can be. People are losing themselves and not even realizing it until it's too late."

I gently take her wrist in mine and lower it, meeting her eyes.

"I lost myself a long time ago. This is my chance to get it back." I let her arm go.

She closes her eyes, her long ashes dark against the deep circles under her eyes.

"Everyone has their price, right?" Her fingers toy with the charms on her bracelet as she shakes her head, swallowing hard. She points to my hands. "You should go re-cover those. You don't want to get an infection."

"Vesper?" I hear a voice call from inside the tent. It's the medic, looking to check up on me.

I follow the sound of the voice. When I look back, Sapphira is gone.

SIXTEEN

Sam drives us back to the gym, and it's almost a joke how normal everything feels as we pull onto the street. The lights are on. People walk out of Aloa's.

I'm covered in antibiotic ointment and wrapped in gauze, and my mind is still reeling from my conversation with Sapphira. I keep replaying it, hoping I'll figure out what I'm obviously missing.

I look over at Sam.

He's quiet, but it's not like his usual silence.

This time, he's afraid, and I feel it coming off him in waves. He throws the car into park in front of the gym. The lights are on. Abagail, Wex, and Roy are probably waiting up for us.

He kills the engine.

Neither of us get out of the car.

He sits there, and I can't read him. "I didn't know it was going to be like that."

"I'm fine, Sam. The medic said it'll heal in a few days."

"I just stood there. I watched it happen. . . ." His words drop off.

I can't stand how his voice cracks; how small it makes him seem. Sam isn't small. Nothing about Sam is small. Seeing Sam act small ignites a fear in me that I didn't know was there.

I shake my head. "I knew I had her."

He looks over at me. "You're hurt, Vesper. And not a little beat-up from a rumble in the Beneath. I had no clue they would let it go that far."

There's something subtle about the way he's talking, like he should have known better. Like he wound me up and let me loose into a web of razor wire. Like *he* used *me*. It's almost heartbreaking, how backward it is. Something in me feels like it's cracking at the sight, but I shut the door against that part of my chest.

I've let this go too far. I knew that before, but I really felt it when I was in the cage. This was never meant to be a friendship. Sam is the means to an end, and I have to stop wanting to tell him everything will be fine, because it won't be. I have to snap out of it, and I have to stop his train of thought. Not just because it's making him feel bad, but because I can't let him entertain the thought of backing out now.

"I signed up for this. I *want* this," I say, looking over at him. The words are even, delivered in even intervals so he can swallow them and digest them and *understand*. "Let's get this straight, okay? You didn't *make me do this*. You didn't *get* me to do anything."

He won't meet my eyes as he shakes his head.

"I know you chose this. You don't think I know that? Damn, Vesper. That's the worst part of this! I was watching you in that mess, and I was equal parts horrified and *proud*—don't you get it? And that's the sick part. Watching you scream, damn, I could *see* the smoke coming off your skin—it was almost too much, but I still stood there, wanting you to tear that girl apart. What kind of a monster does that make me?"

Still not a worse one than me.

I stare at the dashboard. At the scratch in the leather; at the coffee stain beside it. The words bubble up in my throat. "Tell me about Elisa," I say.

I know this will make it harder in the long run, but I need him to focus on what he wants, because if he thinks himself into a self-righteous mood, we're both up shit creek. Also, maybe hearing how much he loved this girl will help me stack immovable objects in front of that door in my chest.

He looks at me like I must have misspoke. "What?"

"What did you think when you first met her? What was

the first thought in your mind?"

His eyes search mine, and he leans back against the door. "I thought she was a thief."

"What?" I ask, and the word comes out as a laugh.

He nods. "She was upstairs during one of my parents' parties. I went into their bedroom to get something for my dad and saw her leaving my little sister's room. She was wearing a black dress. Her hair was a dark blond, all twisted, you know?" He motions at the back of his neck with his hand, indicating a low bun. The streetlights illuminate his face as the memory takes hold. He smiles. "I yelled at her to stop, but she took off. Jumped out an open window onto the patio below."

"What did you do?"

"I followed her. She was fast, but I was faster." He's caught up in the memory, now. I can see it in the way the smile that started slinking up the side of his mouth has reached his eyes. "I caught her halfway through the Thompsons' back lawn, near their pool house. We fell into the grass. I thought I had the upper hand, but she flipped me over and pinned me down." He takes a steady breath. "Her hair had come all loose and . . . and I thought she was going to knock me out or something."

My chest tightens at the sound of his voice. It's softer than I've ever heard it, like the memory is crystal and he's lifting it out if its wrapping to give me a glimpse.

"What did she do?" I whisper. He looks at me, his eyes coming back into focus.

"She just . . . looked at me. And then the sprinklers came on." He smiles. It's the most I've seen him smile so far.

"What was she actually doing in your parents' house?" I ask, genuinely curious.

He blinks like he's coming back to himself. "Oh. Right. Stealing." He reads my face. "She had secrets then. She had secrets even at our closest."

Closest. I imagine Sam, the sunlight on his skin. I imagine her making him laugh in bed on a Sunday morning. I imagine what he must have looked like happy. And I don't want to think that. I don't want to see what a stark contrast it must be to now.

Also I don't want to think of him in bed. I shove the thought out of my mind.

"Is that what you were fighting about? The night she left?"

"No," Sam says. "And maybe that makes me awful, but I never pushed her about it. I knew she was into some shady stuff, but . . ." He stops, looking through the windshield as though he's tasting the words he just said. "You know those people? The ones where they're around and you just feel . . . *whole*, I guess is the word. Your soul feels fed, and you're better for having been around them. I'm sure that makes zero sense."

I make myself look away from him before I speak. "No. It makes sense."

Sam drops his hands from the wheel, and the silence is back.

I say the only thing I can think that will make tonight worth it. The only thing I can think that is true.

"I want to win this, Sam. Help me, okay?"

When he looks up, I feel it in my chest. It's like he's accepted something—the fact that this is going to get ugly and he has to let it. He has to let me do this.

He nods. Just once, and only slightly.

He helps me out of the car. Abagail redresses my wounds, which are already almost completely healed thanks to the medic's magic. Wex makes us soup. And by "makes" I mean he heats it up using Tupperware and a microwave. Sam tells them everything while I sit on the couch next to Abagail.

I fall asleep on her lap as she plays with my hair.

Sometime in the middle of the night, I wake up and hear the bag. Someone must have carried me back up to the loft. Normally, it would freak me out that I was that vulnerable. But here, the idea doesn't scare me as much as it used to.

One two three. One two three.

I know it's Sam, and the thought comforts me. I like knowing that he's downstairs. I like knowing that he's close. Here, alone in the dark, I let myself think that. I turn my face into my pillow, shutting my eyes tight. The pain tonight will fade. But I'm suffering from a completely different affliction.

Because when he talked about someone who makes you feel fed? Whole? Strong?

Yeah, I know that feeling, and it hurt to figure that out.

Because I feel it when I'm around him.

SEVENTEEN

I manage to avoid Sam for the next couple of days. I shower in the gym bathroom, carefully, and stretch my sore muscles. Sam goes to work and then comes to train, but I make sure I'm in the loft. My new hobby is online stalking on the old PC in the corner of the office. I find Ananias on Facebook. Instagram.

He has pictures of him dining at the Petronas Twin Towers of Kuala Lumpur with several friends, glasses held aloft. There's another of him sitting outside a café in Paris, holding a bread crumb out to a pigeon.

I don't know what I was thinking I'd find, but it was more helpful than that.

I punch Sapphira's name in. I find her Instagram account. Or what *was* her Instagram account. It hasn't been active in almost a year. The Sapphira I know and the Sapphira in these pictures don't even seem like the same person.

Sapphira on the steps of her high school, surrounded by friends. A girl with blond hair throws up a peace sign. Sapphira leans on her shoulder.

Sapphira at a football game, her arm linked with two other friends.

I stop as another picture loads. A little boy, probably no more than five years old, sitting on her lap, his head thrown against her shoulder. In his fingers, there's a toy dinosaur. I look down at the caption—"the rare and very dangerous Nolan-osaurus!"

There's a reason I stayed on my own for so long. You can't have people watching your back without them also seeing your scars. Everyone's rubble feels the same when you walk across it, and I know I'm treading over a part of Sapphira she wouldn't want me seeing.

I feel antsy. The room feels too small, like I need to get out.

I click out and push back, and movement on the sparring mat below pulls my attention out the window. Sam shuts his locker carefully, pulling a beanie over his head before picking up a bag and slinging it over his shoulder.

I don't know if it's because I don't want to be alone with my thoughts or because there's something about the way he looks over his shoulder that suggests he doesn't want to be seen—

But I slip my feet into my boots and follow him.

✳ ✳ ✳

He heads down Fifth and takes a left. The streetcar wires crisscross overhead under a cloudy night sky. They hum with electricity, letting out little noises that sound like someone plucking a string. Across the street, a live band plays at a small bistro. Sam looks over, and I stop, stepping behind a tree, thinking he'll look behind him. He doesn't.

I follow him across Broadway, making sure to keep a good distance between us.

I'm going to feel really stupid if this walk is just a stroll and we wind up doing a big circle back to Duncan's. Sam stops at a crosswalk and looks over his shoulder, and I dive behind a homeless man's shopping cart. He's sleeping upright against the brick wall of a club, and he opens his eyes as I trip down next to him.

For a moment, terror rips through me. I'm alone, in the dark. I throw my hand out in front of me, and the pulse in my palm throbs, but I realize that Aldrick was right. All I can do is cage it.

I can't really use it.

"You okay there, hon?" he asks. I nod as I lower my hand slowly, and he settles back and closes his eyes again.

I look at the black trash bags settled high over the cart, watching as Sam stops at a blue metal door next to a mural of comic book characters salsa dancing.

He steps inside. I wait a few minutes, and then I follow.

Inside, the walls are hot pink. A dark wood staircase

twists upward, and I hear footsteps I assume are Sam's. I stay one floor below, chancing a look over the edge of the third floor as Sam takes out a key and opens apartment 408.

I should turn back. This isn't my business. I start down the stairs, but something stops me. Maybe he's hiding something. Something dangerous. I look over my shoulder and notice something next to the door. A little ceramic nameplate sits over a buzzer.

A name?

Slowly, I creep up the stairs and walk up to the door as quietly as I can.

E. Littleton.

E.

Elisa?

This is Elisa's apartment. Wait . . . if they're broken up, why is Sam still at her apartment?

I'm about to turn and run back down the stairs when the door swings open. Sam stands in the doorway, a look I would characterize as distinctly unhappy to see me on his face.

"You're following me now?" he asks, leaning against the doorframe.

"I was worried I was partnered with a freak who breaks into his ex-girlfriend's apartment in the middle of the night, and, wouldn't you know it? I was spot-on."

"Vesper," Sam says lowly, but I back up and hold up my hands.

"It's really none of my business, Sam. Except I feel compelled to tell you that this is *really* fucking weird and girl code mandates that I remind you that this kind of invasion of privacy isn't okay! I mean, I know you miss her, Sam, but *stalking*? Sam, you—"

"Vesper. Please. Can we talk inside?" he asks.

"Oh yeah, I was hoping this would get *more* weird. She'll come home, and we can explain how we're partnering in an otherworldly tournament to win her back. That'll go over well."

"Elisa is dead, Vesper. She died about two years ago," Sam says, his voice a blade that cuts through the air between us with startling precision. I stop, trying and failing to comprehend what he's saying.

"What?" I breathe. Sam steps aside.

"Please," he says, motioning me inside.

My legs are numb as I step through the threshold, my mind spinning.

The apartment is small and warm. The living room is filled with boxes, the kitchen counter covered in stacks of paper. A gray cat darts in and out between my feet.

"That's Penny," Sam says. "I've tried to rehome her, but she always finds her way back here, so I gave up."

"Nice to meet you," I say dumbly as the cat looks up at me with the most gorgeous teal eyes I've ever seen. She lets out a meow, and I find myself sinking to the floor to pet her.

Sam walks into the kitchen. "Want some tea?"

"I want an explanation," I say finally.

There's silence, and then the sound of a kettle turning on. Sam comes back to the entryway and motions for me to follow him.

The walls are a lilac purple. I see the marks on the paint where pictures used to hang. I wonder if Sam took them down. He stops at the coffee table.

"Her family owned this place outright. I used to watch it when she was out on business. Now, I've just been"—he turns to look at me—"packing it up."

"For two years?" I counter.

His eyes narrow. "This is none of your business, Vesper. You shouldn't have come here."

"I know," I reply, because, honestly, I know I've crossed a line. "I was . . . worried about you." The words ring true in my chest, which just makes this all worse.

He sits on a floral wingback chair, crossing his arms over his chest. I sit on the arm of the couch, looking around like the walls themselves will give me the answers I'm looking for.

"I didn't lie to you," he says quietly, and I turn back to him. His eyes are intense. Vulnerable. It makes my skin itch, like the words are rubbing against me, coaxing my dishonesty to the surface.

I shove myself up. "We're partners, Sam. You don't owe me

anything. I just wanted to make sure you weren't checking on your freezer full of dismembered body parts or something. *That* kind of stuff, I want to know. This? I—"

Sam stands, then. "No. Exactly. We're partners, and I feel like shit for misleading you. I just . . ." He stops, and *damn* I want him to stop talking. I should never have come here. My chest heaves as I contemplate just turning and leaving.

"I didn't want to put this whole thing on you. I know enough about the pressure of the cage. Everyone's watching. And the money was enough. I didn't want you to know the whole grisly story of Elisa on top of that. It's too much for me to carry, and I'm not actually fighting." He looks down. "But I wasn't lying when I said I wanted to undo a fight. We argued one night—"

He takes a deep breath and pushes onward. "I was at a title fight downtown, and she got a call. I didn't want her to go, but she did. And I didn't follow her. I stayed. I won. And then I never saw her alive again."

He looks up, and his eyes are shining. I never should have followed him. I don't want to know this. I feel the door in my chest splintering against the weight of his words as they press into me.

"They found her body in the bay three days later. Official cause of death was . . . unknown. I came by after to feed Penny." As if on cue, the cat jumps in my lap. She purrs and throws herself against my hand. "I started sorting through stuff." He gestures around the room.

The kettle screams, and Sam goes back into the kitchen.

I hear the satisfying gurgle of water as he pours the water into the mugs and close my eyes as I scratch a purring Penny behind the ears. This complicates things.

I'm planning on screwing him over, and that was much easier when I thought his pain was something from a Taylor Swift song. But this?

I look around the room. Boxes are marked with years, and there are Post-its on the tables labeled "Receipts" and "Phone Records." Sam has spent years trying to figure this out. This is so much more than trying to repair a breakup. This is life-and-death, and I wasn't expecting that.

Sam walks back in with two steaming mugs, but I stand, dropping Penny unceremoniously to the floor.

"I'm sorry. This was stupid. I never should have come here." I turn, hoping to make a quick exit. But my efforts are thwarted by a cardboard box I don't see near the base of the chair. I trip, careening forward and landing with my face against the wall.

"Whoa—are you okay?" Sam asks, rushing to my side and helping me up.

"I'm an idiot," I say, and I'm not just talking about the falling.

"This place is a hoarder's dream, right now. It's not your fault," he says, but I don't hear a word. I look at the wall,

where a slow line of ink has appeared over the paint. Sam
falls silent as he follows my eyes.

"What the hell?" he asks.

"Umbra ink," I mutter, close to the wall. The coil spreads.
"Writing that can only be activated by the breath of an Oddity."

I push myself to my feet. I run my breath down the wall,
breathing hard.

Dark black words run down the wall as though being
written by an invisible hand.

I step back, and I feel Sam go completely still beside me.

Leave it alone, il mio combattente.

I look to Sam, and he's gone ashen. He takes a couple of
staggered steps back until he is pressed against the opposite
wall.

"*Mio combattente?*" I ask, my voice a harsh whisper, alarm
bells sounding my head. The question bubbles up, but I try
to put it into words.

"Elisa." Sam pushes himself forward, running his hand
over the words. "She studied in Florence in college. She
called me 'mio combattente.' My fighter.

"She wrote this, Vesper," Sam says. His breathing is heavy
as he runs a hand through his hair, and it stands up on end.
He looks back at me, his eyes full of a fire I've never seen.
He's breathless, his chest heaving up and down. "Why would
she tell me to leave it alone?" he asks. He doesn't expect an

answer, so I don't give him one. He runs his hands down the words, like they'll give up their secrets at his touch.

"More than two years. I've searched through all the records. I've tracked down everyone she'd talked to. I sat in the police station all night, just to try to get someone to listen to me. I've looked everywhere. And this was here, all along."

A question stings my tongue like a nettle, and I spit it out before I can stop myself.

"How did Elisa know about umbra ink?" I ask.

Sam freezes and then exhales as he rubs his hands over his face and turns back to me.

"She was a Metalurg," he says finally.

An Oddity who can control metal. She was an Oddity. It makes sense—how comfortable Sam is in the Beneath. How Duncan doesn't faze him at all.

"I've got to take a picture of this," Sam says, disappearing through the kitchen. I hear him riffling through things in the living room.

Questions spin in my gut, but I swallow them back as I look at the words on the wall.

Sam comes back and snaps a picture with his phone before looking back down at me with a smile I've never seen before.

"What?" I ask.

"Kind of seems like a waste of time now, doesn't it? Considering you're about to win this tournament that will undo all this."

My stomach twists. "You know what they say. Don't count your chickens before they win an otherworldly death match."

Sam snort-laughs as he looks at me, and I smile despite myself.

I hate that I love that laugh.

"It's not just that, I guess. Even if you do win . . . I need to know what happened. And Elisa . . ." Sam stops for a moment, like he's deciding whether or not he trusts himself to continue. "She kept things to herself."

"She won't tell you?" I ask, feeling like a snake for saying a bad word against her.

Sam's expression darkens. "Elisa was protective of her secrets," he answers. "But if I don't know how this happened, how can I stop it from happening again?"

"What do you think she was keeping from you?" I ask.

"I don't know. But I have a feeling it got her killed."

He looks at me, and I cock an eyebrow in response. We both take a step back and look at the writing.

I run my hands along the wall, letting out breath. Maybe she left another message. I walk all the way to the bedroom, but nothing else appears.

"I'm gonna need something stronger than tea," Sam says, walking back into the kitchen.

I stop at a tower of boxes stacked perilously against a wooden armoire. I swear I'm not snooping. But something catches my eye. A round metal tin sits on top of downward-facing picture frames. Inside, there are some loose beads and a couple of safety pins. I peer closer, realizing that my fall also knocked something loose.

A false bottom.

With a look over my shoulder to make sure Sam is still in the kitchen, I reach my hand in and carefully lift it.

My breath catches in my throat as bile spins in my stomach.

Underneath, there's a handful of dried queen of poisons flowers. I hear my heartbeat in my ears as I stare at the withered, brittle buds.

I turn them over, trying in vain to count them. How many of these did they leave her?

I jump at the sound of Sam moving around in the kitchen. I set them back down and take three huge steps back, like the dead flowers can reach out and grab me.

Suddenly, the apartment feels too small. Everything feels like it's caving in.

"Sam, I'm gonna get some air," I say, fighting to keep my voice steady. I don't know why I didn't call out to Sam right away. I need to catch my breath.

He leans into the doorway, drying his hands on a dishcloth as he regards me for a moment. "You okay?" he asks.

I nod. "Just feeling a little cooped up. This place is a claustrophobic's hellscape."

He tosses the cloth on the counter. "I'll walk you back. It's not safe," he says.

"Neither am I," I say with a forced smile as I back up.

I need to be alone. I need to process this. Sam looks skeptical, but I hold my fingers up and wiggle them to emphasize my point.

"I don't like this," he says warily.

I open the door and step out. "I'll be fine. I'll see you back there."

I step out and close the door behind me before he can argue further, and then I walk as quickly as I can. I don't want him changing his mind and following me out here.

EIGHTEEN

The night is cool on my face as I walk, and I run my hands through my hair.

Elisa's dead.

That changes things, and it changes nothing.

Perhaps that's why I feel like shit. Or, more than I did already.

It felt like no contest to choose my family over Sam's ruined relationship. It was still a messed-up choice, and so distinctly terrible of me to sit and decide whose heart hurts worst—whose pain deserved relief, as though fissures in the soul could possibly be quantifiable like that.

Not just dead, but dead and, by the looks of it, killed by the Wardens.

I mean, there's a chance she maybe just likes aconite buds. They're pretty flowers. Or she was super into killer botany or something.

I stop at a stoplight.

Or she was killed by the Wardens, and investigating her death could mean poking at something that shouldn't be poked.

I step over a green grate in the sidewalk that's engraved with a smiling mermaid and past a bakery that still has seating outside despite the frigid temperature. I pull my jacket closer as I realize I'm no longer headed back to Duncan's. I can't sit still right now. Not with all this bouncing around in my mind.

My dad told me that my ability to stay alive rested on how well I feared the Wardens.

Yet I find I've just stepped into a mystery that has them written all over it.

I stop walking, looking up at the puffs of my breath as they swirl in front of the light from the streetlamp.

I could just go back to Duncan's, keep my head down, and not mention Elisa again. After all, she's not my problem. *Sam* isn't my problem. I want to win the tournament, take the unraveling for myself, save my family from what I've done, and then disappear.

So why can't I just do that?

I close my eyes as the answer washes over me.

Because I care about him.

I want to help him figure out how he got this thorn in his heart. I don't want to walk away and leave him with nothing.

❈ ❈ ❈

I don't know how long I wander the streets.

When I open my eyes, I'm surprised to find I'm closer to the Grotto than I thought. Across the darkness, nestled into the black leaves of trees, a small light peeks out from the lighthouse.

Sapphira.

A small light beats up against the darkness at the railing of the lighthouse, and my feet move before I can change my mind.

"How are your hands?" Sapphira asks as I open the rusty door. She doesn't even bother to look back and confirm it's me.

"Fine," I answer, stepping up to the railing and taking a seat next to her. I barely notice the shiny red skin on my palms anymore. It's nothing compared to the shredded feeling in my chest right now.

"Long walk from the MMA gym," she says, handing the spiced wine over to me.

"I wasn't at the MMA gym," I reply, taking a pull of the warm liquid before handing it back. I turn to look at her. The moonlight washes her out—she looks like a porcelain doll in this light.

She takes a drink.

"That guy. Your sponsor," she starts, looking over at me. "He seemed really worried about you while you were in the cage."

"You saw that?" I ask. Her jaw ticks, but she shrugs.

The thoughts that all surfaced, flotsam and jetsam stirred up from the storm of a walk I had over here, rise to the top. I reach for the thermos.

"He was worried about his gladiator. You would be, too, if you were trying to bring back your dead girlfriend. I thought they just broke up. But no. No, she's dead. Two years." I'm rambling as I swirl my wine.

"Sheeze. That's . . ." She falters, and I nod, handing the thermos back. "So you two aren't—" she starts, and I shake my head a little too vigorously.

"Hell no," I spit out, knowing that I doth protest too much. Sapphira sucks in her lower lip and cocks an eyebrow but doesn't push me.

A moment passes.

"His girlfriend had umbra ink in her apartment. She left a message before she disappeared two years ago. Do you know any Scribes who might know who helped her leave it?"

"Two years," Sapphira says. She crosses her arms, and I can see her mind working as she rolls her wrists. The dinosaur bracelet charms jingle against each other.

"I found dried queen of poisons buds in a box of her stuff," I blurt. I don't know why I tell her this. I guess I just didn't want to carry it alone, anymore. Just another moment of emotional cowardice.

Put it on my tab.

"You think the Wardens killed her?" Sapphira asks.

I press my lips into a thin line, and she takes that for my answer.

"I think there's a Scribe who has been around here the past couple of years. Let me figure out who," she says.

"Thank you."

Sapphira looks out at the water, her expression clouded. The sound of crashing waves and wind whipped into a fury fills the air as we both look out past the railing.

"Well. It's the least I can do, since you're lending me your history notes before the midterm."

I laugh, not realizing how much I need to. "They're shit, but sure."

She drains the rest of her cup and smirks with a full mouth.

We look out over the water, watching pelicans dive down and disappear over a thin film of fog.

"If I bring her back, will she remember dying? Or will it be like she never died at all?" I muse. I don't think I'm really expecting an answer.

"She'll remember it. An unraveling undoes the direct consequences of a tragedy but leaves the memory of what actually happened. She'd come back, fully aware of what happened. Nothing else would change."

I think about it.

"You'd still have met Sam, if that's the kind of butterfly-effect question you have. Everything that happened up until now will still have happened. Elisa will just appear somewhere, alive. Unraveling doesn't rewrite time."

I picture myself at home with my family, scars healed, house fixed. They would still remember what I did.

I shift in my seat. She can read me too well. I don't like it. "Why is he doing this?" I ask, looking up at the cloudy night sky. "He has unlimited power. Why is he offering it up as a prize?"

"It's not unlimited. Unravelers are bound by rules, just like we all are. They can't unravel their own tragedies, and they can only unravel something for a person who has love for the thing that was lost."

"So it's a gift you can't use on yourself, and you can only use it for good?"

Sapphira looks at me. "I guess you could say that."

"Who makes those rules?" I ask.

Sapphira laughs. "Who said Aldrick can only retain his Stoneskin form for minutes at a time? Who decided that you could only pull out fear? Probably the same who made gravity and tides and all that stuff. No one really knows."

I know what I grew up believing—that there's a power greater than me that set all that in motion. God. But my belief was one of the things that only half made it out of the fire that night. Because why would the God who made bioluminescent algae or white blood cells also make someone like me? Someone who can only bring fear? It doesn't make sense.

She passes the drink back to me, and we're quiet as we watch the fog roll over the water. I lean over and place my head on her shoulder. She tenses for a moment and then lets out a breath as she tips her head to rest on mine. My mind drifts to Sam. On what I plan to do.

This choice is going to leave marks I will wear for the rest of my life.

If I win the final round, I will remember all of this—him— even after I've won the unraveling. I will remember what I've done in exchange for a life free of fearing my true nature.

I shut my eyes as the thought slices down my core like a white-hot blade.

I realize that I've been so worried about what will be left of Sam at the end of this that I didn't stop to ask what—if anything—will be left of me.

That night, back at Duncan's, I lie on the bed and look up at the ceiling. I think about what Aldrick said. How I'm caging my magic, not controlling it.

And how I'm sick of being scared of everything.

I might never be completely at peace with what I am. What I've done. Even if I manage to unravel the darkest secrets I carry—there might always be a part of me that feels out of place.

But I'm tired of being tired, and I'm tired of feeling afraid of myself when there's so much more to fear.

And maybe the best way to undo what I am is to first accept it.

And to accept that Sam and I were never going to be friends. I'm fighting to bring his dead girlfriend back to life—that's what he wants. And I'm going to betray him. I need to focus on winning now. I need to focus on getting home.

I pull out my burner.

Let's do it, I text Aldrick.

A moment later, my phone buzzes.

Hell yes, he answers back. **When?**

NINETEEN

"I don't like this, Aldrick," I say, going up on the balls of my bare feet. They squish against the mat.

"You're not going to like it at first. That's part of the process," Aldrick answers back from across the floor. He's shirtless, his hair piled up in a bun on top of his head.

"I signed up to learn to control this. Not to use people I care about as *bait*," I say, motioning to Wex and Abagail. Sapphira sits next to Sam on the top edge of the cage next to the mat. I look up at them.

"How else did you think this would work?" Sam calls out.

"I don't like when you two talk," I say, gesturing between Sam and Aldrick.

I'd planned on meeting Aldrick to practice somewhere private, but Sam got involved, and then before I knew what was happening, Aldrick was taking off his shirt, and everyone was waiting for me to poke the bear inside my chest.

"No one is forcing us to be here, Vesper," Abagail says.

"I'd like to force you to *not*," I reply.

"You're scared you're going to hurt someone. Facing that fear is part of the process of reclaiming what's rightfully yours," Aldrick says.

"If this gets out of hand?" I start, looking up at Sam.

"Sleeper hold," he replies. I made him promise to knock me out if the magic got away from me. I don't know if that will make whatever terrible thing I pull out go away, but I have to think it can't make it worse.

"It won't come to that," Sapphira says.

"Come on," Aldrick says, motioning me forward. The invitation sends shivers through my limbs, and I feel my magic stretching under my skin. Aldrick lunges forward, grabbing behind my thighs in an effort to pull my feet out from under me. I splay my legs outward, widening my stance and folding my upper body over his.

The magic surges as my fingers grab his arms.

"You feel it?" he grunts as I grab on to him harder, locking my wrists so he can't throw me.

"Yeah," I answer back through gritted teeth.

"Vesper. Just a little. Try."

I take a deep breath, and I know that arguing about this is pointless. I'm going to be out of my comfort zone at some point. It might as well be now.

I unleash the magic, and I feel it plunge into his chest. It digs deep, parsing through memories that echo like a wind chime as my magic brushes past them.

Aldrick! Look out! A woman's voice screams. Glass shatters.

Aldrick stands, and I shift my body until I'm behind him. I lock my legs around his waist, and I feel a deep surge as my magic pushes forward, like I've just hit the gas.

I see glimpses of Aldrick's fear. I'm looking over the edge of the Grand Canyon—heights. I did this with Carl on the first night, but this is different. This time, I can feel the varying intensities of the fears. Usually, I only decipher which one to pull out based on how *I* feel, but now I know how they make Aldrick feel. I can tell which ones will traumatize him versus which ones will make him uncomfortable.

Aldrick shakes me loose finally, and I collapse to the floor. The magic slithers back to me as we both catch our breath.

"Well?" he asks.

Sweat drips down my face. As I look up at him, it runs into my eyes as the realization sets in. I just let it out, and then I pulled it back.

I just nod, and Aldrick smiles.

We work for another hour, and my friends rotate in and I ease the magic out of the cave I've stuffed it into. Little by little, I let it out as we spar.

I dig through Wex and see shadow. His whole life was fear. My magic listens when I call it back, and it doesn't leave any gaping wounds as it retreats.

Sam jumps in, and I try a round without calling my magic forth at all. I say it's because I want to practice varying degrees of using my magic, but it's really because I don't think I can stomach getting any deeper into Sam. Asking Sapphira to help find the Scribe who could find answers about Elisa seems different—safer.

As Abagail swings at me, I block with my gloves and my magic slips into her chest. I see an empty apartment as she watches the ball drop on TV. Loneliness. She drops her guard for a moment, and I get an uppercut in—lucky shot—but I feel the surge in my chest echo the punch, and I pluck at the fear like a guitar string.

Abagail gasps and staggers back, putting a hand to her chest.

"You okay?" I ask, breathless. That was new.

She takes several deep breaths. "It was like . . . for a second there, the fear felt like a knife in my chest."

"We can stop," I say, and Abagail shakes her head.

"Just when this is getting good?" she asks with a smile. I pull the Velcro straps of my gloves with my teeth and tighten my gloves before jumping back in.

She swings her leg around for a roundhouse kick, but I catch it against my chest and hit the back of her knee, knocking her to the ground. The force of my blow sends my magic rolling out toward her in a wave, and I feel it wash over her. That has never happened before, and I don't know what kind of effect it has.

Abagail freezes, and I stop, dropping to my knees.

"Abagail! Are you okay?"

She's silent for a moment but then blinks several times. She nods, and I let out a relieved breath.

"It was like . . . for a moment, I was so scared, I couldn't move."

"Scared of what?" I ask.

"Just . . . scared," she says, smiling.

"Why are you smiling?"

Abagail nods. "Because that was awesome. You just punched fear into me."

I stand and help Abagail to her feet. Then I look up at Sam, who has been watching this whole time. He smiles slowly.

"Is a fear punch even a thing?" I ask.

Sam rubs his hand over his mouth and smiles even wider.

"It is now."

Hours go by, and people who were strangers weeks ago keep putting themselves back in my line of fire, just to show me that I'm not the monster I'm still quite convinced I am.

By the time we stop for Wex and Abagail to take pizza orders, I have to keep swallowing the lump in my throat.

I didn't know that it could be like this—people seeing me, knowing me, and not being terrified of what I am and what I've done.

But I still haven't pulled a fear out yet. I've parsed, I've searched, but I haven't made any of them material.

And they still don't know what I did to my family—not even Sam knows the full truth.

So they don't see you, the voice in my head says.

Aldrick and Sam are in the cage, and Sam is showing Aldrick some release moves.

Roy and Sapphira sit on the bench under "Invictus," talking. I didn't even know Roy was here—he comes and goes like a shadow. Or a stray cat. He's smiling as Sapphira talks to him—it's a rare sight. Sapphira has that effect on people.

Sapphira's phone beeps and she glances down at the screen. When she looks up, she meets my eyes and motions for me to follow her. We slip up the stairs. When we're alone, she turns.

"There's only been one Scribe in the city for the past six years. I found out where he works. Or, at least where he was working as of a month ago. But he was an operative of the Wardens, so who knows where he might have scurried off to."

My stomach roils. The Wardens?

Two months ago, the mere mention of them would've put me on a bus. But I swallow the bile rising in my throat and nod.

"Where?"

"I'll go with you."

I shake my head. "Sapphira, I don't know what this will lead to, and I really don't want you getting mixed up in this."

Her eyes harden. "You don't know where to find him, and you don't know what he looks like."

"Tell me, and then show me a picture."

Sapphira grins, raising her eyebrows.

"Take it or leave it, Vesper."

"Fine. But no Aldrick," I say. She narrows her eyes.

"You want to fight a losing battle? Try to get Aldrick not to help with something. He's not exactly itching to sit around the Grotto, either, with all the stuff happening." She reads the question on my face. "A couple of the Oddities are saying their powers are . . . weird after the first tournament. Others are saying they're just trying to freak everyone out."

"You believe them?" I ask.

She shrugs. "I've never had a reason to doubt Theo. If he says his powers are acting weird, then I believe it."

"Okay. Well, weirdness or no weirdness—I don't think Aldrick should come."

She cocks her eyebrow at me.

"We're potentially dealing with the Wardens, Sapphira. I don't want to put a target on any more Oddities.

"And why are you helping?" I press, because I can't help wondering. I hate how the words sound—so distrustful. Like they're searching her pockets for sharp ulterior motives.

She shrugs. "It seems important to you," she says simply, before looking over at Sam and then back to me. I know that look, and what it means. I ignore it.

She studies me for a moment. I nod.

TWENTY

"The next trial is in one week," Sam says as I wrap my healed hands in cloth, winding it between my knuckles and over my wrists. I know how to do this now. And I am not going to lie, it makes me feel like a total badass.

I watch as he and Roy spar with rubber blades. Sam flips Roy and jabs the tip of the rubber into Roy's kidney. "And, dead."

"Son of a bitch," Roy whispers, jumping to his feet and pacing along the edge of the mat while Sam spins the blade and smiles.

"Anything particular you want to learn before then?" Sam asks, leaning down and grabbing his Moleskine notebook off the bench. He scribbles something down.

I look up into the cage. Abagail stretches, her legs straddled as she leans forward against the floor.

"You should learn some submission moves," Abagail says, wincing as she pushes the stretch and presses her palms down.

"Submission it is then," I say to Abagail.

"Duncan? Can you help me show her?" Abagail asks as Duncan walks in. He stops, looks at me, and then to Abagail.

"I'm busy," he says simply before disappearing into the office.

I'm usually pretty good at being sneaky.

Even before I had to be sneaky. It was a gift. Lindsay and I used to jump the pool fence of the local country club and skinny-dip at least once a week during the summers. We would've kept getting away with it, too, if Lindsay hadn't purposely left her black lace panties hanging from a low-hanging branch of a tree so the hot lifeguards would see them in the morning. Yes, my mom figured it out. Yes, we ended up having to cut our skinny-dipping down to once a month after that.

But I count that as Lindsay's fault. If it were up to me, we would've never been caught. All that to say, I should know how to walk down the stairs of Duncan's at dawn without making a bunch of noise. Maybe it's an off day or something, though, because that hasn't been the case. Today, I've accidentally slammed the door behind me. I've tripped on the stairs. My shoes sound squeaky. They've never been squeaky before.

Even the sound of my jeans, the *swish* of my windbreaker, the zipper on my bag—all sound loud as I creep past the mat. I didn't think I'd be sneaking out on Halloween morning to go chase down answers about the dead girlfriend of the guy I'm screwing over. But that's what I'm doing.

I want to make sure that this lead is real before I bring Sam into it. Also, because I don't know what kind of mess we'll be walking into today. If this guy was an operative for the Wardens way back when, then that could put Sam in some crosshairs.

I know I'm going to hurt Sam, but at least I can make sure no one else will.

I make it to the door. I'm pulling it open when—

"Vesper?"

I turn, looking sketchy as hell as I let the door swing shut and smile at Sam, who is standing by the lockers, pulling his sweatshirt over his head. He's probably been standing there the whole time, watching me tiptoe to the door like a freaking moron.

"Happy Halloween," I say lamely.

"Where are you going?" he asks, pulling off the sweatshirt. It pulls the white tank top underneath with it, and I see a sliver of his skin, where the muscles on his side pull to a V. There's a line of dark hair down his flat torso, disappearing into the waistline of his jeans. Some girls on the squad used to call that a "happy trail." And I suddenly get it. Because my cheeks get all hot and I pull my eyes away because I'm sure he knew what I was looking at.

Eyes. Look at his eyes.

I look up. And his lips are parted slightly, an eyebrow cocked. He for sure saw me. I freeze. He raises both eyebrows, and I realize he's waiting for me to answer him.

I don't have an answer.

At least, not without telling him everything.

"Out," I answer, turning to the door once more.

"Whoa," Sam says, and I know I don't have to stop at the sound of his voice. I can keep going, but something about the way it sounds—almost like he's hurt—makes me stop.

"I didn't know I needed to check in with you," I say, bristling at the way he looks like he's waiting for an explanation. I walk slowly toward him and keep my voice down. This isn't a conversation that needs any more volume than necessary.

I look at him, letting myself really see him for the first time in days. His eyes are bright under his furrowed brow, his face shadowed with light scruff.

He sticks his hands in his pockets. "You don't. I just thought . . ." he starts, and the words trail off as he smiles sadly and runs his knuckles over his lip. "You know? I have no right to be upset if you don't want to tell me everything."

His eyes are guarded, and the way his gaze searches mine just shreds whatever resolve I have to turn and walk away.

He walks closer, and with every step he takes I can feel

the air between us get thinner. The lights are on above him, bathing the curve of his bare shoulders in a white glow.

I want his help, and he's earned my honesty. Well, some of it, anyway. And those reasons sound noble enough that I can overlook the dark, pulsing truth that streaks underneath them like the beating heart of a vicious weed.

I step up, but my foot catches on the edge of the mat.

I pitch forward, and he lunges forward. I stumble straight into his chest.

Seriously? Can I be more of a cliché? *Help me, I'm stumbling and he'll catch me and I'll look up and look into his eyes.* They're green, ringed with gray—a gray and gold that catches the light as his eyes search mine.

And his hands are still on my waist, and he doesn't pull them away.

The moment where it is appropriate for him to pull back passes, and he's still holding my waist. He's still looking me in the eyes, and then his gaze drop to my lips.

For a moment—a corner of a moment, a sliver—I let myself blow onto the embers in my chest, just to illuminate the shape of the thing that has been growing in the shadows of my black, traitorous heart. Just to assess the damage.

How long have I wanted to be this close to him? Did it start the night of the coffee shop? Or the Beneath?

I try to shut the door in my chest. I try to stop the feelings from squeezing the air out of my lungs. I try to remind myself that in a few short weeks, he may hate me more than he's ever hated anyone. I don't want to distill these feelings into words. They're too awful. Worse than that. They're impossible. A stupid, impossible crush.

I'm going home. I'm going to make it so I never hurt anyone else again. This is impossible.

But looking up at him, for a moment . . .

It doesn't feel impossible.

And maybe I'm imagining it, but his hands are still on the small of my back.

My fingers curl against his chest.

For a minute, I let myself believe that this is simple.

He's just a boy with muscles and scruff and that tattoo on the back of his tricep is just a really bad teenage mistake, like our parents always warn us tattoos will be. I'm not a gladiator. I'm not a coward, or a life-ruiner. I'm just a cheerleader, and I've stumbled against him like heroines do in the cheesy movies Lindsay and I always made fun of.

And my shame is hot as the razor-sharp voice cuts through the poison fog I'm breathing in.

This is not your story, it hisses like white-hot steam.

Shame at the thought that I somehow have any sort of claim on him.

Shame at the thought that I still haven't pulled away.

But . . . neither has he. And I know the truth will hurt when I blink and this all slides out of focus. So I steal one more second, and then I pull back.

And here's the moment—I could do the right thing and leave him out of this. I could let him stay on the sidelines and handle this myself. Or I take him with me, bring him with me.

I take a breath, and I tell Sam.

"I found queen of poisons flowers in Elisa's things."

Sam's hands drop as he takes a step back.

"I didn't say anything because I didn't know what to say. I think it just . . . scared me."

Sam nods, processing what I've just said.

I tell him about the Scribe, and that chasing him down might be dangerous. His eyes widen. "So you were going to go do that yourself?"

I stop at the words, and a crushing realization comes over me. Yeah. Yeah, I was. I was about to face my worst fear chasing down a ghost because of . . .

Sam. I was going to do this for Sam.

I want to help him because I like him.

That's just the truth. It's sharp and messy and it's going to break me apart and run me over, and I'm still not willing to pretend I don't feel it.

This sucks.

"I'm coming with you," he says finally.

TWENTY-ONE

The morning of Halloween has always felt weird to me. Something about the way the light breaks, almost as though it sees what lurks at its edge at the end of the day, has always filled me with some sort of strange, heightened wariness.

So just imagine that weirdness put in a blender with four extra helpings of glitter, two seventy-two-ounce bottles of Monster Energy, and a smattering of fake blood—and you'll get a vague taste of what San Francisco is like this All Hallows' morn.

Especially down here at Nob Hill, where people are already lining up for the "Dark Legends of the Bay" tour on the sidewalk outside of the Nob Hill Cafe. The only parking is down the street, and we join the bustle on the tourist-ridden sidewalk. It's freezing, and the fog is thick, hanging over our heads like a threat.

Sam zips his jacket. "How are we going to get him alone to talk to him, assuming he's here?"

"I'm thinking," I say, smiling cordially at a stout older woman who has a camera bigger than her head hanging from her neck.

We reach the front of the door, where a man with a thin mustache and top hat stands talking to a woman in a deep purple dress slit up to her hip bone, exposing fishnets embroidered with bats.

I feel someone come up behind me and touch my back. I jump but turn and recognize Sapphira. She told me she'd meet us.

"Welcome, mortals," Top Hat says, "to the Dark Legends tour. We will be departing in a few minutes, so be sure to buy your ticket and collect your complimentary garlic strand from Zac." He gestures to a man behind him, who holds out a necklace strung with garlic cloves. Sapphira reaches forward and squeezes my hand. I know what that means.

I lean forward. "Sam. The guy with the garlic is the Scribe."

Top Hat continues. "We will leave from here and go directly to Huntington Park, Grace Cathedral, and many bloody spots in between before stopping back at the café— open exclusively for patrons of this tour—and Zac here will tell you all about the establishment's bloody history before you enjoy some *sinfully* delicious pasta or any variety of organic, made-to-order pizzas."

People bustle around us, and when I look back, Sam is gone.

I try to look around without looking panicked, which, by the way, doesn't work.

He left? He left. He didn't leave. He couldn't have just left. Top Hat announces that it's time to leave, and Zac disappears back inside the café. Sapphira and I meet eyes and hang back, letting the crowd slip around us as we step close to the building. It thins, leaving Sapphira and me looking sketchy as hell as we lean against the wall near the glass front door.

"It's open only for the tour. How are we going to get inside? And how are we going to get him alone?" Sapphira asks, her eyes widening as she realizes why I'm looking around. "Where's Sam?"

I'm about to answer when the glass door opens. Sam lets out a quick whistle, jerking his head to motion for us to follow him inside.

"How'd he do that?" Sapphira hisses behind me as I grab her hand and pull her after me through the glass door.

It's warm in here, and I almost let out a sigh of relief but stop as Sam pulls us into an anteroom to avoid two uniformed waiters as they walk by. We press our backs against the dark wood walls.

"How?" is all I say, and Sam shrugs. "Second-floor fire escape. I didn't want to draw attention by telling you so you could give it away with your glass face."

"So you just ditched us?" I ask, irritation mounting. "And I do *not* have a glass face." Why did I say that? Of course I have a glass face.

I know why I said it. Because there's a hint of a smile playing at the corner of his mouth as he shrugs, enjoying my faux outrage.

"I remember how stealthy you were at Aloa's."

"Um. I did fine, thank you very much," I shoot back.

Sam laughs, and okay, if that's how he wants to play this, then—

"Can you two please chill on the flirting for two seconds so we can find him?" Sapphira asks, sticking her head around the corner to make sure the coast is clear. She doesn't even realize what she just said. Her words are a knife in my gut, and the moment for a joking dismissal passes. I just stand there, mouth opening and shutting like an idiot as I stare at the vacuum lines in the carpet. Sam shifts next to me, and it's everything I have not to look at him. To try to read his face. I was not flirting.

Why did I think that? Of course I was flirting.

Sapphira crooks her finger and steps out into the main hall. The whole place is dark wood, stark emerald upholstery, and deep, plush carpets. We creep down the side hallway, and I can hear the distant clang of pots and pans in the kitchen. Sam follows behind me, and I'm too aware of the sound of his breath. The rustle of his black canvas jacket. The smell of the deodorant he threw on before we left.

We stop at an open door. Sam gets closer. I can feel him just over my shoulder. I turn my head slightly, and I know if I look back I'll be inches from his face. Sapphira peeks around the doorframe. She pulls back quickly, nodding.

"Let me," I whisper, volunteering. Anything is better than standing here with Sam's breath on my neck. You know, since every goose bump he elicits on my skin further damns me to that circle of hell reserved for girls who crush on dead girls' boyfriends.

I don't wait for a consensus. I step into the room. It's small—just a little office space. There are papers and Styrofoam cups littered about, and a glass door to my right. Zac is looking over some papers at a desk, and his eyes dart up, meeting mine. I swallow hard.

"Zac?" I ask.

He looks past me and then meets my gaze again. "Who is asking?"

"A friend of Elisa's," I say. I figure it's best to just cut to the chase.

See, this is an example of someone who does *not* have a glass face. He doesn't so much as flinch as I mention her name. After a moment, he carefully reaches out, splaying his long—too long, almost—fingers against the wood as he considers.

Then, quick as it takes me to think, *This is too easy*, he bolts.

Over to the glass door on his left, opening it and sprinting out.

"He's running!" I cry, scrambling after him. Sapphira and Sam clamor after me, and we all spill out into an adjacent hallway just as Zac turns the corner, and we take off after him as he cuts his way through the kitchen.

Shouts erupt as Zac shoves his way through the cooking staff, Sam right on his heels. Mozzarella balls and bowls of romaine lettuce fly, and Sapphira and I duck under a man holding a tray of frozen pizzas. "Made-to-order" my ass.

We spill out of the kitchen and take off up a back stairwell. Zac reaches the top landing, turns to take off down another hallway—

And there's a solid *whack* as an arm reaches out from behind the corner and clotheslines him straight across the chest. Zac's feet lift as high as his waist, and he lands on the carpeted floor with a *thud* and a tremendously satisfying groan.

Aldrick steps out from around the corner, a smirk on his face. He opens his mouth to smile, revealing plastic vampire teeth.

Sam stops as he reaches the top landing, but I stop on the stairs, Sapphira right behind me.

"You're *velcome*," Aldrick says in his best vampire accent as he turns to me.

"What the hell are you doing here?" I spit, feeling Sapphira freeze behind me.

Zac moves to get up, but Aldrick puts his boot squarely on the Scribe's chest and spits the fake fangs into an open palm.

"You said you were going to get coffee, but I didn't believe you. I wanted to make sure the girl I love is safe." He gestures to Sam and me. "Obviously I don't care that much about you two, but I'm glad you're not dead."

Sapphira steps forward, frowning. "You *followed* me? Who does that?"

"Yeah, who does that?" Sam asks drily.

"Can you get off of me?" Zac wheezes.

"No. Shut up," Aldrick snaps.

Yelling wafts up from downstairs—our stunt in the kitchen has alerted the staff to our presence. They'll be here any second.

And we can stand here in this thick, uncomfortable silence, but we don't have time.

"You two distract them, okay? Sapphira and I can handle this." I look at Sam, desperation clear on my face. We can't stand here any longer.

Aldrick raises a skeptical eyebrow. "Please, Aldrick," Sapphira begs. "I'll explain everything later."

Aldrick eyes Sapphira for a moment before taking his huge boot off Zac's chest. Sam pulls Zac to his feet.

"You sure you got this?" Sam asks lowly. I look back at

Sapphira, and she nods once, a smirk on her lips.

"We got this," she says.

Sam doesn't look so sure, but I nod again. "Buy us as much time as you can, okay?" He acquiesces, though I can tell he doesn't like the idea of leaving Sapphira and me alone with Zac.

The noises get louder, and Sam motions to Aldrick. They both head down the stairs, two at a time.

Sapphira and I shove Zac back against the wall.

He looks like he's about to yell, but I reach up and put a finger to his lips. They're moist. Gross. I thought this would be a power play, but now it takes everything I have not to shudder.

Focus, Vesper.

"I wouldn't do that, if I were you," Sapphira says, looking meaningfully at me. "You ever hear of a Combuster? They're like Chargers. But worse." And why shouldn't they be? I am 90 percent sure she made them up.

The Scribe's eyes widen as he looks to Sapphira. He's thinking about calling bullshit—I can see it in his eyes. But something about the word *Combuster* makes him take pause.

"You're lying," he seethes.

"You wanna find out?" Sapphira asks, leaning closer to his face. To drive the point, Sapphira raises her hands. The Scribe flinches.

I lower my finger and wipe it surreptitiously on my jeans.

I'm never doing that again.

"Elisa Littleton," I say. "She had umbra ink on her wall, and we know that you, Zac, are the man for umbra ink."

"I don't know an Elisa," he says lamely. Sapphira raises her hands again, and he flinches.

"Okay! Okay! I'm sorry. She paid me a hundred bucks to leave a note on her wall. I didn't ask questions, okay? I didn't want to know anything about Elisa's business."

My breath catches. "Why not?" I press.

He looks at me like I'm stupid. "Did you know Elisa Littleton?" he asks.

I keep my face blank. "A little."

"I stayed out of her way."

"Unless the Wardens told you otherwise, right?" Sapphira asks. I try to keep my face neutral as I look at her, confused. Why is she asking about the Wardens?

"I don't do that kind of stuff anymore," he says through gritted teeth.

"So they didn't say a word about where they were going? Didn't give a heads-up to their favorite messenger boy?"

What the hell is she doing?

"Elisa must've said something to you, Zac. Some hint about . . . something," I press.

I knew I should've invested more time watching *Law & Order*. This interrogation is going south, fast. But I have to snatch the questions back from Sapphira, because I have no idea what the hell she's thinking, asking about the Wardens.

Zac stares at me, and I bite the tip of my tongue.

"Answer her," Sapphira adds, locking eyes with me. Okay. We're on the same page, again. That's good.

Zac presses his lips together, and Sapphira leans in close. "Have you ever seen a femur after it's been pummeled by a Stoneskin?" she whispers. "They have to pick up the slivers of bone with *needle tweezers*."

"Shit, that sounds awful," I say, turning to face Zac with an exaggerated look of concern on my face.

"Okay! Okay, listen. I heard her on the phone talking to someone named Lynn about a meet-up."

"Lynn Holloway? The Seisma?" Sapphira asks, and I can't control how my eyebrows knit together. How does she know all this?

Zac shrugs. "Sounded like it. They were talking about a cabin in Big Sur."

"You've been there?" I ask.

He shakes his head. "No. But it was an old Warden safe house. We all know where it is."

"Draw us a map," Sapphira orders. Zac reaches into his pocket and pulls out a crumpled old receipt and a purple pen. He turns to the wall and scribbles on the paper for a moment. He turns back around and hands the map to Sapphira. She glances at it and then nods to me.

"Thank you for your cooperation," I say, reciting something

I heard from an action movie. That's what the interrogator said after stabbing a man clean through the hand. Not exactly like that applies here, but whatever. I'm stuck on the fact that we have a lead.

"Come on," Sapphira says, making her way down the steps. The shouts have grown louder.

We find Sam at the end of the hallway. Aldrick is in his Stoneskin form and has torn away the doorframe, jamming the door shut. Shouts rise up from the other side. Sam leans against the wall, arms crossed. He looks way too comfortable for someone about a hot second away from being arrested.

"I'm trying to pull! I'm telling you, it's totally stuck, guys," Aldrick says, shoving the beam deeper into the door with his granite arm.

"*Who are you?*" someone's muffled yell comes through the wall.

"We've told you," Sam shouts back.

Let's go, I mouth, but Aldrick holds up a finger, and Sam stifles a laugh. In the minutes we've been gone, it's like they have become the best of friends.

There's a beat of silence. "Okay, we just looked it up," the voice calls from the other side, "and a '*Mission Impossible*–style kidnapping birthday telegram' isn't a thing. We're going to need to talk to Zac."

"Are you kidding me?" Sapphira sputters. "Let's *go*."

Aldrick checks the door one more time, and we all run.

I squint against the daylight as we burst through an emergency exit and spill outside, but Sam grabs my arm when I stop to try to get my bearings.

"We've got to get away from here. They'll call the cops."

I blink. Blink, blink, blink as Sam pulls me along. Finally, my eyes adjust. Aldrick is leading. Sapphira is behind me.

We turn the corner and stop. We're at some sort of Halloween street fair.

"This will do," Aldrick says, reaching in his pocket before slapping a couple of bucks on a table and grabbing some plastic masquerade masks.

He hands them to us as he looks over Sam's shoulder. "Split up, meet at the end of the street." He pulls on a black mask that covers half his face.

We don't listen. Sapphira and I follow Aldrick. Sam starts heading the opposite way but changes his mind and runs after us.

"Aldrick," I call, shaking my head at a woman offering me a free sample of some pineapple drink.

He doesn't stop.

"Aldrick!" Sapphira yells.

"Not using my real name would probably be a good idea," he says over his shoulder. Sapphira passes me and reaches for his hand. It turns to stone as he yanks away and keeps walking.

"You have every reason to be mad, Aldrick. But *please*, listen to me."

He stops, but only for a second. I can see the anger glittering in his eyes as he looks down at us, then . . . something else. Sadness. We step back between two booths selling agave candy and dark chocolate raisins.

"I don't have a reason to be mad—that's just it. I have no claim on you, Sapphira. And yeah, I felt really creepy following you, because following you was a creepy thing to do. I just—"

"You wanted to protect me. And I wanted to protect you. We didn't want you involved in this, because it could be dangerous," Sapphira says.

"But you told Mr. Muscles?"

"His name is Sam. And you shouldn't talk," I say, motioning to his fitted gray T-shirt. "That's like the pot subtly accusing the kettle of steroids."

Aldrick shoots me a look. I look down at the sidewalk as droplets of water pepper the concrete.

"What happened to 'split up'?" Sam asks as he catches up to us.

Sapphira looks to me, and then to Aldrick. I swear there is brokenness in her eyes, too, as she takes him in.

She holds her hand out to him. "I'm sorry I lied to you," she says. He looks down at it and then takes it. They walk away, leaving Sam and me standing between the booths.

"Shall we walk, or just stand here looking sketchy?"

I don't want to leave them, but he's right. We can't just stand here. We walk together, heading back to his truck.

"So did you get what you needed?" he asks as we stop to look at a table full of ridiculously priced organic honey.

"He knows someone who might know where to find someone who was talking to Elisa," I whisper as we keep walking.

Sam nods, his hope cautious. My phone chirps, and I look down. It's from Sapphira.

   You guys go ahead.

Sam pulls me to the side, under a tarp overhang. I send a reply.

   You okay?

   Yeah. You guys go on. We'll get back.

I show Sam the text just as thunder claps overhead.

"We'd better go then," he says.

TWENTY-TWO

The rain comes down so hard that the truck bed roars, and I'm so thankful for the way it drowns out the metallic rattle of Aldrick's words in my mind and helps me think of anything other than the completely broken look on his face. I pull my legs up and rest my face on my knees.

"You okay?" Sam asks quietly as we stop at a red light.

I don't want him to ask me that, because I can't tell him the truth. I look at him with one hand on the wheel, his voice so genuine that it just makes me remember the lies wrapped around my ankles. I shake my head. He lifts his thumb from the steering wheel, and I know it's an invitation to say more, but I don't.

He looks at me, and I turn my face back into my knees.

Sam nods and whips a U-turn, and I bump up against the car door.

"What are we doing?" I ask, and Sam shakes his head.

"We're not going back to Duncan's. All this shit today, you don't need to hit something. That'll just get you more inside your head."

"Sam, we have a lead to chase down."

"In Big Sur. We can't get there until tomorrow. And we have to eat, right?"

The air is smoky, sweet, sizzling. It crackles like the breeze itself is caramelized around the edges, curling up like melted sugar. It's cold, but the lights strung up above our heads and heating lamps make it bearable. The rain has stopped, leaving just the smell of wet pavement and melted cheese. If there's a combination of smells to soothe the soul—this is it.

There are a handful of food trucks and tables, with people bustling around, licking sticky fingers and sipping frothy drinks. The air is alive with laughter and some distant music. It's far from the sound of shrieking or twisted metal. Police sirens. You know, the sounds I find myself becoming increasingly desensitized to.

"Okay. Twenty minutes, but then we need to get back," I start, but Sam shakes his head and steps out in front of me, turning around as he walks backward.

"No. If there's one thing I know . . . it's the burnout is real. We both need a clear head."

The wind bites at my cheeks as his eyes meet mine. I want

to hold this moment.

I don't want to steal it, this warm feeling in my chest that spreads across my ribs as he cocks his eyebrow. This feeling that things can be simple. That he's a boy and I'm a girl and we're walking. This feeling isn't mine to pocket, and I'm not going to. I just want to borrow it.

Borrow.

No harm in that.

I let myself smile.

"I can't believe you've never been to the StrEat Food Park," Sam says, staring down at me as I look around in wonder. We walk, taking in our different options. I could try dishes from about seven different countries. Considering I always found myself struggling to decide between a Chalupa Supreme or burrito from Taco Bell, this is going to take a while.

I snicker. "Yeah. It's not like I came to San Francisco for the best tourist attractions, Sam. I wound up here in the middle of the night by mistake."

"From where?"

Careful.

"I was in Seattle. I was up there for six months."

"So . . . you don't want to be here. Did you consider going home?" he asks, and he bumps into me slightly. "Indian food?" he asks, pointing to a truck. I make a face.

"Not my thing," I say.

"Going back? Or Indian food?" he asks, doing the

knuckles-on-the-lip thing again. I smile at the easy movement. I wonder if he even notices he does it.

I eye him. "You get what you want," I say, dodging the
question like a freaking pro, thank you very much. Also, he
should eat. It must take a ridiculous amount of calories to fuel
him. I don't want him passing out because I can't choose. If
he goes down, there is no chance of me catching him.

"No, that's not the point. Half the fun is choosing. I'm
going to walk you through this."

We pass a Thai truck and some stand offering organic
soybean burgers.

"How about you?" I ask. "Ever thought about going back
home?"

Sam lets out a soft scoff. "Ah. No. Elisa coming out here
gave me a push, but I was never going to stay in that town.
I just wanted to stick around long enough to protect my sisters."

"From what?"

Sam looks at me. He could tell me it's none of my business.
That would be fair. But he shrugs as he points to a pizza
truck. I wrinkle my nose, and we keep walking.

"My little sister, Cheyenne, um . . ." He stumbles over his
words. His finger finds the necklace he was wearing the night
I decided to let him sponsor me. "She's an Oddity. Was."

Was. My stomach sinks.

"Oh my God. I'm sorry," I say, but Sam shakes his head.

"No. It's not like that. She's alive. She was . . ." He stops walking. "She was ripped."

Sam sees the horror on my face and realizes he's not explaining well. "No . . . she's fine. Better than fine, actually. She was a Midasarene. She—"

"Could turn minerals to gold," I finish.

Sam seems impressed that I know. "Yeah. And my parents, well. They liked that, as you can imagine." There's a sour hatred in his tone. "They used her shamelessly. At first, it was just to get the creditors off our backs. My dad got into some . . . *trouble*," he says, and I know he's being diplomatic. "That's actually why I started fighting. It was all underground stuff, just to help. Not like the money was that good, or anything. I just . . . wanted them to leave Cheyenne out of it. I thought if I could pay things off quietly, they'd leave her alone." He sticks his hands deeper into his pockets and shakes his head. "Nothing was enough. We needed more. More cars, more status. More pieces of modern art none of us liked. I don't know when or how they stopped seeing her as their daughter, even when she did too much at one time and was hospitalized with exhaustion. Or when they stopped seeing my youngest sister altogether. But it was . . . it was a mess until she was ripped." He takes a deep breath.

I look down at my Converse as his world sinks into my skull. My dad's words echo somewhere in the back of my memory.

The Wardens did good things, once. My dad really believed they did. It has been easy to think of them as villains because of the stories I've heard. But I've also seen the fear of Baselines, and I know what that fear can do, because they don't like what they don't understand. The Wardens have done some messed-up shit, but they've also kept us a secret. And this is the first time I've looked in the eyes of someone who has experienced that safety firsthand.

"That's why you know all about our freaky little world," I say. Sam nods and keeps walking. I follow.

"After that, my sisters went to live with my aunt in Oregon. My parents let them go, because . . . well. My sister was of no use to them anymore."

The bitterness in his words is palpable, and I stop for a moment.

I point to the necklace. "She made that?" I ask.

He nods.

His eyes shift as he talks about them, and I recognize the love he's feeling. It's the same thing that I feel for my siblings. It's the same love that's made me desperate enough to want to do anything to have it back.

I swallow down the guilt I feel, shoving it low in my gut.

Sam points to Chinese food, but I can't think about food right now. I shake my head.

"When you said she was ripped, I was ready for the worst," I say.

"Why is that?" he asks, pushing his hands deeper in his pockets. "I mean, I would think that some Oddities would want their powers taken. I know Cheyenne did."

"*That* would be awesome, sure. But it's not that simple. Ripping is extremely dangerous. Trying to rip certain powers can kill." I say the words my dad used.

Trying to rip certain powers can kill.

Sam listens.

"My dad . . . ," I start, and then I realize I'm not quite sure what to say. I've never said the story out loud to anyone. I barely even let myself think about it. But something about Sam talking about his family makes me want to.

"My dad worked for the Wardens once." Sam stops, and so do I. The words sound bigger as they fill the air between us—not a musing or a memory but a fact that comes with consequences. "He was a Harbinger, like me, and when he couldn't do what they expected of him, they ripped him."

"That's barbaric."

"That's the Wardens," I say, looking at Sam as I make myself keep walking. "They wanted him to use his powers on a teenaged girl, Sam. They wanted him to punish a child. My father said no, so the Ripper ripped him, and then left him in some back alleyway in New York. They meant for him to die from the wound. It was only because someone found him and called a hospital that he lived."

Sam stops again, and so do I. His expression is grave.

"I'm so sorry," he says finally.

I swallow, blinking back tears as I remember my dad's scar.

"Rippers might have done some good, at some point. But they're the Wardens' favorite tool for torture, and from what my dad says, they have no love for Harbingers. We're unpredictable. Dangerous."

"That doesn't sound like you at all," Sam says, grinning slightly. I'm thankful for the smile. It means that we can be done with the heavy stuff, for now. And I very much need to be done with the heavy stuff. But I have one last question.

"Wait. Do you know where we could find that Ripper?"

I don't know why I ask that. Maybe I'm making contingency plans in case I lose the tournament. I'd risk almost anything not to hurt anyone anymore.

Sam shakes his head, though I can see he is still thinking about what I've just dumped on him. Sam gestures that we should keep walking but stops himself as he holds up a hand, like he has one more thing to say.

"I'm sorry, Vesper. I'm sorry that you've had to carry that, because it sucks. The whole thing sucks."

I don't know what to say to that, or to the way his gaze is boring into mine, or the way his shoulders are tight with the earnestness of his words. It's been so long since I've thought about how badly it all sucks—I don't know what to say. Or what to do with my hands. So I nod, because it's all I can do.

"We're pretty dismal conversationalists. We need an 'optimism only' option," I joke, and Sam smiles. I realize how rare it's been on him today, and that door I dead-bolted in my chest strains and splinters against the joy that smile brings me.

"You're getting better with your new special brand of mixed martial arts," he offers. "We're going to have to find a new name for mixing magic and punching."

"Let's wait until we see if it works first," I say, ignoring the dread pooling in my gut. "I don't even know if I trust myself to use it on the third night."

"Wait. Happy stuff," he says, pointing to a burger truck behind me.

"Perfection," I say, because it is. A burger. That's what I want.

I order a blue cheese burger with grilled onions, because it's perfect on two levels: it sounds delicious, and I will be forced to stay three feet away from Sam at all times so as to not kill him with my breath.

They call out my order, and I walk up to gather the tray. When I look back, Sam's writing in his notebook again.

"What is that?" I ask, walking back to his bench and handing him his double bacon cheeseburger.

Sam closes it, almost defensively.

I hold up my hands. "Sorry. Don't mean to pry."

But Sam stops, like he realizes he's overreacted. He takes

our burgers, and we walk, looking for the perfect spot to sit.

"It's just something I started doing after Elisa, when things were dark. Duncan told me to start writing down good things. Things to be thankful for. To keep them close, so I could remember them. Like the smell of rain on pavement mixed with french fries."

I want to ask about the dark. I want to ask if he's okay. But we're not talking about sad stuff right now. We're eating burgers. Sam leads me to a school bus that's been repurposed into a dining car. As he makes his way down to a table at the end, I gawk at how perfect this town is. How messy and strange and colorful and human.

I want to remember this. I want to write it down, so I don't lose a moment to time.

Sam and I eat in silence, because there is no way I'm coming up for air with this burger. It's absolutely amazing.

I make a really unladylike noise, and Sam snort-laughs into the straw of his drink.

"Should I leave you alone?"

I toss a fry at him, and he catches it in his mouth.

"This burger reminds me of the ones I used to get at Roger Mac's after games."

"Games?"

I swallow. We've been through so much together that it's easy to forget the he has no idea who I was before that night at Aloa's. "I was a cheerleader. Varsity."

Sam looks at me, and I hunker down lower in my seat, all of a sudden self-conscious. That girl was buried in ash years ago. It almost feels like I don't have a claim on her anymore.

"I can see it," Sam says, idly dipping a fry in ketchup he'd squirted haphazardly onto a napkin. Now I laugh.

"Is it the unwashed hair? The dark circles under my eyes? General aversion to talking to people? What gave me away?"

Sam looks up at me, and I don't like the way he stills, like he's considering what I've said. Like he's thinking me over and I'm getting all stuck in his gears.

What gave me away?

I don't like the way he breathes in like he's going to say something but changes his mind.

I don't like how I like it. I like it a lot.

"I think it's the name *Vesper.* It's unusual. I guess I always just associate cheerleaders with names that are . . . peppy?"

"Way to stereotype, jerk," I laugh through my burger, and he widens his eyes.

"Hey. Cheyenne was a cheerleader, and I've seen some of the stuff cheerleaders can do. No way in hell. I'd be dead four times over. Nothing but respect over here." It's a reverent tone, so I let him off the hook.

"Well. A name that means 'prayer' isn't peppy, you're right. I was born a few weeks too early and spent some time in the neonatal intensive care unit. My parents spent a lot of time, well, praying."

"Hence the name," Sam finishes.

I nod, pulling a pickle out of the burger and sticking it in my mouth.

"I like that. You were born a fighter. Suddenly it all makes sense."

"Does it? Sometimes I wonder if their prayers wouldn't have been better answered if—" I stop, realizing what I was about to say. Sometimes a thought is so familiar that I don't notice when it gets wings and slips past my teeth. Sam stops and looks at me. We said no serious stuff, but it seems like we can't stop veering into the marrow. The origins of all our scars.

"No," he says. It's simple, and it's the best response to that thought that I've ever had. *No.*

I force a smile. I want to get away from this topic. I want get to away from this heaviness. I need to fill this silence. "And what were you? Band geek? Mascot? Linebacker?"

"Wow. Do I have to fit into a box from *The Breakfast Club*?"

"What were you then?"

Sam considers this as he takes a pull from his drink. "I didn't really go to games, honestly. Elisa didn't go to my school, so we just kind of did our own thing."

There. Her name is back between us, a powerful breath puffing away all the unspoken debris that was piling up. I feel better and worse all at once.

Sam smiles as he looks down. "She got mad at me once,

because I just figured we weren't going to prom, which was good because I had too many detentions and was on some lame 'no fly' list. She was so pissed because she wanted to wear one of those ridiculous dresses. And get her hair done."

"Her school didn't have prom?" I ask.

He shakes his head. "No. She was homeschooled. I didn't realize how much it meant to her, so I spent two weeks straight in detention to get my name off that stupid list. And we only ended up staying for three songs." His eyes are far away as the memory plays itself out, and I don't say anything until he blinks it from behind his eyes and turns back to me. I see him then. His hair out of his eyes, looking sharp in a tuxedo with Elisa on his arm, her hair curled, her makeup perfect. I have no idea what she looks like, but still I feel like I can picture her. Them slow dancing, though I don't think of Sam as the type of guy who dances, so I'm sure they swayed from side to side. I wonder how his hands felt on her waist.

My cheeks are turning red. I know it. Abort. Abort. Say something. Say anything.

"You answered my question, though," I choke out. I grab my drink and suck water up the straw. "You were the detention guy."

"I was not."

"Oh, I know the kind of guy who had too many detentions to attend prom, Sam. The detention guy. You were Bender."

Sam stops, considering this. Then he sits back in his seat

like he's just lost an argument.

"Crap. I was, huh?" He laughs, and I toss him another fry. He catches it in his mouth and raises both arms in triumph.

"Ice cream?" Sam asks.

"Obviously," I say, gathering our trash. It's freezing outside, but I could never turn down ice cream.

We get gelato. I get straight chocolate, he gets mint chocolate chip, and we swap tastes as we walk back to the truck.

And I realize that that whole time, I didn't think about the third trial.

I have no idea how long it will be until I feel this again.

If I ever will.

So I savor it. The cold air running itself through every strand of my hair. The way Sam's breath puffs out against the cold. The way he laughs through a brain freeze, and I show him the trick where you put your thumb on the roof of your mouth.

I savor those borrowed moments as we ride home, the taste of mint chocolate still on my tongue.

TWENTY-THREE

I text Sapphira when Sam and I pull up outside the Grotto the next day, but she doesn't answer.

"I'll be right back," I say, unease pooling in my gut.

"I'll go," Sam says, but I stop him.

"I don't think they'll take kindly to a non-Oddity being in their space."

He drums his fingers against the steering wheel, and I know he doesn't like it. But he nods. "If you're not back in seven minutes, I'm coming in."

I walk down the dilapidated stairs and come out on the second level of the parking garage. I'm on my way to the non-elevator when I hear a car door slam behind me.

I duck behind a rusty truck and look out.

A black SUV is parked in front of the elevator. Sapphira steps out of the passenger side, throwing a black bag over her shoulder.

The windows are tinted, so I can't see who's driving. But then the driver rolls down the glass. Ananias rests his forearm on the door as Sapphira steps up and talks to him. I can't hear what she's saying, and I don't want to get closer.

Whatever I thought was going on, it wasn't something that would warrant Ananias driving Sapphira around. Didn't he have minions for that kind of thing?

She shakes her head, and he puts a hand on her wrist. A sinking feeling settles in my gut as I watch her pull her arm closer to her side.

"Sapphira?" I ask, stepping out from the shadow. I don't know if she needs help or not, but I can tell by the look on her face she's uncomfortable.

Her expression falters as she sees me standing there, like she'd hoped I'd stay hidden.

Ananias smiles as he turns his attention to me and steps out of the car in one fluid movement. He slams the door behind him and leans against the still-running SUV. He's wearing dark jeans and a white turtleneck, and he looks weird without a suit. I mean, I've only ever seen him twice, but he's the kind guy you'd think lives in a suit. Like that he even has suit pajamas.

"Aren't you going to introduce me to your friend, Sapphira?" he asks.

"We've met," I answer. His smile deepens as he waves me off.

"But that doesn't mean we've been properly introduced. And any friend of Sapphira's is a friend of mine."

He holds his hand out. I'm still, for a moment, because something about the whole interaction just seems . . . odd. But then again, I'm used to sleeping under highway overpasses. Perhaps I've forgotten proper nonrunaway etiquette.

I keep walking as I close the distance between us, reaching out to take his wide palm. Immediately my power snaps into his palm. I freeze, looking him in the eye to see if he noticed it. I haven't prayed in a long time, but I whisper out a panicked plea that I can untangle myself from him without something happening.

"Vesper, right?" his eyes are locked on mine as I fight to hide the fact that my power has fled up into his bones.

The power wraps around his hand and snakes up his arms, and I hear snatches of the edges of the memory of things. I catch glimpses of fear. *I won't let you do this*, a woman shouts.

"We didn't really get to meet the other night," he continues.

I won't let you, the woman screams again. It's not terror in her voice so much as *rage*. Her voice sounds shredded with it.

I nod at Ananias, forcing my lips up into a smile as I pull my hand back and look down, taking the moment to shut my eyes tight and order my magic to come back to me—preferably with nothing in its jaws.

I feel my power disentangle at my command as it slowly

slithers back into my palms and I breathe a sigh of relief.

"I'm looking forward to your next fight. The investors were intrigued by your . . . unique fighting style. They're very excited to see what you do next."

"Well. We'll see," I say, as the voice of the woman fades into the back of my mind. I chance a look up at Ananias to see if he noticed anything, but I can't tell. His eyes search mine, a hint of a grin on his lips.

"Let's hope." He turns his attention to Sapphira. "When will you be back?"

"Later this afternoon. We're just going to a movie and maybe lunch," Sapphira replies, shrugging as she adjusts her bag on her shoulder.

I keep my face unreadable, though there are questions zipping around my head. I know she works for him, but since when does that entail telling him where she'll be at all times?

He smiles again and then nods. "Be safe."

She nods and grabs my hand as we walk toward the stairwell. I don't turn around, but I feel Ananias watching us until we disappear from his sight.

TWENTY-FOUR

Big Sur is stunning—all forest green and sea blue rushing together, intertwined and not minding that logic says that land and sea are separate. It's enough to take my mind off things for at least a bit.

The trees, with their thick trunks and towering height, silence all of us as we walk through the forest. There's something truly sacred about this place, and it brings me a moment of peace.

Sam halts. I hear his footsteps stop and look up. It's a small cottage, poking out from in between the branches, leaning a little to the left. Almost like it was running and got tangled up in the trees.

"Should we . . . knock?" Aldrick asks.

"There's no need," a woman's voice sounds from behind us. We didn't hear her. I don't know how long she was there before she decided to say something.

We turn. She's slight, with dark skin and white hair cascading down her back in waves. She takes us all in through the sight of a shotgun.

"Whoa," Sam says, and he steps forward, inching in front of me. Yeah, okay. No.

I try to ease myself in front of him, and he grabs the back of my jacket and yanks me back. I want to cuss him out, but we've got bigger problems than his trying to protect me. Like, you know. The twelve-gauge pointed at us.

Sapphira holds her hands up. "We're not here to hurt you."

"I don't care. You're here. This is private property." Her voice is low and rich. The white hair threw me off, at first, but now I can tell she's in her late thirties, maybe.

I hear the cracking of Aldrick's skin, and I know this whole thing could devolve very, very fast.

Sam steps forward. "We won't take much more of your time than necessary, I promise. We just want to ask you about Elisa Littleton."

The woman considers Sam's question, parsing the words out without moving a muscle. Then she lowers the gun.

"You won't take any of my time. You'll leave, now."

She stalks between me and Sapphira, and then right by Sam. She walks toward the cabin.

I look at Sapphira. Truce. At least until we figure this out. We didn't come this far to just quit now.

Sam follows her, and I scramble on the dense forest floor to keep up. Aldrick and Sapphira come after us.

"Let me do the talking," I say over my shoulder, giving Aldrick a pointed look.

"Why are you looking at me?"

"Is your arm a concrete slab right now?"

"She has a gun," he retorts. "Excuse me if I'm a little on edge."

I wave my hand frantically to try to get him to hush.

We're on her steps before she turns around and levels us with a gaze. "You think I need the shotgun to convince you to leave?"

"No. I don't," I say. "Do you think we'd be following the woman with the shotgun if we had any other choice?"

The woman looks at me as she chews the inside of her cheek. Her shoulders lose tension as she searches our faces.

"What makes you think I know anything about Elisa?"

"You talked to her right before she disappeared. Zac told us."

I see irritation flicker across her eyes. "*She* called *me*," she clarifies. "I couldn't help her."

She opens her front door and walks inside. She moves to close it, but I stick my boot in the way.

Any sympathy she had evaporates like water on a hot burner, and she lifts the gun again.

"All right," Aldrick says, pushing his way forward and

shoving the door open with a *crash*. The woman stumbles backward, pointing the gun at Aldrick's chest. He grabs it and tosses it away. "You should've just listened to my friend, here, because she's way more diplomatic than me. So let's try this again. Hi! We're looking for information about Elisa."

We follow him inside.

It's a modest little place, with a furnace burning low in the corner, a bed against the wall, and a kitchen barely big enough to turn around in. We're all crowded in, our body heat filling the place like a violation. I don't want to do this, but I also don't want this trail to run cold. A piece of mail lies unopened on a table. *Lynn Holloway*, it says.

"Big mistake, asshole," she says, pulling a pistol from the waist of her jeans. Aldrick's back is turned, and he's not prepared.

My fingers rip with charge as I hold my hand out, letting the power flow as quickly as it can. I wish I could have more practice, but I already feel a difference—I am using this on purpose. I *called* the magic, it didn't just rip from me.

There it goes, a ravenous mouth careening toward the depths of Lynn's chest. I feel it sink its teeth into the pulsing, living fear in her center.

And I don't hesitate as I yank back. I'm terrified of what will come after, but the sight of a muzzle aimed at Aldrick overrides all my thoughts.

She staggers, dropping the gun to the wooden floor with a clatter.

And then everything goes black.

For a moment, everything is clear. I see a little girl with white hair, huddled in a closet. The air around her is pitch-black. Outside the door, people are screaming.

I blink, and the vision disappears. It's like there's been a blackout, but it's the middle of the day. I can't even see my hand in front of my face, and I can't hear Aldrick, Sapphira, or Sam. It's dark, and it's silent. I keep my breath steady as I take a step forward.

I hear a hiccup of terror in front of me, coupled with panicked, staggered breathing.

"Lynn?" I ask.

She turns, and I can see her—eyes wild, hands outstretched. She's terrified.

"What did you do?"

I look around. The darkness has covered everything in inky shadow, keeping us locked in a pitch-black bubble. Every fear I've ever pulled out has been a thing outside of me, but this is different. I am controlling this.

The room vibrates.

The excitement in my gut mixes with dread as I realize I am excited about this while she's terrified. This thrill of control comes at her expense, and I can see the complete terror etched on her face.

I remind myself that she was about to shoot Aldrick and that I didn't have a choice.

I take another step toward her, until I'm close enough to touch one of her hands. She jumps when I make contact, her gaze shooting around in the dark but finding nothing. I can see her, but she can't see me. Just like I want it.

The vibration turns to a shake, and I remember what she is—a Seisma. She controls seismic activity. Oh, good.

I grasp her hand tightly. Her fingers are cold and shaky. "I'm not going to hurt you, okay? None of us are. But you have to calm down, and you have to help us. Please."

Her breathing steadies. "You're a Harbinger," she says finally, looking over my shoulder.

I nod but then remember that she can't see me. "Yes. And I need you to tell me what you know about Elisa Littleton. Please."

My nerves are taut, stretched as they sustain the dark without letting it grow. The hum of the magic sings through my limbs, and I'd be lying if I didn't say the power made me feel really good.

"Is the 'please' supposed to make me feel better about you keeping me hostage in my own fear?" Her words are light, but her voice shakes. "You could take it, if you wanted. Torture me until you get what you're looking for, like the Wardens' Harbingers. They were monsters. It's a pity no one knows where the hell they are—you would get along with them."

I look at her—the wild fear shining in her eyes even as she forces herself to stand straight. She's looking at what terrifies her most in the world, and still she keeps her eyes open. She stands in its face, even though her clenched fists are shaking.

The vibration under my feet gets stronger.

This isn't who I want to be. With a deep breath, I let the power slip through my fingers, like the tether of a helium balloon. The darkness dissipates, and Lynn blinks as sight floods back into her eyes. She staggers, and the room around us reappears. The shaking stops.

"What the hell was that?" Aldrick exclaims, his arms out to the side. "You guys just disappeared!"

I don't look at him, or Sam. I keep my eyes fixed on Lynn. She makes no move to grab the gun on the floor between us, but stares at me in defiance.

"I am not going to make you tell me anything, Lynn. But if you try to hurt one of my friends, I'll do it again. I am not one of the Wardens' Harbingers. I never would be."

Lynn eyes me. "I've only known one other Harbinger to ever show mercy. It's not in your nature. And he didn't live long. If you flex like that, kid, you'd better be ready to go all the way." Hope flares in my chest as I see sadness in her eyes at the words.

"Are you talking about Brady Montgomery?" I ask quietly, saying my father's name for the first time out loud in almost a year. The words taste foreign on my tongue.

Her eyes widen. "How do you know him?"

I swallow hard. If I misread the sadness in her gaze, this could be a bad move. "He's my father," I say finally.

Lynn narrows her eyes at me, taking a deep breath through flared nostrils. "I don't know why the daughter of Brady Montgomery would go looking for the Wardens. You must have some deep love for Elisa."

I look at Sam, who meets my eyes. I look down quickly, not wanting my face to give me away.

"The Wardens are gone. We're looking for answers about a dead girl," Aldrick says. This is the first time he says it where it sounds like he doesn't quite believe it.

Lynn pulls a pack of cigarettes out of her back pocket and pats one into her palm.

She smiles at him as she plays with the cigarette with her tongue, moving it around like a joystick. There's something about that smile that makes my stomach turn, like Aldrick's conviction is cute or something.

"What did they want with her?" Sam asks quietly. Lynn turns her eyes to him.

"Didn't ask. Didn't want to know."

"Then why did she ask for your help?" he pushes.

"Because I used to work for Ivan," she says, her smirk widening as she sees the look on my face.

"Ivan Illeria? He's dead. He's been dead a hundred years," Aldrick says.

Lynn lights her cigarette with one hand. "The fact that you know so little about the Wardens shows that you shouldn't be messing with anything involving Elisa Littleton."

Sam shifts, and I put my hand on his arm. He stills under my touch.

"Fine. Let's say we believe you. How is Ivan Illeria still alive?" I push.

"I don't care if you believe me," she says, casting her eyes upward and blowing smoke through pursed lips.

"Please." The words fall from my lips before I can think about them. There's no answer if she decides to not give me one. It's a dead end after her.

She lowers her gaze to mine, considering me for a moment. I don't know what she sees in my eyes, but it softens her. She hisses smoke through clenched teeth and runs her tongue over her bottom lip.

"If Ivan sent his ilk after someone, they didn't last long after that. His daughter was a Ripper. A real rat, but he treasured her. Not so much because she was his daughter, but because Rippers are rare, as you know. She had this . . . tattoo on her neck in Hungarian that meant, 'The shadows are a sanctuary. The light is my knife.' She ripped things with abandon. Whatever her dad sent her to do . . . she did it, and she was good at it. We don't know for sure how he's still alive, but rumor has it that he had her pull immortality from a Perpetual and give it to him instead of put it in the Athenaeum, where ripped powers belong." She gives me a sideways glance. "And he made sure she and the rest of her kind took out all Harbingers who didn't want to use their powers for the Wardens."

I go so still, I think my heart has even stopped. This is the response she was looking for. I can tell by the way she puffs smoke up against the ceiling. "He said they were too dangerous. The first time they slipped up . . . he'd find them."

I clench my teeth, and I can feel Sam's eyes on the back of my neck.

Lynn runs her tongue over her teeth. "Still want to find them?"

It was my people he wiped out. My race he culled and put under his thumb. But I know my answer. I know which side of the wager I'll fall on. "Yes."

Because it's not just about Elisa, in this moment.

It's about staring down the monster from my nightmares.

I want to know if they're gone.

I *need* to know that they're gone.

Her eyebrows shoot up, and she squints at me. She looks back at Sapphira and Aldrick. Then, she looks to Sam like's she's deciding something.

"Elisa didn't need me. She wanted to know where to find the Chronicler. He doesn't talk to many people, obviously. We have a history, and I *might* know where to find him." She says *might* with a trace amount of venom that reeks of protective instinct.

"Take us to him?" I ask, trying to swallow the excitement I feel at the thought of the Chronicler being real.

She shakes her head, thinking. "He's fiercely private. You would need to talk to him somewhere where he'd be safe." She considers. "The Festival of the Queen of Poisons," she says finally. "You know it?"

"The one happening next week?" Aldrick asks.

Lynn nods. "Go to that. I'll talk to the Chronicler in the meantime. If I can get him to talk to you, then that would be the place. I can guarantee you only a place like that is anonymous enough to get him to come out for even that limited amount of time. I know him. Agoraphobic doesn't even begin to describe it. I'll find you there and lead you to him, but I'm warning you . . . you'll probably only get a few minutes."

I look back to Sam. His face is tilted downward, but he lifts his eyes when he feels me turn. He shrugs. *It's the best we got*, it says.

I nod as I turn back to Lynn. "We'll do it."

She nods and pulls another cigarette out of her pocket. "Now get the hell out of my house."

Aldrick opens the door for Sapphira and Sam and then exits himself. He looks back, but I put a finger up, asking him to give me a minute. I turn back to Lynn.

"What made you decide to help me?" I ask.

She blows smoke through her nose and licks her lips.

"Brady Montgomery got ripped for refusing to use his powers on me."

I'm still for a moment as her words sink in.

"My dad?"

She nods, looking down as she knocks ash onto her wood flooring. When she looks up, her eyes are rimmed with tears. She shrugs.

"You look like him."

TWENTY-FIVE

"Nope. You go this way, I do *this*," Abagail says, putting her leg behind me and flinging me to the ground. Sam told me to rest today, but I don't want to. I have scabs all over and bruises covering most of my arms. Abagail drops, covering my body with a full sprawl—legs out, so I can't shove her off. But the only thing worse than how much Abagail's takedowns hurt would be sitting around thinking.

I buck my hips as hard as I can and twist my legs, locking her waist with my feet before flipping her over and riding the momentum until I'm over her.

"Nice," Sam says from where he's sitting on the mat beneath the punching bags. His notebook is next to him, pen poking out from between the pages. He's got a cut across his eyebrow, a black eye, and countless scratches and bruises across his cheekbones, but he's fine otherwise. Roy throws his knife against a plywood board on the other side of the gym. Every ten seconds, a sharp *thwack* fills the air.

I close my eyes and the magic seeps gently as I loosen the leash and let it sink into Abagail.

She stops as she feels it. "I will *never* get used to that feeling."

"I got it," I reassure her, because I do. Since the blackout with Lynn, I've been testing the waters with letting my magic out.

"Good. 'Cause I'm not about to let you get off easy," she says with a smirk. She twists over me, getting me in full guard—wrapped from behind, with her feet hooked together over my waist.

I let the magic sift. Wade. Search.

In between things that feel too personal, too painful to exploit for practice—a slamming door and an empty bed—I find something workable.

"Shit, Ves. How you proposing to get out of this conundrum?" Aldrick's voice sounds from the other side of the cage. I open my eyes—he's eating a hot dog and watching me struggle to breathe like it's the funniest thing in the world. Sam joins him at the cage and smacks him upside the head.

"What?" Aldrick asks, affronted. "She said she needs help focusing with distractions. That's what I'm doing."

Sapphira has been working more lately, so Aldrick has been spending more and more time here.

"Like . . . this . . . ," I choke out. Then I tug on the tether connecting Abagail to me, and Abagail screams as she lets go. I turn just in time to see her pull a snake off her arm and throw it to the mat.

"Snakes?!" she shouts, looking totally betrayed as she scales the cage and sits on the top ledge.

"It's not poisonous," Wex calls as he comes up next to Aldrick. He has a hot dog, too. What, did they go get snacks to watch me get my ass kicked?

"Black next to yellow, it's all mellow." Wex points to the snake's stripes as it coils over itself.

"I thought it was black next to yellow, you're a dead fellow," Sam counters.

Wex shoves the rest of the hot dog in his mouth. "Shit, maybe you're right—"

"*Just get rid of it!*" Abagail shrieks from her perch.

This is the part I've been working on. I close my eyes, hold out my hands, and think . . . *It's only fear.*

I open my eyes just in time to see the snake evaporate into nothing.

"Need help down?" Wex calls to Abagail, and she flips him off.

"Nice job, Vesper," Roy calls as he throws the knife once more. *Thwack.*

"Not *nice*," Duncan says, coming out of his office. Everyone turns.

"You were too soft on her," Duncan says. "You'll do her no favors by pretending she's better than she is."

"Whoa, Duncan," Wex starts, but Duncan silences him with a look.

"Her form is all shoddy. Limp arms, and no follow-through."

"Sir, she just pulled a snake out of thin air. That's pretty badass—" Abagail starts.

"You *let* her get to that fear, Abagail. In the cage, the opponents won't be so simple to crack."

Okay. I don't know who took a huge chunk out of the middle of my fuse, but I'm super pissed at his attitude. Yes, he lets me stay here. Yes, he lets me train here. But I don't know what I did to him to make him so mad, and I'm sick of this.

"Then show me," I say. Sweat drips down my forehead. I'm in my sports bra, black leggings, and some hot pink wraps Abagail gave me when I passed the second trial. I'm sure I look like a joke to him. A recovering, homeless cheerleader.

He eyes me, and I hold out my arms.

"Teach me, then. Don't just stand there criticizing me."

Sam looks from me to Duncan, wariness on his voice. "Vesper . . ."

"No," I say, breathing hard. I point at Duncan. "Come on."

Duncan narrows his eyes. For a second, I think he's going to kick me out.

But instead, he pulls his shirt over his head. He slips gloves on and secures the straps with his teeth.

His biceps are as big as my head. How many times can I think *I'm going to die* before it becomes a self-fulfilling prophecy?

He opens the door to the cage and walks in, gesturing for Abagail to leave.

"Fight, fight, fight," Wex jokingly chants.

Roy stops throwing his knife and comes over to watch.

Duncan looks at me. All I get is a slight *You ready?* nod and we're off.

Duncan lunges, and I duck his strike.

He's on his toes.

"You can only run for so long, Vesper," he says.

I do a flying knee, jumping and aiming for his gut, and he swats me like I'm a fly, knocking me backward into the chain-link fence.

"Duncan," Sam says, his tone warning.

But Duncan swings again, and I barely avoid him. This time, I'm ready. I spin, letting the back side of my sparring glove smack him in the back of the head.

Aaaaaand I'm on my back.

I don't even know how that happened. Did I black out?

And he's over me. He didn't even break a sweat.

"And this is where I kill you, should I feel so inclined. You were so busy congratulating yourself that you didn't see me coming."

"I'm not going to die," I spit.

And his controlled veneer cracks, just for a second. "You're messing with things beyond human comprehension and you think you're going to walk away? You're going to get yourself killed. You're going to get other people killed by having inflated ideas about yourself."

That's it. I'm pissed.

I reach up and lock on to his chest. I don't delve deep—not into the darkest parts of him. I don't even dip into his nightmares. I slink under the skin, where I find the things that give the creeps. Things that make people avert their eyes or change the channel. Everyone freezes; I can feel the stillness around me.

He rocks forward, and I shove myself up, arms up.

Standing in the cage, by the door, is a mannequin.

Like, as in . . . something from the mall. It's bare: its arms cocked at its side, its head facing forward. One leg out, the other one back, just waiting to showcase an overpriced dress. And Duncan turns slowly, looking at it with utter horror on his face.

"What happened? The hell is this?" Wex asks. Roy twists the blade in his hand, eyeing the thing suspiciously. But Sam? Sam covers his face. "Oh no."

"Mannequins? You're afraid of *mannequins*?" I ask, letting out a little laugh.

I look at it. We all look at it, unsure as to what to do next. Should we take it to the dumpster? Personally, I think it would be hilarious to stick some gloves on it and keep it here as a souvenir forever and ever.

And then—

AND THEN IT MOVES.

It's head jerks to the side like it heard me planning to dress it up.

"*Shit!*" Aldrick screams, scrambling backward on the mat as Duncan lets out a cry—it doesn't sound that much different from that quick scene in the first Lord of the Rings movie where they're torturing Gollum—as he backs up against the chain-link fence.

The thing takes a jerky step forward, unsteady on its feet as it works its way closer to us. It looks like it's doing the robot—head moving from side to side with each movement.

"Kill it!" Duncan cries.

"It's not alive! How do you kill it if it's not alive?" Wex shouts back.

Abagail stands, openmouthed, as Sam pushes himself to his feet. Roy? Roy just stands there, his eyes wide as he fingers his knife.

Sam rips open the door to the cage and jumps on the thing, knocking it to the ground. Aldrick follows, and the limbs pop off and flop around the mat in wild protest. Wex kicks a leg as it rolls toward him. It goes flying toward Duncan, and he does a forward kick so hard that it dents the plastic.

Sam holds the shoulder joint of one of the arms and beats the torso with it.

Abagail laughs, unwinding her wraps as she straddles the fence.

Duncan kicks the torso with a sort of hilarious panic, like he can stamp the damn thing out of existence.

Sam stops, watching Duncan's frantic movements.

And then he starts laughing.

It starts small, like a snort. And then it spreads, taking over his whole body. Wex stops, too, looking down at the dented mannequin torso. His shoulders move. The laughter infects Abagail, too.

"You think this is funny?" Duncan asks through deep breaths. "My terror is hilarious to you?"

Sam doubles over. Roy pulls his knife out of the mannequin's head, and I see a smirk curl up on the corner of his mouth. I stand with my back against the fence, afraid to move. I do feel bad. It might be *hilarious* to us, but I can see the sheen of sweat on Duncan's forehead, and I know this was an ordeal. I can't laugh.

I shouldn't laugh.

Too late. I snort, but I do get points for trying to pass it off as a cough.

"Explain yourself," Sam says, gesturing to the mannequin.

Duncan runs a hand over his face. "I will do no such thing."

"Come on, Duncan. Do we need to talk about your fear of

the impossible beauty standards women face?" Abagail says, swinging the leg in her hand. Wex howls with laughter. The arm on the ground moves, and Duncan jumps.

"I was a kid, okay? I got lost in a store and the manager turned the lights out and I was stuck for almost an hour with these . . . things," he says with disgust. "I have had nightmares about them ever since."

"Dude, you were in war! Actual war," Sam says, running a hand through his hair, and he looks at me with the same kind of incredulous smile he gave me the first night we met at the coffee shop. I tighten my grip on the fence behind me. I grit my teeth and look down at the mat.

"That should say something about the kind of mannequins that were in that store!" Duncan protests. "Just get rid of it," he snaps at me.

I close my eyes and flick my wrist, and the mannequin disappears. It *worked*. I pulled a fear out and then put it back, *twice*, and no one is dead.

I smile over my shoulder, but Sam's back at his locker, turned away from me.

Wex says something to Duncan, and Duncan flips him on his back in the cage.

I make up an excuse about being tired and head up the stairs to the sound of Wex cracking jokes, Duncan threatening to turn him inside out, and the reassuring *thwack* of Roy returning to his knife throwing.

TWENTY-SIX

I'm in my bed.

My bed.

What?

I sit up.

My bed. This is the comforter with the stripes my mom got me for my fifteenth birthday. I can see the desk by the door. The bleach stain next to my vanity where I spilled nail polish remover on my carpet.

Home.

Home. I'm home.

And I swivel, putting my feet to the floor. My bare feet touch the floor, and the whole room explodes into flames.

I hear screaming, and I can't tell where it's coming from. Maybe me.

I push out of the room. I'm running through flames, but

they aren't burning me.

I hear Carmen screaming. I see my mom tearing down the hallway, calling for me.

I'm here, I shriek.

But she doesn't hear.

She doesn't see me.

And I can't want her to see me. This is my fault. I can't tell her this is my fault.

And then I'm biting my tongue clean through, and blood is dribbling down my chin.

My mom is crying for me.

Vesper. Vesper, answer me. Answer me.

And the flames get higher. Then, someone is walking up the stairs.

It's just a silhouette, but I know who it is, like you know things in dreams. I can feel the fear spinning in my bones. Ivan.

He opens his palm, revealing a queen of poisons flower.

He blows it, and a thousand purple flowers fall from the ceiling. They choke me. My mouth is full of petals and blood.

I fall backward, and the petals cover me. The flames surround me.

The screaming fades.

I sit up in my room at Duncan's drenched in sweat.

Tonight is night three. There's no way I'm sleeping anymore.

I go downstairs. I want to hit the bag, but I don't want to damage anything before tonight.

So I sit next to the punching bags, under the skylight that lets in the moonlight. When I stop moving, the truth of what I fear creeps up like the fog on the bay.

The closer we get to the answer of what happened to Elisa, the closer we get to the Wardens.

Footsteps sound next to me.

I jump when I look up and see Duncan.

"May I?" he asks. I gesture to the mat next to me, and he sits.

Silence.

I don't know what to say. *Sorry I pulled a dummy out of your subconscious, and I'm especially sorry that it turned out to be alive. And I'm sorry everyone heard you shriek seven octaves above your normal speaking voice.*

Nope. I think I'll just sit here.

"That first night you walked in here, I was ecstatic," he says. I go very still.

"Why?" I croak out, my voice still hoarse from sleep.

"Because I saw the way he looked at you. And I thought, for a moment . . ." He drifts off. I want to beg him to continue, but I bite my cheek. It won't help to know. It can only hurt.

"Do you know, I actually don't think about that night in the store that often anymore," he says, draping his hands over his knees. "It was kind of a surprise to see that thing yesterday."

"I'm sorry, Duncan," I say, and the words rush out of me, because it feels good to tell him that. I have felt increasingly guilty since I went upstairs. I just reached in and yanked something out that was *none* of my business. Just because I was pissed.

He shakes his head. "I mean, it *was* a dumb move. But I forgive you."

I look at him and it startles me, how easy it is for him to say the words.

He's quiet for a moment. "I knew one of your kind. A friend of mine in the service. Never told anyone but me, though. She died outside Mosul fifteen years ago."

And it's like I'm starving. Ravenous. I'm choking on questions. He knew another Harbinger?

I had my father, but that was different. He'd been ripped. I'd never been around a Harbinger who still had powers.

"How . . . who was she? *How* was she?"

"One of the best women I ever knew," Duncan says with a deep sincerity. "She had an interesting take on fear. Used it in combat. She thought that fear could actually be a beautiful thing, that fear was the mirror of your deepest love. Take the"—he has a hard time saying it—"the mannequins. Do you know why they scared me so much as a kid?"

I shake my head.

"Because I was alone. I was running around, the only sound the squeaking of my shoes on this polished floor. We were poor, when I was younger. I *longed* for some of the things I saw in shop windows. I *longed* to be one of the elite people who could afford such things. But then, that night, surrounded by thousands of dollars of beautiful things, I was still alone. With things that looked like people but *weren't*. And I realized, in that moment, at seven years old, how much I loved my family and how little the material things mattered by comparison. How much I wanted to hear my sister's voice or watch my brothers sneak in my room to steal my G.I. Joes when they thought I was sleeping."

His words are foreign, a balm that sits on top of my skin but doesn't fully absorb in. A nice notion—but not what I've seen. I've thought of myself as some sort of macabre party trick—a fucked-up Dorian Gray–esque thing—for so long that the thought that I would *add* something to someone's life instead of just showing them the deep, fanged parts of themselves is something I can't understand.

"But I came down here not to seek your apology but to give one."

I turn, startled. What?

"I have been cold to you since you decided to do the tournament on Sam's behalf. And I didn't really stop to think about why until today. Until I saw that mannequin and remembered that night in the store."

Duncan looks up into the moonlight.

"I don't see my family that often. Both my brothers died abroad. My sister, my parents—they handled their grief different ways. We scattered. But these people? Sam and Wex

and Roy? Abagail? They are my family. And I would do anything to protect them."

"I know." Because I do. I have no doubt.

"And if I thought bringing Elisa back was a good idea,
Vesper, *I* would have signed up to fight for Sam. *I* would risk
my life for his. I would *give* my life for his."

I stop. I don't want to hear this. I do. I don't. I do.

"Why don't you think it's a good idea?" I ask, my voice
small.

"Don't get me wrong. Elisa was a beautiful person. Giving, compassionate, and boy, did she *love* Sam. That's why I
think she wouldn't *want* to come back."

I stare at Duncan, trying to compute.

"What?" I want to make sure I understand.

He points to the poem written on the wall.

"'Invictus.' It was her favorite poem. One of mine, too, as
a matter of fact. She painted it on my wall. Without asking,
I might add." There's a smile in his voice, despite his attempt
at a disapproving tone.

My eyes rove over the words, though I've looked at them
so many times that they're burned into my mind. "'I am the
master of my fate, I am the captain of my soul.' Shouldn't that
mean that we *should* undo things?"

"It doesn't say that you're the master of time. Or of death.
Anyone who thinks those things is in for a rough awaken-
ing. No. It's not saying that we are the masters of anything
but ourselves. While it might seem really . . . arrogant? It's

actually very humbling. You control nothing but *you*."

"So you think there's a plan, then?" I ask, looking at the words on the wall. She had beautiful handwriting. Even on brick.

Duncan nods, motioning down to the tattoo on his forearm. There's a crucifix, surrounded by flowers. He looks at me. "So did Elisa. She believed in destiny. God. Whatever you want to call it—the Thing Greater Than Ourselves. Elisa and Sam stayed up till all hours of the night on that couch over there"—he points to a run-down sofa on the opposite side of the gym—"arguing about it. She thought there was a reason for everything."

"I know what it's like to sit in a waiting room and feel completely powerless. When my wife died," he starts, and I feel myself go very still next to him. "I remember the panic I felt sitting in that waiting room, knowing there was *nothing* I could do to change anything. I know what it's like to stand over a casket and feel all the rage a person can feel and know there's nowhere to send it. Nowhere to put it so I didn't feel it. All I could do was bear it, and the thought was almost too much. But that's what we do. We bear it."

"This is the opposite of a motivational speech, Duncan," I whisper, finally turning to him. He smiles, his dark eyes reflecting the moonlight.

"We're not supposed to do things the tournament is offering, Vesper. We aren't supposed to undo things. And this

Ananias has darker intentions than a good business venture. He wants people to think that Oddities can be the masters of the world . . . but we're not. We're the masters of ourselves, and no more."

I close my eyes and let myself remember the vanilla candles my mom would light before Bible studies. I picture Carmen trying on my dresses and Iris borrowing books.

I agree with Duncan's words, but the conviction doesn't seep down into my heart. I am starting to be able to control my power, and I would still do anything to have my normal life back. The desire is marrow-deep now.

"Letting go of that opportunity, though . . . it's easier said than done."

Duncan nods. "I know. But accepting things has its own power, you know. It's just not as alluring as control."

I think about this, but it sounds like bullshit. It sounds like something you tell yourself when you're shackled. Of course it's nicer to think you're more powerful that way.

Duncan clears his throat.

"Anyway. I just wanted to let you know that I'm glad you're here, Vesper. And I see more and more that you care about Sam."

His last words are measured, and I look over at him. His eyes search mine, and I get what he's saying.

He sees it, too.

My face burns.

Does everyone?

"I hope you do well today. I'll be praying," he says as he pushes himself to his feet.

"Thank you," I say weakly as he walks away.

"Duncan?" I call out, and he turns around.

"Do you think there are mistakes in the plan?" He tilts his head in confusion, and I clear my throat. "Do you think that God makes mistakes?" My voice shakes as I voice the question I've been carrying since I first felt the pulse in my palms.

Duncan looks at me, waiting until I meet his eyes to answer me. "No, Vesper. I don't think he does."

He walks away, and I stare down at the mat.

The moon illuminates the mat, and I can still see some remnants of bloodstains.

Though now, I can point out which ones are mine.

TWENTY-SEVEN

I know from the moment we step out of the car that this night is going to not go as I'd expected.

Sam calls the number, gets the address, and we pull up to a parking lot for the third trial. Aldrick and Mavis are there already, sitting next to a railing by a dock. Sam and I walk over to them.

It looks like everyone else is here. Toward the back of the pack I can see Carl, Briony by his side. Mavis sits next to Aldrick. I took the Duster's spot when I bested her time at the shipyard. There are only four of us, now, and there will only be two by the end of the night.

"Baselines wait over there," Mavis says, pointing to a warming tent that was set up across the loading area. It's not so much of a *just in case you're cold* suggestion as much as it's a *kindly fuck off*.

"He's fine," Aldrick says, and Mavis shrugs.

"I have a bad feeling about this whole thing," I say, solidifying myself as the patron saint of *no duh*. I hadn't let myself really think about who I might be fighting tonight, but looking at everyone makes it impossible to avoid. Either I'm fighting Aldrick, Mavis, or Carl. This is a lose-lose-lose situation.

Someone claps twice behind us. "Hop to, my little mutant freak chickadees. Time to go make the monies and do all the traumas, yada yada yada." Tessa.

So that's how I am on this boat. We all walk on board. It has a cover, almost like a ferry. Along the side, the name reads *The Victoria Marie*.

I lean on the railing, the raw wind whipping at my cheeks as we speed off to God knows where.

Sam appears beside me, two cups of steaming-hot coffee in his hands.

"Here," he says, handing one to me.

I take a sip and make a face.

"I know. I can't tell if it's coffee or the chemical they were using to clean the machine," Sam says.

I don't care. I choke it down. It's warm.

We're silent. He could be up with Ananias's investors on the upper level, enjoying hors d'oeuvres and champagne. But I'm glad he's next to me, on this freezing deck.

"Listen, Vesper," Sam says. My heart does this skippity-flip-skip thing, and I don't know if I want to hear this.

And then, I see a dark outline. I know where we're headed.

"Oh my God," I whisper.

Alcatraz.

We're going to Alcatraz.

They separate us the second we pull up to the island.

"Baselines to the observation deck," Tessa says, eyes still glued to her phone as she waves her hand at Sam. He reaches over and grabs my hand.

"You can do this."

I nod, because what else can I do?

I can do this. I can win and then betray him to undo my powers. I am starting to believe I *can*. Can isn't the hardest part anymore. The reality of betraying someone I care about is.

Sam goes left with the other sponsors while Tessa leads the rest of the gladiators up a walkway.

The dark clouds swirl almost purple overhead as I look up. The main prison looms over us. They taught us about this place in school when we had to present on national parks. I've always wanted to visit this place.

But I mean, not necessarily like this.

How Ananias got the okay to do this—I almost don't want to know. If I had any doubt that he has the powers that be in his pocket . . . they're gone now.

"I'd hate to be redundant, but I would like to go on record

that I agree with your 'I have a bad feeling,'" Aldrick says as we walk up to the main building.

I look past him at Mavis, who eyes the barbed wire and abandoned guard towers with the closest thing to fear I've ever seen on her face.

Tessa leads us to Cell Block A, and it's as creepy as I've always imagined. The air is cold and musty, and it feels like it's still and alive at the same time. Don't ask me how.

We aren't friends—we all know that. But there's something primal about the dark of this place; like it's a living, breathing thing that doesn't like being seen. We're all huddled together, our backs pressed against each other.

We all stop as we see it.

In the middle of the lower cell block—someone has set up a cage.

As we get closer, a soft rumble of noise wafts down from the upper levels.

"The investors are up there. How the hell did Ananias pull this off?" Aldrick asks. I look up—there are a lot more people than there were at the shipyard. Word must have got around about Ananias's venture. I scan the crowd, but I don't see Sam. I know Sapphira must be around here somewhere, but I don't see her, either.

"Okay, so—the cells have water bottles and snacks in them . . . you can just chill in there until we call you," Tessa says, looking down.

"I'm sorry, you want us to go into the cells?" Mavis challenges.

Tessa looks up from her phone, annoyed. "We're not *locking* you in. Calm down. There's just not a lot of space in here. The floor plan sucks."

"It's literally a prison," Aldrick answers back, but Tessa is back on her phone. Mavis, Aldrick, and I take a cell. Carl and Briony take the cell next to us. Mavis jumps on the top bunk, and Aldrick sits on the lower. I can't relax, though. The paint is chipping, and the metal is rusted. The walls feel like they're soaked in despair. Like it's a palpable thing here. I lean against the bars and look out the small window at the fog rolling over the bay.

"I never thought I would be praying to fight Carl," Aldrick says eventually.

"Don't get sentimental on me now, Aldrick," Mavis says. She props her feet up on the wall and lies so her hair hangs over the edge of the bunk.

"I'm not sentimental. I just happen to know if I kill you, the kittens on the bluffs will have to go without food."

Mavis sits up and looks over the edge. "Who told you about that?"

"You could just bring them inside, you know. Joey and Lucy would be so stoked," Aldrick answers.

Mavis huffs and turns around, lying back down and crossing her ankles on the wall.

"That's really cool, Mavis," I say, knowing full well that this contribution to this conversation will probably only make her hate me more.

She looks at me from her upside-down position, her eyes narrowed. It doesn't surprise me now, actually. I saw the look on her face after her fight with the Slitter. Hurting him broke something in her. She pulls her gaze from me and stares back at the ceiling.

It's too quiet. The hum of the investors speaking is making me even more nervous.

"What are you fighting for, Aldrick?" I press. If we're paired together, I might not want to know the answer to that question. But right now, I need something to fill the silence.

"What part of this situation makes you think that this is a good time to bond?" Mavis shoots at me, sitting up.

"If I'm up against Aldrick, I'm not walking out of that cage. Maybe I want to know what I'm getting flattened for," I reason.

Mavis smirks. "Fair enough. Answer the girl, Aldrick. I'm curious, too."

Aldrick looks to me, taking a deep breath. "If I win, I'm going to undo something I did when I was fourteen."

"Specifics," Mavis barks.

Aldrick kicks the mattress from below and Mavis jerks upward, barely managing to stay on the bed.

"I was getting there," he says. He looks to me, again, rolling his eyes.

"My family has this long-standing feud with a family of Miasmas across town, back home in Samoa. It's always been a thing—even when I was little, I knew we weren't supposed to talk to them. So when I was fourteen, my Stoneskin abilities showed up for the first time, and I thought I was a badass. There was this Miasma—he was about seventeen, at the time. He was badmouthing my family outside a restaurant, and—" Aldrick stops, working his jaw from side to side. "I hurt him. Badly. I was a hero to half my family, after that, even though I knew what I was doing was wrong. I knew it was wrong as I was doing it."

He falls silent, and I brace myself for a snarky comment from Mavis, but even she is quiet.

"Go ahead, Mavis. Your turn," Aldrick says finally. Mavis turns over onto her stomach, perched up on her elbows.

"I was playing the piano at church when my powers manifested for the first time. A thousand people in my small Southern town saw the piano turn to dust in the middle of 'How Great Thou Art.'"

"That sounds kind of badass," Aldrick says.

"Really?" Mavis asks, her tone sharp. "Yeah, it was badass to go from head of the prom committee to a complete pariah overnight. It was pretty badass when all my former 'friends' started calling me 'the Priestess' and making crosses with their fingers when I walked by. Real badass to lose every-thing."

"I'm an ass. That sounds awful," Aldrick says. Mavis nods.

"It was. I mean, not everyone was a dick. A lot of people from church understood that my magic didn't change who I was. But it was . . . a small number," she says. Her voice is smaller than I ever heard it.

"So you want to reverse . . . ," I say.

She looks up at me. "I want to reverse them all being born," she spits. She holds her menacing expression for a moment before devolving into laughter. "Wow, I can't believe you fell for that. No, I'm not killing anyone. I want to reverse where my powers manifested for the first time. I want what I am to be a secret."

"You don't want to just . . . change being a Demo?" I ask, almost too quickly.

Her eyes flash as she smiles. "Hell no. And I actually like the name Priestess, too. I just . . ." She pauses. "I want my parents to be able to live in peace."

It's quiet, and a low roll of laughter trickles down from the rafters above.

"Priestess. It suits you," Aldrick says finally.

Mavis nods, and then points to me. "Go."

I wrap my hands around the bars behind me. "I'm going to bring Sam's girlfriend back from the dead," I say, trying to make my voice as strong as I possibly can.

"The hot one? Why would you do that?" Mavis snorts.

"We're just friends. I'm taking the money, and he's getting her back."

I make the mistake of watching Aldrick's face as I answer. He cocks an eyebrow. "Just friends?" he asks.

"Yup," I retort.

He licks his lips and smiles. "Okay."

All of a sudden, the lights go out.

The creak of metal doors shrieks through the otherwise quiet cell block. I thought I was maybe getting braver since my time on the run, but here, in this tiny little cell, I realize I can still learn things about myself, surrounded by pitch-black.

And then, I see it.

Glowing red eyes, peeking out from across the cell.

I'm about to bite back a scream when I hear Mavis's laugh.

"Mavis!" I cry, throwing a hand to my chest.

"What?" she asks, feigning innocence.

A spotlight illuminates the center of the cage, where Ananias now stands with his hands behind his back, a smile on his face. I step up to the door, lacing my fingers over the bars.

"Alcatraz. A place for the unfit. A home for the unwanted. A cage for the unworthy."

My fingers tighten on the metal as I hear his voice slip through the dark.

"What a fitting place for our third night—the trial that will determine which of you will get to the finals. Because we don't have to live in bondage anymore," Ananias says, looking up at the sponsors lining the second-story railing.

Ananias smiles and claps twice. "Shall we?"

The investors erupt in cheers, and Tessa jumps up to call names—

Aldrick versus Mavis.

My heart sputters at the thought, knowing I have to fight Carl while also imagining the horror of Mavis fighting Aldrick.

Mavis smirks at Aldrick as she stands. "Shall we?" she asks, gesturing to the open cell door.

Aldrick steps out of the cell to the sound of raucous applause, and Mavis pauses before she turns to me.

"If I get my ass kicked, tell Sapphira that the kittens are under the old lifeguard station," she says.

"I will."

"And that if anyone touches my peppermint creamer in the fridge I will turn their sorry asses to dust when I come back."

I give her a salute, and she flips me off before stepping out of the cell.

Part of me thinks it would be a good idea not to watch, but I know the cheers will just make me imagine the worst.

Aldrick and Mavis face each other in the cage as Tessa

introduces them. The crowd cheers as Tessa signals for the fight to start.

Mavis and Aldrick move toward the center. Mavis takes her gloves off with her teeth, tossing them to the side. Aldrick throws his arms forward, and they crack into stone.

I look up at the railing above, wondering if Sapphira is watching this, too. I almost hope she's not.

Mavis leaps toward Aldrick, but he dodges out of her way. The moment she lands, he slams his hands down on the mat, causing the ripple effect to send her sprawling against the chain links. Her eyes light up red as she pushes off the pulsating links, cracking her knuckles as she launches herself at Aldrick once more. He spins, turning his arm back to its normal skin as he knocks her back.

He didn't use his Stoneskin form. He didn't hurt her as badly as he could have, and her eyes widen at the realization.

"Don't you dare go easy on me," she hisses at him. She swipes her fingers across his chest, turning his shirt to dust. He looks down at his bare chest and then back up to Mavis. The crowd cheers, and Mavis snarls at him.

He snaps back into Stoneskin form and charges her, throwing a left hook and then a right hook, bobbing her swipes. He grabs her hands in his rock-hard grip, and he can't quite get her fingertips to the stone.

She jerks back, kicking him in his still-human stomach. He doubles over, and she frees herself from his grip, spinning and swiping at him one more time, her fingers scooping nothing but air as Aldrick jumps back.

She throws herself at him one more time, and he catches her forearms. She pushes her fingers closer to his neck.

Aldrick strains. He'll be weaker when he loses his Stoneskin form, and Mavis knows it. She just has to wait him out.

Her hands get closer and closer, and Aldrick starts shaking.

I turn around, not wanting to see what comes next. But just as quick, I spin back to the front.

There's a crack as Aldrick slips out of his Stoneskin form. Mavis wraps her legs around his torso, her arms still trapped in his grip as she gets even closer.

Aldrick grunts, straining and losing ground.

I can't believe for a moment I thought Mavis had a heart. But she knows if she touches him in the neck, he will die. And she's still going for it.

I grip the bars as hard as I can, pressing my face between them as I watch.

She's an inch away when she stops.

She locks eyes with Aldrick, and I see something shift in her then. Something passes between them. Aldrick shoves back, and she *lets* him. I don't know if everyone else can tell from up above, but I see the disbelief in Aldrick's eyes as Mavis loses ground and then falls back as Aldrick snaps into Stoneskin form once more. He steps over her, his granite fist curled. Mavis looks up at him, her chest heaving.

Aldrick raises his stone fist, but then stops.

He lowers his arm as he looks down at Mavis.

"No," he says. He looks up at the crowd peering over the railing. "No. I won't do this."

Aldrick reaches down. Mavis secures her glove and then takes his hand. He heaves her to her feet.

"Mavis advances," Aldrick calls, holding Mavis's shocked gaze.

She smiles at him, and tentative applause rings out over the balcony. Mavis and Aldrick turn toward the cage door.

Ananias steps forward, leaving the shadow of the balcony.

"I'm afraid that's not how this works," he says. The applause peters out, echoing sadly in the cellblock.

"If you refuse to finish the match, then you forfeit, according to the contract in the Ledger." His voice is cold—mercy does not make for a good fight. "And so will Mavis, since she pulled her punch at the last moment, deeming her unworthy for this stage of competition."

Mavis opens her mouth to argue, but Aldrick puts a hand on her shoulder.

She swallows back whatever she was about to say, and they step out of the cage.

It was the first bit of kindness—of humanity—I've seen in this competition. And it cost them both the chance of a lifetime.

I watch them step out of the cage. I want to say something,

but Tessa calls my name and announces what I already knew. I'm up against Carl.

I walk up to the cage stairs, and Aldrick helps me secure the wraps around my wrists.

"What was that?" I hiss, referring to his fight.

He shakes his head. "Focus on what you need to do right now, which is kicking that creep right in the ass."

I nod. Aldrick bumps his fists against mine. "You can do this, Vesper."

That's when I see it—he knew Mavis would back down when he did. He wanted to clear the path for me to win.

I open my mouth to say something, but Aldrick shakes his head. "Focus, Vesper."

I nod again.

As I walk up the stairs, I do what Aldrick told me. I focus.

I am closer to the end than I ever thought I could be. I'm closer than I ever thought I could be to ending this terror that lives just beneath my skin. Then I can go home. I can get my life back.

That's what I tell myself as I march across the springy mat to my side of the cage.

I am going to get my life back.

I take a deep breath as Carl smirks at me, his eyes glittering with something between hatred and amusement. A roaring fills my ears as I remember the last fight we had— the helplessness and fear.

Then, something clicks inside of me. The last time I faced him, I was a different person. I was more afraid of what was coiled in my chest than I was of him. My hands shake as the magic hums through me, scraping against the underside of my skin as it reaches for him.

I don't hear Tessa's voice. Carl is still staring at me, so I close my eyes. *It's just fear.*

Then, Tessa raises her hand and Carl hurtles across the cage, letting the stingers descend from his hands, splitting the ACE bandage he has wrapped around one wrist.

He screams as he runs toward me—he's hoping he can scare me into freezing up.

He's wrong.

I sidestep, throwing him to the chain-link. He turns, sneering as he holds up his fists. I'm ready when he throws a jab. I duck, throwing a left hook as I come back around. It catches him right in the jaw, sending a shock of fear through him, just like I'd practiced with Abagail. He staggers backward, his eyes wide as he struggles to catch his breath.

The fear fades from his eyes, replaced by fiery hatred. He lowers the stinger from the underside of his wrist, its black point gleaming with a green liquid. He rushes me again, the stinger launching at my head. I roll sideways, taking my feet. I spin and hit him in the gut with a roundhouse kick. Fear jolts him back from the impact, throwing him against the fence, the stinger limp at his side.

He blinks, fighting the terror that momentarily over-takes him as he shoves himself up to his feet. With a growl, he throws his arm out, his stinger whipping past my head while he jumps forward, swinging his fist at my face. I catch it, careful to avoid his stinger as I twist it behind him and kick behind his knee to knock him to the ground. The crowd shrieks with glee, and I feel a swell of pride.

I throw my weight back as I wrap an arm around his neck, bringing him into full guard as I wrap my forearm over his throat and grip the inside of my opposite elbow. If this lock can make Aldrick tap out, it's good enough for Carl.

I look up at the overhang. I don't know how I can make him out in the dark, but I see Sam. He's crouched before the railing, hanging on the middle bar with one hand—the other is on top of his head as he watches.

Carl grunts under me, spit flying from his lips as he struggles to get free. His free hand flies up to my arm, but I grab his wrist and pin it to his chest, rendering his stingers useless. Just a few more seconds and he'll pass out.

My magic reaches out and sifts around his chest. I can feel it searching, plucking at different memories, different fears. His mother's voice fades into a monster taking lurch-ing steps down a dark hallway. Blood. Taunting faces on a playground. Back to his mother's tinny shriek. But I know now that here's something deep past his ribs—something that will paralyze him.

My magic shifting through his chest makes him squirm, just like it did with Briony, and I use it to my advantage, tightening my grip.

I pull back out. This will be over before I need to pull any fears out of him.

A small, angry poke bites into the underside of my wrist, and I yelp.

What was that? I look over Carl's shoulder at his stinger. I can see it, so where did that pain come from?

My mind gets hazy, like I'm being pulled backward from my thoughts. The shouts of the crowd separate from the spotlight beating down on me. Then, I'm letting go of his neck and falling backward, and he's lurching to his feet.

I shoot up to my feet. Or I think I'm shooting up to my feet. It's taking a while. I'm upright, but then I lose my balance and stumble against the chain-link, the metal biting into my fingers as I stop myself from careening to the ground.

Everything spins as I watch Carl wipe his mouth with the back of his hand. The light glints off his wrist wraps, and then something registers in the warm haze settling over me.

A needle. He hid something in his wraps, and he's drugged me.

Carl stalks forward, his smirk deepening as he sees the stuff taking effect. I shove off the cage wall, but he backhands me down to the mat. The rusty taste of blood fills my mouth. It splatters against the off-white floor of the cage as I cough, pulling myself up to my knees and elbows.

Carl kicks me, hard, and I roll over.

He's standing over me, and I put my hand up, letting my magic streak toward him. I grab a hold of his chest and pull the first thing I can find.

His mother's voice fills the cage, and it sounds very far away.

But I see the horror in Carl's eyes as the noise rains down from above.

"Carl Jeeves, you piece of *shit!*"

Carl's eyes widen as he looks around, terrified. Then he turns his gaze to me, and his face is pure rage. He drops to his knees over me and puts his hands over my throat.

"*Stop it!*" he screams.

I want to slap his hand away, but I can't. The voice in the cage fades back into me as I gasp for breath. I can't find the tether between us anymore, and what I pulled out wasn't that strong to begin with.

Everything slows as Carl's grip on me tightens.

Not like this. It won't end like this.

I put my hand up, focusing my last bit of strength into the whip of fear I lash against his chest. He staggers back, letting go of me. I scramble up, pressing my back against the fence to keep myself upright, and then I see it—the thing I pulled out.

The closest thing I can compare it to in my hazy mental state is a zombie. It looks like a zombie, anyway. It's a human-like monster thing that seems like it was once a woman. Her left shoulder hangs like it was broken at the joint, and she shuffles her feet. Her blond, stringy hair hangs down past her shoulders, and she groans. It's a rattly gurgle, like she's choking. Then, there's a second one. A man, this time, in a tattered football jersey, his rotten skin showing through tears in the fabric. They start walking toward Carl.

I pull myself up, my fingers pulling on the chain links as I stand.

"What did you do?" Carl asks in a terrified whisper as he scampers across the cage, trying to get away from the shuffling creatures.

"What are you afraid of, Carl?" I ask, my vision blurring as I push myself to my feet. My tongue feels numb, but I still have a grip on the fear. I twist my wrist, and the zombies move closer to him. He screams and throws his stinger out at the woman creature. He hits his mark with a disgusting *thunk*, but it does nothing to slow her down.

"You bitch!" he screeches, reaching out and kicking the jersey zombie in the stomach. It staggers, but it keeps going.

A heaviness starts in my chest, pulling me down to the mat. I slide back down against the fence. Carl clears a path toward me, a sneer on his face as he pulls his arm back, ready to launch his stinger at me once more.

I twist my wrist, and more zombie creatures appear. Carl lets out a growl of frustration as he uses his stinger to fight them off. This is buying me time, but I don't know how long I can keep a hold of this fear. The tether I have on it feels like it pulses in and out as the poison settles deeper into my veins.

Then I hear a voice. Sam.

"Vesper!"

I turn my head. Sam is at the cage door, but two of the bouncers are holding him back. His face is twisted in agony as he screams and fights them, trying to push them off.

Trying to get to me.

If he touches the cage, then I forfeit. It's all over for both of us.

It's all over for me, anyway, the voice in my head chimes in slowly.

Everything implodes. The investors' deck erupts in shouts, and someone—maybe Tessa—is saying something over the loudspeaker.

"Time-out," Tessa announces.

I exhale at the thought of a reprieve, and I hold up my hand. Despite my feeling of complete weakness, the fear obeys. The zombies all freeze.

Then Aldrick shoves one of the bouncers away and Mavis reaches up to put a finger to the cage lock. It crumbles under her touch, and Sam rushes in. In one swift movement, he has

Carl by the neck and shoves him back against the cage.

"What the fuck did you do to her?" he yells.

"Guards!" Ananias's voice sounds from above. I hear the clicking of guns.

"Sam!" I bark out. My tongue still feels numb.

"Winning, asshole. Deal with it," Carl spits back.

Mavis pulls her gloves on and helps me sit up.

Ananias strides into the cage. With a snap, the guns above us lower. He looks at the zombies with interest, leaning in to inspect them.

"A Harbinger," he says, his voice full of awe as he looks back down at me. I meet his eyes, which are alight with something I haven't seen in them before. He looks genuinely excited.

"Tessa, would you please escort our guests to the yacht for intermission?" he asks. There's a shuffle above us as the guards lead the investors out. Once the door behind them closes, Ananias's smile drops. I chance a glance upward.

"There has been an accusation of unsportsmanlike conduct," Ananias says, stepping around the female zombie to get a better look at Carl.

"They're lying," Carl spits.

Sam reaches into the folds of Carl's wraps before Carl can stop him. Sam holds a small syringe up to the light. "Last I checked, Chiggers didn't manifest their powers via medical-grade syringes," Sam hisses as he steps closer to

Ananias, still holding the syringe up between their faces.

Ananias eyes the syringe, and then looks to Carl with a heavy glance dripping with disdain. ·

"Is this true?" Ananias says. Carl opens his mouth like he might argue but then just stares at Ananias, defiant.

I try to open my mouth and say that I want to finish the fight—that I just need a minute, but my brain feels like it's full of cotton.

Ananias shakes his head. "This has held up the proceedings long enough." He looks to the guard behind him. "Get him off the premises."

As the guard walks over to take Carl, I turn to Sam.

He touches my face as his eyes run over me. "Are you okay?" he whispers.

I nod, my head clearing a little. Whatever Carl gave me wasn't designed to last too long. Just long enough to win at whatever cost.

"You shouldnthavvedone . . . ," I slur.

Aldrick holds open the cage. From the corner of my eye, I see something—

Carl, shaking with rage, eyes full of something I haven't seen before.

He flexes his wrist, and his stinger lowers.

With a shout, he raises his wrist to throw his stinger right at Sam's chest.

I don't think. I throw both hands up. More zombies appear,

filling the cage and blocking Carl's stinger. The ones I had frozen start moving again, all shuffling toward Carl.

The cage smells earthy and wet, like damp soil mixed with a sour, moldy scent. Growls fill the cell block, and the cacophonous roar echoes off the prison walls. Carl's eyes widen in terror.

Ananias, Mavis, and Aldrick all bolt for the door.

"Come on!" Aldrick calls to us. Sam tries to guide me out, but I shake him off.

I hold my hands up, trying to get them all to freeze again. But they don't listen. I can't get a hold of my power enough to make them stop.

They are all heading toward Carl as he swings his stinger around wildly, knocking a couple down in the process but doing nothing to stop the horde coming his way. He starts to climb up the chain-link fence, but his shoes are too bulky and won't catch the metal. He reaches down to untie them, but the monsters are coming too fast.

More keep appearing, filling the cage slowly. One turns toward Sam, its jaws snapping wildly. He kicks it back.

"Aldrick! Get them out of here! I'll get Vesper! We have to make sure none escape!" Sam calls. Aldrick nods, pulling Mavis down the cell block.

"Vesper, we have to go," Sam whispers fervently, turning back to me. My hands shake as I try again to make the fear disappear. Nothing.

More appear, pushing Sam and me farther back against the edge of the cage.

"Vesper, we have to go *now*," Sam calls.

Forget magic, then. I can get to Carl myself. I launch myself forward, but Sam grabs me and lifts me up, dragging me toward the cage door.

Once we get outside the cage, Sam sets me down but doesn't release his grip on me.

Ananias stands at the top of the cage stairs. I thought he'd be long gone, but instead he stands on the stairs just outside the cage, watching.

Carl shoves through the zombies, falling just shy of the door as two zombies grab his shoes.

"Help him!" I plead.

Then Ananias closes the cage door.

"What are you doing?" I shriek.

"No time," Ananias states simply as he walks to the bottom of the steps.

"We have to help him!" I try once more to call the fear back. The poison is fading, but I'm still not strong enough. I shove myself forward, raising my hand, begging my magic to work. Sam tightens his grip around my waist, and we both fall to the ground as I double over in my fight to stop him, running my nails over his skin. "We can't just leave him!" I shout, but a sound stops me. Carl lets out a bloodcurdling scream as the creatures overtake him. He looks up at me, and the terror in his eyes is the last thing I see before Ananias steps in front of me.

"You shouldn't have to see this," he says, raising his hands.

A thick emerald-green wall rises out of the ground, blocking the horror from sight.

Ananias steps back as the screams die down.

I kick, clawing at Sam until he lets me go. I hit my hand against the wall. It's glass.

"It's done, Vesper," Sam says quietly. I know it is. Carl's cries have stopped, overtaken by the gurgling roars of the monsters I created. I hit my hand against the glass, though my fist feels small and inconsequential against the cold enormity of it.

Then, it's just silence. Normally, that would make me feel better, but I know they disappeared because Carl is no longer here to harbor the fear.

I turn around, my fists clenched as I look at Ananias. "How could you do that?" I ask. My voice comes out in a horrified whisper.

Ananias brushes his hair out of his face. "Nothing happened to him that you didn't want."

"What?" I scream, lunging at Ananias. Sam doesn't stop me this time. I shove Ananias squarely in the chest, not giving a second thought to the fact that he's the most powerful Oddity in existence. His eyes lock on mine, absorbing my shove like it's nothing.

"He cheated and then tried to kill your friend. Didn't you want this?"

"No!" I shriek. I had only wanted to stop Carl, not kill him. I hate the white-hot tears that spring to my eyes as I scream. "That wasn't for us to decide!"

Ananias stares down at me. "Is it not? What do you think we're doing here, Vesper? What are *you* trying to do here?"

I step back, the force of his words like a slap across the face. Sam is silent, his hands on his hips while he catches his breath.

"It's done," Ananias says. It's not full of menace. He's not threatening me. He's just saying the truth as he sees it. As he creates it.

I sink to the step in front of the cage and cover my eyes as Ananias turns on his heel and stalks away. Sam kneels down next to me and wraps his arms around my shoulders, but I shake my head. I don't know what happens now. I can't even think about it.

"Please let me be alone now, okay?" I ask. "I'll meet you down at the water in a few minutes."

Sam seems unsure about the idea of leaving me alone but nods and walks away.

When I hear footsteps again a few minutes later, I look up, ready to tell Sam I need more time. But I stop when I realize the person standing in front of me is Sapphira. I can tell from her drawn expression that she saw the whole thing.

She walks me to the yacht, where I know I'm expected. I'm the champion, after all. I am the Oddity who made it to the final fight.

We get down to the water's edge, and I look up at the yacht, with its civil, golden glow.

Sapphira puts her hand in mine, and I jump at the contact.

"You're shaking," she whispers.

"I just . . . I can't go up there right now," I say, walking closer to the water. "I just . . ." My voice comes out in racking sobs. My lungs stagger under the weight of tonight, and I can't catch my breath.

I lean down and put my hands in the freezing water, washing the blood from my fingers. I know it's cold, but I don't feel it.

I can't feel anything.

Sapphira is next to me then, her hands over mine as I scrub blood from my fingers.

"It's not your fault," she says finally. I bite back the sob that floats up my throat.

"I just need . . ." I collapse into a sitting position in the water, still rubbing at my hands even though there's nothing there.

She lowers herself into the water next to me, wrapping her arms around my shoulders as I dissolve. I don't shove her away.

❋ ❋ ❋

I don't know how long we sit there, quiet. Eventually, she helps me up and we both walk to the shore, collapsing on the sand next to the yacht. Neither of us want to go up. I shiver, though I don't feel cold.

She brushes a piece of hair from my eyes. "None of this is your fault."

"It is," I say. "I'm a monster, Sapphira. I'm—"

"No. You're not. You saved Sam's life. Carl tried to kill him twice tonight."

I shake my head, the words boiling in my chest despite the freezing air around me. "Not just that. I signed up for this whole thing intending to *betray him.* I still am. I am going to ruin his life to reverse something I did. I—" I stop myself from finishing what I was going to say. I swallow the words. "I *care* about him, and I will still break his heart to fix my own mistakes. Only a monster could do that, Sapphira."

Her eyes burn into mine, and she clenches her jaw. At first, I wonder if she's as disgusted with me as I am. She grabs my face with both hands. I shut my eyes tight.

"You are *not* a monster— Look at me. You aren't."

I open my eyes.

"Doing something monstrous to protect someone you love doesn't make you a monster. It makes you human." Her voice cracks at the last word, and I reach up to take her hand in mine.

"Why are you working for him?" My words are soft and pleading. Desperate.

"Do you still think the Wardens are the worst things that could happen?"

"Vesper," Sam calls me from the ramp. Sapphira drops her hands and I stand, dusting the sand off me as much as I can before I realize it's hopeless. I look like a wreck.

"Sapphira. Aldrick is looking for you," he says as he reaches the bottom of the ramp. He looks past me.

She stands, running a hand through her unruly hair. She walks past me, gently touching my arm as she goes.

Sam looks down as we're left alone by the water.

"There's a gala at the Palace of Fine Arts the night before the final fight. He made an announcement up there. Formal. You're expected to attend, now that you are, as he put it, 'the face of this tournament. Your final opponent will be picked from the Ledger at random, since . . .'"

There's no one left. Mavis and Aldrick were disqualified. And Carl is dead.

"It is complete bullshit. You're the last one standing. This whole thing should be over."

I don't if I'm in shock, or what, but the words float past me. I hear them, and I don't. My eyes are fixed over his shoulder, at the fog rolling over the water. I should be mad, but right now I feel so detached. I remember the look in Ananias's eyes as he let Carl die. Ananias is pulling the strings here. I see that now. And honestly, part of me is relieved that I don't have to face the decision of the Unraveling yet. Another round means I don't have to face that choice yet.

"Ananias said there would be a final round. There's nothing we can do about that."

"Vesper. We should talk." He reaches for my hand, but I step back.

"I need a minute."

I don't look at his face. I can't bear to read his expression right now. The night is filled with the lapping of the water and distant foghorns, but somehow it's unbearably silent between us.

"I'll meet you up there then," he says after a moment.

I don't move until he's gone. Then something pricks at the back of my mind. The way Sapphira had touched my arm.

I walk back over to where we were sitting, and, in the sand, I see it. Writing.

The devil you know.

TWENTY-EIGHT

I don't sleep.

I can't.

Every time I close my eyes, I see Carl.

I hear the snapping jaws of a terror I released and couldn't put back.

I feel the light of the yacht when Sapphira and I eventually went up to the deck. I feel the blanket Aldrick put over my shoulders. I hear the mild-mannered applause of the investors who were safe on the boat, eating chocolate-covered strawberries as I unleashed hell inside that prison. I feel the icy breath of the sea that washed over me as I stood on the bow of the ship and watched Shaders block a construction crew from view as they cleaned up the mess in Alcatraz so no one would ever know we were there.

And I see the words. The ones that make no sense.

I don't chance texting Sapphira, worried that Ananias might intercept the messages. She clearly doesn't want him to know that she told me anything.

Still, the words haunt me. *The devil you know.*

I grab my gloves and go downstairs. Moonlight pours in through the skylight. I walk over to the mat, stopping with my toes just on the edge of the glow.

I don't want to step into it.

I can't.

This barreling feeling in my chest is rising, coiling around my throat and pulling tighter and tighter.

It's so cold that I can see the steam of my sorrow spinning in the moonlight.

"I am the master of my fate, I am the captain of my soul."

I want to laugh at the words. I am the master of this clusterfuck, and I am the captain of this train wreck.

Doing something monstrous to protect someone you love doesn't make you a monster. It makes you human, Sapphira had said.

No, but I am a monster because I remember the feeling I had when I pulled the monsters out of Carl—pride. Pride at my power. Pride at my strength.

And then it quickly derailed, and now he's dead.

Just last night Duncan and I sat here, and he told me that he'd pray for me. I don't think God listened. My hands shake as another sob bubbles up, but I swallow it down.

"Vesper?" Sam's voice comes from the dark beyond the

moonlight. I didn't even know he was here. He must have been sleeping on the couch again.

Or not. He doesn't look like he's slept, either.

I wipe the tears off my face with the back of my hand.

"Yeah?"

He just stands on the other side of the shaft of moonlight. He's wearing a dark hoodie and black sweatpants. His hair is longer than I've ever seen it, and he's got a five o'clock shadow.

"You okay?" he asks. It's a whisper.

I nod.

"Liar."

He steps closer, and I step back. It's instinct, because it's not just the blood of the trial that kept me awake but a question.

And I want the answer so badly that I ache with it, but I've never been so scared of a question in my entire life.

He holds his hands out, confused.

I can't look at him. I turn, walking past the cage. I don't know where the hell I'm going. Upstairs. Outside—anywhere is better than here. Anything is better than talking to him. I am not going to talk to him. We are not going to talk about this. He follows me.

"Vesper. Talk to me."

I whirl around.

"Why did you stop the fight?" I whisper. Okay. I guess we're talking about this.

"I told you. Carl injected you, and I knew—"

I shake my head. "You didn't know that. You couldn't have known. It just looked like I was getting my ass kicked, which isn't exactly a rare occurrence these days, so cut the shit."

It's like I slapped him.

And for a moment, I wonder if he's really thought about his reason. If he even knows why he jeopardized getting us both thrown out of the competition—getting himself killed. But he swallows hard, and I look down. I can't look at his face. I can't let him look at mine.

"I couldn't let you— I couldn't . . ." He falters. "I couldn't let you."

"Couldn't let me what?" I press, looking up. "Couldn't let me get through it on my own? Couldn't let me figure it out? Couldn't let me get through this round? It wasn't just *your* chance you were throwing away, Sam. It was mine, too. And I didn't ask for your help, so please tell me what you *couldn't*—"

"*I couldn't let you die.*" The words aren't a yell. He doesn't raise his voice. But the words stop me dead in my tracks. They rattle my bones. His voice almost breaks me in half, and I have to cross my arms to stop from busting open and falling apart. My scabs pull, and I feel blood seep into my sleeve. Tears swell at the back of my throat, but I swallow them down.

"I'm not another damsel you need to step in and save, Sam."

"I don't think that."

"Oh?" I choke out, finally giving oxygen to the notion I've been fearing for the past couple of weeks. "Because if this is some sort of fucked-up catharsis where you heal whatever is shattered in you by saving me—"

"You didn't see the look on your face. You were dying in front of me," Sam cuts in, and his voice is strangled as he steps closer. Something in me snaps.

"I'm not a stand-in for Elisa."

"I didn't say you were." His voice is ragged and low. He regards me for a moment before turning around and taking three lumbering steps away from me. He whips back around. "Believe it or not, not every decision I make has something to do with her."

"Oh, it doesn't? Look around, Sam. She's been gone for more than two years, and still: *everything* you do revolves around losing her."

"Careful," he says. His tone is the quiet hush of a razor cutting air.

But I don't want to be careful. I want to swing out and hurt him so badly he never looks at me in the eye again. I want him to hate me now and get it over with.

"Everyone is worried about you. You're the best fighter in this whole gym and you just . . . stopped. You fucked up once, but that doesn't mean you pull the brakes and stop living."

I've spent the last two months hitting bags, sparring pads, and people.

But none of my punches land quite like that one. Sam steps back, blinking several times as he lets out a shuttering laugh that holds no humor at all. The sound chills me.

"Says the girl who hasn't talked to her family in over a year because of an accident," he spits back. I reel from the truth of it, letting out a slow breath through my clenched teeth.

Sam steps forward and points at the ground.

"We're partners in this. You were in trouble. I made a judgment call."

He saved my life. I know he did. But I'm pushing now, because I need to. I need to shove him as far back as I can. He narrows his eyes.

"That's right. We are business *partners*, Sam, and you made a call for the both of us."

"Is that what we are? Business partners?" He crosses the mat in two seconds, and he's in front of me again.

"Isn't it?" I hate how my voice shakes.

I *need* him to tell me we're partners. I need those words to be a white-hot cauterizer on something open and raw that's been blooming in my chest since the night of the first trial.

But he's not saying what I need. He's looking at me, his eyes searching mine as he steps closer. I feel his breath on my face and the heat of his chest. I swallow hard as goose bumps bloom on my skin. I hope he can't see.

I want him to see.

I don't want him to see.

I do.

I can't.

If I don't shove him away from me now, I won't have the strength to do what I need to when the time comes.

He steps closer, and I hold up my hands.

"This has worked for us, Sam. This—" I move my finger between our chests. "We've used each other for what we need, and we both know it. I should've stopped it when I had the chance, but . . ." I swallow the tears that bite the back of my throat. I shrug. "But shame on me for using you to feel normal again, even just for a little while. And shame on you for using me to stem your own bleeding." The last words erupt from me, because I can't stand how true they sound. I can't stand how easy it was for me to start falling for him. He steps closer, but I push him back as hard as I can.

It barely moves him, though he reels from the force of it. And I trip a wire, because he lets out another laugh. It bursts from him as his eyes fill with tears and he brings both hands to his head. He steps closer to me. There's no humor in the sound. It sounds like thunder, threatening and low. It sounds like something breaking.

"You are doing the opposite of stemming the bleeding, Vesper." He drops his arms and takes one more step. I take a step back, running up against the chains of the cage. He puts his arms up, threading his fingers into the cage on either side of my face.

A tear rolls down his cheek. I could shove him away. I should shove him away. I can feel his eyes on me, and I know I shouldn't look up. I should walk away, I should—

I look up.

He's close enough that when I turn my face up to his, our lips are inches apart.

"I would give *anything* to have what you just said be true," he whispers. "Maybe then, I could sleep."

And his eyes are on mine, searching, and it feels as though he's plundering the deepest, most shameful thoughts I have. And I'm letting him. His eyes are drinking me in, and they drop to my lips.

My heart thumps hard in my chest as I clench my fists.

Enough of this.

"My only focus now is fighting to bring back your dead girlfriend," I say, the lie rolling out of my mouth like it's nothing. "Besides. Even if I wasn't . . . I don't feel that way about you, Sam," I say, the words cutting my mouth on the way out.

He's still as he lets his gaze drop to the ground, and I wonder if the words hurt him as much as they hurt me.

I'm a liar. I'm a liar, and the lie fills me so completely I wonder if I'll ever taste anything other than the bitterness of it. If I'll ever be able to open enough windows in my soul to air out the terrible stench it's leaving on my bones.

"You're right," he says, meeting my eyes once more. Something in him hardens, and it's almost like I can feel him closing off. His lips twitch. "I'll let Wex take over your training tomorrow, and we'll keep it professional from now on." He lowers his hands and steps back.

It takes everything I have to push off the cage and walk away.

Across the mat, up the stairs. Once I'm back in the room, I look down through the window.

Sam stands outside the cage, his arms up, fingers wrapped in the links.

He looks as broken as I feel.

TWENTY-NINE

The Festival of the Queen of Poisons is lit.

And by that I mean both figuratively and literally.

There aren't usually parties allowed in national parks, but what the hell. We weren't supposed to be able to have gladiator battles in a shipyard or on Alcatraz, and we did that, so.

I'm not shocked about that.

But I am shocked that there are so many people here.

Thousands. There are string lights strung up in the trees, and a bonfire below on Pfeiffer Beach.

Baselines and Oddities are here, but you can't tell who is who, since most people are covered in paint, masks . . . both. A deep beat pulses from the cliff, where someone's set up a dance floor. Music mixes with the electric air, and everything feels like it's come to life. Even the skin of the trees is drenched in glitter, and they glisten like they're in on a secret. Someone has filled the forest with little pockets of couches, chairs, and coffee tables covered with ice buckets and bowls of grapes and passion fruit. They're all set up on top of thick rugs, and chandeliers dangle from the tree branches above. They look like places for civil conversation, but that's not what some of them are being used for. I blush and look away.

I walk past tents and tables with Abagail, since there was no stopping her once Sam mentioned it. And then there was no stopping Wex. Or Roy. "It'd be better to have them as backup if things go sideways," Sam said. I agreed. Added bonus? There wasn't enough room for us in one car, so I opted to ride with Abagail to save myself from a long amount of time in a confined space with Sam.

It's been two days since the third trial, enough time for every poisonous thing in me to clot. After my midnight talk with Sam, I took a step back. Something inside of me limped into a corner and curled up, and I let it.

I'm going to help him figure out what happened to Elisa. I owe him that much.

Then I'm going to win this thing, and I'm going to undo what I am.

Abagail and I walk by two Fire Furies make a show of spinning fire on their palms as two shirtless guys roast marshmallows on the open flames.

And all over, queen of poisons flowers hang from the trees, a defiance.

Two women walk by dressed in gossamery blue gowns.

"Hold on, Amanda," the taller one says, waving her hand toward the ground near her friend's foot. A small dust devil appears, knocking a stray piece of trash loose from the bottom of her friend's sandal.

Abagail stops, eyes wide. "That is. So. Cool," she whispers.

"You should be used to this by now. How many times have you seen Duncan just . . . disappear?"

"Enough that it doesn't even faze me anymore. But I've never seen this many different powers. It's—" She stops to look at an Electrode kissing what I think is a Shifter. He has horns, so I'm hoping he's a Shifter. We've got bigger problems if there are actual demons on the loose.

"Bathroom!" Abagail exclaims, pulling me toward a small trailer.

I follow her, all the while keeping an eye out for Sapphira. I haven't heard from her, and I'm starting to get worried. The bathroom—because someone erected an actual *bathroom* here—is packed with girls checking themselves out in the mirror. Abagail and I squeeze through the crowd until we get to the last sink near the exit.

"Yikes. Isn't it supposed to be cold?" Abagail asks, using her hands to fan her sweaty armpits.

I crane my neck, looking for Sapphira. Nothing.

"They probably had Stokers infuse heat veins in the dirt. This whole section of the forest is like a giant electric blanket."

Abagail stops fanning herself. "No shit? That's the coolest thing I've ever heard. But it's not exactly helping," she says, examining her dress. It's a shiny gold cocktail dress with a draping back. She's wearing black gladiator sandals with leather straps wrapping up to her thighs, and she has a metallic band tied around her forehead, securing her spiral-curled hair.

"You look amazing," I say, and I mean it.

She turns to me, eyeing me up and down. "You do, too."

"You're cute when you lie," I say, scrunching my nose. I opted for a simple black dress and a little mascara. I've got no one to impress, and I don't feel like dressing for anything but battle, if I'm honest.

I want to meet the Chronicler, get answers about Elisa, and then end this.

We leave the bathroom, and I see Sapphira next to one of the many trash can fires that have sprung up between trees. She looks stunning in a sapphire-colored dress that hangs off her shoulders, paired with combat boots. Her eyes are smoky, and she has dark jewels hanging from her ears, her hair loose down her back. We're closer to the dance floor and announcer podium, and the music roars through the forest. Aldrick comes up next to her, and she threads her fingers through his.

Despite the ache in my own chest, I smile. Finally.

I open my mouth to ask her what the hell the writing in

the sand meant but stop as Sam comes up beside me.

"Found 'em," Wex says, taking a deep pull from a glowing neon curly straw.

I chance a look at Sam. I haven't seen him in anything but workout clothes, and so the sight of him in dark jeans, boots, and a tight black shirt throws me—he looks different. Good different. We lock eyes, and I look down.

"You guys know how to throw a party," Roy says. He's holding a clear cup full of a swirly purple liquid. He lifts the cup to take a drink, but stops as he looks over my shoulder.

He clears his throat, pointing. I turn.

A figure with a golden half mask and white dress stands behind me. I know it's Lynn from the white hair.

"You have twenty minutes," she says. "Follow me."

"We'll guard the drinks," Abagail says, her voice wary. Which makes total sense, since we're about to follow a strange masked woman deep into the woods.

I nod, trying to give her the most assured *We got this* face I possibly can before following the strange masked woman deep into the woods.

The string lights peter out once we push past the party, and the forest transforms from a fairy-lit shindig into a dark, mossy kingdom adorned in deep, lush green. The trees are monstrous shadows towering above us. A chorus of crickets' chirps and owls' low, mournful calls accompany our steps.

Aldrick and Sapphira walk behind Lynn, their fingers still interlocked.

Sam is behind me, and I don't look back.

The moon is out, but it is still so dark that I can only see her dress and hair as we walk.

Suddenly, she stops, crouches to the ground, and runs a hand over the forest floor.

The ground opens up in front of her feet, gently sloping to reveal a walkway into the earth.

"Don't ask anything you don't want to know the answer to. Don't expect to get the answer to everything you ask. Don't ask about anything regarding Baselines—she won't know. And don't," she says, turning to us, "ask anything twice. The answer no means just that. No."

I stop. "Wait. She? You said 'he' back at the cabin."

Lynn smiles. "Why would I tell you anything to help you get closer to her if she didn't want to be found?"

Aldrick stops. "How do we know you're not lying to us now?"

Lynn just smiles and walks down the ramp.

We have no choice but to follow.

I thought the Chronicler lived in a house. A cabin in the middle of the woods like a hermit, or something. I was not expecting this. We head downward for what feels like forever, and I look up, trying to tell myself to take deep breaths. To not think about how far under the ground we are.

And how close we are to the San Andreas Fault.

Okay. That was an unhelpful thought. That was the *worst* thing I could've thought of.

We walk into a grand cave, all sandstone with moss poking out between the bricks. In the center of the room, a huge waterfall falls like a sheet from an unknown origin in the shadow, landing in a grand pool with shallow edging. Vines hang from the ceiling, and lit torches line the walls in the small amount of space that isn't covered by shelves loaded with books.

Books, everywhere.

The room is massive; so big that I can't see the ceiling. It's just shadows, leaves, and books. It's so gorgeous that for a moment, I stop walking, just to take it in.

"Vesper," Sam calls.

We walk around the waterfall, and I look into the collecting pool below. I watch the curls of steam coil over the stone floor, stopping just in front of the bookcases as though it has brushed up against an invisible barrier. Some sort of magic protects the books from the water. Brilliant.

The pool looks like the night sky, dotted with stars and the whisper of fading rain clouds. Confused, I look up, thinking it must be a reflection.

But the roof above is closed.

It's just magic.

I turn, and there she is.

The Chronicler sits in a chair.

Wait.

A chair. Like a La-Z-Boy. With polka dots.

I stop, looking behind me, confused. I was thinking she'd be some bald mage in a white robe and some huge-ass talisman around her neck.

But no. She looks about my age. She's wearing black skinny jeans tucked into knee-high riding boots. And a striped cardigan. Like, one I've seen at Anthropologie.

Her hair is in a messy bun atop her head, and she has wide-framed glasses. Her peachy blush perfectly complements her olive skin. She writes in a journal with a purple pen with a fluffy blue bauble at the end. I look closer at the bookshelves. They're notebooks. Journals. Spiral-bound, hardback. Hundreds, thousands of journals, all containing her visions. Our histories.

"Tiffany?" Lynn asks, and Tiffany regards us all before closing the journal and sticking her pen in her hair. "They're here."

Tiffany the Chronicler gets up from her chair and crosses her hands across her chest before nodding at Lynn.

"I'll be waiting outside," Lynn says. She walks back up the ramp, and then it's silent, save for the sound of the waterfall.

Okay, who is going to talk first?

What's the protocol here?

I step forward. "Um."

What do I say? *Your Majesty? M'lord?* "I like your cardigan."

Sam turns around slowly, giving me a look of disbelief over his shoulder.

But it works, because Tiffany smiles. "Thank you."

She looks at all of us again, taking a second longer on Sam than the others.

I mean, okay. Not necessary, but okay.

"Lynn tells me that you want to know about Elisa Littleton," she starts, narrowing her eyes. "I've thought about this a lot. Elisa was . . . complicated. There's no way I can show you *her* without showing you *everything.*"

"What's everything?" Sam asks, his face is unreadable. I would give anything to know what he's thinking right now.

"I still have nightmares," Tiffany continues. "Don't ask questions to which you do not want to know the answer. It's a luxury I wish I had," she says, turning and walking to the far wall, her boots clicking on the stone as she approaches one of the towering bookcases. "At least, I've been wishing that since Ivan came into power over the Wardens." She lifts an arm and runs her finger along the spines of her journals, stopping at one in the middle. She pulls it out and turns back to us.

"How is he still alive?" I ask.

She looks at me, sadness etched on her expression. "You'll see."

My heart sputters in my chest. Fear pricks at the back of my neck, and I fight the urge to run.

I shake my head. "Wait. Since Ivan's been in power? How old are you?"

Tiffany smiles coyly but doesn't answer. *Don't expect to get the answer to everything you ask.*

"So you can never turn it off?" I ask, my eyes roving over the thousands of journals lining the walls. "You see everything that happens to all the Oddities and then you . . . write it down?"

Tiffany walks to the waterfall and sets the journal next to it, making sure to center it on the floor.

She nods. "So you imagine how much I'd be worth to someone like the Wardens. All their secrets—exposed. But I am not for them, because they lost their way long ago. I hope you will see that."

"So you don't think they're gone?" I ask. She meets my eyes, and then drops her gaze to the floor.

Don't expect to get the answer to everything you ask.

She flips through the journal in her hand. "I don't have many visitors. Only the worthy can find me; only those who are seeking true knowledge. That gets more and more rare with every passing century."

Century? Wait. *How old is she?* "I wish to remain hidden, and Ivan is a large reason for that." Her voice hardens, as do her eyes. "But Lynn asked me to do this as a favor.

Considering her mother was one of my best friends, I'll do it." She ignores the question on my face. She motions for us to join her on the other side of the sheet of tumbling water.

"Now, I don't see these things like I'm witnessing a story. It's more like . . . I'm *there*. All at once, and a little at a time. It's confusing, but that's the only way I know how to describe it. So you won't hear an explanation as much as you'll just . . . know it. Like I do."

Something about her voice is heavy with a sadness as she takes a deep breath.

"Are you sure you want to know this?"

"Yes," Aldrick says, and none of us disagree.

She holds her hands out, and the torches on the side of the walls go dim.

Then she reaches down, holds her hands over the paper, and then throws them up, like she's pulling the words from the page and splashing them on the waterfall.

Sam grabs my hand as we plunge, and I don't stop him.

And then, I'm no longer in the cave.

I'm in front of stone doors. They're at least three stories high, with engravings of wolfsbane lining the outer sides.

The doors groan and stretch, opening to reveal a vast room—bigger than this one, filled with rows and rows of shelves.

Each shelf holds hundreds of jars. Some are metal, some wood, some glass. In the glass ones, I can see a pulsing, writhing light, each a different color.

I realize at once what this is.

It's the Rippers' Athenaeum. It's real.

It's breathtaking. Gorgeous the way bones are. Startling in their perfection; startling in the way that only invites awe through death.

There's a man. He walks between the shelves, and something about the walk tells me who it is. Just like the Chronicler told me I would . . . I just *know*.

Ivan.

He wears a black cloak, his face obscured by the hood.

I move with him as the story carries me onward.

Then he's out, in a hallway lit by veins of light stretched through the concrete in the ceiling.

Which one did you take this time? a voice calls as soon as he steps out of the doorway.

It came from a girl. My age, maybe a little older. Arms crossed over her chest, her fitted leather vest has the collar popped up to her chin. Her hair, a dark blond, is woven back from her face. Her chestnut eyes are dancing with revulsion as Ivan turns to her, almost like he forgot she was there.

The one we discussed.

The girl pushes off the wall.

That was not a discussion.

She walks toward him.

My sisters let you do this for centuries. They let you in and looked the other way when you plucked powers from this place at your sole discretion, but I won't.

He gives her a level look from under the hood, and I can't tell if he's proud of her or rageful. Impressed, or irritated.

And I get it, just like Tiffany said I would. All the pieces fit.

Ivan was taking powers from the Athenaeum. He was taking the powers for himself. That's how he was still alive, all these years later. He stole immortality. He didn't take them all at once, not enough to raise alarm from the other Wardens.

But slowly.

Do you hear me, Father?

He walks away, and I see the girl's face. I see the sorrow and terror there. Agony at what her father was becoming.

It was his daughter, the Ripper.

She walks to the aconite-bud doors and pulls them shut. They creak as she puts her hand on them.

Light snakes out from her fingers.

She's locking it. Of course. Only Rippers can get in to the Rippers' Athenaeum.

The image blends and fades, and I hear screaming then.

It's terrible. It's a razor along the inside of my veins; a fist pulling my lungs down.

It's a mother, cradling her unmoving child in the dark of a nursery.

A brother, finding his sister unmoving in her bed.

✳ ✳ ✳

And another.

And another.

Different houses, different shades of night plummeting in through the windows.

Another. Another another another, over and over again. I see bodies. Unseeing eyes, reflecting moonless skies.

Different countries. Different people, different loved ones in their arms, all with the same strange dark burns on their skin.

Same scream.

The scene fades, and the scream blends into a cry; something feral.

The Ripper shoves open the doors to Ivan's court—a large obsidian room. He sits at the head of a table of elders in robes. The Wardens.

Mascara cascades down her face, her hair wild.

You did this, she breathes, not bothering to hide the tears slipping down her cheeks, out her nose. Over her full lips. *I forbade you from taking the Seeker's magic. You lied to me about which power you took from the Athenaeum.*

The sinking feeling in my gut mixes with understanding. Seekers are like Trackers, but you can find anyone based on one criterion. One attribute.

Ivan motions for the rest of the Wardens to leave the room. He stands as they exit.

They were the dangerous ones, he answers.

They were innocent! the Ripper screams. The veins in her temples strain with rage as she shoves a chair to the side. It clatters against the stone. *But you sent our deadliest after them, anyway. Children, even. While they slept.*

They were Awakeners. Tailors. Miasmas with deadly, untraceable poisons. Metalurgs. Anything Ivan deemed dangerous. And they were snuffed out.

There's a pause as she considers—and a thought settles over her beautiful face.

I won't let you do this, she says.

Ivan is unimpressed at the Ripper's show of emotion.

If we waited until they did something, it would be too late. Wiping up messes is the way of yesterday. Making it so the messes never happen is the way of the future.

The Ripper stops, like something is dawning on her. Like she's making a decision.

If killing innocents is the way to assure our future, then we don't deserve our future.

She looks up at him, a gold light ringing her irises as she revs her power.

You. You don't deserve a future.

There. There it is—the first moment of fear in Ivan's eyes.

What are you doing?

The Ripper's hair dances around her head as she raises her hands.

Stop. Stop this right now, Ivan says. He still thinks he has control of the situation.

She lifts her hands, and his assured expression fades. He tries to run, but she is too quick.

She snaps her hands into fists and twists.

You can't. You can't do this, Ivan chokes out. *You will die.*

The Ripper tightens her fists, and Ivan clutches his chest.

And then your only way into the Athenaeum goes with me, Father. You'll be powerless. More powerless than those mothers whose screams I hear in the darkest night.

No, Ivan starts, but the Ripper pulls her hands to her sides with a shriek that cracks the walls around her, and Ivan falls to his knees.

Different shades of light slither out of his nose. His eyes. His mouth and ears.

His power, slinking away from him like poison out of a wound, straight into the Ripper's chest. The powers he was born with. The ones he stole.

It absorbs into her with a *whoosh,* and the table in front of her flips, along with the chairs, crashing against the walls with a loud *crack.*

The room shakes, and she lets out a scream. She opens her eyes, fully aglow with the different shades of light she took from Ivan.

And that's when I realize.

Ripping certain powers can kill.

That rule isn't just for the one losing the power—it is for the Ripper, too.

Taking all that power from Ivan at once; an Oddity hundreds of years old . . . she knew she wouldn't survive it.

A choking sound slips from her throat, and the light from her eyes fades.

She crumples to the ground and doesn't move.

Ivan looks up, his face red.

No, he gasps, crawling to the Ripper.

No, no, no, no. He touches her face, then gathers her up in his lap, burying his face in her neck as he lets out the same scream as those who had lost the ones he killed.

The skin-tearing, soul-shredding sound of a parent losing a child.

After a moment, he pulls away. He wipes his hand over her face, and then he sets her limp body on the floor and stands.

He motions to the overturned table with a flick of his wrist, and nothing happens.

He tries again.

Nothing.

He has nothing.

One of the Wardens comes in through the side door, a hood pulled low over his head. *We felt something, Ivan. What just happened?*

Ivan looks down at his daughter.

Her eyes are open, her lips parted.

She's dead.

The Warden steps forward. He doesn't know what to say.

I'm ... I'm so, so sorry, he stammers. *I will start the preparations for her burial right away—*

But Ivan shakes his head. *No. She will go into the harbor.*

The hooded Warden is silent. Horrified. *But, Ivan—*

Ivan whirls around. *She was my daughter, and I say she goes into the harbor. There is no room for traitors in the family crypt.*

He looks down at her.

And no room for weakness in my service.

Ivan steps over her body and strides toward the door.

What should I do, then? The hooded man asks.

Ivan looks over his shoulder.

Find me another Ripper.

The light fades and swirls, curling in at the edges. And then we're back in the Chronicler's cave.

She lowers her hands, and the waterfall becomes just a waterfall again.

We're quiet as we struggle to process.

What did I just see?

What did I just see?

I look over. Aldrick is silent, his hands clenched at his sides. Sam runs his hands through his hair as he steps back, silent. Tears rip down Sapphira's cheeks as she stares at the waterfall.

I look to Sam, and understanding washes over my face. Elisa must have been one of those innocents Ivan killed. One he deemed dangerous, for whatever reason.

"I told you it was bad," Tiffany says, her voice small as she leans down to pick up the journal.

"So that's what happened?" I say. "He was pulling power from the Athenaeum and his daughter ripped him."

Tiffany nods.

"So where is he now?" Aldrick asks, and Tiffany shrugs.

"That's just it . . . I haven't been able to see him since he was ripped. I haven't been able to see any of them. The Wardens have all been in hiding since then."

"Why don't the Wardens just pick a new leader? Like someone from that table?" Aldrick asks, and Tiffany shakes her head.

"Ivan has a hold on the Wardens that transcends his power as an Oddity. They were all linked. When she ripped him . . . she ripped them all. They won't want to broadcast that they were weakened like that. Or that such corruption was rampant in their ranks."

"So what is he going to do?" I ask.

"What I suspect he has been doing. Looking for another Ripper to open the Athenaeum so that they can regain their former power. He still has the entirety of the Wardens at his disposal, so he is still rather formidable. But he's not eager to share with the world that he has no power left. Or that it was his daughter who made it so."

I look to Sam. He's silent. Staring straight ahead.

"Thank you for showing us," he says. The words are robotic. Hollow.

My whole heart sinks. There's no closure in his eyes. No peace. I was a fool to think this would end in anything but pain.

Tiffany pulls at the end of her cardigan awkwardly. "I'm sorry," she says, shrugging sadly as she heads back to her chair. She pulls the fluffy pen from her hair before she sits down, her eyes glazing over as she starts to write furiously once more. It's over.

THIRTY

The party is still in full swing when we get back. The music is a dull throb in my bones, but the melody doesn't register.

Elisa was killed by the Wardens.

The Wardens, who ordered hits on innocent Oddities.

Ivan was stealing powers from the Athenaeum.

We're silent as we walk back, all trying to process the depth of what we just saw.

The Wardens were as bad as we'd feared, and they're gone.

Not of their own choosing, but because they were betrayed, which means that they will probably be looking for a way back. It's only a matter of time before Ivan finds what he's looking for.

So even if I win, if I fight to undo my powers—one day, they will find me.

One day, I will pay for what I did. I will pay for fighting in this tournament. We all will.

I'm damned if I do, damned if I don't.

Sapphira walks up beside me as we pass through the trees, deeper into the party. I slow down slightly and look over my shoulder. Her eyes are far away, tears rimming her full lashes. Once Sam and Aldrick are out of earshot, I turn to face her.

Something in me snaps. I'm so sick of secrets. What have they done for me so far besides break my heart and ruin my life?

"What the hell does 'the devil you know' mean, Sapphira? Why won't you just talk to me?" I ask, my frustration at everything barreling into my tone. I know I shouldn't, but I'm angry.

Her eyes are unfocused, and I see a chaos within— something is ripping her apart.

"Sapphira?" I ask, my voice softer now.

She blinks, and then slowly licks her bottom lip. With a sniff, she meets my eyes.

"It means nothing, Vesper."

I open my mouth to argue, but she shakes her head.

"I was wrong. The devil you know is just as bad as the one you don't."

She meets my eyes, and then shrugs as tears fill her eyes and she pulls her bottom lip between her teeth to stop them from quivering.

"How can we be good in a world that's just . . . not?"

Her voice is small as she regards the night sky. A hopeless feeling curls up my gut like smoke. I don't have an answer for her.

"Sapphira. You were trying to tell me something."

"I was being stupid, Vesper. I was hoping for something that will never happen—you know the feeling, right?" she spits bluntly, dropping her gaze to mine. "It was a dead end."

My eyes fill with tears. The party rages behind us; the boys we've lied to and hurt stand waiting, silhouettes just out of reach.

And for what?

All this, this searching, this hoping . . . for nothing. No closure. No hope. Just the memory of screams that will be forever burning in my memory.

"I want a drink," Sapphira says finally, her eyes clearing at the thought. "I want one of those purple sparkling things that Wex had. Tonight? I want to pretend to be the girl I was before everything fell apart." Her voice gets louder as she wipes the tears from her eyes.

She looks at me expectantly and holds out her hand.

I don't know if it's the heartbreak or the fear or the disappointment, but I take it.

I reach the booth with the pretty drinks and hit my hand on the table like I've seen in old westerns. The woman with the purple eyelashes looks at me like *Excuuuuuuse me*, so I set a twenty on the table as a tip. I pulled it from my stash before we left, meaning to spend it only in an emergency. This feels like an emergency. She hands me my pink drink without another word.

It's tasty, but not tasty enough for how fast I'm drinking it. Whatever.

Sapphira laughs as she chugs hers next to me.

I down more until the world is pleasantly warm and I'm tucked in just right. I'm not drunk—I remember getting drunk with Lindsay in her mom's basement, and I am not yet making finger pistols with the accompanying *pew-pew* noises, so therefore I am not yet drunk.

But I'm warm. And I feel . . . I feel good.

That's the interesting thing about being totally and completely screwed either way, isn't it?

It doesn't matter.

So I should eat, drink, and be merry. For tomorrow I may literally die.

Or I may win, and leave Sam with nothing.

I have the drinking part down . . . so now I need the merriment. And I know just what I need.

Abagail comes up behind me. "Hey. You okay?" she asks. "Sam told me it was rough down there."

I look at Abagail, and how her lipstick is smudged just a little. Get it, Wex. I snort and put the back of my hand to my mouth.

All of a sudden, the music turns. The beat is infectious, filling my body with its pulse.

"Vesper?" Abagail asks. I look up. "You okay?"

"I do not want to talk about it. You still got that eyeliner?"

We crowd in the bathroom, Abagail and I squeezing into a corner. I look up, and she smudges liner around my eyes and puts on another coat of mascara. The alcohol is like pleasant cement in my limbs as I tap my toe to the beat pounding through the wall against my back until Abagail tells me to be still. She takes the band out of my hair and pulls a travel-size can of hair spray out of her bag and spritzes my roots. She smears color onto my lips and helps pin my dress back, using the tie from my hair. After a moment of consideration, she steps back and smirks.

"Oh hell yes."

Abagail steps aside, and I look at my reflection in the dim bathroom light.

Eyes rimmed. Lips pink. Cleavage—I forgot I even had that—prominent. And for a moment, I'm me.

I'm Vesper Montgomery. I worry about my GPA and have a curfew. I have a crush on a guy in my third-period class. I'm normal.

It won't last, but I'll take what I can get.

And then I'm out in the night, the music rattling my bones. Beckoning.

And you know what? Hell yeah. I'm here for it. I don't know where the others are, and I don't care.

I grab Abagail's hand, and we cut through the trees, and I'm giggling even though everything just fell to shit. Everything is going to burn, so I'm going to have some fun tonight.

The dancing pit is full of sweaty, writhing bodies. A Specter has conjured glittering snakes of pale light that coil and bend over the dance floor, casting strange, intoxicating shadows over everything. There's glitter trapped in the steam that clashes against the outside cold.

Abagail and I jump in, and we smash our bodies together as we dance.

She lets out a whoop, and I do, too.

I don't know how long we're there. One song blends into another, and my muscles burn. Some guy has asked if he can dance with me. He's cute, and I like that he asked. Also, he smells nice and has good moves, so I decided that I'm going to take the small wins where I can get them. Sweat drips down my back as the song changes again. I look up and realize we're on the edge of the dance floor. There are chandeliers in the trees rimming this clearing, sending soft light dancing onto the forest floor. My eyes catch something.

Sam.

He's alone, sitting on a wingback chair under a tree, beer in hand.

He doesn't look pleased at the sight of me. And a thrill jolts up my core at the thought, and I swing my hips wider against my partner, lifting my dress a little more as I flip my hair. I'm so basic, and I'm sure if I was 100 percent sober, I'd care.

But I'm not, so I don't.

He doesn't care, either. I have to remember that. He doesn't care. He can't.

I turn to dance facing my partner, just to let Sam know I'm not focusing on him. The lights above turn purple and red as the song changes again, a deeper, more dirty beat rolling out of the speakers. The guy pulls me closer. I let my head fall forward.

The music spears through my chest, and all I want to do is forget. I want to let everything fall away.

But the sound of the screams I heard in the Chronicler's recollection rips through my skull, and I lift my head from his chest as the thoughts swirl around in my mind, clearing away the alcohol-induced haze.

The look of rage on the Ripper's face.

The limp hand of a daughter in a mother's arms.

"Hey, you okay?" the guy before me asks.

"I just need some air."

"We're outside," I hear him mumble as I push off him.

With no clue where I'm headed, I push into the darkness between trees, walking under chandeliers strung up in tree branches, ignoring the bodies strewn on blankets near the roots.

Tears trip over my bottom lashes as I reach a clearing.

There's so much death rattling around my heart, so much tragedy and darkness—I feel like I'm drowning in it. I thought I could chase the shadows away, but they are too deep to be scattered by a pink drink and some club music.

I'm seventeen. I shouldn't be able to pull fear out of people. I shouldn't have to decide which heartache is most worthy of healing.

I should be home. I should be manning the bouncy castle at my church's Thanksgiving festival with Carmen. I should be sending screenshots of ridiculous Tumblr posts to Iris just to hear her crack up in the next room. I should be yelling at Jack when he dive-bombs my bed in the morning when Mom sends him to wake me up.

I shouldn't be feeling things for Sam when he's still in love with Elisa.

When I've been so hell-bent on betraying him. On ruining his life.

I fall to the ground. The second my hands touch the ground, veins of light illuminate the ground, spiraling outwards. They stretch up the trees, wrapping up through the branches, fingers of bright sparks that rip through the darkness. In moments, the whole clearing is blazing with the soft, golden light. The veins streak through the ground, intertwining just inches below the moist earth. Tendrils of illumination reach up through the flowers that bloom at the base of the trees, scattering different colors against the tree trunks.

Lumineers left these here. My touch activated it.

I know that; I know there's a perfectly rational explanation for it. Still, my breath catches in my throat. It's the most beautiful thing I've ever seen.

I press my palm down on the ground, careful as I touch it. It's warm—but not hot. It feels good against the cold night, and I lie back, letting the veins of light heat my back as I look up at the pinprick stars in the night sky.

Duncan believes there's something watching out for us, something that will make sense of all this chaos. My parents did, too.

They named me after that hope.

Right now, I don't feel it, but I want to. As I lie on fire and stare up at diamonds, I want to believe in miracles. I haven't prayed since before the fire. Fear is a weed that choked out that part of me, slowly but surely. I became lean on terror, weaned off the thickening fullness of hope.

"I don't understand any of this," I say, and my throat feels thick with sorrow. Fear. Rage. "I don't understand any of it," I repeat, and hot tears rip over the sides of my face, mingling with my temples.

"Vesper?"

I sit up, startled. Sam stands there, looking down at me, his eyes wide as he looks around the clearing.

"What is this?" he asks, breathless.

"Lumineer veins. Lumineers control bioluminescence."

"It's gorgeous."

I nod, wiping the tears with the back of my hand.

"May I?" he asks, and I nod. He steps softly over to where I am and then sits.

"Oh," he says, jumping slightly before settling back.

I let out a small laugh. "Yeah. It's warm."

"What were you doing out here?"

I look at him and then to the sky. "Praying."

He smiles, and the light from the veins make him even more beautiful than usual, if that's possible. My heart seizes. I look up at the sky, because the beauty up there is less devastating. I can't focus when I look at Sam.

"And?" he asks.

I consider. "Nothing yet."

"Keep waiting."

I pull my eyes from the stars reluctantly, looking back to him and fully knowing the danger I'm putting myself in.

"Prayers get answered in strange ways," he whispers.

"How can you say that? You saw the complete evil cesspool we're dealing with. The death. You saw what happened to Elisa. They killed her because they feared her. Her, and dozens of others. They're monsters."

I look down. I don't have to remind him—he knows.

"I'm sorry," I whisper. It's no louder than the breeze that's playing with my hair. "That didn't help anything, did it? Getting answers?"

His eyes lock on mine, and he shakes his head. "No. Getting answers didn't help."

"I'm so sorry, Sam," I whisper. "I thought I could make it better."

His eyes drop down to my lips, his face drawn tight.

"I wanted to make it better," I mumble, and I'm leaning in now. Leaning closer.

"Vesper," he whispers. His voice is hoarse with longing, and . . . apology? I pull back. "I . . . ," he starts.

Oh my gosh. I misread this. What am I thinking? He just found out why his girlfriend was killed two years ago. Embarrassment floods my veins. I lean back, staggered by the mortification ripping through me. "I'm so sorry," I say, shoving myself to my feet. The cold whips my skin, and I gasp at the loss of heat. But he grabs my wrists before I can run. I look back down at him, and his eyes burn into mine, his jaw clenching and releasing as he takes a deep breath.

"Stay, Vesper," he says. It comes out a strangled whisper, and I sink back down to my knees, keeping my eyes on the warm light pulsing through the ground. He pulls me closer, and I want to shove him off and tell him to forget it, that I'm not his Band-Aid, his distraction, or his redemption. But I don't.

Don't look up. Don't look—

Shit. I look up.

Because he's looking at me in that way he does, and then he's dipping his head to mine, and then I taste his lips. Softly, at first, and he exhales against my mouth like he's coming up for air. It's tentative, my wrists still locked in his hands, a taut suspension between us.

And then it's not soft at all. And I fall down against the heated forest floor, and he's over me, claiming me with a feral hunger, loosing an animal noise in the back of his throat that absolutely sets me on fire. His tongue meets mine, and I move against him like he's *my* redemption. I bite his lip, and he drags a rough hand up my thigh.

He runs his mouth down my neck, and I lift his shirt, inching my fingers up his ribs. Counting him; claiming him.

He kisses me like he's starving, and I realize that I am, too.

He pulls back, setting his forehead against mine.

"I have to stop," he whispers, but I guide his mouth to mine again, and he growls in submission, giving in to me. We exist in this shadow, all light and earth, the steaming heat of our bodies a rebellion against the cold night. It can't last, so I memorize it. The feel of his tongue; the taste of his lips. The sounds of his groan echoing against the back of my throat.

When he pulls back, he looks me in the eyes, and I can see how green they are.

"I think we have to talk," he says, his gaze lowering to my mouth, distracted. I love that he's distracted, but I hate the words, because I know they're true.

I press my hips up against his, and he lets out a sound I've never heard before and want to hear again. He falls against me, and I gasp, putting my hands against his chest as he deepens his kiss.

My palms pulse, and I feel a strange tug.

"Let's talk," I whisper against his lips.

He nods, taking a deep breath as he raises himself up. "But we should probably talk vertically," he whispers, swallowing hard. "Or we won't."

I nod, trying and failing to swallow down this dizzying pleasure that's spinning through my chest. He stands, reaching down to help me up. I stand, adjusting my straps. I stop as I realize he's gone very still.

I look up.

Abagail, Wex, and Aldrick are standing next to the clearing, their eyes wide with shock.

"Oh. Um . . . ," I start, realizing that there is absolutely no coming back from this. I'm all twisted and smeared and tangled and flushed. I look to Sam, and he glances at me before looking back to the group.

"Guys," he says, but stops when he realizes they aren't looking at us.

They're looking past us.

I turn just as I hear twigs snapping in the dark.

A figure steps out of the shadow and into the light.

Her hair is twisted back in a low side ponytail, her black leather vest unzipped all the way to her sternum. But it isn't the way she looks at Sam that startles me. It's not even the fact that I've seen her before, or that horrible, sinking recognition as I see the faint outline of words tattooed on her neck.

She's the Ripper from the vision.

Ivan's daughter.

Neither of those shock me like the word that comes out of Sam's mouth.

"Elisa?"

Elisa. Elisa the Ripper, the one from the vision the Chronicler showed us, the one I'm fighting to bring back. Elisa, the girlfriend whose body was found in the harbor. They are the same girl.

And I pulled her out of him somehow. Sam takes a step forward, his shaking hand out. He takes another step, but she vanishes into thin air.

He turns, his expression melting as he looks at me, and I start to piece it together, messy scraps of flesh and shadow.

I run.

I hear Sam follow, but I don't slow down.

I run through the dark, tripping over tree roots until I find myself on the ledge overlooking Pfeiffer Beach. I sink down next to a tree and bury my face in my hands. The sounds of the bonfire—shrieks of laughter and raucous singing—rise up from the sand below, where the party is still raging.

"Vesper?" I hear him approach, and I shove myself to my feet.

"Don't take a step closer," I spit, hating how my voice warbles with sobs. "You *lied* to me."

Sam shakes his head. "I didn't."

"You told me she was a Metalurg! And you fed me that bullshit story about how you met, how she was a thief—"

"That was true," Sam says, stepping forward. I step back. "We met the night she ripped my sister. What she was stealing was Cheyenne's power. Saving her life."

I remember the story he told me in the car.

What was she actually doing in your parents' house?

Oh. Right. Stealing.

I shake my head in disgust, shutting my eyes tight.

Official cause of death was unknown.

It all comes together. The queen of poisons buds in her apartment weren't given to her by the Wardens. They were hers. She gave them out.

Everything comes spinning into focus, and I shut my eyes. Two years ago.

That is when the Rule of Shadow ended. The Stirring. Ananias didn't reverse it.

Elisa did—by ripping the Wardens.

Sam's voice brings me back to the moment. "Vesper. I didn't

know that she was *that* Ripper, okay? When I found you, I didn't know. I just knew she was *a* Ripper, and I wasn't about to use that as a selling point when I knew how you felt about them." He runs his hands through his hair. "I didn't know. I didn't know she was Ivan's daughter. Lynn mentioned the tattoo, but I'd hoped that maybe all Rippers had the same one."

"But you knew. You knew when you saw her in the Chronicler's vision."

He swallows hard and looks down. "Yes."

"You should've told me right away."

"I should have. I was scared."

Terse words, back and forth. Shot for shot. He doesn't flinch.

I've heard enough. I can't believe I thought I could kiss a boy and not bring down the entire world.

"And then you, what"—I stop, making sure I can push on without crying—"make out with me as a distraction?"

I start to walk past him, but he steps into my path. He's mad now.

"*Distraction?* Vesper, do you realize what happened back there? Do you even understand?"

I clench my jaw. When I don't answer, he continues. "You pulled my fear out of me. I guess we were so—" He doesn't finish the sentence because I think he knows it won't help his case at all.

"Yeah. I know what happened. It almost always happens

when I'm pissed, but I didn't realize it also happened when
I—" I blush, hard. I'm not finishing this sentence in a mature
fashion, that's for damn sure.

"Piss off, Sam," I sputter finally. I want to get out of here
before the real tears begin.

Because I can't let him know what that kiss meant. I can't
let him see how badly this hurts.

It's obvious what just happened. His greatest fear is that
Elisa would catch him cheating, and so she did. My skin
burns where his lips touched, and I wonder if it will ever heal.
I can get mad at him all I want. I can lay this at his feet and
kick that bag of shit at him, but I knew what was happening.
I knew about Elisa, too. I am, after all, fighting to resurrect
the girl who just crossed the boundaries of time and death to
catch me making out with her boyfriend in the woods.

I walk past him, into shadow. Aldrick is there, along with
Sapphira, who looks confused when she sees the tears streak-
ing over my face.

Sapphira reaches for my hand, and I take it.

Sam moves to follow, but I hear Aldrick stop him.

Don't even think about it. All it took was him hurting me
once, and now he's on Aldrick's shit list.

Sapphira walks me to the Grotto's van, and we both climb
in the back. I don't say anything, and she doesn't expect me
to. I swallow, and I still taste Sam in my mouth. This is when
the pain comes, as raw and loud as a cracked bone. Sapphira

wraps her arms around me and cradles me against her chest.

And I cry and cry and cry over a boy who has broken my heart.

We're as normal as we've ever been.

And man, does it hurt.

I go home with Aldrick and Sapphira. I fall asleep in the van on the way there, exhausted from the tears and alcohol. Hours later, when we finally get back, I feel Aldrick wrap his arms around me and cradle me to his chest and carry me inside, laying me in the bed I slept in that first night.

I dream of Sam's kisses leaving aconite flowers in my mouth. I spit them out, and they spark as they hit the ground.

THIRTY-ONE

I stand in front of Baldwin Hospital, and I still don't know how I talked myself into coming here.

I needed to get away from everything.

What I really need is to get away from myself, but that's not possible, so I hopped on an Amtrak.

I don't have the strength to keep this up. I need to remember why I started this in the first place.

No pictures. No phone calls.

Sam is too deep in my bones for that to work anymore.

I need to see Carmen.

And it's this thought that pushes me inside, past an elderly couple with an *It's a Girl!* balloon. Through the second set of automatic doors. Up the elevator.

In the hallway.

Outside the door that reads *Mary Lou Wiles Memorial Recovery Center.*

I don't let myself think. If I think I will talk myself out of this.

I hit the button, and the doors open.

I step inside. I don't know what I was expecting, but it is lighter in here than I thought.

There's a room with kids holding bouncy balls, all playing and laughing. To my left, there's a group meeting. A girl with a wrapped arm is talking.

A little boy walks past me, his neck wrapped in bandages, led by a nurse in pink scrubs. He looks me up and down before motioning for me to come closer.

I kneel, slowly, as he inspects me.

"Are you hurt?" he asks softly.

And the words hit me right between the ribs. I can't tell if I let out a soft laugh, or a sob, but I nod.

"Yeah. I think I am," I say. "Have any tips on being brave? You look like you've got it down."

He purses his lips and pulls a sticker off the back of his hand. He puts it on mine, nodding once.

I nod back, and the nurse beckons him along.

I look down at the sticker. It's a bear hugging a heart. *I love you beary much*, it reads.

What am I doing here? Why did I think I could do this? This is selfish. I'm gonna come in here and kick up dust in Carmen's life to make myself feel better?

I turn, and there she is.

Across the hall, talking to a guy in a gray sweater. Her

eyes drift from him for a half a second and find mine, and she freezes, her mouth open. She touches the guy's arm to excuse herself, and I try to make a run for it.

"Vesper?" she whispers in disbelief.

I'm out the doors and in the hallway, and I'm pressing the elevator buttons with this sort of frantic panic, as though it's going to make the elevator be like *Oh shit, she's serious, better speed this up.*

But it doesn't come.

Instead, I hear Carmen behind me.

She doesn't say anything, but I can tell that it's her by how she breathes. She breathes the same.

I turn.

The left side of her face is a raw pink, her eyelashes and eyebrow gone. The side of her mouth is scarred together. Her eyes are bright with tears as she steps toward me, arms out. I try to take a step back. I don't deserve her touch. I don't deserve her forgiveness. But she redoubles her effort, grabbing the front of my sweatshirt and yanking me close. I crash against her, and her hand goes to the back of my head, and we sink to the linoleum as I dissolve into sobs.

"Let me at least call Mom," she says. We're outside in the courtyard, by the fountain. She bought us coffee from a cart near the entrance, where she knew the barista by name.

I shake my head and fiddle with the lid of the cup.

"I can't do that, too. It was hard enough coming here."

She sits sideways, with her feet tucked under her as she looks at a family of ducks wading in the water. It's overcast, and she has her hood loose over her hair.

We've been over everything. She told me that when I left, Dad came clean about Oddities. He told my family the truth. She told me about her skin grafts, and it was everything I could do to not cry at the pain she went through. I told her everything. Where I went. What I've been doing.

We aren't okay. I know that much. I disappeared for almost two years, and I have a lot to answer for.

"You broke our hearts, you know," she says.

"I know."

"You don't."

I laugh humorlessly. "I don't. I know that I don't know. I ruined your lives. Our home." I stop as she puts her hand on mine.

"That's not what I'm talking about. We could give a shit about the house. We all lived. That's what mattered. But we lost you, and that's what we couldn't heal from. Jack is still mad about it. I think we all are. But you're still thinking of the loss as the house. Or the things inside. Or me." She gestures to her face. "But it's that at the end of all the smoke, Vesper, you weren't standing with us."

I run a tongue over my teeth, not sure what to say to that.

Partially because I don't know what it would mean if I believed it. That kind of grace and forgiveness isn't computing. My hands are too dirty, and I'm not ready to touch it.

"It started as just running not to look back, you know, but it didn't stay that way. I didn't want to come back empty-handed. I thought I could . . ." I stop, knowing the next words might sound crazy to her. "Fix it."

Carmen takes a pull from her coffee and shakes her head. I guess she's had a while to adjust to thoughts that sound crazy. After all, her little sister did burn down the house with her mind. "I'm glad you didn't find a way to 'fix it,' Vesper. There's nothing to fix."

I give her a look, and she shakes her head. "Oh, you can screw yourself if you feel bad for me. Is that what this was all about? Please, please don't tell me you broke our parents' hearts and fought in an underground fighting ring because you *pitied* me."

There's an edge in her voice for the first time, and I freeze at the sound of it. She shifts on the bench.

"Do you know I always thought I was a coward? My whole life." She watches the mallard dive under the water, his emerald neck shining in the light. "You were always the one attempting double-backs on the trampoline. Iris watched scary movies with Dad like it was nothing, and Jack didn't cry that one time he broke his arm. Remember that?"

I did. He'd crashed his bike in the cul-de-sac next to our

house and walked home with a compound fracture like it was nothing.

"I was the one who slept with the lights on even though I was sixteen. I was the one telling you all to be careful, to watch out. But that night?" she takes a deep, shaky breath. "You know how this happened?" she asks, pointing to her face.

I'm about to say *I'm a fucking freak of nature* when her voice cuts me off. "I ran back for Jack. He'd been mad at Mom before he want to bed and locked his door. It melted shut and he couldn't get out. I heard him and went back. I was scared shitless, Ves, but it wasn't even a question. And I kicked that door in. I found out who I was that night. It cost me." She motions to the burns. "But I don't want to give that back."

It's almost like she can see my hesitancy, because she squeezes my hand.

"I wouldn't give it back. More than that? It isn't yours to take. I don't know what you were looking for before you came home. But believe me when I tell you that the only thing we wanted was you."

I take a shuddering breath because this is the first time I don't think about the fire and want to throw up. I don't know how to process this.

"Are you going to stay?" she whispers. "Dad will be here in a little bit to pick me up."

My heart staggers at the thought of facing my father. I shake my head.

"Not . . . right now. I have to go home to Sam." My head shoots up, realizing my slip. "No, shit, I don't mean—"

But Carmen smiles warmly and takes my hands in hers. "You did. And that's good, Vesper. You don't realize . . ." She stops, taking a deep breath and blowing it out through pursed lips. "You were gone before you were gone, do you know what I mean? You stopped cheering. Stopped talking to your friends. You hid in your room. Stopped being . . . Vesper."

Tears prick the back of my eyes, and I shut them.

"I think its bullshit that you left."

She lifts my chin. "But I don't think it's bullshit that you found someone else to make you feel like you're home again."

The tears roll down my face. "I think I fucked it up, Carmen. I really fucked it up."

"Then go unfuck it," she says simply. "Life's too short to not."

She leans in and kisses my forehead. Someone calls her name. "Give me a minute?" she asks, and I nod. She skips away to go give a group of younger kids a hug. One throws her arms around Carmen's neck.

I scrawl a note on her napkin, and then I slip away before she can stop me.

I sneak behind the line of trees that lead to the parking

garage, but a sight stops me in my tracks. I duck farther behind the leafy coverage.

My father is walking away from the coffee cart in the hospital courtyard. He looks the same, his salt-and-pepper hair brushed back from his high forehead. His jeans are still tucked behind the tongue of his worn-out hiking boots, and I'm sure Carmen still teases him for it. He crumples the receipt in his hand as he raises the cup to blow on the coffee.

I'm struck then at how right he was. About everything. About the Wardens never really being gone. About my powers being dangerous. About the havoc it can wreak.

Because I can't change what happened with Sam. He loves Elisa, and he wants her back. And I can't betray him. I know that now. I think I knew it when I saw him stare at her in the woods—the look in his eyes.

I lean on the trunk of the tree, shutting my eyes and trying to push away the memory.

Carmen doesn't want this reversed, but what about my dad? Does he still fear me?

I watch him walk across the courtyard, and I know there's only one way to really find out.

Carefully, I step closer, making sure to stay hidden in the shadow of the trees. I hold my hand up and let out a low exhale. A single strand of power slips from me; I feel it as sure as I feel the breath leaving my lungs.

It streaks across the open air, curving around other people

in the courtyard until it finds my father. The power sinks into his back. I stop, then, wondering if he felt it. He looks up as the magic slips between his shoulder blades, but he doesn't stop walking. I close my eyes and sift through him, as quickly and quietly as I can.

I follow the sound of crackling fire, because I know that's where I'll find the fear of that night. That's where I'll find the fear of me. I find it—a memory that glows orange and smells like ash. I wrap my magic around it, peering inside.

I see Carmen, lying on a gurney in the ambulance. I see Iris, covered in black smoke, Inigo in her arms. I see my mom holding Jack as he sobs into her shoulder.

It's almost too much, and it is everything I have not to pull out and run. But then the fear shifts. Next, I'm seeing the empty ambulance, my pulled IVs dangling lifelessly off the edge after I'd run away.

What do you mean she's gone? my mom's voice cries.

The fear shifts, and I see a hospital waiting room, with an empty chair between Iris and Jack. I see the inside of a police station, where my mom is yelling at a detective behind a desk to *do something.*

The fear swirls, and I see countless iterations of the same thing. An empty space at the table. My mom looking at a picture of me, tears streaming down her cheeks.

It takes me a minute to realize that the fear isn't of *me.*

My father's fear is of *losing* me.

I pull out so fast, I almost don't realize what my power is ripping through. On my way out of my father's fears, I see another vision. The alleyway. I see the man stopping, his silhouette turning under the fluorescent light. *If you can't serve us, then you're of no use,* the man says.

I swear the voice is familiar, but I can't stay in any longer.

I yank out of my father as hard as I can, and then fall to my knees, gasping for breath. The dirt is damp, and it soaks my jeans in seconds as I dig my fingers into the bark of the tree and fight to catch my breath.

When I look up, I see my father. He turns around, his eyes scanning the trees. He felt that; he had to. I lost my subtle touch at the end.

My mind spins, and a vise clutches my chest as understanding wraps around my cracked heart.

I've spent so much time running and hiding and planning and trying to find some way to repair what I am and what I've done that I didn't see the damage I was doing.

Tears slip out of my eyes as I let both hands fall to the wet grass.

I never wanted to hurt anyone ever again, but Carl's dead. My family was just as shattered by my wordless disappearance as they were about the fire.

And Sam.

I let myself fall alongside someone who never wanted me as more than a gladiator. I let myself break off pieces of my soul as I fell deeper into whatever I felt for him while planning to rob him of the girl he really loves. I've been so afraid of the monster inside I didn't see the monster I was becoming.

I pull up two fistfuls of grass as I sit upright, blinking the final tears over my bottom lashes.

I can't betray Sam. I won't. He wants Elisa, so I will bring her back. I will give him the life he wants, and then I will have to turn around and face the shattered pieces of mine. I will face what I've done.

With a grunt, I push myself up, dusting the grass off of my wet jeans.

I don't get the happy ending here. The sooner I accept that, the sooner I'll find my ending. Whatever it may be.

I sink farther into shadow, not chancing a move until my dad turns back around and makes his way to Carmen's bench just as she returns and sees the napkin. The realization that I'm gone slinks over her shoulders, but I think she knows I'm still watching her, because she puts both hands over her heart.

THIRTY-TWO

I take a cab to the court gala. I didn't want to ride with Aldrick. I wanted to be alone. We pull up, and I peer out the window at the people in tuxedos and gowns walking up to the Palace of Fine Arts, a gorgeous museum on the outset of the peninsula. Torches light up the tree-lined walkway, casting the gorgeous pillars and arches into strange, bewitching shadows.

"Honey, you sure you're at the right place?" the driver asks me. He's a nice guy. Kind of reminds me of my grandpa.

"Yeah, why do you ask?" I grin at him in the rearview mirror and take another deep pull from my red Slurpee; I asked him to make a stop at 7-Eleven on the way. "Don't I look nice?" I give myself an exaggerated once-over. I'm wearing the cut-up *300* shirt I wore for cheer practice, the holey one with a ripped-out Gerard Butler screaming into the rain on the front and "DEATH BEFORE DISHONOR" on the back. I haven't showered since before the festival last night, but I did make sure to put on some of Sapphira's acne spot treatment that I decided to not wash off. My hair is in a topknot, and I put on as many of Aldrick's bracelets as I could find. That, paired with my paint-stained Northview High sweatpants and Converse, make me into—if I may so myself—a fucking *vision*. I also haven't washed these clothes since my last grappling session with Wex two nights ago, so I smell even better than I look.

Because, sure, Ananias said I had to show up in formal attire. But I'm so, so tired of playing by the rules when they've done absolutely nothing for me. I've got no one to impress. I've made it to the final trial no matter what I wear to this, and I'm not shaving my legs for these assholes.

I give a queen's wave to a polished couple walking by, making sure to smile broadly with my Slurpee-stained teeth. The cab pulls up to the curb, and I unwrap a Twinkie as I hand the fare to the cabbie. Oh right. I also stuffed my pockets full of Twinkies.

"You know, dear, I'll tell you what I told my daughters," he says, craning his neck to look back at me. "It's what's on the inside that matters. So you walk in there with your head held high. You're God's creation, and don't you forget that."

I shove the whole Twinkie in my mouth. *"Fank oo,"* I say, with half mock seriousness and half genuine appreciation. I climb out and watch him pull away. That was nice. I wonder if I'll come across that kind of kindness again before I bite it.

I pull another Twinkie out of my pocket and unwrap it as I meander up the walkway to the museum. I'm getting strange looks as I take a bite of Twinkie and chase it with a slurping pull from my Slurpee.

"This the party?" I ask a woman in a sleek silver gown. She looks me up and down, trying and failing to hide her horror.

"Sorry, so rude of me. Want one?" I ask, pulling another smashed Twinkie from my pocket. She leans back in disgust, and I shrug as I make my way past crowds of people and closer to the steps of the museum.

I pop the lid off my Slurpee and dip my Twinkie in the ice before shoving the whole thing in my mouth.

"Vesper? What the hell are you doing?" I hear a voice gasp behind me, and I spin, letting my drink slosh over the side.

Sapphira is in a black gown that hugs her every curve, cut deep over her chest with a solid strap of fabric connecting the diverging lines just under her collarbone. Her hair is slicked into a low ponytail, and her blood-colored lips contrast against her minimal eye makeup.

I swallow hard. "Hey, girl!" I say, tipping my drink back. The ice gathers, rushing toward my face in one swoop, and I cough and sputter as I get Slurpee in my nose. "Where's a trash can?" I ask, Slurpee dripping down my face.

Sapphira grabs my hand and yanks me down the walkway, keeping to the shadow. Little clusters of tuxedos, smooth hair, and glittering gowns part for us. We go right instead of left, into a building opposite the domed arches where the party is happening. I hear a stringed quartet echoing over the stone.

We walk down marble hallways, and she pulls me into a small bathroom. She pulls a duffel bag from under the sink and opens it. There are brushes, curling irons, and all manner of makeup.

"Wow. You came prepared," I joke.

"Ananias likes his employees to look the part," she says. "Is this supposed to be some kind of statement?" she motions to my sweatpants and wipes under my eyes with the warm washcloth.

"Sure, if the statement is 'Here's your headliner—watch her make every wrong decision.'" I pull Twinkies out of my pocket and hold one out to her, and she smacks it out of my hand. It hits the wall, hard.

"I'm here," I say, defeated. Because that's all I can say. I'm here. I'm going to fight for Sam and give him what he wants.

Sapphira pushes a stand of hair off my forehead, her eyes heavy. "You still haven't told me what happened," she says, wiping some sort of cleanser across my forehead.

I haven't told her that Sam's girlfriend is the Ripper. I don't even know where to start. "It was a shitshow. I don't want to talk about it right now."

Sapphira sets the towel down, the dark circles under her eyes barely hidden by her professionally done makeup job.

"You look how I feel," I say.

"I'm just really tired," she says, motioning for me to sit still. She swipes brushes on my eyelids and over my cheekbones, runs her curling iron over my hair, and then pulls a dress off a hanger on the back of the bathroom door.

"My spare. Put it on."

I don't argue. I slip out of my sweats and pull the sky-blue gown covered in crystals up over my body. The fabric feels like silk, and the straps rest on my shoulders like they were made for me. Sapphira pulls a spare pair of heels from her bag and tosses them to me. I strap them on, straightening as she looks me up and down, adjusting a piece of hair before nodding once. I look at my reflection, hardly recognizing myself. My eyes are rimmed with shimmer, my mouth a full pout of crimson. Somehow, she's turned my mess of tangled hair into a side-swept chignon at the base of my neck.

Outside, the quartet starts playing a lively song, and Sapphira goes on her tiptoes to look out the window.

"It's starting soon. We have to go," she says.

I follow her out into the hallway, our heels clicking on the marble floor. We're almost to the door when I stop.

"Wait," I say, looking down. "My phone. I left it in the bathroom."

She looks eagerly out the door, out into the firelit garden. She's nervous.

"You go," I assure her. "I'll meet you out there."

I head back, stopping to adjust my hair before I grab my phone off the counter. I've just opened the door when I hear footsteps. Shuffling.

As quietly as I can, I close the door, leaving it open just a sliver.

Ananias and one of his guards stop at a door across the way, one marked *Curator's Office*.

He punches a code into a keypad on the door and disappears inside. He's only gone a moment before he appears again, straightening his suit jacket and whispering to the guard, his jaw set, his eyes intense.

The guard nods once. Twice. Then Ananias walks down the hall, past the bathroom. I let the door close all the way, barely trusting myself to breathe until his footsteps fade. I press the door open a sliver, peering out.

The guard is still in front of the curator's office, his hands clasped in front of him.

He's guarding something. Alarm bells sound in my mind. I know something's shifted in Sapphira—there's something she's afraid of but won't tell me.

The devil you know.

I lift my hand and the magic swells under my skin. I go as slowly as I can, letting it stretch languidly across the hallway until it's at the guard's chest. With a hitch in my breath, I dive into him.

He shifts uncomfortably and looks around. I pause, but after a glance up and down the hallway to assure himself he's alone, he settles back against the door.

I close my eyes, sorting through the things he fears. Dogs with bared teeth. Flying in an airplane.

Then, I see Ananias's face. I lean into that fear, plucking at it gently like a harp string. He's afraid someone will get into that room. He's afraid of failing Ananias.

A small swell of excitement bubbles up in my throat. I just have to get him to step away from the door. I let the magic move around in his chest, gently strumming the fear he has of dogs.

The sound of a growl sounds down the hallway, giving way to a sharp bark.

I almost feel bad as I see the look of sheer terror on the guard's face. I stroke the fear again, and the sound rings out down the hallway once more, closer this time.

He draws his gun and steps away from the door, sweat beading on his temples.

"Who's there?" he asks, and I swallow back a snort.

My magic brushes deeper, and the growl gets louder, sounding in the hallway perpendicular to this one.

The guard weighs his options before stepping away from the door and stepping down the hallway in search of the vicious dog that doesn't actually exist.

I only have moments. With one push, I open the door and slink across the hallway. I let my magic stretch, chasing the sound of the guard's rubber shoes on the floor. My magic spears him from behind, sifting until I find the fear of someone getting into the room. I pull it out, and the door he was guarding pops open with a soft hiss.

A thrill shoots across my shoulders, and I can't help smiling as I step inside and close the door behind me.

I did it. I'm controlling this magic. It's not controlling me.

Focus. I have to focus now. I don't have much time, and I still have to figure out how to get back *out* of here without being seen.

I squint into the dark as my eyes adjust. A dim desk light is on, illuminating a sparse office. There's a desk across the way, but no chair.

On it, there's a leather briefcase.

At least, it looks like a briefcase. Sort of. I step closer, my gown swishing around me as I get closer. Scratch that. It looks too . . . *old* to be a briefcase.

With a deep breath, I reach out and rest my thumbs on the gold locks. They spring open at my touch, and my breath catches in my throat.

A light-colored leather-bound book sits inside, a circular seal stamped deep on the cover.

A quill, surrounded in a swirling chain, tightening toward

the end of the point. Blood drips off the end, splashing onto the paper below.

The Ledger. The one I signed, earlier.

With shaking hands, I open the book. Contracts. Hundreds, one right after the other.

I stop at a name: Rebecca Hannah.

She was a Miasma the first night who was knocked out right before me.

I, the undersigned, agree to fight for the Tournament of the Unraveling.

My eyes skim the paper—I recognize the waiver I signed the first night.

I flip through the book. Another page has a name written in purple ink: *Tessa DeLaney.* Even she's bound to him. I flip through the pages, irritated. It's all the standard waiver.

I let my head drop, exhaling sharply. I snuck in for nothing.

I lift my head, and something stops the breath in my throat.

Words are slowly appearing on the page, spreading like a stain.

Umbra ink.

I, the undersigned, agree to bind my power to the Tournament of the Unraveling. Upon my losing or forfeit, I surrender my powers to Ananias Ventra.

My heart takes off in a wild gallop. My fingers dig into

the edge of the table as the words sink in.

When you lose, Ananias owns your powers.

My mind skitters, trying to piece everything together. It all comes rushing back.

Theo saying his powers had vanished.

The glass Ananias conjured around the cage in Alcatraz.

Ananias took his power when he lost.

I flip through the book, looking at the dozens of contracts of the fighters who have lost the tournaments so far. How many powers does Ananias have now?

I turn the page, and a name stops me cold.

Sapphira Raina Savrey.

Sapphira. This is a different contract. I lean forward to read, but footsteps sound in the hall, and I shut the Ledger as quietly as I can, closing the briefcase and backing up slowly. I slip back out into the hallway, letting the door close softly behind me.

Sapphira was right.

The devil we knew, the Wardens, were better than this.

I spin and run straight into a solid chest. My heartbeat runs wild, panic spiraling. My mouth opens to let out a scream, but Sam covers it with his hand.

"Ves. It's me." I almost didn't recognize him. He's wearing a dark suit, and his hair is brushed back. The panic subsides, but my heartbeat doesn't slow down.

He lowers his hand, looking over my shoulder. "You didn't

come out with Sapphira, and I got worried."

I grip his arms and look up at him. "Sam."

Sam's face tightens, though his eyes are confused. "We have to get out of here and back to the party. We're not supposed to be in here."

I nod, my mind still racing. The jingle of keys sounds behind us, along with squeaky footsteps. The guard.

Sam looks down the hallway. There's nowhere to go. He'll be here in seconds.

"We won't be able to get out of here in time. He'll know something's up, Sam," I whisper.

Sam turns back to me and meets my eyes. Something in him shifts. I know it happens quickly, but it doesn't feel like it. It's like I see his look go from worried to resolute to . . . something else.

It doesn't have a name, but it has a feeling. It feels like a drop on a roller coaster, like the heat of a match burning too close to fingers. My skin tingles as he steps closer and pushes me against the wall, his rough fingers on my bare shoulders, his green eyes lit like emeralds that have been resting on a bed of hot coals.

"Play along," he whispers, and then his lips are on mine. It's not like the first kiss. There's nothing tentative about this, nothing sweet. Part of me wants to shove him off, to tell him to go fuck himself. To tell him that I learned my lesson last time.

But another part, a hungrier, louder part, takes over.

His tongue presses against my lips, and I open my mouth against his, tasting him as his hands run down my ribs, his fingers burning me through the fabric.

I bite his lip and he gasps into my mouth, his unshaved jaw moving over mine like he's claiming me. And my fingers run through the back of his hair like I'm fine with that.

He nips at my bottom lip and I'm against the wall, my leg around his hip, his hand under my knee and—

"What's this?" A flashlight shines in our faces, and the spell is broken.

Sam sets me back on the ground—when the hell did he lift me up?—and holds a hand up to shade his eyes.

"We were just looking for privacy," Sam says, putting on his best *Aw, shucks* grin.

"This isn't a hotel," the guard barks. "Make yourselves decent and get out."

I lift my strap back into place—when the hell did it fall down?—and Sam grabs my hand.

"So sorry about that," he says to the guard.

The guard escorts us out. I look back over my shoulder. He's still behind us. I want to tell Sam what I've found, but the guard is too close. I can't risk him hearing me. I bite my lip hard and focus on the sound of my heels clicking on the concrete.

Sam reaches over and puts an arm around my shoulder,

pulling me close. To any outsider, it might look like we're having a sweet moment. His lips brush against my ear. "We need to talk."

I look over my shoulder again—the guard is still behind us, suspicion in his glare as we lock eyes.

I turn back around. "We need to be alone," I whisper. We continue on the winding walkway back to the party. We reach the firelit dome, and we both stop.

Inside the dome, the painted concave ceiling is lit by floating candles, kept aloft by several Levitases that sit on steps that line huge planters alongside the columns.

Ananias stands on a lofted stage on the far side, and he's looking at us. In fact, everyone in the dome is looking at us.

Everyone.

Ananias steps off the stage, and the crowd parts for him. He stalks toward me like a jungle cat eyeing prey. It's everything I have to not recoil as he reaches me.

"Vesper Montgomery is the challenger in our championship round tomorrow. I will be announcing her opponent before the fight. Once you see what this one can do, you will *not* be disappointed," he adds, turning to the throngs of people. I see some of the investors I recognize, but there are dozens of new people.

A string quartet starts a song in the corner, and Ananias holds his hand out to me.

"Let's start this night off on a civilized note, shall we?"

I look quickly to Sam, whose jaw is locked as he gives me a look that tells me this is my choice. I have to play it cool. At least until I figure out my next move.

I take Ananias's hand, and he pulls me close. The rest of the room either pairs off or edges to the side of the dome, where Levitases guide trays of floating champagne.

The cello echoes off the lofted ceiling, and it sounds mournful. Ananias puts one hand on the small of my back, and I look away. Stokers make their way among the guests, acting like human heat lamps, moving their hands around bare arms and backs to heat the air. Across a still, black lake, a row of houses sits facing the museum. Two Shaders stand at the water's edge, arms up. No one can see us.

"Nervous?" he asks quietly.

I can't avoid it anymore. I turn to face him and pray he can't see the look of—what am I feeling? Hate? Rage? Fear?

All three, maybe.

He wanted us to believe he was our liberator. He wanted to let us believe we had nothing more to fear.

"No," I lie, looking up in his hazel eyes.

"I'm sure Sam is excited. A Harbinger fighting for you— I'd like those odds."

I look down. "We'll see."

My heart is fluttering wildly in my chest, and I hate myself for being afraid.

Ananias puts a finger under my chin and raises it. I look

up, fighting the urge to yank away from his touch.

"Don't look at the floor, Vesper. You were meant to keep your head held high."

I can't pretend. I force a smile on my face and drop my hand from his.

"I'm going to get a drink."

Ananias doesn't let me go right away. His smile deepens, and I worry he can see right through me. That he knows I know.

Sam's voice cuts through the din then, and it's like a light in the darkness.

"Mind if I . . . ," Sam asks, gesturing to me.

Ananias looks from Sam to me and then gives me a slight bow before disappearing into the crowd.

Sam leans close. "I didn't know where you were. I tried calling Sapphira, but she told me you didn't want to talk—"

I shake my head. "Sam, listen—"

"What happened in the forest—"

I know what he's going to say. He's going to apologize and try to tell me he thinks I'm great and all this other stuff that's supposed to make me feel better, but I can't deal with that right now.

"Sam. Shut up for a minute," I breathe. He stops, looking down at me as I take a shaky breath, and I lean in. My lips brush his ear as I tell him what I found, and I feel his grip tightening on mine with each word.

When he pulls back, I see the fear in his eyes. He understands.

"What are we going to do?" he asks, looking over my shoulder at the crowd.

"I'm going to do what I told you I would. I'm going to bring Elisa back."

Sam shakes his head. "We can't, Vesper."

I move away from his touch. I wasn't expecting that. "We can. And we will."

I try to pull away, but Sam grabs my hands and brings me closer. "Vesper. Shut up for a minute."

He sets his hands gently on the side of my face as he sighs, like the sight of my guarded gaze causes him physical pain. "You don't understand," he says, leaning down to meet my eyes. The torchlight dances against his skin, his face crumpled with desperation. My breath feels like it's been stolen from my lungs. For a second, I forget the shadows around us. I forget everything except him. I reach up, pressing my hand to his cheek. He closes his eyes and presses his hand over mine.

I savor this moment. I breathe it in, drinking the scent of the champagne on his breath and the warmth of his skin on mine. He leans closer to me. "I know I didn't tell you the whole truth."

I pull back. "Hold on, Sam."

He sees the worry in my eyes. "I know you feel like I lied. And that there's nothing real between us—"

I laugh. It's loud, and a couple of the dancing partners stop to look. I press my lips together. It's now or never. I steel myself.

"There is no us. There never was."

His jaw twitches. "You don't mean that."

My throat burns as I stare at him. "I was going to betray you, Sam. The whole time, I planned on taking the unraveling for myself."

I've said terrible things to him, but this is something different entirely. This is a breaking of something precious. This is the shattering of the glass hope I've coaxed out of the dark corners of my heart.

This can't be unsaid.

This can't be undone.

But I know if I didn't tell him, I might lose my nerve. I might try to tell him what he means to me or worse, let him start to tell me what I mean to him. And that will make doing the right thing harder.

And I can't let this get any more difficult than it already is.

He tilts his head as he steps away from me, the weight of my words knocking him back.

I break free of him, walking to the edge of the party. I come up behind one of the pillars, snatching a glowing drink from a tray as I pretend to admire a floating candle. I step out into the dark, blocked from view and press a hand to my mouth, trying to stifle the tears that bite the back of my throat.

I stop as a figure breaks away from the party. Ananias pulls a cigarette out of his pocket and steps out to the water's edge. Suddenly, I have an idea.

I step farther into shadow. It might be crazy, but this might be my only chance. Ananias blows smoke out over the water. I lift my hand, my magic smoothly leaving my palm.

"Vesper. You didn't follow. I was so worried—" Sapphira hisses as she comes up next to me. I don't break my concentration as I look over at her.

Without looking, I let my magic slip through the dark. I feel it latch on to Ananias.

"You were right about the devil we know, Sapphira," I say.

I press into him. It's murky. Dark. There are the echoes of screams, the sound of squealing tires. Blood.

No. I need something better. I brush up against a fear toward the surface. It's not his deepest fear, but it's the one he's thinking about the most right now. In his mind, it's the loudest.

"Vesper. What are you doing?" she asks.

I give Ananias's fear a slight tug, and I see him flinch just as Sapphira goes down next to me. Aldrick is there then—he must've been watching from inside.

"What happened?" he breathes, his eyes full of fear as he lifts her head to his lap. I fall to my knees next to him, the wet grass soaking through my dress.

The fear is still out, I feel it pulsing in the open air. She's out cold. I put my hands on the either side of her face.

She's . . .

I stop, noticing the absolute stillness of her in my arms. Aldrick feels for her pulse.

"She's dead."

Panic flutters in my chest, gasping breaths wrenching from me as I look around.

"I'm going to get help," Aldrick chokes out.

Ananias's fear sticks in the back of my throat. I look up at him by the water. He blows smoke through his nose, but nothing's changed.

Nothing's changed, except —

I look down at Sapphira. Ananias turns, his eyes fixing on me, and then on Sapphira.

"Aldrick. No. Wait."

Aldrick's eyes lock on mine.

"What happened?" Ananias calls, running over to us, keeping to the dark.

He drops to his knees next to me; the fear is so thick I think I might choke on it. I force myself to breathe in. Breathe out.

It's just fear.

"What did you do?" he asks, the terror in his voice unmistakable. *What did you do?*

The words come fluttering back like a bat in the night, bringing with it the memory of my father, earlier.

Of the first fear I ever pulled out.

The weight of it crashes into me, and I see it all play out in my skull. Wet stone and blood. The man in the suit walking down an alleyway.

The vision expands, revealing the fear in its entirety, as if it were huddled in my mind like a trip wire since I brushed through my dad this morning.

I see it as though I'm standing outside myself, taking in the whole scene as if I'm there.

My father lies on the ground, twenty years younger than he was this morning and gasping for breath. His chest is bleeding, spilling through his fingers onto the concrete. Lynn, her hair white even as a teenager, stands with her back pressed up against the brick wall, eyes wide as she watches my father bleed out.

The man turns around now. He always stopped halfway, but now I see him fully.

The recognition punches the air out of my already-still lungs.

"Ivan," someone calls from the mouth of the alley.

It's Ivan.

The name that's been haunting my nightmares.

Except it isn't a new face, and it's not obscured by shadow.

This face is handsome. A little younger, but I recognize him.

It's Ananias.

✻ ✻ ✻

I fall out of the vision, my mind spinning as I try to piece it together without giving myself away.

He kneels across from me. Ivan, the head of the Wardens. It's Ivan. This whole time.

I shut out the thought. I need to focus on Sapphira right now. I need to bring her back.

I breathe out and let the fear dissipate. It slips back into him, and Sapphira sputters, her eyes fluttering open.

He reaches out to touch her cheek, and I see it, just above his cuffs . . . the ones he keeps pulled as far down as possible.

The Ledger's mark. Realization slams into me so hard I almost can't breathe.

Ivan is a Ledger? How is that possible?

I stop, thinking about the fear I pulled from him. It was losing control. Losing the power the tournament gave him.

Losing . . . Sapphira.

It all clicks into place.

Sapphira dying is Ananias's fear. Ananias isn't the Unraveler.

Sapphira is.

Aldrick sighs in relief as my eyes flit up to meet Ivan's, and, in that moment, I know he knows what I've done. He pulls his cuff down, over the mark.

I push myself up to my feet, taking a step closer to Aldrick, as though I can protect him from Ivan's wrath.

The moment between us crackles, alive in anticipation. I should run. I should scream.

"You couldn't just leave it alone," Ivan breathes, almost like he's disappointed.

Then he lifts his hand and a small dart hits me on the neck.

Everything goes black.

THIRTY-THREE

I wake on a cold floor, and my head aches. It takes everything I have to sit up. I'm in a cell. There's a window cut into the stone above me, and a sliver of moonlight cascades in.

"Sapphira?" I ask.

"She's fine," a voice says from the dark. The other side of the bars.

Ivan leans into the light.

"Aldrick?" I ask.

"Also fine."

I try to conjure the tingling in my palms, but nothing comes. There's a hollow sleepiness in my blood that chills me to my bones.

"Don't even bother using your magic. The Miasma's poison gave you a nullifying dose that will last all night."

"Where are we?" I ask.

"Like it?" Ivan asks. He wraps has hands on the bars and

leans his head down, stretching his shoulders. He grunts in satisfaction before straightening.

"I borrowed the idea from the Romans. They had cells under their fighting rings, too. We're under my newest development—a model replica of the Colosseum. Normally, my gladiators would spend the night in the four-star victor's suite I had prepared, but that's not where we're at."

He opens the cell door. The clunk of the metal echoes painfully off my aching head, and I scramble back against the far wall as he steps inside. He stops when he sees how afraid I am.

"I'm not going to hurt you, Vesper, if that's what you're worried about."

As though to prove his point, he kneels down so we're eye level. He tilts his head, trying to meet my eyes. I finally look up at him, ignoring the screaming terror as the words play over and over in my head. *Ivan. It's Ivan.*

"You tried to kill my father," I rasp out.

The accusation doesn't affect him. He takes in the words and then looks at the stone wall on the far side of the cell.

"I didn't want him to die, Vesper. But you know what your powers are. You know how dangerous they can be. I was trying to protect him."

"You left him bleeding out in an alleyway behind a Laundromat," I spit, the rage taking place of fear in my chest.

Ivan purses his lips. "I was young. I was . . . vengeful." He considers it for a moment and then shakes his head as though to clear a thought. "I did a lot of things I regret."

I shiver in the corner, and he stands. He leaves the cell for a moment and then returns with a blanket. He holds it out to me, but I don't take it. He drapes it over my shoulders anyway. The warmth makes me want to sigh in relief, but I don't want to give him that satisfaction.

He leans with his back against the bars.

"Where's Sam?" I breathe out, my eyes searching the cells on the opposite aisle behind Ivan. He laughs. It's humorless—almost bitter.

"Oh, you don't worry about Sam. He's safe. My daughter made sure of that."

I lean forward, too enticed by answers to guard my expression. Ivan must like the look of interest on my face, because he stands straight and then leans forward.

"Oh yes. Sam Hardy has been a thorn in my side since before my daughter betrayed me. But she used the Chronicler—who *also* has no love for me—to find a Vigilant to put a protective spell over him. I was never to touch him. I was never to speak of her to him. And in my lessened state, I am no match for it."

"Lessened?" I press.

Ivan smirks and shows me his wrist. "Before I had access to the Athenaeum, I was just a Ledger. So when she *ripped* me"—he says the word like it's a curse—"she left remnants of the power I was born with. It took months, but I nursed it back. And I worked with what I had."

"You mean you tricked Oddities into signing over their powers to you," I say, not bothering to hide my disdain. Sometime since I woke up, I realized he is going to kill me. He wouldn't be telling me any of this if he was planning on letting me go. Somehow, the fear of that doesn't register, and I'm thankful. I know it will, eventually, but it lets me be present for answers.

He smiles. It's slow, and almost sad. "It was not as effective as the Athenaeum. Tricking Oddities to sign over their powers was exhausting."

He paces the cell.

"And, I found, kind of useless. A year of searching, and Sapphira was the only Oddity of any real power. Even with a tournament designed to draw the best and brightest, all I found were Miasmas and Stoneskins. Then in walks my daughter's Baseline boyfriend, and I realized I could have it all again."

My stomach sinks at the thought of Ivan recognizing Sam.

"I thought about just having Sapphira go offer to bring her back, but the spell prohibited that as well, since it was on my behalf. Damn rules."

"Why didn't you just use Sapphira to bring Elisa back yourself?" I ask.

Ivan stops walking then and turns to me.

The answer creeps over my spine. "Because you need love to unravel. And you didn't love her. Your own daughter."

His lip curls at my words. "She took everything from me. How could I love someone like that?"

"Love is unconditional. You love someone for who they are, not what they do," I say, and Ivan crosses the room toward me in two strides, kneeling in front of me with a finger pointed inches from my face.

"See? That was the problem, Vesper. You. Those notions. I thought my problems were over when Sam entered the tournament, but I realized they were only getting started. Because the more he felt for you, the more I lost my one tether to Elisa."

"So this is all about bringing her back," I choke out.

Ivan's smile widens, like there's a joke I'm not getting.

"It was," he whispers. "But I've come up with something better."

He pushes himself to his feet. "I'm going to give you the opportunity of a lifetime, Vesper Montgomery. A chance to have everything you want."

"You don't know what I want," I say, though my voice comes out softer and less convinced than I mean it to. I shove myself to my feet, tired of looking up at him. The blanket drops to the floor.

Ivan smiles again, and it's the smile of someone who is holding all the cards and is about to lay them on the table.

"You want your powers gone. You want your family to be safe, and you want Sam. I can give you all three."

Everything in me stills. I want to tell him to piss off. I want to look less interested, less desperate. But I can't help it—I'm curious, and he sees it.

With a flick of his wrist, he holds the Ledger. It's materialized out of nowhere.

"Sign your powers over to me, Vesper. I'll take them from you. I will promise that your family—your father—will never be bothered by the Wardens, ever. I will assure safety for Sam, and most of all—no Elisa. You can even say that I made you do this. Either way, you're Baseline, and you get the boy of your dreams."

As he speaks, glowing words fill up the page, copying what he is saying. He waves his hand, and the book floats right in front of me.

"You would give up the only chance to see your daughter again?" I ask. It's genuine. I saw the pain in his eyes in the Chronicler's memory. Somewhere deep inside, he did love Elisa.

He steps closer. "There are two powers in this world, Vesper. Love and fear. Sapphira's unraveling is bound by love. Even Elisa, my own treasure, betrayed me because of love. But you?" He steps closer, over the book, and his features are illuminated by the words. "You are fear. It's limitless. And perfect."

The glow of the book soothes me, and I let myself drift closer to the page. I would be Baseline. I could go home and never hurt anyone again. My family would be safe. And Sam. I wouldn't have to betray Sam, and he wouldn't blame me. Ivan holds out a pen, and I reach across the pages and take it.

I take a breath as another thought slips into my mind, cold and clarifying.

"You will reinstate the Wardens?" I ask.

Ivan's eyes harden. "You've seen what happens when we aren't in charge, Vesper. Oddities need boundaries, or the world will eat itself."

"So what will happen to those who like their freedom? What happens to the Oddities in this tournament?"

"Worry about yourself, Vesper. I believe the offer on the table is more than fair."

Home, but at the cost of giving this power to someone who desires fear more than love. Sam, but at the cost of his choice.

I don't know where it comes from, but the line from "Invictus" flits across my mind.

I am the master of my fate, I am the captain of my soul.

I couldn't control the fire. I can't control the fact that I'm a Harbinger. I can't control who Sam loves, and I can't control what happens tomorrow.

But I can control this.

No.

I lift the pen, gripping it so hard that my knuckles go white.

Then I set it down on the page.

Ivan's eyes flicker, revealing a hint of rage he quickly checks.

"What are you doing?"

I step back, letting the cold stone sooth my bare shoulders. "No."

He slams the book shut. "What do you mean, *no*?"

"I am not letting you have this power. Ever."

Just like that, all traces of humanity disappear from his eyes.

The fear that he is going to hurt me flares in my chest, but then I remember—he can't. I'm protected as long as I'm in the tournament. This isn't part of the tournament, so he can't kill me here.

I see the hate boil up in him, and just as quickly—it goes still. He's impossible to read, and it's more frightening than the rage.

"You are making a mistake."

I nod. "Probably."

He steps closer. "I'll give you the night to think about this, Vesper. And think carefully. Tomorrow, you will lose the fight, and then I will have your power anyway. Then, I will have your power and you will have no protection. Don't throw your life away."

With that, he turns. He slams the cell door, and I'm alone.

I go to the lighthouse in my dreams. The rain is pouring as I creep up the steps. Sapphira sits, looking out at the water. I try to hug her, but I can't reach her. I call to her, but she doesn't turn.

And then everything blends from cool to warm, and the screams in my throat subside as long-forgotten memories bubble to the surface, warming me with their light—bits of goodness rimmed in shimmer and warmth to wrap around myself on the cold stone floor.

The day Carmen, Iris, and I made a lemonade stand and no one showed up, so my mom dressed up in her most ridiculous outfit—one of my grandmother's old church hats, the rims of my dad's old glasses, and fake hillbilly teeth she got from a dental convention—drove around the block, and showed up at our stand with a coin purse full of change. *I'm here to buy some lemonaaaaddde*, she said. We almost peed ourselves, we laughed so hard.

My dad teaching Iris to read in the light of the fireplace, handing me M&M's as little bribes to not read over her shoulder and say the words before she figured them out herself.

Lindsay and I walking through downtown to the pancake house on Saturday mornings after a sleepover, because neither of us had our licenses yet.

The echoes of "Happy Birthday." The smell of sunscreen and watermelon. The crackle of a bonfire on the beach. The first laugh after a good cry. Bumping fingers with a cute boy in the popcorn bin in the movies. My dad singing hymns too early in the morning and my grandparents' collie, Oliver the Wonderdog, getting too excited when we came to visit and—

I don't know what wakes me, but I uncurl my body, stiff with sleep, and sit up.

Moonlight pours through the barred windows, splashing on the ground. I look over. I scoot, pushing myself into the light, turning my face up to meet it.

I imagine it spilling over my skin, soaking my pores. I imagine it is confused as it brushes up against the dried tears on my cheeks. I imagine that it's full of whispered messages that the world outside is still the world outside, that couples are kissing with it slipping between their mouths, that it's still crashing over late-night get-togethers, getting lost in the frenzy of firelight. That somewhere, it is roving over the skin of a pregnant belly, whispering against the imprint of a foot or a hand. Somewhere, it's slipping through the glass of a child's bedroom, coaxing them from the edge of a nightmare.

I'm glad I didn't miss this. This strange, beautiful thing in the middle of my cell. Nothing has changed. My heart is still cracked like a piece of hard candy some kid stepped on.

Everything is still shit. But here? In this moment? I'm alive, and for the first time in my life, I am calling the power inside of me *mine*.

I was always afraid of the thing inside of me, this beckoning shadow that seemed too powerful to ignore. But I know now that the worst monster one can become is the one you *choose*. I've spent too long fearing what's inside of me.

Something shifted when I refused to sign that book. I had everything I ever wanted right in front of me, and I found it wasn't what I thought.

I am a Harbinger.

I look up at the night sky. Purple clouds streak across a navy blanket pinpricked with specks of glittering light, and I push myself to my feet.

"God," I whisper.

It's been a while. Like, a long while. And I don't know if I'm still mad at him or if this is because I'm going into the fighting pit tomorrow, but I feel like I should say *something*.

"This has been really, really fucked up," I start out loud. "All of it. Every move I've made feels like the wrong one. Everyone I've loved has gotten hurt. All of this has been for nothing, and I'm mad and I'm thankful and I'm pissed and I just wanted to tell you that I've been so focused on what I would change, what I would reverse, what I would have done differently, that I didn't stop to think about the things that were just . . . perfect."

Walking the StrEat Food Park with Sam. The sound of his laughter. The feel of his lips.

"Did you just say *fuck* during a prayer?"

I jump at the sound of a voice coming from the other side of the bars.

"Is that how you always pray? Because that would explain our shit luck," Sam says, stepping into a shaft of moonlight.

I blink, not sure I am seeing what I think I'm seeing.

But Sam is standing there.

I cross the cell, certain I'm still dreaming. But when I get close and he reaches through to cup his hand on the back of my neck, I gasp and jump back. "You have to get out of here, Sam!" I hiss, looking down the dank basement hall.

"You're here, then I'm here," he says.

"How did you get in?" I ask, and he just smirks. It pisses me off. "Get *out*," I plead, and he steps closer to the bars.

Sam reaches through the bars once more, and I don't stop him as he threads his fingers gently through the hair at the base of my neck. A couple of the bobby pins Sapphira put in the bun come undone and fall to the floor with a soft *clink*.

"We aren't leaving here without you," he says, his voice low.

I shake my head, but Sam tightens his fingers around my hair. His eyes bore into mine. "You were right. This was for me. All of this. It had nothing to do with Elisa, because if I'd stopped for one second—one *fucking* second—I would've remembered the thing I loved most about her. I forgot *her*. Her spirit. Her will. Her unshakable faith that everything happens for a reason, but that we're not powerless. And if I couldn't see that? Then I should have seen the other reason when we visited the Chronicler. She died putting an end to carnage. It is only because of her that more innocents didn't die at Ivan's hand. She stopped him, knowing full well it would cost her her life."

I shake my head. I can't hear this. I can't let my heart go there.

"I saw her, Sam. I saw her walk out of the trees when I pulled her from you. I know your fear was her walking in on that—"

I start to pull back, but Sam yanks me forward, forcing me to meet his eyes.

"I'm trying to tell you that I'm in love with you, dammit."

I can't hide the look on my face that tells him exactly what I didn't want him to know.

"I wasn't afraid of Elisa seeing me *cheat*. I was afraid of her seeing that I fell in love again. I was afraid of moving on, Vesper."

He reaches around and pulls his Moleskine out of his back pocket. Cracking it open in the moonlight illuminates his writing. *Reasons Life Is Good.* He hands it to me.

And I can see them.

It starts simply—with: *The sunlight at Duncan's.*

Then, in different ink: *Hot coffee with Wex.*

The girl sitting across the way at Aloa's.

Then, something shifts. A new pen. The start of a new column. The entries get closer together.

The way she says "crap." Her hair in her eyes.

Farther down:

The way she gets mad. Her laugh. That look when she swings and misses with Abagail.

Her voice. Her smile. She smells like rain.

Then, just one word, below all the others. Bigger than all the others.

Vesper.

I close the book. Sam takes it back.

"I'm in love with you, Vesper, and I have been for a while. And I'm sorry if you ever thought that I was using you to make myself feel less, because that couldn't be further from the truth. You made me feel more in two days than I did in the two years since she died. And I *know* you're not interested. But I had to tell you. I couldn't—"

A door opens on the far end of the block. Sam and I turn around. Mavis stands with Aldrick. Abagail and Wex stand behind. This is a rescue mission.

"How'd you know where I was?" I ask as Abagail tosses Sam a key.

"Sapphira came to get us," Sam replies, popping the cell door open. Once I'm free of the bars, I grab the front of his shirt in my fist and pull him to me. His mouth crashes against mine, his arm tightening around my waist.

"Okay. Run for lives now, tonsil hockey later," Mavis snaps.

I stop, looking at the people who just risked their lives to save mine.

I shake my head, and I step back into the cell. Sam's face falters, and I hold up my hands. "I can't leave."

Then, a thick metal *clunk* sounds throughout the cell block. A door opening.

"You have to get out of here," I whisper, stepping farther into the cell.

Sam reaches for me, but I slam by cell shut and grab the key before he can stop me.

"What are you doing?" he cries, pulling on the metal.

"If I leave, it's the end of everything, Sam. I have to fight."

"Sam!" Abagail hisses as the sound of approaching guards grows louder.

"Vesper. Open this door. We're leaving."

I shake my head, tears running down my face as I meet his eyes. I reach through the bars and set a hand on his cheek. "You have to let me do this, Sam. You have to trust me."

There's a battle in his gaze as the footsteps get closer, but something shifts in him. I see it. He trusts me, even if he doesn't have all the answers. He opens the notebook and scribbles something on a piece of paper.

"If you're going to fight, then put this in the Ledger," he

says. I take the paper as he slides it through the bars. He doesn't let go right away but uses the paper to pull me closer. He kisses me one last time.

The footsteps are almost upon us now.

I watch as the people who came to rescue me leave.

And then, I'm all alone.

THIRTY-FOUR

Dawn breaks, and I haven't moved. I feel rather than see Ivan on the other side of the bars.

"Can we end this, Vesper?"

Sam's paper is still folded in my hand, unread. It doesn't matter what it says. I have to do this.

I turn, giving him a look rather than words. He understands me, and a steely indifference crosses his expression.

He knows what I've chosen.

I sit in the cell all day, watching the shadows stretch through the bars.

Around dusk, I hear the crowd start to gather. There's a dull roar of voices echoing down to my window. The air feels electric with anticipation. The sun is setting when I hear someone outside my cell. I look up, and Sapphira stands in the doorway, all in black.

I push myself to my feet.

"'The devil you know.' You knew who he was the whole time," I say.

She takes a staggered breath. "I wanted to find the Wardens to stop Ivan. But then . . . I realized at the Chronicler that they were the same. I wanted to warn you, but my contract wouldn't let me say anything. I did the best I could."

The devil you know. She'd been trying to warn me that Ananias was a monster. She just didn't know it was the same monster we'd been afraid of our whole lives.

I step closer and see that her eyes are red. She's been crying.

I feel the pulse back in the center of my palms, and I know the poison has worn off.

"Why would you sign the Ledger, Sapphira? Why would you give someone like him access to your power?"

She smiles sadly. When she looks up, her eyes are full of tears. With a deep breath, she lifts her arm to show me Nolan's bracelet.

"My brother was killed by the Wardens. He was an Unraveler, like me. But he was young and couldn't control it. They came for him, like it showed in the vision. Ananias told me that if I signed over my powers, he would find a way to bring my brother back. But now I know . . . he was the one who killed him in the first place."

Everyone has their price. Her voice echoes in my mind, and I understand.

Her face crumples, and I cross the cell until I'm directly in front of her.

"I'm so sorry, Sapphira."

She shakes her head. When she opens her eyes, her gaze is fierce.

"You have a chance to get what you want, Vesper. You should take it."

Outside, the crowd gets louder. I know she means that I should take Ivan's deal. That I should walk out of here unscathed, with everything I want. I know she wouldn't blame me for signing the Ledger and disappearing.

I can't exactly put a finger on the feeling running through my chest right now. It's not courage, but it's something like it. I think it's the knowledge that there's a purpose to this. I am not a mistake. I am not something to be dulled.

"That's exactly what I'm doing," I tell her. She considers, then looks up. She reaches behind her and tosses me a pair of leggings and a black tank top.

"Well. You can't kick ass in an evening gown," she says.

The dull thump and thunder of the ground crowd makes the whole place shake, but it still feels quiet as I wait in the mouth of the pit.

It's twilight, but the torches stain the world with an orange haze.

"You know what you're going to write in the Ledger?"

Tessa asks me. I hand her the paper. "Just write this down, okay?"

She looks at me, confused, but nods as she takes the paper. I remember that Ivan has her bound, too. She talks into an earpiece as she steps away. I peer out.

Suddenly, all of Ananias's investors make sense. We're in an arena the size of the Colosseum in Rome. Stone overhangs bursting with queen of poisons flowers line the balconies that stagger upward in amphitheater seating. Rose petals flit down from the top row of seats, a strange contrast to the dust that will no doubt be covered in blood.

The gate in front of me lifts, creaking and clanking as it pulls upward.

Across the way, a twin gate does the same. Beyond that, there's a silhouette in the darkness. My competitor, whoever it is.

I step a little farther out, narrowing my eyes as Tessa motions for me to enter.

My competitor steps toward the night, and my breath stops in my throat.

Ivan.

It's Ivan.

But, as he crosses the threshold into the ring, he shifts. He changes.

And he becomes Aldrick.

I stop walking, lead filling my gut. He has the Shifter's

powers from the first night, and he wanted me to see it.

He wants me to know it's really *him* I'm facing.

The leader of the Wardens. The Ledger with the powers of a dozen other Oddities magically bound to him.

He really meant it when he said I wouldn't make it out alive.

He's going to see to it.

Tessa steps in front of me, raising her hands, and the whole coliseum falls silent. My eyes search the crowd until I find Sam.

"Ladies and gentlemen, welcome to the inaugural fight in the Arena of the Queen of Poisons!"

The crowd erupts, and I look up at the night sky. I close my eyes and think about the cool breeze brushing my bare neck. I think of my family. I think of Sam's kiss.

"The final trial of this tournament will commence on my word. Ready?" she asks, looking up at the crowd. Her voice carries, echoing through the stands.

It's now or never.

"GO!"

Ivan throws his arms out, turning his arms to stone. He runs at me, his eyes glinting. He looks like Aldrick in every way, except I know Aldrick would never look at me with such hatred.

He swings, and I duck, jumping and rolling to the side.

He brings a massive boulder-size hand down, and I barely

roll out of the way in time. The crowd's reaction is so loud it feels like it's going to splinter the ground.

I can't match his strength. I have to figure something else out, and quick.

With a deep breath, I sprint to the edge of the ring. He follows, a smile on his face as he takes his sweet time.

He's enjoying this.

I put my hands on the stone wall of the ring and close my eyes, letting my magic slip through the stone. I don't know what I'll find, but I have to try.

My power slides through the wall and to the crowd on the other side, gliding over the bodies as I search. I've never tried this with so many people before, but I splay my fingers and feel my magic respond, splintering off as it explores. Hundreds of people, thousands of fears.

My mind blends through visions of x-rays on an illuminated screen to a growling wolf glaring from behind a dead tree. I see a closed-in box, with a hand frantically scratching at the wood, and then a pair of yellow eyes peering over a windowsill.

Ivan gets closer. He swings Aldrick's arms, and I've got nothing. My search becomes more frantic—darkness. Cemeteries. Bank statements full of red lettering. Then, I stop at the sight of an open field. The air crackles under a blanket of black clouds.

I open my eyes. Ivan is a foot away, his arm cocked back.

I wrap my small tendril of power around the fear and whip it out of the person's chest, letting a scream rip from my lungs as I swing it into the arena between us.

A bolt of lightning hits the ground between us, and Ivan flies backward. He lands on his back halfway across the arena and then rolls to a crouch.

Aldrick's smile looks all wrong on his face as he stands.

I push off the wall, feeling the fear in my hand like a metallic whip. I bring my hand around in an arc, and lightning rains down, landing inches from Ivan. He holds his arms up and turns to stone as a wicked lash of lightning hits the ground near his feet and slithers up his legs.

It doesn't affect the stone, and I feel my grip on the lightning fear slipping.

Ivan rolls his shoulders and crouches. His body writhes, and then he's Briony—the Fire Fury from the second night. The crowd gasps, and then erupts in applause.

They probably think my opponent is a Shifter.

"You can still stop this before it gets to the point of identifying your body through dental records," he says, and it comes out in Briony's tinny, hateful voice.

I grit my teeth as my power skitters over the audience, searching for a fear to counteract what I know Briony can do.

He blows a kiss as he crosses his arms over his chest and then throws them outward. A tunnel of fire shoots out from his ribs, heading straight for me.

Got one.

I drop to my knees and put my hands on the dirt, summoning a fear lingering in the back of an adrenaline junkie's mind. A rumble starts from somewhere above us, a phantom threat.

Ivan manipulates the fire, and it becomes a wall, careening toward me.

But I have something better. A sheet of snow, thick and roiling, spins out of the ether above us and meets the fire in a scream of steam. The snow arcs over my head, and I feel harmless chips of ice against the back of my neck as the avalanche's frigid breath blows past me, rendering the fire useless.

I open my eyes in the aftermath, the steam covering the ground around us.

With a shaky breath, I push myself to my feet and wait for the next attack.

Ivan steps forward, now in Riles's body. The Slitter. He rolls his wrists, and his hands turn to blades. He cracks his knuckles, a sickening *pop* sounding from his hands.

The crowd is going crazy. Their shouts are almost deafening, and they've started a stomping beat—*thud thud thud.* Clap. *Thud thud thud.* Clap.

I fight to catch my breath. I look up, finding Sam in the stands. His face is drawn.

I can keep pulling fears from outside, but I know Ivan will

keep shifting. He will keep adjusting. And I know I can't keep going forever.

Ivan's close now, the smile gone from his face as he slashes the air.

I lift my hands, sending my power streaming toward his chest. It finds him, and I hear the echoes of screams. I see darkness. But just as quickly as I have him, I lose him. He brings a blade across the air in front of my neck, and I hear the whisper as the knife slices the air.

I can't get a hold of his fear this way.

I have to get closer.

I look up at Sam, who seems to know what I'm thinking just by reading my face. Or maybe he knew what this would come to before I did. Either way, he meets my eyes and nods.

Once.

Ivan rushes at me, arm cocked back for another attack, but I roll under his reach, jumping up just in time to throw myself forward, wrapping my hands around his waist.

It's a classic Jiu-Jitsu takedown, and Ivan wasn't expecting it.

He falls, letting out a cry of rage as he hits the dirt. I'm careful to avoid his blades as I slip around, wrapping my arms around his neck. My legs slide around his waist, locking one of his arms against his side as I interlock my feet.

I waste no time, letting my magic slip into his chest. I

sift through, and different images rip across my mind—
blood-covered hands. A ship leaving a harbor.

I'm delving deeper when I feel him transform again. His
body shifts under mine, and the bodily change is enough for me
to lose my grip. Ivan pushes my arms aside and scrambles away.

"What did you do?" he asks, and the familiarity of the
voice stops me cold.

He turns, and it's not Briony. It's not Riles. It's my father.
Ivan's taken on the physical appearance of my dad.

"What did you do, Vesper? You ruined everything." His
blue eyes dance with hatred as he looks me up and down,
disgust plain on his face.

He circles me, and my mind trips over itself. I know this
isn't real. I know this isn't my father. I know this isn't my dad.
But the look on his face is one I've feared for so long, it almost
doesn't matter.

Ivan doesn't have a Harbinger's powers; I know that. This
is just my father's physical appearance. He can't pull my fear
out, but he doesn't need to.

This isn't real. It's just fear. It's just fear.

"You're a monster, Vesper," Ivan says in my father's voice.

It's just fear.

I ball my fists. With a scream, I lunge forward.

Ivan mixes my father's appearance with Riles's blades, and
he swipes at me. I bob and weave like Abagail taught me,
ducking the blade and coming up just in time to throw an

elbow out, catching Ivan right in the jaw. He sprawls backward and then holds his palms out. Carl's stinger lashes forward, and I knock it sideways as I launch myself on top of Ivan. The fear splinters out as my knees hit him, and he's rocked back by the grip of terror that momentarily overtakes him.

I get a hold of his deepest fear before it slips through my fingers. I let my magic snag on another one just as he wrenches free from my grasp and rolls over.

I do a shoulder roll backward, taking my feet and looking down at him.

Ivan's there, and he looks like Ivan. Because I just took his fear of being seen and brought it out. He still has access to all the rest of the powers he's stolen, but he'll use them while looking like himself. The crowd will see Ivan.

He clenches his teeth as he stands, lumbering toward me with his fists clenched and in Aldrick's stone form. He swings at me, and I dodge it. He anticipates my next move—a lunge to the left. He switches from Stoneskin back to his regular hands, but when he runs his fingertip over the ground next to my foot, I know he's using Mavis's Demo magic. The ground buckles, and I fall.

He leans down, blowing dust from his palm. The Duster from the shipyard. I choke on the glittery poison, and my limbs feel heavier than usual. I stagger, struggling to get up on my feet.

Ivan takes his time. I hear his footsteps approaching as I slowly crawl away. He stands over me.

"I told you that this was painful. And to think . . . it all could have been avoided."

With a heave, he kicks me hard in the stomach. I gasp, falling over on my side as the wind leaves my lungs with a *whoosh*.

He leans closer to me then, gripping my hair in a clenched fist as he brings his face down to mine. I look up, trying to find Sam in the crowd, but I'm facing the wrong way.

I'm not strong enough. He's going to win, and then the whole world will suffer.

"Your power will be mine, Vesper. And while your bones slowly break down into the same dust that lines this coliseum for years to come, your magic will be with someone who can wield it. Someone who deserves it."

I finally raise my eyes to meet his, and a new spark lights in my chest.

No.

No.

My father was right—it's dangerous. I've made huge mistakes. People have been hurt because of me. It makes me afraid of getting too close to someone. It's a burden.

But my father is also wrong. This power isn't all evil. I used it to realize my family still loved me. I've used it to save Sam. Aldrick. And, in the past several weeks, I've learned to control it. There is good that can come from it. Duncan was right—fear is the mirror of love. And if this power has to be inside of someone, it should be inside of someone who understands that.

I'm not afraid of this anymore.

That thought is all I need to muster the strength for one last thing.

His hand is still gripping my hair when I pull back. He loses his balance, and I twist to the side, grabbing his arm and rolling so it's between my legs, with one calf under his jaw, and the other across his chest.

A perfect arm bar.

I press my hips upward, extending his elbow backward.

He lets out a violent scream, and it's enough to know he's distracted.

I only have a moment.

I don't let my power slip this time. I don't let it trickle.

I slam my power into his chest like a fist, not caring what kind of damage I cause; I go for the deepest fear he has.

I grip it with my magic, and pull as hard as I can. I feel the fear manifest in the air.

Ivan goes limp beneath me, and I roll off him.

His eyes are open, but there's no light behind them. He looks to me, and the purple rings under his lashes are dark and pronounced.

He looks like what I'd expect a powerless person to look

like. Because that's his greatest fear. Powerlessness.

For a moment, as long as I can hold it, Ivan has no magic. And he knows it.

He smiles, contempt etched on his expression as I stand over him.

"You can't hold it forever."

I shake my head as my other hand reaches out toward the audience, searching until I find the fear I'm looking for, and a knife materializes in my hand.

I lean over him.

"I don't need to hold it forever. Just long enough to kill you," I say, leaning down to press the blade against his throat. I pause.

"What are you waiting for?" he rasps.

I feel the two fears I'm maintaining thrumming in my chest. But, for the first time, I don't fear them spinning out of control. I don't fear at all.

"Yield," I say quietly.

Confusion spreads over his face, and then he laughs. "You're this close, and you can't finish it?"

"I don't need to kill you in order to destroy you," I whisper.

He raises his head, and blood pools around his throat. "You do, Vesper. Believe me. You do. That's what power is. The one with the least fear wins. And right now, you're afraid to do what you need to do."

"And you're not afraid?" I press the knife tighter against

his skin, and hesitancy colors his gaze.

He is quiet for a moment and then leans back against the ground.

"I yield."

Wind whips through the stadium, stirring up dust as the final fight comes to a close.

I am still for a moment, poised over Ivan.

"This is over," I tell the silent crowd. "Leave."

They don't move, and the creak of the cell doors sounds through the stadium. Mavis, Sam, Aldrick, and Sapphira walk into the stadium. Sam breaks into a run, and grabs me around the waist, spinning me around in a crushing hug.

"You did it," he whispers.

Mavis looks up at the crowd and pulls one glove off with her teeth.

"You heard her. Get out!" she says, motioning to the ground. The thought of a Demo bringing down the whole stadium gets people moving.

I hold the powerlessness over Ivan, keeping him on the ground until everyone is gone and Sam is standing beside me.

"What now?"

A rumble starts, low in the ground, deep beneath our feet.

I look over to Mavis, but she holds her now-gloved hands up. "That's . . . not me."

Sam grabs my hand. "Um . . . we should go."

"What is it?"

"My unraveling is happening. And we need to go."

He pulls me behind him as the rumbling intensifies.

Ivan doesn't move. He just lies there, looking up at the sky.

"We can't leave him!" I cry out to Sam.

"If we stay, we die!" Sam calls back over his shoulder. And I know it's true. Sam grabs my hand and we run, sprinting across the dirt just as the foundation cracks in half.

I stop for a half a second, turning to scan the stands. They're empty. Everyone got out.

Sam yanks my arm, and I turn and run with him. The others follow. Into the doorway, through the hallway with the dungeon cells. The ground is splintering, gaping wounds appearing in the floor as the metal doors of the cells bend and crack.

"Sam, what the hell did you do?" Mavis shouts from behind us. We skid past the door leading into the front lobby. Sam grabs my waist as we reverse our momentum.

We jump over the turnstiles, booking it into the parking lot. My lungs are about to burst, but I pump my arms as the entire structure cracks in half, collapsing in on itself with a sound like a shriek and a clap. The ground buckles and shakes, and Sam and I lose our footing on the edge of the parking lot, rolling onto a nearby sliver of grass between two rows of abandoned cars. The concrete base groans, taking longer to give up than the rest of the stadium, but eventually falls inward with one last sigh. I watch as a small crack, thinner than a pencil mark, stretches, pushing as far as it can before giving up at the curb.

The Arena of the Queen of Poisons is gone.

Mavis wipes her eyes, surveying the destruction. Aldrick hugs Sapphira.

A cloud of dust rolls over us, and we sit up, coughing as we survey the destruction. The entire coliseum is a pile of rubble. Small fires have sprouted up, spewing lines of smoke into the sky. In the distance, I see a figure running.

Ivan.

I stand, ready to chase him down. Ready to knock him to the ground and punch his face in until my knuckles are raw. But Sam grabs me and pulls me back.

I look to Sam, and he reads the question in my eyes. "I unraveled Ivan. I made every contract in his stupid Ledger moot. He's powerless—no one belongs to him anymore," he answers.

Sapphira's eyes widen, and she looks at Sam as his words sink in. Then she throws herself into his arms. He's startled at first, but then hugs her back. Aldrick joins in, knocking them both over.

Abagail grabs Wex and they both jump in. Roy announces that he's not getting involved, so Mavis reaches out and trips him.

And I didn't think I'd be laughing today. I didn't think I'd be laughing ever again.

But here I am, in the shadow of rubble and destruction.

And I'm happier than I've ever been.

THIRTY-FIVE

THREE MONTHS LATER

The sound of a school bell cuts through the spring air, and it's weird how the sound of it still makes me feel like, *Shit, I'm late*, even though I have never gone to this school.

Even though I took my GED last month, and so I don't really need to go back, ever again. I'm sitting on the hood of Sam's truck, leaning back against Sam's chest. We're parked at the far end of the parking lot of Tanglewood High School, tucked in the shade of the blooming jacaranda trees.

Aldrick leans on the tree trunk, his arms folded against his chest as he watches the steps as students spill out, talking and laughing. A girl does a rail slide on her skateboard, and a teacher blows a whistle, giving her a *Not on my watch, missy*, look.

I take a deep breath and look up through the leaves. I

didn't think I'd be alive to see this, and I didn't think it'd be this . . . okay. I didn't think I'd ever have these days again, these warm-wind, bonfire nights of dizzy kisses and salt-stained skin.

I never thought there'd be a time when I went home, not ready to move back in but ready to talk. Ready to be told how much I've been missed. But that's what's happened. My family and I FaceTime once a week now, and my mom and dad are coming to visit next month. It's slow going, but it's going.

The Tournament of the Queen of Poisons shook the whole world. Pictures of the collapsed coliseum were all over the news. News shows begged the "gladiators" to come forward, but we opted not to. I was done being in front of the public eye. Briony did, though. She showed up at a radio station and told them all about it. About the Beneath, and the Wardens. So maybe she's not that bad. Or whatever, I still think she's the worst. But that's not the point. She called for Oddities to come forward, and several did.

And by "several," I mean hundreds. All on the steps of the Capitol, all ready to talk to the Baselines. All tired of living in the shadows. We're here now. No longer a myth. It's not smooth sailing, by any means. There have been a few riots. Groups calling themselves the New Wardens and the Basecamp have emerged, leaving scrawled threats on garage doors and billboards. But hate isn't new. We'll deal with it.

Aldrick straightens, his eyes focus on the steps. I lightly tap Sam's knee before sliding off the van's hood and walking up beside Aldrick.

She's on the steps.

Blue jeans, white shirt that hangs off a shoulder, hair in a messy bun held up with a pencil.

Sapphira.

Math book clutched in her arms. When she sees us, a smile slips up her lips.

She crosses the parking lot. Aldrick reaches out and pulls her in for a kiss.

Sapphira hands him her books and turns to look at us.

"Guys, it's considered not cool to have your family waiting for you after school."

"It's your first day!" I say, holding my arms out.

Sapphira rolls her eyes, but I can see the happiness and ease in her shoulders. She wanted to go back to school, and now she can. She's not normal—not by a long shot, but she's closer.

"I'm seventeen years old," she says as Aldrick pulls her in for a hug.

"So no more notes in your lunch?" he asks.

"Don't you dare stop those," she says.

Later that night, I walk down to Aloa's to get Sam and me some coffee. We're going to talk about college and look through some brochures.

I walk back, loving the sound of my heeled boots on the wet pavement.

I reach the door of Duncan's, balance one grande on the lid of the other, and stop.

Because there it is, pinned next to the Open sign.

An aconite bud: its purple bud dry, despite the rain. It's fresh.

I pull it off the door, letting the pin clatter to the pavement as I turn, eyeing the parked cars on the street. Whoever did this is likely still around.

I knew Ivan wasn't done with me.

So I tuck the flower behind my ear before I pull the door open. I hold it open with my boots as I turn around and look down the dark, wet street.

We're watching, that flower says.

But whatever question they leave, whatever threat they pose—I have my answer, and I see it as I hand my boyfriend his coffee and read the handwriting of a brave, kickass woman scrawled on the wall of my home:

> *It matters not how strait the gate,*
> *How charged with punishments the scroll,*
> *I am the master of my fate,*
> *I am the captain of my soul.*

I stare into the dark, unafraid of the shadows and what may be lurking within them.

I give a mock salute to whoever's watching before I take a pull of my coffee and disappear into Duncan's.

ACKNOWLEDGMENTS

First, thank you to my God. Thank you for Your mercies and Your plan. Every good thing I have comes from You.

Writing would still be only a dream if it wasn't for my husband, Ross. Seven years ago, he bought me a writing desk and told me to chase this impossible thing. He woke up early and stayed up late to protect me from doubt that prowled at my door. I am blessed to be your wife.

To my Aryn Bear and Liam Robin—I thank God every day for your kind hearts and strong spirits. When the time comes when the world pushes, push back. I will always be in your corner. And to Baby Girl kicking me as I write this— thank you for keeping food down long enough for me to finish this book.

An additional note to all three of you—yes, I say adult words in this book. No, it doesn't mean you can.

A ridiculous amount of gratitude goes to my agent, Bri-anne Johnson, whose unfailing support puts wind in my sails when I feel like I've gone stagnant. Your vision cleared a path for this book to exist, and I cannot thank you enough. Allie Levick, you make the hustle look easy, and I'm so thankful for you and the whole incomparable team at Writers House.

To the whole team at Katherine Tegen Books—thank you for believing in my strange little story about a girl gladiator. Claudia Gabel, for your guiding hand and kind words. I'd be lost without my copy editors—Stephanie Guerdan, Kathryn Silsand, Erica Ferguson, and team. I'm sorry I say "just" in every paragraph. I'm working on it. A special shout-out to my beloved Melissa Miller, who took a chance on an untested writer and helped her make a book out of a sentence. To the lovely Mary Pender—thank you for being in my corner.

Dad—thank you for walking me through the woods when I was lost. Thank you for putting in hours at your desk so that I can sit at this desk and write down dreams. You told me that fantasy stories can ask the questions we can't ask ourselves . . . you were right. Mom—you were given a strange kid who couldn't be more different than you, but you never tried to change me. Thank you for letting me check out vampire books from the library. Thank you for marching me to the bus stop in your cloud pajamas and for taking me to get chocolate pie after therapy. You both show me what love is daily.

To Hannah, Rachel, and Becca—thanks for doing life with me. Carmen is a mix of all of you, and that's how I knew how to write an awesome sister. Sue, Ross, Marie, David, Bri, Victoria, Emilia Belle, Elaina, and (soon) Jack—thank you all for being the best family a girl could ask for. To the Rutherfords (all thirteen of you), for reading early drafts of early stories and fanning the ember of hope I had burning in my heart. To the Janadi family, for hugs and coffee and making me cooler by association. Aunt Lin, thank you for always believing I would get here.

To my clan—Amanda Jaynes, for inspiring 90 percent of the inappropriate teen antics in this book. Hilary Miller and Jillian Denning, for fighting for these dreams alongside me. Thank you both for Duke's, reading my shitty first drafts, and endless text chains. I can't wait to see my name in your acknowledgments, soon. Brittany Sawrey, for doing it first and showing me how. I love you, your heart, and your stories. Isaac, for your title ideas, my clean kitchen, and many of my meals. To Ashtyn, for giving me all caps texts of excitement when I need it and lending me your killer story sense. To Kate Angelella, for telling me to shoot for the stars and believing I could actually do this weird career. Landon—for being an effing force to be reckoned with and a reliable source of Shia LaBeouf gifs.

To Dr. Arai and Luke—thank you for the prayers, chocolate, and general badassery.

To Rachel Simon, Olivia Hinebaugh, Andrew Munz, Cat Scully, and Nikki Roberti for surrounding me with talent to catch up to. Michele Gendelman and the whole writing group—Kaci, Avan, Chris, Melinda, Ren, Dennis—you all are freaks and I'm glad to know you. You make my stories and my life better.

And to the teachers who shaped me. Mrs. DeLong, thank you for your gentleness and prayers. Mr. Theriot, thank you for showing me what it looks like to love books with a passion. Also, thank you for never sending me to the principal's office when I walked into class barefoot and on the phone. Andy Guerdat, for showing me how to find a story's soul. Dr. Julianne Smith, for tireless advocacy. Thank you for turning me into an English major. You changed the trajectory of my life, and I am blessed by you.

To all the readers—we need you now more than ever before. Reading makes your head smart and your heart strong. Fill up, seek truth, and fight to make the world better.